SEESAW MONSTER

ALSO BY KOTARO ISAKA

Kotaro Isaka

SEESAW MONSTER

Translated from the Japanese
by Sam Malissa

THE OVERLOOK PRESS, NEW YORK

This edition first published in hardcover in 2025 by
The Overlook Press, an imprint of ABRAMS

Abrams books are available at special discounts when purchased in quantity
for premiums and promotions as well as fundraising or educational use.
Special editions can also be created to specification.
For details, contact specialsales@abramsbooks.com or the address above.

English translation rights arranged through CTB Inc.
Translation from the Japanese language by Sam Malissa
First published by Harvill Secker in 2025
Originally published by Chuokoron-Shinsha in Japan as *Seesaw Monster* 2019

Library of Congress Control Number: 2024951582

Printed and bound in the United States

10 9 8 7 6 5 4 3 2 1

ISBN: 978-1-4197-7707-3
eISBN: 979-8-88707-419-1

ABRAMS The Art of Books
195 Broadway, New York, NY 10007
abramsbooks.com

SEESAW MONSTER

'THE NEWSPAPERS ARE ALL BUZZING about the Japan–US trade wars, but no one's talking about the mother–daughter-in-law wars under my roof.'

Such was my lament to Watanuki, who sat opposite me at a corner table in the *izakaya*. He sipped his beer and laughed drily. 'Do you want people to be talking about that?'

'Well, not exactly, no.'

A bunch of guys and girls who looked like college students were chanting coarsely, urging someone to chug. The speakers were playing the new hit from the idol group that sings and dances in roller skates.

'I get what you're saying, though.'

'You do?'

'Sure. Everyday problems might not make the news, but they're still a major headache when you're going through them.'

'Exactly!'

I leaned across the table, beaming with appreciation. I could have hugged him.

The world is full of terrible misfortune. I even feel bad summing it up with a banal label like 'misfortune' – things like the JAL plane that crashed a few years back, or the volcanic eruption in Colombia, or that ceiling collapse at the disco. Thinking about all the people who suffered deep pain and loss in these incidents, my problems seem like tiny little scraps of garbage. I'm not saying that I'm the most unfortunate wretch in the world, or that I wish the Japanese government would spend as much time worrying about me as they do about the price of beef and oranges.

But even garbage scraps can pile up, and when that happens the pillars that support your spirit can start to splinter and crack, and it'd be nice if someone would offer a few words of quiet encouragement: *Hey, your pillars are looking a little shaky, you okay buddy?* That was all I wanted.

So when my coworker Watanuki, who started at our pharma company four years before me and was someone I really looked up to, said I was looking down and did I want to go out for a drink, even that was enough to chase away my cloud of gloom. But to hear that he understood where I was coming from – I nearly wept with gratitude.

'So you all live together?'

'At first she was supposed to live on her own, but after my dad died I was worried about her being alone. My mom's never really had a job besides some piecework at home, she doesn't know how the world works. So I brought it up with my wife and she was so kind—'

You're right, it'll be hard for your mother all by herself.

Miyako, my wife, had smiled as she'd said it.

It could even make my life easier; she can help with the housework.

'Sorry, Kitayama, but you were being naïve.' Watanuki's tone was firm. 'It's not like your wife could have said no. She didn't want to look like a selfish daughter-in-law. But think about how she really felt. She probably wasn't too excited about it.'

It was true. I had just hoped it would all work out.

Although it's not like I expected my wife to be happy about living with her mother-in-law. Quite the opposite. I knew that it was a serious thing to ask. And since it was serious, I didn't think that she would put up a front and hide her true feelings. I also don't think I pressured her into it.

'She probably didn't want you to resent her, and figured she could tough it out.'

'I told her she should say no if that's what she felt.'

'Yeah, but it can be hard to say no. You know, it's funny, when you ask someone if they're okay, they usually just nod and say, "Yeah, I'm okay." Like canned dialogue. Even when you're not okay, maybe you're feeling sick, it doesn't seem to be getting any better, but still you end up just saying, "I'm okay." It's weird how that works.'

I thought back to English classes. *How are you? I'm fine, thank you.* An exchange of set phrases. Was that what had happened?

'Also, I bet your wife didn't start out thinking that she wouldn't get along with your mother. She probably thought that you'd all figure out living together, that she could make it work.'

'See, you really get people, Watanuki.'

'Please. Hey, does your wife know the most important things a daughter-in-law can say to a mother-in-law?'

'The most important . . . what, "Would you like some tea, your dinner's ready, how about some dessert?"'

'No, it's not a food thing. It's: "You're right. I didn't know that. You're so good at this. Let me take care of that."'

I turned those phrases over in my head. *You're so good at this* felt like obvious flattery, but then again it's not like anyone would get mad about being told that. 'So she just has to say that stuff and they'll get along better, huh?'

'It's not exactly the old saying *sickness starts in the mind,* but it is true that friction and misfires in communication are a matter of words. People always look for the hidden message.'

'The hidden . . .?'

'You know, like the real meaning behind the words. For example.' Watanuki paused, like he was reviewing the examples he had stored in his head, but only for a moment. 'A mother says to

3

her kid, "Little so-and-so's already learned his multiplication tables!" So how does the kid feel?'

Ahh. I nodded. 'He assumes that what she's really saying is, "Why haven't you learned it yet?"'

'And when there's an underlying meaning, people pick up on that. That's one way we're still better than machines.'

'Oh,' I said, remembering, 'that reminds me of something Dr I. said the other night.'

'The internist?'

'Yes. I took him for dinner in Akasaka and then for drinks in Roppongi. He said, "Seems like everyone is doing the night-out-in-Akasaka thing. Oh by the way, I recently heard about a doctor who got taken on a private jet up to Hokkaido for ramen." What he was saying was that he'd like the same kind of treatment.'

'I mean,' Watanuki says with a chuckle, 'it's pretty plain to see what he wanted. Nothing underlying about that. There is no limit to people's desires. Anyway, when it comes to interpersonal exchanges, in most cases there either actually is a hidden meaning, or somebody suspects there's one. Women especially are good at sniffing it out. They're very sensitive to what might be lurking behind the words.'

'No kidding.' There were countless times my wife had gotten upset over the simplest of greetings or apologies from my mom.

'You're stuck between a rock and a hard place, my friend. I don't envy you. And both of them are very important to you, I imagine.'

'Watanuki, I—' I could feel my eyes getting moist.

Watanuki noticed too, and smiled ruefully. 'I can tell you're having a tough time, Kitayama.'

'I feel like it's starting to affect my health.'

'Hell of a thing to say for someone who works for a pharmaceutical company.'

'Do we make any drugs for this?' I sighed. Then I opened up

about the stress from hearing my wife and mom complain to me all the time, day in and out. *Listen to what Mother said to me today* from the one, and, *Can you believe what your Miyako said?* from the other. They reported it casually, masking their grievances as conversation. And I would tell them, *Don't worry about it,* or, *I'm sure she didn't mean it like that,* but I had said those things so many times they no longer had any effect.

It's probably not fair to hold people to what they've said in the past, but before we got married my wife shared with me that she had always wanted to have a family, because her own parents had died when she was young. And she didn't just say it once, she said it all the time, like a comedian with a catchphrase. And every time she did I was overjoyed.

Miyako had grown up in a town by the sea in Chiba. She lost her parents in a boating accident, so she was raised by relatives. Their household wasn't exactly overflowing with warmth and love. From her insistence that we put her on my family registry and residence certification, I gathered that she didn't want her aunt and uncle to know where she was.

So when she told me, *Naoto, I want your mother to live with us,* I believed her.

I had no reason not to.

When we were dating, she asked what my mom was like. I figured that it would make her less nervous and manage her expectations if I gave it to her straight, rather than putting my mom on a pedestal. So I told her my mom was generally calm and composed, but this sometimes made her seem chilly; that she was sociable, but a lot of that was just her being a meddling gossip.

Miyako immediately responded that this was no problem. 'I was basically neglected growing up, so a family that's close enough to have some meddling sounds good to me.'

Despite what she said, I was still cautious, telling myself that

5

we wouldn't know what was inside until we took off the lid. But I never thought it would be like this, never imagined that the difference between lid on and lid off could be so extreme.

'It doesn't matter how much of a people person someone is,' Watanuki said, 'once they're actually in a situation with someone, well, stress can start to build up.'

'I wonder if that's it. In their case, I think it's a question of basic compatibility.'

'Mom and wife are just incompatible, huh?'

'Yeah.' I nodded. 'From the very first time they met, it's been, let's say, strained.' I swear I've felt the air between them crackle with static.

'They're just different types, I guess,' Watanuki said. 'Women can really tell when someone isn't their type, and then there's just no getting along.'

'What about you? Do your wife and mother get along?'

'My wife made it clear before we got married that my mother wasn't going to live with us, so that was that. Anyway, my mom's got her own thing, she's always traveling abroad or busy with one of her hobbies.'

'Must be nice.'

'But she has zero interest in her grandkids. She's kind of a cold one.'

I let out a sad little noise. Of course everyone has their problems and the grass is always greener, but the word 'grandkids' hit me in the chest and settled like a lead weight.

Miyako and I were having a hard time getting pregnant.

Which was making things worse between her and my mom.

I could hear my mom's unkind words in my head. *Your father always used to tell me I would live a long life and enjoy my grandchildren. But now it looks like I'll never get the chance. When I die and we're together again, what am I supposed to tell him?* It wasn't just once either, she said this all the time, like she was a rival comedian with her own catchphrase. Every time I heard it I wanted to shout at her to leave me alone.

I know it hurt my wife whenever she heard my mom say it. And her pain turned into arrows that made a pincushion of me.

'Stop worrying about her so much,' my mom would say, irritating me even more. 'She's not as fragile as you think.'

'Must be tough getting an earful from both of them.' Watanuki understood what I was going through.

'Unlike the Japan–US trade wars, this isn't affecting society, so I guess I shouldn't complain.'

'Hey, everyone needs to vent, from the people at the trade ministry and the foreign ministry on down.'

At that point we got into company gossip. The division chief was having a fight with his girlfriend. A woman in Watanuki's cohort got a rich college kid to buy a Soarer so he could drive her around in it, wheels-on-call.

'While we get to hang out with docs-on-call. Hey Kitayama, how's your body holding up?'

'What do you mean?'

'We entertain doctors, we take them out, we eat a lot, we stay out late. You're still young, but if you run yourself into the ground, you won't be any use to anyone.'

'If I get diabetes I can sell our drugs with the authentic perspective of a patient.'

Watanuki laughed at my joke, but not heartily. On the taxi ride home it occurred to me that when he asked about my health he was probably more worried about himself.

As I approached my house my steps grew heavy and my face tightened, but then I saw that the lights were out and felt a wash of relief. Even with the blackout curtains drawn some light would seep from the cracks if there was a lamp on inside. Zero light meant that my wife and mom had gone to sleep. People don't complain when they're asleep.

I gingerly unlocked the door and slipped into the living room with as little noise as possible. Whenever I get home I take off my jacket and tie and relax on the sofa for a bit. It's like a ritual, or like the credits at the end of a film. I'd be fine without it, but I wouldn't feel quite right.

When I turned on the light someone was already sitting on the sofa and I nearly jumped out of my skin. It was my wife, Miyako.

She hadn't been dozing, either. She was sitting up straight, making her look a little like a ghost. I scare easily, and almost shrieked at the sight of her. 'What are you doing sitting there like that?'

'I was watching TV. I turned it off just before you came in.' Her earphones were on the table, the cord stretching to the television.

'And you were sitting in the dark?'

'If I leave the lights on, Mother gets upset.'

'I'm sure she's asleep. Isn't it supposed to be bad for your eyes to watch TV in the dark?'

'Really?'

'I mean, it's bad for your eyes to read in the dark.'

'They said that's not true,' Miyako declared. I had heard no such reports. 'They kept you out so late. Do you want something to eat?' She got up and headed toward the kitchen.

There was no room whatsoever in my stomach. Besides that, though, I was sure that her waiting up for me meant that I was about to get an earful of her troubles. My work for the day wasn't quite done.

'Your balloon's all full, huh?' I asked.

'Yeah,' she said, nodding.

8

The unhappiness of living with her mother-in-law just built up and built up, day after day.

'Imagine a balloon,' she had once told me. 'An invisible balloon that I pump full of my frustration. You're busy with work, and I'm just here in the house all day. So there's no way to let anything out of my balloon.'

It made sense. And it wasn't hard to guess why she chose that as her metaphor.

Because balloons can burst.

'I do my best to deal with it on my own, but my balloon is so blown up,' she said, spreading her arms to show how big, 'it's going to explode. So I need to talk to you before that happens.'

'Let out some of the gas.'

'I'm not sure it's right to talk about Mother in terms of gas.' It was encouraging that she showed this little bit of care for my mom's feelings, until a moment later when she added, 'She's more like poison gas.' Hearing that just blew up my balloon.

'So what happened today?'

'It was about kids.'

'Aah.' Only the heaviest, most sensitive topic.

We didn't worry about kids when we first got married. We figured that in the natural course of living together as a married couple it would just happen. I got home late most nights because I was usually out entertaining doctors, so more often than not the timing was off for us to get intimate, but we reasoned that all we had to do was schedule it.

Mom started to give us a hard time after we had been married for four years. Although she had already been making comments now and again, like when Dad died the year after we got married, and Mom said, 'If only there were grandchildren at the funeral to brighten things up a little.' She would disguise her guilt trips as general statements that would be hard to argue

9

with, but it was clear enough that she was disappointed in us for failing to give her grandchildren.

'This afternoon, Mother was watching TV. It was a crime drama, and in the last scene the actress is on a cliff and she shouts "It's not my baby!"'

'Let me guess, she was the killer?'

'How'd you know?'

'If I was a screenwriter I wouldn't give a big line like that to a supporting character.'

'Well, it was about kids, and I immediately got this pit in my stomach and thought, *Here we go*. And sure enough, right on cue—'

'Mom just couldn't hold back.'

'She says, "That reminds me, Miyako, have you ever been tested?"'

Fastball, no curves.

'That reminds me, she says, as if she isn't *always* thinking about it. "Tested? What kind of test?" I asked her, playing dumb. She had nothing to say to that.'

I had advised my wife before to fight back when my mom took swipes at her like this. If she just sat there and took it all the time her frustration would just build up, and Mom would press her advantage. *You can't always be on the defensive*, I had said. *Sometimes you need to counterpunch.*

'Mom can be a real handful.' But I could see that Miyako was in a foul mood, so I hastily amended, 'Not so much a handful, more like she's really mean.' She was waiting for me to say more, so I adjusted my wording again: 'She's not just mean, she's the worst.'

I must have finally satisfied her, because her expression relaxed a bit, and she gently chided me, 'It won't do much good to call your own mother the worst.'

'Yeah, you're right.' I didn't feel like arguing. 'Oh, hey, I got us a reservation at a nice restaurant for your birthday.'

'Really?'

Miyako's birthday was in a month, right near Christmas, so all the good spots were booked up. But the owner of a restaurant I brought my doctors to sometimes got in touch and let me know that there was a cancellation. Things must have gone sour between some guy and the girl he was planning on taking there. According to the owner there are college kids making reservations for a big Christmas date at fancy hotel restaurants half a year in advance. I wondered doubtfully about what kind of college students do that, and what kind of adults they'd become.

'Let's also stay at a hotel that night,' my wife said.

'Wha—?'

'Why not? It's so rare we get to go on a date. Once in a while it'd be nice to just relax.' Her eyes floated up to the ceiling, on purpose or unconsciously, I couldn't tell, but it was clear enough that "relax" meant getting away from Mom.

Of course I felt the same way. I needed to relax just as much as Miyako did. I'd never say it out loud, but I was pretty sure that I needed to relax more than anybody else in our household.

What gave me pause was whether we'd be able to get a room at a hotel. Anywhere that was even a little nicer would be all booked up, and it's not like we were going to go to some cheap motel. Although I imagined that even the motels would be full.

But if I explained all that to her it would be like dousing her hopes with cold water. I'd be dousing myself too, and I didn't want to be cold and wet.

'I can't wait until my birthday.' Before I realized it Miyako was standing right beside me. She wound herself into my arms and pressed her chest up against me. I started adding things up in my head: all my built-up fatigue, the late hour, what time I had to wake up in the morning, all the steps involved in getting physical; but then I thought that what was needed at that moment wasn't calculation but heat, and even though that judgment itself was a kind of calculation, I hugged Miyako close.

She was tall for a woman, and while she looked slender she had strong muscles. As a kid she was sporty, big into basketball, and she often still went for a run early in the morning, saying that she didn't want to get soft. Mom wasn't crazy about this, and more than once had said to me that she always thought I would settle down with someone more feminine. Naturally, I never shared this with Miyako.

I ran my hands over the curves and dips of her body, but suddenly she pulled away and looked toward the doorway behind me.

What happened? I asked with my eyes.

'Nothing, I just thought that Mother might be awake.'

'I'm sure she's asleep.'

'You're probably right,' she said, but her face was tense, as if she was imagining my mom upstairs with her ear pressed to the floor.

I held in my sigh. Then I thought back to the first time I met my wife.

Seven years ago, I took the Shinkansen from Tokyo to Osaka. I barely made it aboard before it pulled away from the station. It was just after I had started at the pharmaceutical company; I wasn't used to the pace of business and always felt like I was scrambling to keep up. Weekends were for sleeping and regaining my energy, but that day I had a college friend's wedding. And I overslept.

I jumped on the first train I could, which would get me to the wedding just on time. The moment I sank down in the seat I felt a wave of relief and went back to sleep.

After a while I became aware that someone was sitting next to me. I felt them leaning on my shoulder and opened my eyes. It was a woman. Miyako Shiota, who is now my wife. Her head fell forward and she jerked awake with a little 'Ah.' Then she looked at me. 'Sorry about that.'

'No, no, I'm sorry,' I answered. She was wearing a long skirt and a blouse, a clean look that was properly grown-up. In a word, she was really cute, and I was feeling lucky to be next to her. That sense of good fortune was like a warm bubble around me, and it almost lulled me back to sleep. Just as I was about to close my eyes again she asked:

'Where are you headed today?'

'Osaka' was on the tip of my tongue, but I was so exhausted that I wondered if I had even bought the right ticket, and I started fishing for it to check. It wasn't in my pants pocket, or in my jacket that I had hung by the window. I would eventually find it in my bag, but at that moment I couldn't locate it anywhere, and I started feeling sheepish about fumbling through all my belongings, so I tried to say something clever: 'I'm headed to tomorrow. To Japan's future.' But it wasn't clever, and didn't even really make sense.

She was silent, and I felt my face getting hot. She must have wanted to say something to dispel the awkwardness, so she asked, 'Are you going to get something when the snack cart comes by?'

'Maybe I'll get some green tea,' I replied.

'Tea, that's a great idea.'

I wasn't expecting such an enthusiastic response. I turned to look out the window.

The scenery flew by. It felt like the speed of my day-to-day hustle. I would go to a hospital, greet the doctors, pitch our new drugs, write a report, get yelled at by my boss, read an academic paper, each day flowing into the next before I had a chance to even exhale. Exactly like the old saying, *time flies like an arrow*. I worried that I was hurtling through space and would go *thunk* into the target without even knowing what had happened.

There was a commotion nearby. Two rows ahead of us a group of middle-aged men in facing seats seemed to be having a party. Their shouts and cigarette smoke filled up the train car.

More than just being annoying, it was vaguely threatening.

A loud voice is enough to scare someone, Watanuki had once told me. *It's an instinctive animal reaction. When men have something to say, they want to say it loud. This frightens the women. That's the way it works. If you say something as if you're the boss, people treat you like the boss.*

The girl pushing the snack cart came down the aisle and the rowdy men stopped her to order this and that. When she asked for payment they demanded a discount, laughing vulgarly. 'No dice, huh?' one said with an edge in his voice. 'You some kinda high-class chick?'

I glanced at the woman beside me, who would eventually become my wife. She had been watching the scene unfold but was now looking down at her lap. There was concern on her face, but it was clear that she understood she couldn't do anything about the situation.

'Excuse me,' I called out to the girl with the snack cart. 'I'd like to buy something, can you come over here, please?' I thought I could help her get away from the group of drunks. In other words, a hasty and simplistic plan to play the hero.

Just as I expected, the snack cart girl said she needed to attend to another customer, apologizing and quickly finishing the transaction with the group of drunk men so she could come over to me. I felt satisfied that my little intervention had settled things. I was also hoping that the woman sitting next to me noticed my achievement.

'What'll it be?' asked the cart girl.

'Green tea.' But then I felt a little bad about just ordering a tea after I had called her over. Without really thinking about it, I asked, 'Do you have frozen tangerines?'

I didn't expect one of the drunken men to follow her over. I hoped that he would pass by and head to the bathroom, but instead he plunked down in the empty two-seater in front of us. 'You shouldn't butt in, friend,' he sneered at me. 'We were in the middle of shopping.'

He stared hard and his voice was rough. If you took a snapshot of the scene, the caption would be *Trouble brewing*.

Then he leaned closer and said, 'That's a tasty-looking woman you got with you,' apparently mistaking us for a couple, his tone both lewd and mocking. The snack cart girl had vanished with my payment, leaving me holding frozen tangerines.

'She's not tasty-looking,' I shot back. Of course, I meant that she wasn't my girlfriend, we weren't together, but I didn't get any of that out, and there's no doubt that it didn't land quite right.

Out of the corner of my eye I saw the woman next to me looking both surprised and annoyed.

'No, no – I'm not saying she's ugly, I just mean that we're not together.'

'Well, why didn't you say so! C'mere, babe, have a drink with me.'

I couldn't follow his logic in thinking that's how things would play out, but I suppose his actions weren't driven by logic. It was much more a threat than an invitation.

She stiffened, not saying anything at first. Her face was pale. He reached out to grab her. In that instant, I shot up to my feet.

'Please leave her alone.'

His eyes flashed dangerously. He must have been used to pushing people around. *Now I've done it*, I thought, but there was no going back.

The reek of liquor wafted off of him. He was saying something to me but I couldn't process any of it. It felt like being cursed at in a foreign language.

This guy's bad news, I thought, but then he also reminded me of the doctors and their often-outrageous demands. They'd get drunk and puff themselves up and dangle a contract in front of us. I wondered if this guy might even be one of our clients.

'Leave her alone,' I said with more force than before. 'I was about to start trying to hit on her, so I'd rather you not take her away.' Then I added, 'I'll give you this.' I put one of my frozen tangerines in his hand.

He didn't seem to know how to respond to that. But it must have worked, because he just said, 'Uh – thank you,' and went back to his seat. The other tangerines I was holding had started to thaw.

The woman next to me looked understandably flustered. 'Well,' she said, cocking her head, half-cautious, half-bewildered, 'I guess I should be thanking you.' The corners of her mouth twitched a little, though I didn't know if it was from fear or laughter.

I was so embarrassed, my mind went blank, and I didn't even register that we had stopped at Shizuoka. I cleared my throat theatrically and was about to start talking to her again when a man in a suit entered the train car and came over to our row. 'I think you're in the wrong seat?'

I resumed searching for my ticket – this was when I found it in my bag – and checked the seat. 'Ah, sorry, I'll move.' I had the right seat number but the wrong train car. Taking my bag, I quickly got up to go. My bag must not have been fully shut because I dropped both my business card carrier and the wedding card with the money inside, but I didn't realize it at the time, and I hurried off without them.

After a little while she came and found me in my seat in the other car. 'You dropped these.' And that's how we met, and started dating, and eventually got married.

'Miyako, do you know what happened to the book I left here?'

Setsu Kitayama, my mother-in-law, said this to me the moment I came downstairs, which immediately annoyed me. I knew that behind her words she was also thinking, *I could have asked you earlier if you hadn't taken so long to come down.*

'No, I don't. What book was it?'

'It was Perrault. His fairy tales.'

There was no shortage of mysteries about Mother. One was her love of fairy tales. I didn't know much about the genre, but my basic understanding was that good people were always rewarded and bad people got what was coming to them. She read so many stories like that, but somehow she made no effort to change her own bad nature. It was bizarre.

How could she not notice how mean she was, how spiteful? How could she not see the resemblance between herself and the fairy-tale villains? Maybe reading about a wicked woman being punished gave her a contained thrill, like with a rollercoaster or a horror movie.

'Miyako, have you ever read Perrault's version of "Sleeping Beauty"?'

'That's the one where she gets cursed and sleeps for a hundred years, right? Then after a hundred years she gets woken up by a prince.' *Obviously,* I wanted to add, but I held back.

'You know, the end of the story is all about cannibalism.'

It sounded like she was trying to provoke me. I smiled coolly. I never knew that 'Sleeping Beauty' went there.

'Well, I definitely left my copy right here.' She made a square with her fingers about the size of a paperback, holding it over her place at the dining-room table, directly opposite the television. 'I certainly didn't move it. And yet it's gone. I wonder what happened?'

I had no memory of touching her book. It was true that I did often move her things, because she couldn't follow the extremely basic rule of putting things back when you take them out. Couldn't, or maybe just wouldn't. But I hadn't touched this book.

What happened to it, I wonder. Miyako, do you know?

Did you move it somewhere without telling me?

If you're going to clean up you could at least let me know.

When we first started living all together, I did my best to attend to all of Mother's requests and needs. I bent over backward solving her problems, explaining situations, dispelling her concerns. But eventually I just couldn't be bothered to expend the energy.

Saying nothing, I took a few steps around the living room, making a brief show of looking for her book. Then I just let the subject drop and started vacuuming.

When I was done I started getting ready to go out food shopping. 'Don't forget the toilet paper,' I heard her say. 'And make sure you get it at the cheap place.'

One time when I brought home toilet paper she demanded to see the receipt. Apparently there was another store that sold it for fifty yen less. 'I suppose she thinks money grows on trees,' she grumbled, seemingly to herself. Then she started in on me: 'You know, Miyako, you really don't understand how the world works. If you hadn't married my Naoto, I wonder what you'd be doing with your life right about now.'

It was one of Mother's favorite lines of attack. *Thanks to my son you have it easy. Not everyone gets to have the relaxing lifestyle of a housewife.* Always trying to make me feel guilty.

Recently she had hit on a new idea: 'I bet you'd just be dancing away at a disco.'

It pissed me off how certain she was that if I were on my own I would have gotten sucked into a flashy, indulgent lifestyle.

I had never been one to show off. I was much more suited to putting my head down and focusing on my work. It was true that thanks to my husband I didn't have the day-to-day stress of going to a job, but it irritated me how she acted like being a housewife meant that I was just relaxing all the time. And she had been a housewife too!

When I finished my shopping and came home, Mother was out. There was a note on the table: *I'm at the neighbors'*.

She must have meant the Furuyas, who lived in the house next door. They were the same generation as her, now living on their own after their sons got married and moved out. They were nice enough, but it didn't help that they were always talking to Mother about their grandchildren. She usually came home in the mood to be a grandmother.

I found a book on the little shelf next to the bathroom. It was Perrault's fairy tales, the one Mother had been looking for. Most likely she set it down there when she was washing her hands and forgot about it. And yet she was going on about how she certainly hadn't moved it. Convenient for a false accusation. I decided to leave it there. It seemed likely that if I touched it I would be blamed, somehow.

Just then the doorbell rang. I looked through the peephole and saw an unfamiliar man standing there. He was a little older, maybe in his late forties or early fifties. I opened the door.

'My apologies for coming by unannounced like this,' he said politely, dipping his head. He was short, but his shoulders were wide and his body looked solid. 'Does Setsu Kitayama happen to be home?'

'And you are?'

He apologized and offered his card. It had the name of a life insurance company, under which was printed Ichio Ishiguro. 'I have been discussing insurance plans with Ms Setsu.'

'Oh?' It was the first I had heard of it. It was hard to picture someone as breezy and entitled as my mother-in-law having any interest in life insurance. But there was something slightly refreshing about the idea of her thinking about our future. 'Well, I'm happy to talk if it's something I can help you with.'

'No, I need to speak directly with Ms Setsu.' His tone was mild. He spun on his heel and started to leave. But then he stopped and came back to the door. A look of curiosity shone on his face, different from his previous businesslike air. He was rubbing his right earlobe. It was a rather large earlobe. 'Your eyes are blue.'

He stared directly into my eyes. There was zero sense of awkwardness or impropriety. It was more like the simple awe of a child who had found a rare insect. It didn't make me feel uncomfortable at all. 'That's what they tell me.'

Since I was young, people had commented on the blue of my eyes. That their color made it seem like I was staring at the sea.

'Did either of your parents have the same?'

'Both my parents died when I was little.'

'Ah, that's right.'

That's right? It was a strange thing for him to say. For a moment I thought that I had misheard, but then it's not crazy for an insurance salesman to discuss deaths in the family. It was possible he heard it from Mother.

'Whereas Ms Setsu has large ears.'

'Does she?' I knew that her ears were large, and a little pointy, but I didn't want to give the impression I was interested in the subject.

'Do the two of you get along?'

'What?' My brows knit, without me meaning for them to. *Why would you ask that?* I almost shot back. 'Did she say something to you?' The thought of her complaining about me to a complete stranger, a salesman, made me furious.

'No, no, no.' He waved his hand back and forth, completely earnest. 'I apologize if I gave you the wrong impression. That's not at all what I was getting at.'

'Then what?'

'Ms Setsu, your mother-in-law – what did you think the first time you met her?'

'What?'

'Is it the case that prior to meeting her you felt confident that you would get along reasonably well?'

As if I remember that, I thought. It was like asking me about the original colors on a canvas that had long ago been covered over by thick black paint. But then I actually had the sensation of peeling back layers of crusted pigment inside my head. *That* is *what I felt,* I realized. That's right. I was certain I'd get along with Naoto's parents.

'If it's the parents of the person you love, you should be able to make it work,' I began. 'Now, I wouldn't think something so naïve. Relationships between people are difficult. It doesn't matter what type of person someone is, you're not always going to go the same way; sometimes you collide, and resentment keeps building up.'

'That is exactly right.' Ichio Ishiguro nodded, looking pleased. 'Any living creatures inhabiting the same space will eventually clash with one another. In human relations, there is no such thing as unconditional compatibility. Loving married couples who later heap abuse on one another and eventually divorce, pupils who come to despise the teachers they once revered, trusted teammates who are suddenly at each other like snakes and scorpions. It is not at all uncommon. On the contrary.'

'That's why I never just assumed I would get along well with my in-laws. On the contrary! How can I put it . . .'

'I know what you are trying to say.' Ichio Ishiguro no longer seemed like an insurance salesman. 'The one who can live with a bear is the one who knows how dangerous the bear is. The one who believes innocently that their love for the animal will make it all work out, they do not stand a chance.'

'That, exactly.'

'You are well-versed in human relations, so you thought that if you approached the situation with reason rather than emotion it would work out. But once you were actually in it, things did not go quite as you expected, did they?'

I was about to nod emphatically – that *was* how I felt – when I caught myself. I was being far too open with a man from an insurance company who I was meeting for the first time. But still it seemed like the words were being pulled up out of somewhere deep inside me.

'There was really nothing you could do,' said Ichio Ishiguro. He sounded sad, and there was real sympathy in his eyes. But there was also a hint of satisfaction.

'Sorry?'

'It was never a question of your skills and abilities, or your spirit. Nor those of Ms Setsu. She said the same thing the other day. She said that she was certain she would get along with her son's wife.'

'So, sounds like it's my fault.' I thought I could feel little flames crackling to life in my head, or my heart.

'Indeed. Well, no, not just you, it is the both of you. You and Ms Setsu cannot get along.'

'Why not?'

'Your chemistry.'

'Chemistry?' That didn't feel like it answered anything.

'A certain deep-rooted chemistry.'

'Deep-rooted? What are you even talking about?' Suddenly I snapped back to reality. I had lost my composure. This was not something I wanted to discuss with a stranger, a man from an insurance company. 'Next you're going to tell me it's a grudge passed down from my ancestors.'

I said it sarcastically, thinking it might get a rise out of him, but surprisingly Ichio Ishiguro didn't seem the least bit perturbed. He narrowed his eyes. 'Yes, that is precisely what it is.'

I wasn't following, and said nothing. He went on.

'What about your father-in-law?'

'My . . .?' I thought of Naoto's dad.

'You got along relatively well with him, didn't you?'

Just then a woman from the neighborhood who taught piano lessons walked by and said hello. She eyed the man standing on my doorstep as she passed, part wary and part curious. As if that were his cue, Ichio Ishiguro apologized for taking up so much of my time and left through the front gate.

I had thought that most insurance salespeople were women, although I figured there must be some men too. For the first time I felt a flicker of suspicion about Ichio Ishiguro. But as I went back inside and sat in the living room, I kept thinking about what he had said.

On a quiet night six years ago, my father-in-law died from a fall down the steps at a shrine. He had just turned sixty and was still full of energy, a picture of health. His frame was slight but he was steady on his feet from the exercise he got as a professional gardener. We didn't live together but every time I saw him he was kind to me. He would tell me about the people he knew, nothing special, but he seemed to enjoy it so much that it made me happy too, and I chatted along. I would say we didn't have a bad relationship at all. Of course, he had a tendency to look down on women slightly, and I could tell there was part of him that saw daughters-in-law as being a bit like maids, but that was less about his character than the man's world he came from. I was able to look past that, in the spirit of *Hate the sin and not the sinner*. On the rare occasion that he was in a bad mood and lashed out at me it didn't even bother me that much. There's no such thing as a relationship with zero friction. So if you're able to let someone blow off steam and just have it roll off of you, there's no harm in that.

But for whatever reason, that's not how it went with my mother-in-law. Every single word out of her mouth lit a fire inside my brain. No matter how hard I tried to keep my cool and douse the flames, they never went out. My sense of calm would just burn up. With her it wasn't *Hate the sin and not the sinner* but *When you hate a monk you even hate his frock*. I wasn't sure why this was, but I suppose that they just had different natures, or maybe that there's more natural opposition between people of the same sex.

The words I spoke earlier flashed in my head: a grudge passed down from my ancestors.

I took the laundry out of the washer, put it in the basket, and brought it upstairs to the balcony to dry. While pinning my socks to the clothesline, I thought back to when I first met Naoto.

It was on the Shinkansen, seven years ago. I got on at Tokyo and took my assigned seat. It was an aisle seat, and at that point the window seat was supposed to be empty. The man I was meeting would be getting on at Shizuoka. At least that's what I had heard, so when I got to my seat I was surprised to find a man already there. What's more, he was asleep. But it only threw me off for a moment. In our line of work, the first order of business was to always remain cool and collected.

First I had to confirm his identity, so I pretended that I was dozing too and gently leaned on him to wake him up. Then I asked: 'Where are you headed today?'

And he answered: 'I'm headed to tomorrow. To Japan's future.' That was the password. He was supposed to have gotten on at Shizuoka, so something must have happened to necessitate a last-minute change of plans.

But I had to follow procedure, so I gave him the next code prompt: 'Are you going to get something when the snack cart comes by?'

If he had responded with *Yesterday's beer* then confirmation would have been complete and we could proceed to share information and discuss the mission.

Instead, he said, 'Maybe I'll get some green tea.' Once again I was thrown off. Of course I didn't show it. I looked at him carefully. He didn't seem to be playing any sort of game. I realized that he didn't know the passwords after all. He was just a regular passenger. The fact that he happened to say *To Japan's future* was just an extreme coincidence. I guess it could happen. I had no doubt that if I told my supervisor about this he'd say, *Well that's why we use two passwords.* I could see him asking me to present on this in future seminars at the Agency.

This man next to me must have just taken the wrong seat.

It would have been easy to let him know that, but I didn't, partly because of what happened with the rowdy passengers giving the snack cart girl a hard time, but beyond that, I just wanted to sit with him some more.

I kind of liked him.

There was no shortage of men around me who were handsome, athletic, cool-headed and capable. Compared to them the man sitting next to me seemed delicate, unkempt, and unreliable. But there was something about him. Maybe it was just chemistry. Whatever it was, he put me at ease, and I liked the way that felt.

I also liked how he stood up for the snack cart girl. As an agent, my most important duty was to complete my mission, and no matter what I encountered along the way, if it was unrelated to my mission then I couldn't afford to get involved. It didn't matter if someone was abusing a puppy or kidnapping a child; I had been trained to ignore it if it didn't have to do with my mission. Whereas this man sitting next to me seemed to be motivated by nothing more than a simple sense of justice. It was endearing, and I thought it was hilarious when he gave the drunk guy a frozen tangerine.

And he also said that he wanted to hit on me.

My chest fluttered.

I suppose that was the beginning of the end of my career as an agent.

The person I was supposed to meet to get information about my mission got on at Shizuoka as planned, and pointed out that Naoto was in the wrong seat. As he got up to go I was worried I would never see him again, so I made a split-second decision and stole his business card holder from his bag. I never imagined at that moment that I would marry this man and quit the Agency. Although actually that's not true. I wanted to live a peaceful life, and I wanted it to be with him.

It turns out my hunch was right. Naoto was the ideal partner for me, and we never had any problems between us.

Where I miscalculated was with my mother-in-law. I had been through extensive training on interpersonal communication, so I thought it would be no problem to live together with her. But I couldn't have been more wrong.

There was friction between me and Mother from the first time we met.

Up until that point I was optimistic. A few days beforehand I made a show of fretting about whether or not she would like me, but in fact I wasn't worried at all. I had faith in all the training the Agency had given me.

Even though the Agency was run by the government, or more likely specifically because it was run by the government, the men tended to get the main jobs while the women got support roles. No one even saw the bias, it was just accepted as the way things were, so at first I was given tasks like scheduling for the other agents or entertaining foreign dignitaries. It was obvious to anyone paying attention that men who were less talented than me were getting better assignments, which was infuriating. I brought it up with my supervisor and he heard me out but did nothing.

It's not like there were no successful female agents at the Agency. There were even a few highly skilled women who had made their way into the upper ranks. They were treated as almost legendary, which felt a bit silly. I would hear stories about them that had been passed down over the years, but the fact that a woman making it to the top was seen as so remarkable was just proof of the inequality.

I didn't want to quit or run away from the challenge, and I reasoned that getting paid to learn combat skills and interrogation techniques was a good deal, so I stuck with it.

Eventually I got the recognition I was looking for.

I was especially good at bomb disposal and gathering intelligence from targets through observation and questioning. People are just like explosives: if you follow the emotional fuse gently, patiently, you can get the outcome you're looking for.

At least that's how I thought it would go.

Compared to covertly gathering HUMINT, handling my boyfriend's mother should have been a piece of cake.

I arrived ahead of schedule at the hotel lounge where we were all supposed to meet. Keeping someone waiting creates psychological discomfort, and I wanted to do everything I could to avoid that with Naoto's parents. At the same time, getting to an appointment early can give you an advantageous position. I thought I was ahead of the game.

But they were already there waiting for me.

'We got here too early,' said Naoto's father kindly. 'We've got nothing but free time so we always head out much earlier than we need to.' He seemed friendly, but his wife had a sour look on her face. She glared at me and exhaled with annoyance.

27

I was surprised, but it wasn't a major setback. I apologized politely for being late.

'Oh, everyone's here already,' Naoto said when he arrived, flustered at being the last.

'When you're introducing your girlfriend to us don't you think it's more appropriate that the two of you come together? This is our first time meeting this young woman.' Naoto's mother still had that same sour expression. She would barely look at me, which told me that she already didn't like me. We had barely spoken, so it couldn't have been about anything I'd said or done so much as my general vibe and appearance. Or maybe she had already decided we were enemies because I was dating her only son.

'Sorry, I had a thing I had to do for work, even though it's Sunday,' Naoto explained.

'Naoto suggested that I wait for him so we could come together, but I told him I'd be fine on my own. I didn't want to keep the two of you waiting, and anyway I was eager to meet you.' I was trying to cover for Naoto and butter up his mother at the same time.

'People who say they're fine on their own are usually people who can't do anything on their own.' There was clearly a barb in her voice. Many barbs, in fact, each one with a label that read DISTASTE – that was how obvious it was that she didn't like me. It was enough to make even me shrink a little, but I tried to keep my emotions in check.

Yes, it's true that I sometimes overestimate what I can handle, was what I wanted to say with a blush and a winning smile. But instead, what came out of my mouth was: 'I don't think there's any need to be so nasty.' With a baiting tone to boot. The words and feelings I thought I had stuffed into a box were in rebellion and on the loose.

Finally she looked at me.

The hairs stood up all over my body. I was off balance from my emotions getting the better of me, which almost never happened. I'm not sure if I was more upset with myself for losing control or afraid of her reaction.

'My, my. And what is that supposed to mean?' Naoto's mother's voice was chilly. 'Tell me, what did you mean by that?'

If I look away, I lose.

I surprised myself again by thinking that. This shouldn't have been a situation where I was worried about winning or losing. So why had that feeling crept up?

At that moment I felt a breeze on my cheeks. We were indoors, so there shouldn't have been any breeze, but I felt it, cool on my face.

And I also caught a whiff of the sea. I guessed that it must be coming from the food at another table, but of course I couldn't go and check.

'Come now, dear,' said Naoto's father, who still had the same friendly demeanor.

'Mom, you do seem to be a little prickly today. You're scaring Miyako.'

'Oh, I'm not so scary.' She smiled for the first time. 'Am I?'

'No, you aren't,' I answered, but that must not have been what she wanted to hear, because she stared daggers at me.

She's a tough one, I thought. *The usual tricks may not work on her.* But at the same time I felt that building up our relationship and winning her trust would be a worthwhile challenge.

Naoto's father tried to ease the tension by asking me questions about myself.

I was honest about everything that I could be, and for the things that I couldn't (basically anything to do with my work at the Agency), I lied.

It seemed like we were on track to end the meeting with no more mishaps. But of course, that's not how it played out.

'Excuse me, miss, you dropped this.' A waiter in a crisp black vest was standing beside me, holding out a napkin. I thanked him and took it, saying that it must have fallen off my lap. Even without looking at Naoto's mother I could tell that she was gazing at me severely, aghast at my sloppiness for having dropped the napkin. It seemed that she wasn't even willing to overlook a minor infraction. Rather than feeling angry I just reflected that I couldn't underestimate her. This struggle would be long and hard.

As I was opening the folded napkin I noticed a triangle drawn on the corner in black ink. It took me by surprise, but I didn't let it show.

Making a mildly embarrassed face I whispered to Naoto, 'I'm going to the bathroom.'

I left the lounge and walked past the hotel reception toward the restrooms.

The mark on the napkin was one of our codes. We laid out detailed plans before any mission, but things had a way of not quite going according to plan. We used a number of simple codes in order to adjust on the fly, like hand signals in baseball.

The triangle meant: *New information; meet at nearest bathroom.*

There are a limited number of places where we could meet without drawing attention. Movie theaters, elevators, escalators.

I spotted a bench by the entrance to the bathrooms and figured that was the meeting spot. I sat on one end. There was a man already seated. He looked up when I sat down. 'Hey there,' he said. It was an agent who had joined up the year before me. He wore a suit and a friendly air. 'What a coincidence. You here on business?'

I should ask you the same, I thought, then recalled the mission his team had been on for a month. They were after a foreign operative who had gone to ground.

We had many methods of exchanging intelligence without

speaking, or we could communicate while making it seem like we were muttering to ourselves. But I suppose he judged that in this situation it made the most sense to act as if we were co-workers who had bumped into one another.

'I'm with my boyfriend, meeting his parents over in the lounge.' There was no need to hide that.

'Oho. Isn't that nice.'

'And you? Business?'

'You could say that. I heard that my client is moving forward with their plans.' He smiled indulgently, looking for all the world like a businessman accommodating the whims of a difficult customer. But the operative he was after had a new kind of nerve toxin and plans to release it in public, so I imagined he was fairly stressed.

'What kind of person is your client?'

We were on different teams, but we all provided mutual support. Everyone at the Agency had the same primary goal, broadly speaking: the national interest. When it came to factors that affected the national interest, most were connected at the root. Dig down below any threat and you would find either the Americans or the Soviets, or both. Whether we liked it or not, we agents had to cooperate with each other.

'Good question. I couldn't say exactly what sort of person they are.'

'I'd say that's a problem.'

We knew that one month earlier the nerve gas had been brought into Japan from the Soviet Union. We also had intel that the plan was to release it in Tokyo at the cost of many human lives, but according to what we knew it wasn't supposed to happen for some time.

Had the time come? And was the target site this hotel?

'Is there anything I can do to help?' I asked, but I could imagine the answer.

Sure enough, he replied, 'No, it's my job. I just thought I should let you know. I don't want your party to get caught up in it.' He shrugged. 'Maybe there's another place you could enjoy each other's company.'

He was telling me to get somewhere safe.

Our work was different from police work. If the police knew about the threat of mass casualties they would lock down the area and evacuate every last person in the hotel.

But our priorities were different. More than the safety of average citizens or the stability of public order, our first responsibility was to uphold the national interest. Individual lives were less critical.

In this particular case, the objective was to make it seem like Japan had no knowledge of either the operative or the experimental nerve gas. We had to hide this from both the Soviets and our friends the Americans. Especially from the Americans.

That was why we had to avoid making a big scene when apprehending the operative. The Agency could not maneuver in the open. It was often the case that we had to pretend that we knew nothing.

I went back to the lounge and scanned the room. I recognized several agents dressed as hotel guests. The waiter was probably an agent too.

'So, tell me what you're good at. Can you cook, or do needlework?' Naoto's mother asked me when I returned to my seat, her expression flat. It was clear enough that she was mocking me, asking if I had any accomplishments and assuming that I didn't.

I kept my distaste from showing on my face. Ordinarily I would be able to let something like that just roll off of me, but knowing that the foreign operative could be lurking nearby was throwing off my concentration and making it harder for me to keep my cool.

I told her I was as good as the next person at cooking and

sewing, but because I was agitated my tone was probably a bit sharp. No, I definitely sounded irritated.

She stood up and asked, 'Where's the bathroom?' Like she couldn't figure it out.

I told her where it was and she left the lounge. She had a busy way of walking that came across as forceful. If there was a competition for aggressive walks she would be a leading contender.

Happy that she was gone, I turned to Naoto. 'Actually, when I went to the bathroom before,' I began, speaking loudly enough so that his father could hear as well, 'I overheard something about a pickpocket on the loose.'

'What?'

'It's a little unnerving, can we maybe go find some other restaurant or café?'

I just said it as it occurred to me, and I realized that it wasn't the best pitch, but it was good enough. It looked like Naoto wasn't quite following.

'Pickpocket? As in, someone who picks your pocket?'

His father still seemed relaxed but his curiosity must have been piqued because he started to swivel his head around to see what was going on.

We didn't have time for this.

Naoto's mother reappeared. She waddled forcefully through the room, jostling the chair of a little old lady. The old lady in turn nearly knocked her own bag off her table, but Naoto's mother didn't even seem to notice. She just came back over and sat down across from me. 'And what were you talking about?'

'We, uh, thought we might go to a different place,' Naoto said, and explained why.

His mother made a dubious look, showing well-worn furrows on her brow. She avoided my eyes. 'A pickpocket? Is that even a real thing?'

'Actually I overheard some people talking about it in the lobby just a few minutes ago,' I said. Then she turned her gaze on me, like she was trying to run me through. Her look was so sharp it almost hurt.

'Is that so? Or is it perhaps that it's inconvenient for you to be here?'

'Inconvenient for me?'

'Perhaps there's someone here that you don't want to be spotted by?'

'Someone I'd rather not be spotted by?' I had no idea what she was talking about, and ended up just repeating what she was saying.

'Like maybe there's a man here you're also dating on the side.'

The insinuation in her voice didn't sound like she was joking. I could tell she thought she had caught me.

It took me one second to figure it out.

I realized she must have seen me talking to my coworker by the bathroom.

'Maybe your other man is here and you're panicking?' Her nose-breathing was excited, and she showed a hint of a smile.

When had she spotted me? I held back from clicking my tongue. She had asked where the bathroom was before, but she knew exactly where it was.

'Mom, you watch too many TV dramas.' Naoto didn't seem the least bit suspicious. If anything he looked happy.

My mind was racing. I wanted to defuse the misunderstanding, but more than that I needed to get us out of there. Compared to letting Naoto and his family get caught in a catastrophe, the man-on-the-side issue seemed less significant.

I tried to think of different ways I could solve this.

That's when things started happening in the hotel lounge.

People around the room were getting up all at once, acting as if they were just guests going about their business: paying the bill, heading out to the lobby to look for someone, going to make a call at the payphone. They were all agents, but they all looked like they were behaving perfectly naturally, which was still impressive even though I expected nothing less from them. But I must have been the only person to know that everyone was focused on the same goal.

'Sorry, are you even listening to me?'

It was Naoto's mother. She startled me. I began stammering an apology, but I could see in her eyes that she was angry.

'I can tell that you're hiding something.'

'There's no need to scare the girl, dear,' Naoto's father said, attempting to intercede, but it didn't look like it had any effect on her.

'He's right, Mom. And anyway, we should leave, in case there really is a pickpocket.' Thankfully Naoto didn't seem to be buying into his mother's suspicions.

'Let's just go somewhere else,' I said.

'But our drinks haven't come yet.' No sooner than the words were out of her mouth, Naoto's mother reared up. 'Hello, waiter!' she shouted, waving her hand. She was so loud and aggressive that everyone at the nearby tables turned to look at her.

'Mom, no need to shout!'

'Quiet down, will you?' Naoto and his father both whispered at her, trying to calm her down, but she just got louder.

'Hello, waiter, hurry up!' She looked back over her shoulder and gestured forcefully.

I could see a waiter rushing over from behind her. In his haste while threading through the tables he bumped into one.

It was the same little old lady from before. A spoon fell off the table from the impact. The waiter immediately apologized, even as the spoon was falling, but the old woman's hand shot out and snatched the spoon before it hit the floor.

Incredible reflexes.

Nobody else seemed concerned, but it didn't sit right with me how quickly she reacted.

She looked like nothing more than an elderly lady, but her hair could have easily been fake. She was focused on her plate, eating some dessert-like thing, but she could have also just been trying to make it seem like there was nothing to see. She still had her little bag on the table.

She checked her watch, then stood up to leave.

Something wasn't right.

All my fellow agents were gone from the lounge.

I was the only one there to handle it.

Before I could think about it any more I said to Naoto, 'Sorry, my stomach's hurting.'

'Are you okay?'

'It must be nerves.'

'Well, my mom can be scary.'

'Are you saying this is my fault?' cut in Naoto's mother. The waiter had arrived, so she turned to him. 'I'm still waiting for my café au lait. Hello? My café au lait?'

The waiter muttered an apology and dipped his head.

I told Naoto in a low voice that I needed to go to the bathroom again, then I left the lounge.

The old woman seemed to be heading for the bathroom, walking at a brisk pace. By that point I was pretty certain. I hurried to close some distance between us, then called out to her in Russian.

She slowed down for a moment. It was only the briefest moment, but there was no mistaking it. I had taken her by surprise and her body had reacted, although she tried to play it off like nothing had happened, and she continued walking. I strode forward, getting closer. Timing it just right, I extended my right leg and tripped her from behind.

'Are you okay?'

I hoped it looked to anyone who might have seen that I was rushing up to help an old woman who had fallen. Before she could regain her footing I was on her, gripping her tightly by the wrists.

'If you try to move I'll break your arm,' I whispered to her.

A bellman hurried over. 'Is everything all right?'

'Oh, yes, she wanted to go to the bathroom and I'm just helping her out,' I answered brightly. I had punched the old woman in the ribs so she couldn't talk, she could only grimace in discomfort.

Luckily there was no one else in the bathroom. I forced her into a stall.

She whimpered pitifully, making me wonder for a moment if she wasn't actually just some poor old woman. Which was exactly what she wanted. She wriggled out of my grasp and whipped around, her hand reaching out toward me. Something flashed: a needle. I dodged and chopped my hand hard at her elbow. She recoiled.

I held my breath. All I could do now was act. I jabbed my fingers into her solar plexus. When she opened her mouth to wail I yanked out a length of toilet paper, balled it up and stuffed it in her mouth like a gag. Then I took out some wire and a pocket lock, tied up her thumbs and threaded the wire through the toilet pipes to hold her there. Her white hair had fallen off: it was a wig after all, and quite well made. She may have been small, but she was actually a young woman. I looked inside her bag and found several small plastic vials.

I locked the stall and then climbed up and over the door. I flipped the *out of service* tab on the outside of the stall.

Luckily, it didn't take long to reconnect with my fellow agents. The man in the suit came from the elevator bank. I saw him notice me, but he was on duty and just walked past. I called out to him.

His eyes widened, giving me a look like I shouldn't be trying to speak with him in the middle of a mission, I should have just pretended not to know him.

But I had to tell him: 'Your client is in the ladies' room. I'll leave the rest up to you. I just happened to run into her.' I handed her bag over to him. 'The thing you were looking for is in here. Those valuables.'

By which I meant the explosive device.

It seemed clear that the other agents had received bad intelligence and had fallen for a decoy. And while they were busy with that, this operative disguised as an old woman planned to make her move.

I went back to the lounge. Checking my watch, I saw that not too much time had gone by, but when I found Naoto he was alone.

'Sorry. Mom got annoyed and left. Dad went to go find her.' He looked embarrassed.

Maybe things would have gone better with my mother-in-law over the years if I hadn't done all that during our first meeting.

Of course, I had to do it. If I hadn't gotten involved, there would have been a nerve gas attack. They said as much at the Agency. I was praised for rendering one last valuable service before retirement.

But that had nothing to do with Naoto's parents. From their perspective, the woman dating their son met them for the first time and kept getting up to leave. I must have seemed incredibly rude.

I suppose I made a terrible first impression. I failed. Any time things aren't going well with Mother, which is to say most of the time, I think back to that initial failure.

Only, now, I've started thinking a little differently.

I keep remembering what the life insurance salesman Ichio Ishiguro said when he appeared at my house.

He talked about a certain deep-rooted chemistry between myself and my mother-in-law. It felt like he was hinting at something, but rather than trying to plant an idea in my head it was almost as if he was uncertain of how much he should actually tell me.

If our relationship is governed by ancient connections, then it doesn't much matter what kind of a first impression I made.

On the other hand, I wasn't prepared to fully accept the idea of a generational grudge. Because if that were true, then things might never get any better.

'You know, your father really helped me out,' said Dr O. as he walked along beside me.

'Sorry?' I answered stupidly. It was blue sky overhead and green grass all around us on the fairway. His energetic pace with a bag full of clubs hoisted on his back didn't seem to fit my image of a doctor who worked inside all day. 'I think you're in better shape than I am.'

'My son handles everything at the hospital these days,' he said with a smile, 'while I'm just golfing all the time – so I've gotten a little sturdier.'

O. Hospital was a prominent and long-running institution. Dr O. had recently given over control to his son and daughter-in-law, but he was still an influential voice in the medical community. Up until then I had never had a proper conversation with him, I just knew his reputation for being eccentric and stubborn. That's how people talked about him in the pharma sales world. People said that he was a peculiar sort, that he didn't accept invitations to go out and be entertained, that he just wanted to hear about the new drugs and would get annoyed if you tried to talk about anything else. Whereas his son and daughter-in-law were supposed to be much easier to talk to, and my colleagues were glad he had handed over the reins to the new generation.

But once I actually met him, I didn't get the sense that Dr O. was at all stubborn or peculiar. I mean, we had only played golf over one morning, and so far only nine holes, so it's not like I'd had that much exposure to him, but he seemed to me like a completely normal, sensible person.

It didn't even take me very long to come to my interesting conclusion.

Thinking it was odd that someone didn't want to be taken out to a fancy bar – that struck me as us salesmen being out of touch. It made perfect sense that all a doctor might want from a pharmaceutical sales employee would be information on drugs, and that he'd get irritated at someone who wasn't focused on providing that information.

Dr O. was shorter than me, with thinning hair and plenty of wrinkles, but when he played a good shot his face would light up like a little boy's.

'The old man sure can play golf,' Watanuki said admiringly when it was just the two of us in the break after the front nine.

'He does seem to have great coordination.'

'But Kitayama, why would he have asked for you to come along today? Any idea?'

'None.'

It was true. O. Hospital was handled by Watanuki's team. Watanuki had been out drinking in Ginza with Dr O.'s son, now the head of the hospital, and the son had apparently asked about me and said his father wanted us to go golfing.

Watanuki had cocked his head in puzzlement – *Why Kitayama?* – and I was similarly confused. Although I had no reason to refuse, so there we were.

On my first drive of the tenth hole I pushed out, sending the ball off to the right. But Dr O. did the same, so we both ended up having to leave the cart path and make our way across the fairway. That's when Dr O. brought up my dad.

'So you know my father, Doctor?'

'Actually,' he said, his face creased in a smile, 'we were in elementary school together.' My dad came from Gunma Prefecture, but he had never told me much about his early years. It's not that he had anything to hide, necessarily, he just always used to say sheepishly that his childhood was nothing special, with nothing particular worth recounting.

Dr O. told me that he and my dad were in the same class for several years. 'Your father taught me how to study.'

'Really?'

'Yes, oh, he knew how to study. Not me, I was useless. Especially when it came to memorizing anything. History lessons went in one ear and out the other. I thought that ancient stories didn't have anything to do with me. Whereas your father knew all about history, and he would tell me all about how Emperor Shomu did this and Minamoto Yoritomo did that.'

'Sorry,' I said, for some reason feeling it appropriate to apologize.

'No, thanks to him I took in an interest in history! Suddenly the historical figures weren't just two-dimensional names on a list of dates; I felt that they were real people, like us, who stood on this earth and lived full lives. Emperor Shomu and Yoritomo and all of them actually had stories. If your father hadn't helped me make the grade I never would have become a doctor. That's why I always consider myself in his debt.'

'I'm sure he didn't help you all that much,' I said, waving off his praise for my dad. 'I'm more impressed that you can remember something like that from so long ago.'

'No, your father was very kind. I was always full of bluff and bluster, nobody really liked me, but your father still helped me out.'

41

My dad had a mild disposition, and because he had always worked so quietly and diligently as a gardener it was easy for me to picture him as a child meekly sitting on the edge of the classroom.

Dr O. went on. 'You know, I saw your father six or seven years back.'

'Oh? I didn't know that.'

'We just bumped into each other on the subway. And it really was a coincidence, because I usually drive rather than take the train. But right away I knew it was him.'

From my perspective, even though this man had handed over his business to his son, he was still Dr O. of O. Hospital, a powerful figure and a client we had to do our best to take care of since he was key to the health of our firm. Finding out that he was friends with my dad left me confused as to how I should act.

'We hadn't seen each other in a long time; I was thrilled to reconnect. He probably just wanted to get home, but I coaxed him to come with me to a few places I like for some drinks. While we were out together, you came up. The fact that you work for a pharmaceutical company.'

'I see.'

'Only he wouldn't tell me the name of your company, which strikes me as being very much like him. I think he felt uncomfortable with the idea that my relationship with him would lead to me giving any special attention to his son's company, that is, your company. He even said he was holding it back for your sake. Very circumspect, truly. He said something that made me think: just like with raising trees, if something can grow without intervention then it's best to let it do just that.'

As I listened along, I recalled that at the time my father had made no mention of meeting Dr O. Once in a while he would ask me how things were going at work, but he never pressed for any additional details.

'On the other hand,' Dr O. said, then settled in to take his next shot. He looked down at his ball where it lay in the rough and squared up. I took a step back to watch his swing.

His club arced around and connected with a satisfying *pock*, launching the ball into the air.

'On the other hand,' he continued, 'medicine is a small world, and there aren't that many people named Kitayama. It didn't take me any time to figure out who you were. But I had promised your father I wouldn't bother you, and I was busy planning my handover to my own son, so I decided not to meddle.'

Which explains why I'd never had any contact with him. 'Then may I ask what prompted this invitation today?'

My ball had rolled into the rough as well. I selected the same iron that Dr O. had used, lined up the angle back to the green, took a practice swing, then took my shot.

I meant to just chip it lightly, but I landed a more forceful hit than I planned and sent the ball flying. Watching it melt into the blue backdrop of the sky sent a wave of well-being through my body.

'Well, I recently heard that your father had passed.' Dr O. and I started walking again. He looked forlorn at mentioning it, almost helpless, like a lost child. It surprised me, because I would have thought that doctors are desensitized to death.

Dad's funeral was a modest affair. Our neighbors the Furuyas and other people from the area came to pay their respects, along with some people for whom he had done gardening work over the years, but it was by no means a large-scale memorial service, which felt right for an unassuming man like my father.

'I'm sorry no one got in touch with you to let you know he had died,' I said to Dr O. 'I had no idea you were friends.'

'Ah, please don't worry about that – we were just elementary school classmates, after all. But I was curious, how did he die?'

I looked up, not quite to the heavens, but enough to take in the

43

blue. The sky was like an endless ocean, clean and clear, washing away any trace of negativity. It didn't feel right to talk about death under a sky like that, but at the same time its massiveness somehow made me think of all the people out there who were at that very moment suffering through illness or on the threshold between life and death.

'I'm embarrassed to say – and it's probably weird to say that I'm embarrassed but – he fell off a shrine. Sorry, I mean, he fell down the steps at a shrine. He tripped and fell down a stone stairway.'

Dr O.'s expression darkened, for the first time. 'Was it an accident?'

'That's right. Just one of those random things.'

The truth is, I did have a hard time accepting my dad's death at first. In the past he had been injured on the job, like when he fell off a stepladder and broke his wrist or got tangled in thorns while tending to a rosebush and emerged all bloody, and I kept feeling that the shrine incident was just another mishap. Like he would get better and I would see him again soon.

'So he wasn't sick at all?'

'No, he wasn't.' As we headed back in the direction of the green I started to wonder why Dr O. was pressing me about this.

When we reached the green Watanuki and his partner from O. Hospital had already arrived in their golf cart.

For the rest of the round Dr O. barely spoke, despite golfing very well. It was noticeable enough that Watanuki pulled me aside at one point and asked, 'Kitayama, did you say something to piss him off?'

'No, I don't think so,' I said nervously. All we had done was talk about my dad. It certainly hadn't been my intention to upset him, although it was possible I said something that he didn't like. I couldn't be sure. Which was common enough. I was very rarely sure about my own mistakes.

Luckily, just before we wrapped up for the day I got confirmation that his darkened mood wasn't because of me. We had finished our game and brought our things back to the parking lot, and Watanuki ducked off to the bathroom. While I was waiting for him, Dr O. strode over to me. 'I'm not sure if I should ask this . . .'

'What can I do for you?'

'Was there anything at all strange about your father's accident?'

'Strange?'

'Do you think anyone else was involved? Any foul play?'

'Um, what exactly do you—?'

'I told you we met for the first time in a long time. That day, your father said something that stuck with me.'

'And that was?'

Dr O. grimaced. I had the feeling I was about to be diagnosed with a serious malady. The blood seemed to drain from my hands and feet.

'We were drinking, so I thought he might have been making a joke, but when you told me he had an accidental fall I wondered.'

Can you tell the difference between murder and accidental death?

That's what my dad had asked.

Dr O. didn't know what he meant, so Dad had continued: 'I've just been wondering, if I were to be pushed and fall to my death, for example, what would people think had happened?'

'What did you say to that?' I asked Dr O.

'I said that it's the police's job to figure that out,' he answered with a rueful laugh. 'Motives and foul play, that's police territory, right? But if it were murder, as long as nothing looked out of place, maybe everyone would just think it was an accident. After all, the police can't afford to investigate every little detail every single time someone dies. But when you told me your father died in an accident, well . . . and not just any accident—'

'He fell down the steps.' It seemed like such a silly way to die that I couldn't suppress a nervous laugh.

'I wonder if he had some kind of a premonition.'

'A premonition?'

'That he'd have an accident. That is, if it even was an accident.'

'Sorry?'

'I feel bad suggesting something so awful, but is it at all possible that he was pushed down the stairs?' But after a moment Dr O. waved his hand. 'You know what, never mind. Forget I said anything. Your father had been talking about accidents and murders, so the possibility popped into my head. But thinking about it, he probably just had a fall.'

With that, he thanked me for a pleasant day of golf and headed for his car.

Almost as soon as he left, Watanuki returned from the bathroom. 'Looks like he wasn't pissed off after all. It actually looked like you two were getting along well. I think he must like you.'

'I'm sure that's not true.'

'No, you scored some points for sure, buddy.'

'What do you mean, points?'

'If you can get the top man at a big private hospital to like you, then you're sitting pretty. You're better at this than I thought.'

I'm sure that Naoto was just sharing with me casually, reporting how his golf day with the important doctor had gone. He was probably happy that he had gotten friendly with one of the celebrities in his world. *Hey, listen to what happened today*, was his attitude as he told me.

'Turns out he and my dad were in elementary school together.'

I could understand why this would be a pleasant surprise

for Naoto, but I was stuck on what his father had asked this doctor:

Can you tell the difference between murder and accidental death?

It didn't sound like a random question. I wondered if he had played it off as a joke but was actually interested in knowing a physician's opinion.

Why would that have been?

It didn't take me long to reach a conclusion. What if my father-in-law was afraid that he would be murdered, and that it would be made to look like an accident?

He was a craftsman at heart, a gentle man, and the only enemies he had were the beetles and bees who built their nests in his gardens. Who could have possibly borne him any ill will?

But even as I asked myself that, I already knew the answer.

The next day, after Naoto left for work, I got started cleaning the house. I may share the house with my mother-in-law, but I end up doing most of the cleaning. And though I used to do it my own way, she was always complaining that it wasn't right, that I was leaving it dirtier than when I started, so now I just do it how she says she would do it. I know how to disarm a bomb, so following a specific set of cleaning instructions is no big deal for me. But still she starts in on me every so often. 'Miyako, I just don't know how you can do this so sloppily,' she said, faking playfulness.

'I'm just doing it the way you showed me, Mother.'

'If you did it the way I showed you there wouldn't be this much dust left over.'

Like a coach saying, *You wouldn't lose if you followed my plays, so if you're losing you must not be following my plays.* Since I married Naoto and we moved in with his mother I've mastered the art of expressing my angst through heavy sighs.

I got angry, and then I got ready. As nonchalantly as I could I said, 'The other day a life insurance guy came to the door.'

'Insurance?' She seemed momentarily thrown off. Then she narrowed her eyes. 'Was he trying to sell you something?'

'He said he was looking for you.' It wasn't a lie. The man who had introduced himself as Ichio Ishiguro had claimed to want to talk to her about insurance. 'Are you shopping for a policy?'

'Don't be silly. Such a dark thing. The very idea of life insurance assumes you're going to die!'

Yes, Mother. Dying is what human beings do. I almost said it, but it was so stupidly obvious I just let it go. Instead I asked, 'But, wait, didn't you say you have insurance now?' I knew we had never talked about it before.

'No, I never said that. I don't have any. Do you?'

Here was my opening. Nice and easy does it: 'What about Father? Did he have insurance when he had his accident?'

Her face hardened. 'Why? What is it you're getting at?'

She sounded annoyed, but I had seen a flash of fear. It was obvious she was trying to cover it with indignation. When I was an agent I had endless training on interpersonal negotiation. They hammered into me all the techniques for knowing when someone's lying, or for leading people to the conclusion that you want. In a contest like this between me and Mother, it was pro versus amateur.

'I feel like Naoto once said something about his father having had a policy that paid out. Was that life insurance?'

'Naoto? How would Naoto . . .?'

How would he know that? she seemed about to say. Which was basically a confession that she knew he'd had one but thought her son didn't know. Even though it seemed perfectly reasonable to me that if someone's father had a life insurance policy then they might be aware of it.

I considered pushing harder but decided against it. I didn't have the proof that I needed to finish her off, and it would be meaningless to press any further if she had room to wriggle out of it. I had to keep my ammo for when it would be most effective. No sense in using it up prematurely.

I switched on the vacuum cleaner to cut off the conversation. Mother seemed agitated that it was left hanging in the air, but she wasn't going to pursue it any further either. She stalked around as I vacuumed. She must have been especially peeved because eventually she went into the garden and started tidying up, which she almost never does.

It felt good to land a blow on her for a change, though I wasn't exactly happy about what I was learning.

That night, when she was out with the Furuyas, I asked Naoto, 'How many years ago did your father die?'

'That's a funny thing to ask out of nowhere.'

'I saw a show on TV today that had an accident kind of like his, so I was thinking about him.' It was easy for me to make up small fictions like that. 'And you went golfing with that guy the other day – a doctor, right? – who was your father's classmate as a kid. That's probably another reason it was in my head.'

'I guess it's six years now? It still doesn't even feel real.' He looked over at the little altar in the corner. There was a photo of his father with a young man's smile.

'I don't really know too much about what happened, but I was wondering why your father was at that shrine at night.'

'It's just what he did.'

'Go to pray at the shrine?'

'No, karaoke. On the other side of the shrine was a little place he liked.'

Back then was around the time they started making karaoke boxes out of shipping containers. Apparently my father-in-law would cut through the shrine grounds to get to his spot, when he had some free time for singing.

'And he took a bad step on the stairs.'

I started asking more details about the accident, but not

forcefully. I didn't want Naoto to think I was looking for something, so I circled around what I was after, gently, obliquely, sometimes probing, sometimes confirming, unspooling the answers.

He said that his father fell late at night when no one was around, so the body wasn't discovered for several hours. Which means that we still didn't know what actually happened.

'So there probably weren't any witnesses.'

'I imagine my mother heard everything there was to hear from the police.'

When the call had come, his mother was at home in bed. Although there's no one who can confirm that she was actually sleeping.

While we were talking, Naoto had been taking something out of his bag and assembling it on the table.

'I got this at work. There was an extra one lying around that nobody needed.'

'Like we used to use in elementary school!'

'Yeah, an old balance scale.' Naoto played with different combinations of brass weights, making the pans clank left and right every time he shifted the balance. 'I know this is the whole point of the scale, but I love how when you have the same weight it levels off so perfectly.'

'We'd all be in trouble if it didn't.'

He used tweezers to place a tiny pellet of aluminum on the right pan, which started floating downward.

I pictured a seesaw in a playground at a park. One side sinks, then the other, and if you push off the ground the back-and-forth only gets wilder.

I thought about balance.

When I was at the Agency, there was one meeting where I said to my superior, 'If we don't change the way we do things, we'll never outmaneuver the Americans.'

The meeting was about Operation Ivy Bells. The US used wiretaps on undersea cables near Okhotsk to spy on Soviet communications. The plot was uncovered thanks to a double-cross by an NSA agent and the Soviets scrambled to deal with it, but it was just as much of a surprise to us in Japan. We had zero intel that such an operation was going on in our backyard. From the US perspective, Japan was a subordinate partner, so naturally they didn't tell us everything, but still this felt like we had been caught unpleasantly unaware. It forced us to recognize that though the US was our ally they wouldn't be fully open with us, and it led to Japan getting more serious about intelligence and counterintelligence.

My thought was that we should use the talents and resources of the Agency to strengthen our position against the Americans, maybe even try to pull one over on them.

My supervisor tried to calm me down. 'It'd be tough. No matter how good our baseball teams are in Japan, we still couldn't win in the major league; this is kind of the same. Beating them is nothing more than a pleasant dream.'

'I bet soon you'll be seeing Japanese players winning in the majors,' I said testily.

'It's one thing to say it,' he snorted, 'but I'm telling you, you're dreaming.'

Part of me felt a chilly scorn for him, but then he added something that I had to acknowledge was true: 'It comes down to a question of balance.'

It was the height of the Cold War, and there was no point in asking which side was right or wrong. Both were developing and stockpiling nuclear weapons, each one egged on by the other, only neither was doing it to win the war – they were doing it to maintain balance.

If either side became too powerful, the foundation would crumble. An evenly matched tug-of-war was the best outcome.

'Competition has its benefits, but it also has its downsides,' my supervisor added.

'When the competition is fierce, everyone gets stronger.'

'That's true. But a society based on competition isn't necessarily always and only a good thing.'

'How do you mean?'

'No matter who wins, it always leads to backlash. People are motivated by emotions, not logic. There may come a time soon when sports festivals at school have nice, polite races where everyone runs next to each other. To keep things steady and even.'

'What's the point of a sports festival without competition?'

'*You* can think that, because you'd be one of the ones winning the race.' He paused a moment. 'We don't need to beat the Americans on this. If we do it'll only engender bad feelings and make them put up their guard. That's why we have to keep a lid on everything the Agency does.'

I thought back to this as I watched Naoto play around with the balance scale. A scale should stay even. Whereas a seesaw goes up and down, and no one tries to make it balance out.

I imagined a giant scale with myself in one pan and Mother in the other. Of course the scale was tilted in her favor. Which I understood – in the relationship between a woman and her mother-in-law, there's a difference in status around age, and also because the daughter-in-law is the one entering the household from outside. Understanding your place and keeping a low profile when infiltrating an organization is one of the first things they teach you as an agent.

So why couldn't I be content with my position?

How come I always lost my cool when it came to her?

Why is it that I always wanted to upend the seesaw?

Maybe because of a grudge passed down from my ancestors.

No sooner had I called up the words of the insurance salesman Ichio Ishiguro, than my view suddenly expanded. I had been in our house with the window curtains drawn, but all of that vanished. Or, no, it didn't vanish; it was replaced – by a blank sky over white ground stretching off into the distance. Underfoot, all around, was sand. I could feel the wind and taste the sea salt. I realized I was standing on the shore, and looked about wildly, not understanding. Behind me was an enormous living thing splayed out horizontally. *A whale?* In the next moment I could hear a rumbling, like a great crowd of people drawing closer.

'Miyako, are you okay?'

Naoto's voice startled me. We were in the living room. Where we had been the whole time.

'Going somewhere, Miyako?'

Mother called out to me after I was done with the dishes and the rest of the housework. I hadn't even started getting ready to leave yet but she'd guessed correctly, which sent a chill through me. Asking her how she knew didn't seem like the best play, so I stayed silent and just cocked my head, playing dumb.

At that she said, 'Your makeup's a little different.'

I had to try hard not to let my irritation show.

I didn't intend to do my makeup any differently, but I was planning on going out, so it's possible I had taken a bit more care than I would if I were just staying at home. I was actually impressed that she noticed such a minute variance. Then it made me think of the time shortly after we had first met when she noticed my eye color, squinting like she was looking at something disgusting. 'Your eyes are so light they're almost blue. Why is that?' I bit my tongue to keep from asking why her ears were so big.

'I'm going to see a friend who works at the hospital.' It was the story I'd come up with to cover my going out.

'Really? It's so rare for you to go see friends.'

'More of an acquaintance, really. I'm, um, going to talk to her about fertility treatments.'

Not having luck starting a family had been a blow for me, and I didn't love using it as an excuse, but it did seem to work well when dealing with Mother. As I'd expected, she was at a momentary loss and then backed right off, saying, 'Ah, I see. Well, in that case . . .'

She still couldn't help launching a barb, something about me finally getting serious about kids, but I let it roll off me as I walked out the door.

I took two trains to get to the café I used to frequent back when I was with the Agency. I went to the table in the back where the man I was meeting sat waiting, looking put out.

'I have to get back. It would help if you showed up on time.'

He was an analyst who had started about six months before I retired. I didn't know how old he was but he looked like a frail college student, he was pasty-faced, with a head shaped like a gourd. His physical feebleness wasn't camouflage either, he really wasn't suited for any work that involved moving his body. But when it came to SIGINT, IMINT, OSINT, basically anything involving communications or imagery or public records, he was as good as they come.

'Then hurry up and let's get started.'

'Seriously, put yourself in my shoes.'

'Isn't keeping a poker face the first thing they teach you?'

'When I want to communicate that I'm upset I make sure that I look upset. They're really keeping a close eye on us these days. These internal audits . . .'

'More than before?'

'Finding stuff out is what gets them going. Now any time I use my disk drive a little indicator light goes on.'

'This is the only time I'll ask,' I entreated.

He owed me one anyway.

It was from that dustup with the Russian nerve toxin. This pale fellow was the analyst on duty. Meaning he was the one who took the bait on the bad intel and overlooked the operative who had been disguised as an old woman. If the whole thing had blown up into a major incident, responsibility would have fallen with him. And whatever official consequences there were would have been nothing compared to the blame he would heap on himself. Ever since, he's been grateful for my intervention.

'Well, what you asked about was just an accident. All I did was look into police records, so it wasn't even that big of a deal. Nothing to do with the nation,' he said. 'I couldn't bring any documents with me, you'll have to settle for an oral account.'

In other words, get ready to remember what I'm about to say. 'Got it.'

He proceeded to tell me all about how the police had handled my father-in-law's death, based on the records that remained. It was declared an accidental fall down the steps at the shrine, and there was nothing in the records that suggested any suspicion of murder.

'Was it very dark that night?'

'I looked into that. It was right around the winter solstice. According to meteorological data, there were no clouds, and running a simulation of the time and location of the accident shows that the moonlight would have been bright.'

'A big bright beautiful moon, huh?'

'Well, I wouldn't put it that way, but in any case it wasn't pitch dark. Of course someone can take a fall even when they can see just fine.'

'I guess so.'

'As for witnesses . . .'

'Were there any?' That would make this whole thing simple. Then there'd be no doubt that he didn't just fall.

'Yes. But about that . . .'

'What about that?'

'The one witness died shortly thereafter. Hit by a car. Seems to have wandered into traffic.'

I sat silently for a moment. I had the sensation that, rather than my former colleague, it was my mother-in-law sitting across the table, staring at me with eyes devoid of any warmth.

Several days later, I found myself in the hallway of my own home, suddenly dodging.

In front of me was a man whose right hand held something that flashed in the light. Before I even registered that it was a blade, my body moved of its own accord. Like footwork in boxing. He slashed the air where I had been, his momentum pulling him forward so the knife blade caught the wall.

Right away, I smashed my knee into his ribs.

I kneed him harder than I intended to, but I knew the reason why.

I was angry that I would get an earful from Mother.

She always spotted any tiny ding or dent if I bumped anything while cleaning. It was uncanny how she found any excuse to peck at me.

Miyako, what's this mark on the wall? Always insinuating it was me who did it.

The man fought through the pain and swung his knife again. This time I kicked him in the shin.

His leg buckled for a moment, then he lurched back up, which is when I noticed that he still had his shoes on inside my house, which really made me lose my cool.

I would be the one to hear about it if the floors were dirty.

A few minutes earlier, the doorbell had rung. 'Registered mail, seal please,' came the voice from outside, so I opened the door. I probably should have been more on my guard. It's easy enough to trust someone dressed like a postal worker, but when I was still an agent I never would have been caught unawares like this.

He burst through the door and pushed me into the house. My personal seal went flying.

Knife in hand, he advanced, trying to intimidate me. I skipped backward, maintaining distance between us.

The hallway was perfectly fine for everyday life, but for combat it was tight. Basically just a space between the entryway, the staircase up to the second floor, the living room, and the tatami room.

The man advanced. Not a face I recognized.

He must have been a trained fighter, the way he maintained his stance. I calmed my breathing and bladed my body, right arm forward.

His eyes were slightly askew, like he wasn't quite seeing straight.

'Why did you come after me?' I demanded.

He didn't answer.

'Who sent you?'

You know exactly who sent him. I could hear my own voice scolding me. *Are you just hoping it isn't true?*

When you get close to the hive, the bees attack. That's what my supervisor used to say at the Agency. The more you stick your nose in somewhere someone doesn't want it, the more you run into trouble. On the other hand, if the bees are attacking that's proof you're near the honey.

I once said back to my supervisor, 'Can't catch a tiger cub

without braving the tiger's den, right?' But he shook his head ruefully. 'Close, but not the same thing.'

Either way, the fact that I was being attacked meant that someone was on the alert. And angry. I was getting close to the hive.

But whose hive?

No need to play dumb.

A few days ago I went through Mother's things. She was at the movies in Shinjuku with the Furuyas, a rare chance that I didn't want to miss.

Had my father-in-law's death from falling down the steps at the shrine really been an accident? At first I kept going back and forth, wondering if I was overthinking it. No matter how much I didn't like my mother-in-law, imagining she was involved in murder felt like more than just indecent speculation; I had the strong sense I was violating some basic rule of upright human conduct.

But new things were coming to light that fostered my suspicion.

First, there was the matter of the witness.

There was no one at the shrine steps the night that my father-in-law fell, but apparently someone did see him walking through the grounds.

My former colleague had told me that digging any further would attract attention at the Agency. 'I really hope this will be enough for you. If you absolutely need it I can see what else there might be, but if we can I'd like to keep it to this,' he had said. So I did some digging of my own. It turned out that when I started casually asking around, no one thought it strange that Mr Kitayama's daughter-in-law should be wondering about his death, and it wasn't that hard to get a few more details.

The witness was an old man who people called Santaro, though that wasn't his real name. People described him variously as a homeless guy who wandered the neighborhood, an older man who collected trash and took it somewhere to sell, and a toothless fellow who survived on leftovers from the bento shop.

But nobody who talked about him appeared to have any problem with him. A gentle guy, always smiling. Picked up the rubbish that gathered after a rainstorm, always the first to start shoveling snow from the sidewalks in the winter.

And Santaro also saw my father-in-law right before his death.

When the police were investigating the scene, Santaro had apparently come up to them and told them that he might have been the last person to cross paths with the victim of the fall. As far as the cops were concerned, though, it was just a routine accident, so I'm sure they didn't question Santaro especially deeply.

The next time I was talking with Naoto I found a way to work Santaro into the conversation, asking if Naoto knew where he was now. It's a pretty specific topic to just work into a conversation without seeming obvious, but back at the Agency they drilled us on that kind of stuff until I was sick of it.

'Who?' At first Naoto didn't seem to remember the man. But then he got it: 'Oh yeah, that guy. I remember at my dad's funeral—'

'Oh, he came to the funeral?' It was shortly after Naoto and I got married, and my memories of the funeral here at the house were pretty vivid.

'No, no, he held off. He stayed outside.'

He must have not wanted to put anyone out by joining the service, given that he wasn't exactly what you would call hygienic. He had stood outside the house, hands clasped in prayer.

'He sounds like a good person.'

Of course, there's really no such thing as a good person or a bad person. It's easy enough to say that everyone has their good side and bad side, but it's tough to say what good and bad even mean. In my job I judged people based on whether or not they were dangerous to the state, but that wasn't based on any clear metrics. Even during the Cold War the divisions between East and West were often blurred.

'Yeah, he was a good guy. I kept inviting him inside but he refused. Then he started going on about how he thinks he was the last person to see Dad alive. They passed each other on the shrine grounds. He even said they said hi.'

'Wow.'

'He was upset because he thought that if he had stopped Dad to talk maybe he wouldn't have had that fall, but I told him that even if he had stopped him Dad might still have had his accident, that he shouldn't beat himself up.'

'So what happened to Santaro after that?'

'He died. Maybe six months later. Traffic accident.'

Yep, I almost said. This corroborated my information. 'Life takes all kinds of twists and turns, I guess.'

'Really. Mom was shocked too. She had just met with Santaro, right before he died.'

'What?' I was a little too loud. 'Mother did that?'

'Yeah. I mean, I say met with him; it was more like she bumped into him in the street and said hello. It's like a weird pattern, right? Well, pattern, that's not quite right. Just that before my father's accident Santaro ran into him, and before Santaro's accident my mother ran into *him.*'

I kept quiet.

I wasn't as simple as Naoto, to accept at face value that all of this was just a coincidence. Or maybe it was that my theory was the simple one. Between my father-in-law's accident and Santaro's accident, there stood Mother. It was easy to see the connection. It was all I could see.

'She must have been shocked when he died too.'

'Mom was pretty upset about it. You know her parents also died in an accident. She must have felt like she was some kind of vector for bad luck.'

I managed not to shout out loud when I heard that. In fact my expression barely changed, though I admit that it did change a little. Still, I thought I deserved some credit for keeping my cool.

Mother's parents also died in a fatal accident.

A traffic accident, before Naoto was born.

'Same as Santaro.'

'That's why I'm guessing she must have been shaken up when he died.'

'I see.'

So that was the second detail that roused my suspicion.

And the next thing Naoto said only made it worse, giving more life to the dark picture I was putting together.

'Mom's parents, my grandparents . . . I guess them dying actually helped, in a way.'

'Helped?'

'Dad was acting as their guarantor, so he took on their debts.'

I remembered something I had heard, one of the Greek philosophers who taught that standing for someone else's debts is a sure way to ruin the relationship. Seems that the troubles at the intersection of people and money go back thousands of years.

'But when Mom's parents died, their life insurance money came in, and they were able to cover the debts Dad was carrying. What's that they say, disaster turns to good fortune, right? Or, if your horse runs off it may bring back more horses? That doesn't quite fit either . . .'

The conversation went off in another direction, but I kept thinking about it.

Once someone learns a method that works, they tend to go back to it whenever they're in trouble. If you were to formulate a law for it, it would be the Law of Repeatable Success, and if you were being less formal you might just call it your superstition or your way of doing things. Either way, people usually lean on what's worked for them in the past.

I pictured Mother's face.

'Oh by the way, apropos nothing,' I started. Of course it was apropos something. 'Has your mother ever had financial troubles?'

'Mom? Why do you ask?'

'You've told me that when your father died your mother did everything she could to save money, at least I think I remember you saying something like that,' I lied.

'I wonder. I don't really recall.'

Did she need the insurance money? Was she in a tight spot? I didn't ask the questions floating in my head.

So what did I do instead?

I started by going through her chest of drawers.

I was looking for her bank records. I knew of two different accounts she had because she sometimes asked me to help her handle deposits and such; it didn't seem likely that either of those held any secrets. If she was hiding something, it would have to be in another account.

Starting from the bottom drawer, I made my way up one by one. Most of what I found was clothing she no longer wore, though there was some jewelry scattered here and there. For a second I had the sensation that I was a cat burglar after jewels.

I finished searching the whole cabinet and checked the time. She said she'd be back near five, so there was still another hour. I headed upstairs, to the room in the northeast corner of the house that my father-in-law used as a study when he was alive. It certainly wasn't a study anymore, just a small room a few paces square, with a few shelves crammed full of books and dictionaries, an old massage chair, and unused exercise equipment. It's not like I wasn't allowed in there, but no one went in unless they were looking for something.

I checked the shelves end to end.

There was a set of the complete collected works of some author. Next to that were several photo albums. I flipped through one of them and found snapshots of Naoto when he was a boy, which I got lost in for a while.

It's natural to want to look at pictures of your partner when they were a kid, but young Naoto really was cute. Seeing his suntanned skin and white smile, the pictures of him waving the class flag at Sports Day, I felt a pang for how wholesome my man's childhood seemed to have been. Of course there were some silly shots of him sticking his tongue out and making faces, but I felt that my husband had lived his boyhood years to the fullest.

Naturally the albums were mainly family photos. Two thirds of the pictures showed only Naoto and his mother, likely because his father was behind the camera, but his absence made me feel uncomfortable.

And in many of the shots, Mother's gaze was slightly off to the side, in some cases looking away completely. They must have gone on regular trips together because the scenery showed all manner of famous sites around the country. In a number of pictures, she had a pinched look on her face, as if she were saying, *Are you done yet?* Annoyed, as if even the brief moment before he pushed the shutter felt to her like a waste of time.

I put away the photo albums and scanned the next shelf, where I found a sketchbook.

The pencil landscapes were actually really good. There was a fluidity to the lines. Same with the still lifes of fruit. I kept flipping pages and found illustrations of animals that looked good enough to be in a children's picture book.

Did my father-in-law draw these?

Further back in the book were playful scribbles and shapes in crayon, probably by a young Naoto.

'Goodness, I haven't seen that in a long time.'

The sudden voice behind me nearly made me jump off the tatami.

It felt like my blood was draining. I managed to compose my expression before turning around.

'Mother! You're back?'

'I said around five, didn't I?' There was clear scorn in her voice.

'Is it five already?' I said, but that didn't seem right to me. I had been trained to keep track of time while working. It couldn't have been more than thirty minutes since I'd marked four on the living-room clock.

As if she could sense my annoyance and frustration, she said, 'Oh, were you looking at the clock downstairs? I only just noticed, it's an hour behind.' I didn't miss the slight flare of her nostrils. She was feeling her advantage.

It wasn't the first time the clock had ever been wrong, but I couldn't help wondering if she had changed it on purpose. If she said she'd be home at five and then turned the clock back to throw me off.

But why?

To give me the house to myself for searching and then catch me in the act? For that to be the case she would need to know that I suspected her.

I couldn't imagine she knew.

But then, the sharpness of Mother's intuition was not to be underestimated.

'I was cleaning,' I began evenly, but she cut me off.

'Cleaning?'

She who hesitates is lost. 'I passed by before and noticed some dust on the floor in here.'

'Oh, how observant you are.'

'I just happened to notice. So I figured before I vacuumed I should tidy up the floor. Um, this sketchbook—'

'It's mine.'

'You're very good.' This wasn't just an empty compliment. It was clear she knew what she was doing.

'I used to draw to take my mind off things.' She spoke brusquely, clearly not wanting to talk about it, either because she was embarrassed or because she was irritated.

'I found a photo album too. Naoto when he was young.'

I took it off the shelf and showed her. 'Oh, *these*!' Her voice went up a few notes. Even Mother, who was almost always sour around me, seemed to soften at the photos of her son as a boy.

'This must have been at his school culture festival?' I pointed to a photo of Naoto on a stage in some kind of costume.

'Yes, that's right.'

She started telling me about the photos, a bit flat, even sounding slightly annoyed, but I nodded enthusiastically and asked questions, showing that I was interested. After all, my mother-in-law is still a person, someone's child, someone's mother. She took out other albums and flipped through those too, sharing stories from the past, and I started to lose sight of why I had come into my father-in-law's study in the first place.

Then three days ago, I was on the back porch when I noticed a piece of laundry in the garden.

Must have fallen from the second-floor balcony.

I slipped into my flip-flops and stepped out to get it.

Something fell down from above, about the size of a volleyball, black, dropping right in front of me.

I thought it was a human head.

A split second later the head shattered at my feet. With a loud crack it splintered into flying shards. Something black came spraying out – it wasn't a bomb, I realized, but a planter.

I looked up.

Nothing out of the ordinary on the balcony.

I ran back inside and up the stairs, trying not to make any noise.

'Miyako, such a stern face,' Mother said from where she was ironing in the living room, her eyes hard. She insisted that she hadn't noticed the planter fall. 'You're not hurt, are you?' she asked, but her concern didn't exactly strike me as sincere.

There were several potted plants on the balcony. It looked like the one that fell was the one on the end, the planter with a tulip bulb inside. It's true it was perched on the edge, but it was hard to imagine it suddenly falling.

'Maybe there was an earthquake.'

'No, Mother, if there were an earthquake wouldn't all of them have fallen?'

She looked annoyed, maybe because I had rejected her suggestion, or maybe because she wanted to hide her disappointment.

'It was that bird!' she shouted, jabbing her finger at the sky. I couldn't believe she would try a line that a child might use to distract their parent and avoid being punished. 'It's always landing on the railing,' she said, now waggling her finger around the balcony.

'You're saying a bird knocked it over?' Was she being serious?

'It could happen!'

'Sheesh . . .'

Not my sharpest retort, so I tried to cover by crouching down and looking at the planters. They were lined up on a steel rack. There on the shelf was a snail.

When I was an agent we had wilderness training, on the premise that we might have to survive while roughing it, so I was comfortable with insects, reptiles, and amphibians. I stared at it, closer, my mind emptying out, until all at once it felt like I was about to be sucked into the swirl of the shell.

I followed the spiral down, down into the center, and it swallowed me up.

Falling, twisting. Then I looked around and saw I was standing on the shore, white sand all around.

Before me was a forest, lush and teeming. Beyond the trees rose a rocky crag.

The smell of the tide.

I turned around. There on the beach was a huge, glistening mass, so enormous I held my breath. It was as if the shore had swollen up unnaturally, a boil on the skin of the earth. Carefully, I drew closer. I noticed a large red mark, then realized it was a wound, bleeding, and finally understood that this was some kind of living creature. A whale? An injured whale that had washed up on the shore? The whale I had seen before.

'Miyako, don't tell me you think the snail pushed the pot over.'

The voice floated me back up the spiral, away from the beached whale, back to the steel rack on the balcony. I was already there, had never left, but I had the strong sensation of being spat out from the swirl of the snail shell, like my body was being forced through a pinhole opening.

The snail crawled toward the planters. Of course there was no way it could ever have knocked one over. I stood, not even bothering to answer my mother-in-law.

She leaned out over the railing and spotted the shattered fragments of the pot in front of the porch, then looked at me with concern. 'Well, that would have been *awful*. I'm so glad it didn't hit you.'

'Ah, uh, yes. It fell right in front of me, really surprised me.'

'You're not hurt, are you?'

I looked her in the eye, trying to grasp what she was feeling. I couldn't tell if she was worried, disappointed, or wary. I had confidence in my ability to see through a poker face, but Mother's expression didn't reveal a thing. Maybe I'd grown rusty in retirement.

No, said another part of me.

If you want to read the weather, you need to be calm when you look at the sky. With Mother I was always off balance, my inner seas raging, and maybe the crashing waves disturbed my read on the situation.

If it was just the falling planter, maybe that would have been the end of it.

But the next day when I was shopping in Shinjuku, someone bumped into me from behind at the intersection and nearly knocked me into oncoming traffic. I knew I couldn't just explain it away as a coincidence.

I whipped around in time to see who pushed me. Clearly not Mother. A chubby man in a suit, sweating profusely as he ran off. It might be that he was just in a rush to get somewhere and knocked into me by accident. But my internal alarm bells were ringing, and loudly.

And then today, a confrontation with this knife-wielding postal worker, or anyway a man dressed as a postal worker.

He shifted his weight back and forth slightly. So did I, keeping loose for the next strike.

I gauged his breathing. Slightly heavy.

He was no amateur, but I was pretty sure I was better.

I could take him.

The problem was how to avoid damaging anything in the house.

There was already a slash on the wall. I wasn't going to suffer any more vandalism.

Miyako, you're ruining my house!

Imagining her criticism lit a rage in my belly. It wasn't so much boiling water as it was the foulest stinking magma. I simply cannot stand to be subordinate to her. No woman like that is going to beat me. No human being, period.

But *why* do I get so mad?

What is it about Mother that makes me lose my cool?

The man in the postal uniform advanced.

He punched with his left. I guessed it was a feint to set up a thrust from the knife in his right, which is exactly what happened. Dodge the left punch, block the right stab. The blade clattered against the wall of the narrow passage.

I stepped backward, maintaining my stance, one step, then another.

Just as he lunged, I grabbed the bathroom doorknob and whipped the door open, right in his path.

He barreled into it. Not wasting a split second, I pushed the door hard from behind. He hit the floor.

I darted into the bathroom and grabbed a towel from the rack, then stepped back out to find the man on his knees, hauling himself up.

You need to be quicker than that, my friend.

Unsteady on his feet, he stabbed again, like it was the only thing he knew how to do. Holding the towel in both hands, I caught his oncoming hand at the wrist and wrapped it up, then wrenched his arm behind his back. The knife fell to the floor.

I kicked his legs out and forced him to the floor, face down, then pressed my knee into his back to pin him.

'What is this about? What are you after?'

She hired you, didn't she?

Watanuki must have a top-class alcohol filtration system, because no matter how much he drinks his face stays the same even shade. There's barely any change in his behavior.

Very different from me. I turn red on the first sip and pretty soon feel like I'm not myself.

'How're the Kitayama domestic relations going? Still that mother–daughter-in-law friction?' I was touched that Watanuki would be thinking about me, but at the same time put out that he would bring it up in front of Dr O.'s son, recently made chief of his father's operation.

The young hospital director didn't seem surprised, though. Watanuki must have already told him what was going on. 'Ah, it's the same thing over at my place. Tough being stuck in the middle.'

We were in a small private room at a restaurant famous for its sukiyaki and shabu shabu. It had recently been written up in a magazine as being a great place to impress a client and had been fully booked since. Watanuki had no problem getting a table for him and Dr O. the younger, no doubt through someone in his extensive network, and he had invited me to come along.

'You're stuck between your wife and your mother too, Doctor? I can't imagine that.' I turned up my solicitous surprise to 200 percent.

'The doctor's wife, the vice director of the hospital, she's strong-willed.' Watanuki nodded.

Strong-willed wasn't exactly a compliment, and in fact sounded a lot like a criticism. I wondered if it was okay for him to say something like that, but the hospital director wasn't perturbed in the slightest. Maybe griping about his wife to Watanuki was one of the ways he liked to blow off steam. Apparently they were very close.

'It's really something else how our young doctor friend puts up with her.'

'And my father's always on my case too. I'm not just stuck in the middle, I'm beset on all sides! And they're always closing in. My dear Watanuki, you're the only one who understands me.'

'You're really working hard, Doc. That's why I'm saying you should let loose and relax, eat some good food after a long day.'

'Almost everyone I deal with at the hospital is a patient. It's all sad-sack energy. Of course I'm exhausted. And my wife being like she is, and Daddy doesn't understand anything. Oh, right, that reminds me. You.' He pointed at me. 'I heard you and Daddy hit it off.'

Word must have gotten to him about our golf day. I told him that our fathers had been at elementary school together.

'Well, either way, Daddy came home from golf in a good mood.' He looked sour. 'Good for you, you passed inspection.'

'Oh, um, it was nothing like that.'

'Our Kitayama is very quick when it comes to getting in good with people.'

That was not something I usually heard about myself. I doubted anyone else ever thought that. I'm pretty sure that was the first time anyone had ever said it.

'Yeah, well, you'd do well to remember that I'm in charge of the hospital now, so it doesn't really matter whether my daddy likes you or not.'

'Oh, yes, of course,' I answered right away, but the doctor's stare was so hard and unnerving that I added, 'It's not like he's retired in name only and still pulling the strings,' which I probably shouldn't have said.

'What's that supposed to mean?' He stared harder. I could see the muscles around his eyes firing.

Watanuki started talking about how tasty the meat was, drawing the young doctor's attention back to the feast.

The shabu shabu really was delicious, so for a while I focused on swishing the cuts of meat around the boiling water with my chopsticks while they talked. Or I made like I was focused on the meat. They appeared to have a closer relationship than I had guessed, and they peppered their conversation with confidential information and candid complaints about work. I kept wondering why they would be saying all of this in front of me. I swirled my chopsticks around diligently, trying my best to project that I wasn't listening.

'What's even fun anymore, Watanuki, huh? Got anything fun for us to do? Something it'd be fun to buy? I pretty much have everything I could want. Got a golf club membership and everything. I can totally understand how that guy felt who bought the Van Gogh. I mean, I can't buy anything like that, but that feeling of wanting to buy something to make people notice, I get it.'

'How much was that, more than five billion yen?' Watanuki said. 'Nowadays it feels like there's nothing that Japan can't buy.'

'The power of Japanese money! It's amazing. It makes me feel awesome!'

'And why is that?' It felt like this was a routine that they had done before. Like Watanuki knew what the doctor wanted him to say.

'Because a little country like us is putting the pressure on a giant like America. We may have lost the war, but we work harder than they do, so we're winning now. It feels so good. I bet soon a Japanese person will buy one of the big Hollywood studios. Then America's famous film industry would be ours. People criticize us Japanese as being economic animals, but it's not like we're cheating anyone. It's just money. There's nothing so straightforward as money.'

'You are right about that,' Watanuki said appreciatively. 'There was that thing recently, the medical examination reservation thing, right?'

I had heard this story on the news. Older folks who needed an exam but didn't have any medical emergency and were basically in fine shape had to sit in the waiting room forever to be seen by the doctors, so one hospital set up exams by reservation. But the reservation had a fee. People who paid the fee could see a doctor without having to mix in with the masses. It turned out to be in violation of health insurance laws.

'It makes perfect sense to me,' said the doctor. 'If you pay more, you get better service. Money is a number. Not like, I don't know, humanity, or effort, which are invisible. Money's easy to understand. It's fair.'

'It's tough to understand something that's invisible.'

'I know, right? Here, like this.' No sooner had he said this than the young doctor produced a wad of cash and peeled off several ten-thousand-yen notes, offering them to me and Watanuki. It felt like being a little kid getting some spending money from a relative, only less wholesome.

I glanced over at Watanuki and saw him enthusiastically accept the money, so I did the same.

There's too much money. Just too much money.

The words sparked to life in my mind. Who had said that again?

It was Miyako.

And when was it? I guess it was one night when I came home late and she waited up to sit with me while I ate. I had been out entertaining some people from the university hospital at several different bars and restaurants. 'It's like I don't even know how much anything's worth anymore,' I had said.

And Miyako answered, 'There's just too much money.'

'Yeah, it does feel that way. And it's like the company's saying, "Keep spending, keep spending."'

'Do you know where the most money is right now?'

'Like where is it physically?' Did such a place exist?

'The banks. The banks are holding all the money. But if all

they do is hold it then it doesn't grow at all, so they lend it. They lend it and lend it. Even if someone says, "Hey, I don't need money now," the bank says, "Well, if you don't borrow now then we'll never lend to you again." '

'Really? They lean on people like that?'

'When you get a hot potato you have to pass it on, right?'

'I'm not following.'

'The government keeps launching public initiatives, so land values are skyrocketing, while corporate taxes are going down, so of course companies have more money than they know what to do with.'

'Thanks to that, my and all my coworkers' salaries keep going up. Some of the guys in my cohort are starting to buy condos as investments.'

'Well, everyone keeps building condos like it's nothing.'

'My coworkers aren't the ones building them.'

'Property values keep rising, so developers figure they should buy now. Then once they have the land they figure might as well use it. So they build a high-rise, some condos. Once they have condos, they need to sell them off. People who already have somewhere to live don't need condos, but they'll probably buy one as an investment. You'd probably make money off of it, so everyone buys.'

'You make it sound like buying a condo is a dumb thing to do.' My tone might have been a bit spiky.

But Miyako was calm. She was always calm. 'The other day I saw something on TV about the South Sea Bubble.'

'Was that a Friday-night thriller?'

She smiled and shook her head. 'In eighteenth-century Britain, the national debt was too high so they created a company to try to take on some of that debt. That was the South Sea Company. They thought it would be able to make money, but it didn't go so well. So they started selling stock in the company. One of the company directors, John Blunt, had two rules.'

'Two rules, huh?'

'One: doing whatever possible to bring up the value of company stock was the only way to increase profits.'

I was just impressed that back then they even had the notion of public companies and stock prices. 'And two?'

'The more confusion there is, the better. Make it so that people can't understand what you're doing.'

'*More* confusion is better?'

'The South Sea Company devised a mechanism to inflate the price of their stock, betting that if people saw the price go up they'd buy it. Then that would drive the stock price up higher, which made even more people want to buy because they thought they'd make money. Doesn't that sound like Japan today? The general feeling is it's all right to buy, you'll make money off of it, and nobody's worried. Real estate is taking off and everyone is living a life of luxury.'

When she said that I started to think that maybe Japan today was a lot like the South Sea Company. 'So what happened?'

'In the rush to cash in, all these small fly-by-night companies popped up, backed by South Sea stock. That was a bit too much for the authorities, but as soon as they forbade it the stock crashed. It dragged down the whole market, anyone who owned any stock suffered major losses. We can calculate the motion of heavenly bodies, but not the madness of people.'

'Isn't that Newton?'

'Apparently Newton said that when he lost a pile of money in that crash.'

'I don't love hearing that even Newton got sucked in.'

'At the time everyone had some vague sense that it couldn't go on like that forever, that it would fall apart sooner or later. But they ignored that, because they wanted to believe that it would go on for just a little longer. And that feels exactly like Japan nowadays.'

'So, uh, is this your theory, Miyako?'

'Come on, I couldn't come up with something like that. I saw it on TV.'

'Sure you could. You're smart.'

'First time anyone's ever told me that.' The way she smiled and scrunched up her eyes was adorable. I wanted to throw my arms around her.

'I've always thought you were smart.' It was true. She spent her days busily taking care of the house and didn't seem much interested in politics or the business scene, but from time to time she would share something that was really very insightful. She'd always say she heard it from some pundit on TV or read it in a magazine, but it was usually a fresh take that I hadn't heard elsewhere. If I asked her what show she'd seen it on she always claimed to forget.

'Well anyway, all these slapped together companies buying into the South Sea Company created a speculation bubble. And that's the South Sea Bubble.'

'A bubble as fleeting as a dream,' I said, pretty sure that that was an old saying. Thinking about it some more, I didn't see how Japan could be in the same situation. We were talking about more than two hundred years ago, when samurai still ran the show in Japan. We've learned a lot since then about government and economics, and I doubted we would be happily pumping up a bubble that was just going to burst. 'But I'm sure that they have plans to keep things from collapsing.'

'Sure, there are people planning. But plans don't always go as planned. And sometimes you can't do anything – like there's a runaway train, and you know that you've got to find a way to stop it, but there's nothing you can do, so you just wait for it to crash.

And it's very hard to see a bubble when you're right in the middle of it.'

'I wonder. You think the Japanese economy will take a bad turn?' I couldn't even picture what that would look like.

'Of course it will.'

'Wait, you really think so?'

'And I don't even think it's that far off. There'll be a steep decline that will last for ten or twenty years, and everyone will just keep hoping we can go back to how it used to be in the good old days.'

'What good old days?'

'The ones we're in right now. I bet people will spend decades wishing to get back to this irregular economic situation we've got today.' She seemed so sure of what she was saying that I didn't know how to reply.

I didn't think Japan's winning economy would last forever, but it was just so hard to imagine things getting bad. It felt more likely that the Cold War between the US and the Soviets would turn into a hot war – I'm not sure if hot war would be the right term for it, but in any case that felt like a more realistic possibility.

'Hey, Kitayama, quit zoning out! Did you hear what the doctor said?'

'Oh! Uh, sorry!' I snapped back to the present.

The young hospital director popped a piece of beef into his mouth and spoke as he chewed. 'No, no, it's fine if he zones out. It's the sharp ones like you I have to watch out for, Watanuki.'

'I hope we can still be friends, Doc,' Watanuki simpered.

'You'll be taking over the O. Hospital account.' Watanuki gave me my new marching orders at the nightclub we went to next, after the young hospital director had said he wanted to bask in some youthful energy. I knew that clubs like this were popular, but I had never been to one before. Of course, Watanuki seemed to know the routine, and he pulled me along as I ogled the gaudy brass decorations at the door and shrank from the bouncer eyeing my outfit.

The place was full of young people dancing, masters of their domain. We were the ones who were out of place. But Watanuki and the doctor didn't appear bothered as they sat down on a sofa and took in the sight of the young men and women swaying in the thrall of the Eurobeat.

'I love this! I love it.' The doctor couldn't sit still for very long and soon jumped up and onto the dancefloor, where we lost sight of him.

'I wonder if he'll be all right,' I said, though I have no idea what I was worried about.

'Just let him do whatever he wants. It's our job to let the doctors do what they want and make them feel good.'

'Uh, yes, right.'

'Know what makes doctors the happiest?' Watanuki had to shout over the high-volume synth and vocals.

'Blowing off steam?'

'Making money.'

'Oh?'

'If they're making money, they're happy.'

I laughed uncertainly. There are all kinds of different doctors. I couldn't tell if Watanuki was joking.

'Just kidding! Of course, what makes doctors happiest is helping their patients,' he continued, but his expression was so flat I still couldn't tell whether he meant what he was saying or not. And then: 'Kitayama, you'll be taking over the O. Hospital account. You seem to get along well with Dr O. It should work out perfectly.'

'What should work out perfectly?'

'Don't worry about it, buddy, it'll all be great. O. Hospital is in a strong financial position, by which I mean they're making money, and the young doctor is the way he is. So it should actually be a pretty easy gig. They'll keep buying our drugs without us even asking for the order.'

It threw me off, getting this assignment in a club, directly from Watanuki, without going through HR or management.

I caught a glimpse of the young doctor dancing up a storm, dripping sweat.

O. Hospital is making money.

Would it still be making money with someone like this at the helm? I wanted to ask Watanuki, but I kept quiet.

'That must have been very difficult for you.' Ichio Ishiguro spoke words of sympathy but his face was devoid of emotion.

The last time we'd spoken it had been at the door, but this time we were sitting at my dining-room table.

Things were finally starting to quieten down after the knife-wielding intruder episode from the other day. Mother had come home to find me holding the man pinned down, so she'd called the police, which started a whole other mess. Naoto came home from work early, worried sick about me, which would have made me happy except that after the police took the intruder away they started in with their investigation, asking me all sorts of questions about what had happened. I couldn't tell them that I'd handled the man with no problems, so I said that I just got lucky and hit him with the bathroom door while I was trying to get away.

'So the attack was just a random robbery then?' Ichio Ishiguro sipped his tea.

'I guess so. He apparently forced his way into several other houses before mine.' I was repeating what the police had told me. 'And I hear that they can't really question him.'

'Ah, because he has some sort of mental handicap,' said the insurance man with a grimace. 'Recently there's been a rash of arson attacks to try to drive up property values, have you heard about that?'

'What does property value have to do with this?'

'Arson is a very serious crime. It seems that people are getting individuals who are difficult to question to start the fires. People with brain damage, for example. Also minors.'

'So what does that mean for my case?'

'That there is someone pulling the strings.' He said it with such certainty that I was momentarily at a loss. Then he quickly added, 'Perhaps you have had the same thought?' Which jolted me in a different direction.

'What is going on here?'

Mother had been very concerned about me. She threw a fit at the sight of the intruder, asking if I was hurt, if I was okay, if I needed to go to the hospital. Seeing the intensity of her reaction made it plenty clear that she actually cared about my safety and made me feel guilty for suspecting her as the mastermind behind the attack.

But before long she was back to her usual bile. *Miyako, he didn't do anything funny to you, did he? Miyako, why do you think he chose our house? What must the neighbors think? If only you hadn't been home when he came* . . . It was obvious that she cared more about the court of public opinion rather than her daughter-in-law's well-being, and I felt the door in my heart that had been opening slam right back shut.

Ichio Ishiguro was spreading pamphlets across the dining-room table. 'Not many people ask to buy insurance for their daughter-in-law,' he said with an impressed air. As if he were complimenting my performance as a daughter-in-law.

'After this incident she must have gotten worried about something happening to me. I guess if I'm attacked again and we have a policy then Naoto and Mother would get the money.'

'I sincerely doubt that sort of thing will happen to you again. If another strange man breaks into your house and attacks you I would suggest you look into a ritual cleansing.'

'You're saying I'm cursed?' My own words jogged a memory. 'Actually that reminds me, last time we spoke you said my rocky relationship with my mother-in-law is because of a grudge passed down from our ancestors. Is that what you'd call a curse?'

Ichio Ishiguro cocked his head and asked, with a completely straight face, 'I said that? Are you sure?'

'Yes.'

'And you are sure it was me?'

He was clearly just feigning ignorance, but he stuck to it. Instead he changed the subject, although it sounded like in his mind the new topic was related: 'It's like that story you often hear, the one about the People of the Sea and the People of the Mountain.'

'That story you often hear? I've never heard of it.'

'They have been at odds since time out of mind. At first they were only struggling over a small area, but those that carried their blood have spread far and wide, and carried the struggle along with them.'

'So it's one of those things where the parents teach their children not to trust anybody from that one family?'

'It was that simple at first, most likely, but over time it became a part of their being.'

'Don't tell me it got into their genes.'

'A cat who has never seen a snake is still frightened by ropes and other snake-like objects.'

'But this is different from natural enemies in the animal kingdom. Both sides are humans, they're the same type of organism.'

Ichio Ishiguro nodded. 'And yet this is how it is. How it always has been.'

'Always?'

'Two opposing essences that must stand opposed, no matter what. People of the Sea and People of the Mountain should never meet. When they do, without fail, there is a collision. They simply cannot understand and accept one another.'

'Maybe Oda Nobunaga and Akechi Mitsuhide were another case of sea people and mountain people.' Of course I was just joking, but Ichio Ishiguro's demeanor remained unchanged.

'The struggle between mountain and sea has manifested throughout history, across the whole world.'

'So they never have a showdown?'

'Sometimes they do, for a given place and time. Indeed, there are cases where the conflict reaches resolution, for a while. They still do not see eye-to-eye, but making peace can serve their purposes.'

'But there are more cases where they don't work things out.'

'It is often the case that one side crushes the other.'

I was starting to grow wary of this insurance salesman. No one in their right mind could sit there and say these sorts of things with a straight face. I wondered if maybe he was about to pull out a knife and attack me. I was watching for any sudden movements. Or maybe his aim was to use his fantastical story to lure people into a cult. It wasn't outside the realm of possibility.

But then he began talking about insurance as if nothing unusual had been said, and I almost wondered if we had ever even been talking about the two rival tribes.

After he had explained the policy, I surprised myself by saying, 'About what we were discussing before.' Why was I still interested? I wasn't sure, but I couldn't keep myself from asking.

'Before?'

'About the sea and the mountain. So, someone from the sea people, if they had a child, that child would be a sea person too?'

'That is correct. One born to the People of the Sea is part of the People of the Sea.'

'And what if a sea person and a mountain person got married and had kids, what would those kids be?'

'I doubt that they would ever become close enough to marry one another, and if they did they would not likely be able to have children.'

He sounded so much like a specialist in an obscure field taking questions from the floor, I almost laughed.

'If that's the case then it has nothing to do with my friction with my mother-in-law,' I reasoned. There was some appeal in explaining our rocky relations as being the result of conflicts handed down through the generations. At least the theory made it easier for me to accept how quickly I lost my composure around her. But if that were the case, then Naoto and I wouldn't get along either. It would mean that he and I were on opposite sides, one sea and the other mountain, which would make it rather tough for us to fall in love and get married.

'Is there anything else you would like to ask me?'

I wasn't sure if Ichio Ishiguro was referring to the story of the sea and the mountains or the insurance policy, so I vaguely answered, 'Nothing in particular.'

That was me, in my gym uniform, wearing a big smile. The photo was old and faded, the sky no longer blue. But to me, looking at it in the present, it all seemed to shine brighter than it did when the photo was first taken.

My friend and I were looking proud, flashing V signs at the camera.

It was back in sixth grade. I could tell even without looking at the date on the photo. Flags from around the world hung down on diagonals. Right after the relay race. I could remember it clearly. To be precise, I could remember it clearly as soon as I saw the picture in the album, which I found on the dining-room table when I came back from work in the middle of the night. I saw the photo and reconnected with the memory.

In a relay race against five other schools, our second runner stumbled and dropped into fifth place, but I was the next runner, and between me and my friend who ran after me we made up the gap and finished in first. Our classmates were exultant, the two of us were on top of the world, and for the next several days the school treated us like heroes.

The photograph captured our expressions and let me experience the memory again, but it didn't tell me anything about the person who took the photo. I think it must have been my dad. He was probably in a good mood too. I looked through the darkness of the living room toward the small altar.

This one moment in elementary school might have been the high point of my life.

Is that true?

Memories of junior high started to sprout up like potatoes from the earth.

On the way home from school one day, I came across my friend being threatened by a bunch of bad kids. The same friend I'd won the relay race with in that stupendous turnover. We weren't in classes or clubs together anymore and had grown apart. I pushed down the memory from sixth-grade graduation when I had thrown my arm around him and said, 'You're my best friend.' I pushed it down deep and hurried by. I imagined him watching me leave him there, and kept my face lowered for fear he might catch my eye.

After that, any time I saw him around school I felt deep shame. I don't think we ever talked again.

Seated at my dining-room table, I breathed a heavy sigh.

'Oh, welcome home,' said a voice behind me. It was my wife, coming downstairs from our bedroom.

'Did I wake you?' It was past midnight. 'I tried not to make any noise.'

'No, no, just going to the bathroom,' she smiled, and in fact that's where she headed.

Soon she came back. 'You always work so late, poor guy.'

'Yeah, I guess it's no good.'

'Lack of sleep leads to all the world's ills.'

'Is that an old saying?'

'I don't think it's a saying, but that is how the body works. If you don't get enough sleep it breaks down both your body and your spirit. I saw something on TV about it.'

'That TV is pretty smart,' I said, but once again I got the sense that Miyako was coming up with all this on her own.

'Do those pictures bring back memories?' She nodded at the photo album in front of me, sounding pleased. 'I found it in your father's study the other day.'

'This was the best time of my life,' I said earnestly, but she seemed a little miffed at that, since it didn't involve her, so I reassured her clumsily, stammering that I didn't mean it like that.

'Tell me about it.'

'Tell you about what?'

'Seems like you've got something on your mind. Why not try talking to me about it? It might make you feel better.'

Before I could say anything, she pulled out a chair with a clatter and sat down across from me.

'It's nothing. Work stuff.'

'You're in charge of a new hospital account, right?'

'Yeah, O. Hospital.'

A month had passed since I had taken over for Watanuki. The work itself wasn't very hard. Spending all my energy keeping the

85

young hospital director happy was rough on the body, but that would be the same with any account. Watanuki had handed over a very stable situation with O. Hospital, where I didn't even have to do much to get them to renew their contract. All I had to do was keep that stable foundation in good shape.

'The new head of O. Hospital – that's the spoiled one who just gets by on Daddy's success, right?'

How does she know that? I wondered. The spoiled one who gets by on Daddy's money was an awfully subjective judgment, very hard to quantify. I felt a little wrong affirming it. 'Did you hear that on TV too?'

'Rumors, just rumors. The housewife rumor mill is a scary thing.'

'But O. Hospital isn't in our neighborhood. I wouldn't guess people would be talking about it.'

'Don't underestimate how fast and far rumors will travel,' said Miyako with a chuckle. 'So what's bothering you? It's obvious something is, I can tell just by looking at you.'

I rubbed my hands across my face, as if I was washing it.

It's a question of having to look the other way, I almost said.

'Hang on, quiet.' She touched a finger to her lips. I made a questioning face and she glanced upward, clearly listening. She was worried that Mom might be awake.

'By the way, I found out that Mother is very good at drawing.'

I asked how that came up. Apparently she had found Mom's sketchbook too. I had recollections of Mom saying she used to study illustration, but I didn't know she was any good.

'Yes. Who knew she could capture the little details so well?'

Miyako was usually so easygoing, but her voice dripped with disdain.

Why can't my mother and my wife just get along?

I can't just look the other way.

86

People can't live without breathing. It seems I can't breathe without sighing.

There was a black handkerchief on the ground, so I turned at the next corner and waited. Before long a man in a suit walked up, checking his watch. 'Do you have the time?'

'So you guys never change up your signals?' Black handkerchief means make the next right turn and wait.

'The signals change every day. But if I didn't use an old one you wouldn't get it.'

'And what might you need with an old-timer like me?'

We had been together at the Agency. He didn't seem to have aged at all. He called me out of the blue, using all the codes we used to use, and arranged a meeting.

The sudden summons had surprised me, but when I was still working I would sometimes get in touch with retired agents too, so I didn't imagine it was any kind of emergency.

'About your friend the analyst,' he said, and named the young man with the head shaped like a gourd, the one who had helped me with my investigation of Mother.

Oh that, I thought. *Sorry about that, there was something I was trying to find out about an accident my father-in-law had, so I asked for some help,* was on the tip of my tongue. *It was only once, just a little poking into police records.*

But before I could say any of that, my former coworker continued, 'He was attacked.' My breath caught in my throat.

On his way home from work he had been hit by a car and was in a coma.

'Hit-and-run? And you don't think it was an accident? You said he was attacked.'

'A little while ago he had indications that someone was tailing him and was just about to start looking into it. Then the hit-and-run.'

'So,' I began, and then came out and said what I was thinking: 'Am I a suspect?'

'We're checking out why someone might have come at him now, and we found that he was accessing a few databases in an extracurricular fashion.'

Yes, that. 'I'm sorry, I—'

'You had him investigate your husband's father's accidental death, right? This is against the rules, of course, but we get it. A friend asks for an easy favor, anyone would do it, so we take it in our stride. Only he was, shall we say, passionate about gathering information on you and your family.'

'Passionate?'

'How many times did you meet to hear what he was finding?'

'Just one time.' When he'd shared with me what he'd learned about my father-in-law's death from the police records.

'Well, he kept going after that. We have the records of it.'

In my mind's eye, I was picturing Mother.

My former coworker watched me carefully. If nothing else he could see that I wasn't telling him everything. But at the moment I couldn't bring myself to start getting into everything about her. 'Am I a suspect in this?' I asked again.

'No, if anything we're worried about you,' he replied. 'You were attacked the other day too.'

'The postal worker.' The man who burst into my house swinging a knife. It was being treated by the police as a random break-in, not targeted, but now there was the connection to the analyst. 'Do you think something is going on?' Even as I asked, I had a clear idea of what it was.

'If we find anything I'll get in touch. Same goes for you.' With that he handed over a card, made to look like a salesman's.

'Wait,' I said before he could leave. 'Now that I'm retired, any chance you could erase my file?'

'Information is gold. Unless there are extenuating circumstances, we never erase anything. Might have been easier when everything was on paper, but nowadays it's all disks.'

'Guess the history classes of the future will marvel about how we used to write words on paper.'

On my way home, I held a conference with myself. From my days as an agent I had picked up the habit of challenging my own opinions in order to reach a more objective conclusion.

I suspect Mother.

But she had no reason to go after the analyst.

Well, I did ask him to check out the circumstances surrounding my father-in-law's accident. And then he continued investigating on his own – I'm not sure why, although maybe he found something that made him suspect my mother-in-law too. And then maybe she found out about it.

Theories on top of theories. It's all just theoretical.

But it *is* true that people around her have a habit of dying.

Anyone who has people in their lives will eventually have people around them dying.

No, this is more than usual. Her parents died in a car accident. Her husband fell down the steps at a shrine. The homeless man Santaro was hit by a car after meeting with her.

You're saying Mother had something to do with all of those? So what was her motive?

At the very least, she got the insurance money from her parents' death.

Would she have killed them for that?

More than two-thirds of all crimes are motivated by money. And then there's the testimony from that nurse.

. . . I had gone to speak with the former head nurse at the

hospital morgue where my father-in-law had been taken after his accident, once I found out that Santaro and Mother's parents had also ended up at the same place. It made sense that they were all taken there since it was close to where they all lived, but still it stood out to me. Though the hospital had since closed after the director passed away, I was able to locate a handful of women who had been nurses there.

It was a large hospital, so I didn't have high hopes that the nurses would remember patient names or their families. And in fact most didn't recall anything about a Mr Kitayama. But then I spoke to the former head nurse. 'Actually, I do remember the name Kitayama – there was a rumor that Mrs Kitayama and the hospital director had something going on.'

'Something going on?'

'The nurses would sometimes spot Mrs Kitayama and the director having private conversations. All the nurses were women then – doesn't that strike you as odd nowadays?'

I agreed with her and chatted about gender roles in the workplace for a bit, slowly leading the conversation back to what I was looking for. But all I was able to find out was that Setsu Kitayama and the hospital director had been seen discussing something secretively on a few occasions.

But the notion of gender relations sent me off in a different direction.

What if Mother had been asking the hospital director for something?

. . . And what do you think that might have been?

Concealing the cause of death. My father-in-law, Santaro, their deaths might not have been accidental. They may well have been homicide. Maybe she was asking for the hospital director's help in covering that up. Isn't that a possibility?

But would the hospital director have so easily tossed aside his oaths as a doctor to lie about that?

Maybe Mother found his weak point and leaned on him.

Are you that determined to see her as the villain?

. . . My internal interlocutor seemed exasperated.

It's not that I want to see her as the villain. It's just that any way you look at it there seems to be something going on.

When you worked at the Agency, didn't you learn never to judge a book by its cover?

Yes, I know how important it is to work without bias.

And you really think Mother would go after the analyst? Because he was doing a little digging into the past? It's even crazy to think that she could arrange for an assassin disguised as a postal worker.

I had to concede that my other self was probably right about that.

But I still didn't—

She cut me off.

What if you're ascribing her too much power, simply because you don't get along?

Is it possible I hated my mother-in-law so much that I was doing everything I could to turn her into a super-villain?

In the dark of the dance floor, lights flashed, dazzling. It was like a wild new universe kept being born and then winking back out of existence in time with the Eurobeat.

The young hospital director sat next to a voluptuous girl he had found somewhere, going on about his accomplishments and telling vulgar anecdotes with an insinuating air. I played along as much as I had to to keep him happy.

You seem pretty good at this kinda thing.

I knew exactly who said this. It was my younger self. The me I saw in the photo album on the dining-room table the other night, back in elementary school. What I couldn't quite tell is if he was impressed or mocking.

Looks like you're having fun. That lady wore her naked outfit, huh?

Revealing bodycon dresses didn't faze me anymore. All I could do was shrug at my elementary school self.

'Hey Kitayama, I'm gonna go dance!' The young hospital director started making his way to the floor. Swinging his body, he kept bumping up against the girl in a way that didn't look at all accidental. He was like a supplicant who believed in the healing power of young women's sweat, diligently performing a ritual.

I had a coworker who said doctors were like kings in little castles. They spend most of their lives at their practice where the majority of the people they interact with are patients who need them and call them 'Doctor,' and they don't really know anything about how the world works.

But you could say the same thing about us – we don't really understand the world either.

We spend most of our lives running after doctors, taking them out at night and playing golf with them. It isn't just in my line of work; any kind of job will have its own little sectioned-off world where people spend all their time. There are only so many different experiences a person can squeeze into one go-round.

At least doctors help people get better when they're sick, which is clearly a good thing, better than what most people can contribute to society.

That's why I didn't feel right judging the young hospital director when he acted all horny in front of me.

Oh okay, I get it, so taking this doctor out is important work.

My younger self sounded relieved that his future job would have some value.

Before, I would have said, 'That's right, this *is* meaningful work.' I would say it to hear myself say it, to wave away the question of whether it was okay for me to spend every night playing so extravagantly, the feeling that I should be spending more time with my family.

But now I had a new dimension of doubt swirling around in my head.

What if O. Hospital – what if the young director – was involved in fraud?

The first time the doubt flashed in my mind was a month ago, at the same club.

I might have even been at the same table. I watched the hospital director, lost in his pleasure dance, drunk on the energy of the young, and I thought it was a wonder this guy kept his operation in business. Then something jumped out from my memory: one time, passing by the waiting room at O. Hospital, something I heard an older man say.

'It's wonderful how empty it is here, there's never any wait.'

At the time I didn't make anything of it, and I was actually surprised that I even remembered it. But then I turned it over some more, and reflected that having both an empty practice and robust earnings went against the laws of nature.

Come to think of it, any time I visited the practice the reception area and the exam rooms were decidedly uncrowded.

How could the business be doing well?

It was still just a vague doubt, until I found a way to work it into a conversation with Watanuki. 'Our friend the young director always seems to have free time, but he also seems to be making good money,' I said.

I expected Watanuki to respond with cool confidence, 'The times you go aren't the busy times,' or else with a cynical retort, 'It's his job to fritter away Daddy's money,' but instead he said something unexpected: 'What's up, Kitayama? Did you see something?'

'What?'

Then his stern expression broke. 'C'mon, man, I handed you a cushy setup, don't overthink it. Just follow the routine, right?' His tone was playful, but I noticed that his smile didn't reach his eyes.

So could there actually be something going on?

Despite my suspicion, there wasn't a whole lot of information I could gather. The most I could do was get a sense of O. Hospital's business health and what other companies they worked with. It wasn't like I could just launch an investigation. But what I could do was guess, and that wasn't difficult at all.

Fraudulent insurance claims.

It wasn't a new scam. I had heard about it plenty of times. A medical practice doesn't see any patients but they file paperwork as if they do and then claim the payments from the insurance companies. There are different ways it happens, including using lists of national health insurance IDs bought on the cheap from homeless folks. In those cases, it's almost always some rough types compiling the lists, yakuza or similar.

It's like the rising land prices on the news – you know it's actually happening, but it feels like it has nothing to do with you personally. I resisted the idea. O. Hospital? Couldn't be. I wasn't even going off of any hard proof, it was all just conjecture based on circumstantial evidence.

During the time I was debating what, if anything, to do, I encountered that photo from elementary school. That brought two characters back into my life: my boyhood self, flush with victory and grinning ear to ear; and me as a teenager, who looked the other way when a friend was in trouble.

When someone's doing something bad you gotta say something. So declared my younger self.

But the teenager would answer back, *Trying to be a goody-two-shoes just gets you in trouble. Sometimes you gotta look the other way. Right?*

The young hospital director came back to the table, dripping sweat. I shot to my feet to welcome him. Such gestures were clearly overblown, but he seemed to like it, so there was no need to hold back.

There was no sign of the woman in the tight red dress. 'Where's your, uh, your lady friend?'

The hospital director was sulky. 'Who knows. She disappeared.' I guessed that she had found someone she liked better and attached herself to him instead. I didn't know exactly what to call her – non-discriminating?

'Kitayama, next time bring your wife along.'

'My . . . wife?'

'Yeah. I'm tired of the women here, they're worthless. Their asses are up for grabs.'

It was clear he was angry at having been left high and dry. His typical pattern when he felt bad was to find some way to talk down to me and patch up his damaged self-worth with a tacky sense of superiority. But I wondered why he felt like he had to involve my wife.

'I mean,' he continued, 'I figure your wife must be one of these plain types. That's what I prefer. White rice over fancy food. She may be plain but you never get tired of her. I bet she knows her place, too. Am I right?'

'Doctor, please don't talk that way about my wife,' I protested, but he probably heard it as me feigning protest while playing along.

'I'm not talking about her in any way, I just want you to introduce us.'

'Um, I don't think it's necessary to bring my wife into it.' I fought down my indignation at having to deal with this level of insinuation.

'Yeah, okay, I guess not. Fine.'

Something about the way he said it caused a crack to open in me, with what felt like an audible pop.

'But come on, Kitayama, thanks to me you're getting ahead at your job. Don't worry about it, just do what I want.'

I wanted to tell him that O. Hospital wasn't the only place where I did business, but I kept my mouth shut.

There were people looking at me. I could feel it. My younger selves, boy and teenager, were waiting to see how I would react.

Take a good look, kids, this is what your future holds. It may not look great but there's no need to be disappointed. This is important work, in its own way ... I needed to hear myself express that.

But this guy is doing something bad, right? Faking appointments?

I don't know that for sure, I replied. No, nothing's certain, I stressed a little more forcefully.

'The other day I heard from another doctor. He works with a different pharma company than yours, Kitayama. They really take care of their doctors. You know the doctor who was flown to Hokkaido for ramen on a private jet? That guy.' The young director's eyes were flinty and his voice had an edge. He was always like that when he was saying what was really on his mind. 'I heard that the pharma rep for this doctor is setting him up on a date with his own girlfriend. "Do anything you want with her," is what he said. Although I figure that the pharma guy found some girl who works at a massage parlor and is just passing her off as his girlfriend.'

I felt a flash of revulsion at the thought that just because a girl works at a massage parlor he would think it's okay to tell someone to do anything he wanted to her. And I had a feeling I wasn't going to like wherever this conversation was headed.

'So I said to him, "Why settle for a date with your rep's girlfriend if you can have his wife?" Am I right? A girlfriend might leave you any time, but a wife who made vows, now that's exciting. I think you know where I'm going with this. Don't make me come out and say it.'

With my younger selves looking on, I knew that this was the limit. There was no way I could push my feelings down and let this go any further.

Before I even really knew what was happening, I said, 'Doctor, there's something I'd like to ask you.'

It was a bomb I was debating throwing and I had no idea of the range of the explosion. But suddenly I was ready.

Do it, said my boyhood self. The teenage version of me watched closely.

'Something you want to ask me? If it's about a sexually transmitted disease, sure, I can check you out. Despite appearances, I am a physician.'

Hearing this just urged me on.

'It's about the matter of fake patient examinations.' I was hoping to use a polite tone and frame the question abstractly, but it ended up being fairly direct.

I watched the bomb fly from my hand and arc through the air, leaving me with a weightless feeling.

The young hospital director froze for a second. Shock registered on his face, his body stiffened, his expression turned sour. Then he clicked his tongue. Shock, stiffen, click. That told me everything I needed to know.

My vision narrowed.

But I couldn't turn back now. There was only forward, for myself and my younger selves watching. The die had been cast, now all I could do was see how it landed. I was open to any outcome. I pictured my wife, Miyako, and I hoped I wasn't doing the wrong thing.

'Fake . . . patient examinations?' I had never seen the young director's face twist up quite so much. It frightened me. I almost squeaked an apology and retracted my question, but I felt my past selves standing strong in solidarity.

Don't panic. He's just making that face to cover up that you scared him. He's cornered so he's making it look like he's angry.

My boyhood self was calmer than I felt.

'Yes, fraudulent claims made on exams that never happened.' I didn't go so far as to ask if O. Hospital was doing this, or had ever done it. All I did was line up the key words. It wasn't even technically a question, or a judgment. Basically just letting a few words hang in the air. My plan was to watch his reaction and make my next move accordingly.

The hospital director made a groaning noise and puckered his lips sharply.

I had no idea what he might say or do next.

Or what I should do, for that matter. I had said what I felt I needed to say, and I didn't regret it, but wasn't sure about what should come next. I had launched the plane into the air without knowing how to land it.

The director looked suddenly sober as he opened his mouth to speak. 'Does Watanuki know about this?'

'No, uh, not yet.' I had told myself that I would consult with Watanuki before making any kind of a move, but the way the situation unfolded, I had left the runway without him.

'Well then I suggest you go speak to him about it. For fuck's sake.' He exhaled forcefully through his nostrils, back to looking down on me.

The analyst was out of his coma. When I heard about it from my suited former colleague (after going through the usual extra steps to arrange a meeting), my first thought was that I would finally be able to get to the bottom of Mother's involvement. I imagined he would be able to tell me about who had put the analyst in the hospital.

It felt like there was finally going to be a reckoning in my power struggle with Mother. My side of the seesaw would settle on solid ground while she was left dangling helpless in the air.

But when I met him at the agreed bench in Yamashita Park, I learned that it wasn't at all what I'd thought.

The analyst had been a double agent for the Soviets, and when he wanted out they got angry and tried to have him killed. I felt like I had ordered fried rice and been served a parfait. I even said, 'This isn't what I asked for.'

'What do you mean, not what you asked for?'

'Never mind. So you're saying he was attacked by our friends at the soba shop?'

The soba shop was code for the Soviets. The burger joint meant the Americans. I always thought it was too simple a code so I never used it when I was an active agent, but now that I had retired I figured it was fine.

'Yep.'

'Then that means it has nothing to do with me, right? And the fact that he was looking into my family issue?'

'It does have to do with that.'

'What? How?'

'Your final go-round.'

'My final . . . ?' But before the words could leave my mouth I figured it out. The first time I met Naoto's parents. When I happened to discover and apprehend the Soviet operative with the nerve toxin. It was after I retired, but I suppose that would count as my last mission. 'So when the analyst got the wrong target—'

The story we had all been told was that he had fallen for the soba shop's misinformation and led our agents astray.

'He did it on purpose. It was intentional bad analysis.'

'And not just a rookie mistake?'

'That's just what he made it look like.'

I thought about the analyst and his gourd-shaped head. He kind of felt like a little brother, lovable even if not 100 percent reliable. But it turns out he was a skilled spy who pulled one over on all of us. Even hearing it from my former colleague, it didn't feel real.

So the next thing I heard unsettled me even more.

'And it seems like he was involved in the attack on you at your home.'

'What?'

'That's the connection to your final go-round. Their operative was supposed to use the smuggled nerve toxin to cause confusion and chaos in Japan, but you stopped her.'

'I generally try to stay out of other people's love lives, and same with their nerve toxin plans.'

'Seems the analyst was blamed for the failure of the plot.'

'By the soba shopkeepers?'

'Yeah. And he decided to pin it on you, to take some of the heat off. Probably told them the plan could never have worked as long as you were around.'

'That's giving me a lot of credit.'

'Something along the lines of you being a top agent who would stop any future operations.' Which meant that they decided they had to get rid of me and sent that fake postman to take me out. 'Having a good reputation can be a liability.'

'So they took one shot at me, it didn't work, and that's that? I'd imagine they would have been a bit more persistent. I mean, one try and then giving up . . .'

'You're not wrong. But according to the analyst, he told them that they shouldn't come at you again. He must have felt bad after all.'

'Guess I owe him a thank-you.'

'And after that episode he decided he was done being a double agent.'

'Put in a request to be traded to another team?'

'Yeah, if this were baseball.'

It's not like he could just say that he was resigning and they would thank him for his service and let him go. They must have been going back and forth, and in the middle of it he was targeted with a hit-and-run.

With that, my former colleague said that it looked like there was nothing else to this case and reminded me not to tell anyone about any of it. He looked relieved as he left. As for me, far from being relieved, I had the feeling that the puzzle I was almost done putting together had been blithely overturned and scattered. I sat there for some time, trying to pick up the pieces.

I had been so certain that Mother was behind the deaths of my father-in-law and Santaro, and that she sent someone after me to stop me from investigating. Same with the analyst getting hit by a car.

But with the new information that the false postal worker was a Soviet assassin, it was clear enough that Mother had nothing to do with it.

'What is it? Is there something wrong? Something wrong with me?'

Mother was sitting on the sofa watching television and turned to ask me this at a commercial break.

'Why do you ask?' Yes, there are plenty of things wrong with you, as far as I'm concerned.

'I keep feeling you looking at me.' She narrowed her eyes, not even trying to hide her distaste. 'Maybe you're trying to see if I have any new gray hairs.'

'Come on, Mother, you know you don't have very many gray hairs.'

It was true. Her hair was full and black. Most women her age would be dealing with thinning and graying, but not her. Her skin still had a youthful luster too. It was almost like she was stealing someone else's nutrients. Maybe that's why my skin was so dry. I had all sorts of theories about her.

You were so certain that she was guilty of murdering her family members. Now that you've found out it's not true, maybe you're a little disappointed.

It was my other self, poking fun at me.

True enough, the intruder masquerading as a postman wasn't on her payroll after all.

But I'm still not sure about my father-in-law and Santaro.

. . . Even as I said this to my internal interrogator, I had a strong sense of being a sore loser.

Are you that determined to make her the villain?

The insurance salesman Ichio Ishiguro popped into my head. According to him, there was an ancient antagonism between Mother and myself that went beyond any personal feelings. As if I had asked why cats chase mice or why dogs and monkeys fight, and he responded with a fairy tale about how the Chinese zodiac signs were chosen. But at this point I couldn't even laugh off how ridiculous it all seemed.

'My husband always used to make fun of me for it. "Your hair is tough and you have so much of it," he'd say, "you should at least put it to good use. Make paintbrushes out of it," he'd say.'

'Well, you are good at drawing and painting.' I was trying to find some equilibrium in the conversation, but I actually was impressed with the pictures I had found in her sketchbook.

'Drawing pictures never made me a single yen.'

'Were you doing it for the money?' I intended it lightly, but as soon as I said it I thought about the accidental deaths around her and the insurance money she had collected.

'No, nothing like that. It was just a hobby. Well, a housewife like me has plenty of time, so I didn't see it as a problem.'

'There's nothing wrong with drawing as a hobby.'

She fell silent, looking at me intently.

'What's up?' Uncertainty flashed through me.

She shrugged. 'It's just that I feel like you're being honest with me for a change.'

'I'm always honest with you.'

'Of course you are, dear.'

It was clear she was taking a dig. I fought down the wave of anger that surged within me.

Three days later, Naoto and I went out together for the first time in a while, poking around the brand stores and boutiques in Ginza. We were enjoying ourselves, but I didn't fail to notice that his color was off, like he wasn't feeling quite right. I worried that if I took my eyes off of him he might collapse.

'What's wrong?' he asked, though that should have been my line, and I felt bad that I hadn't asked him first. 'Looks like you've got something on your mind.'

'I'm just fully focused on being with you,' I said with a smile. 'It's so rare we get a chance to go on a date.'

While we waited for a crossing light to change I spotted a news story on a digital billboard about the Emperor's deteriorating health. My whole life had been during his reign, the Showa era, and it somehow felt like it would always be the Showa era. Last year when he fell ill and had stomach surgery, the first Japanese emperor to ever undergo such a procedure, there was a definite sense of historical significance, but after that the gravity of the situation seemed to lessen and things went back to normal. But then his symptoms returned with greater severity. *Self-restraint* became a watchword in Japan. Festivals were canceled, the enthusiasm of TV commercials was toned down. The national mood was glum. In a group-oriented society it seemed appropriate to share in the sadness of others and shun those who didn't show proper respect. Some were declaring that it had nothing to do with them and kept doing whatever they wanted, without a thought to the fact that others were going through a tough time, and that didn't seem right.

'What about you, Naoto, are you all right? It's your day off, maybe it would have been better to just relax at home.'

'No, no, I'm fine. I'm glad we get some time together like this.'

I was thrilled to hear him say that, but I also picked up a note of despair.

'It's rough at work?' I didn't need to ask to know that. It was plain to see – from how late he was coming home each night, from how ragged he looked at the end of the day, from his depressed mood when he left in the morning. I wasn't trying to draw out a full confession or anything like that, but it seemed that my question made his face twitch and cramp. He gritted his teeth through a contorted smile, a textbook picture of grinning and bearing it.

'Yeah, I guess it's kind of rough,' he replied with a shrug. I could tell that he was at the end of his rope.

Naoto was worn down from all the late hours, the lack of sleep and the bodily exhaustion. I was worried about him, but it seemed that if he could get a different assignment that was a little less physically intense then it would solve the problem. On the other hand, I had noticed that he was sighing an awful lot, and there seemed to be something on his mind in addition to the physical weariness, some burden he was bearing, I thought I'd started seeing something like fear in his eyes.

'How's it going with O. Hospital?' When I heard that Naoto

got a new account, I did a little research. The previous director was well liked and had a good reputation, but his son was apparently an elitist snob. It made me angry that Naoto had to cut into his time with me taking care of a spoiled brat, but it wasn't the end of the world.

'Um, what?' Naoto seemed wary. 'Why are you asking about O. Hospital? Do you know something?' He was obviously thrown.

'I just know it's your new assignment so I was asking about it, no deep meaning or anything. But the way you're reacting to my question . . . is there something wrong?'

'Oh, uh, no . . . no,' he muttered, gazing off into the distance.

Ginza Avenue was crammed with people, and the road seemed like a river of taxis flowing by. It was all hubbub and competition, exactly the opposite of a peaceful natural scene that would calm the nerves.

'What would you say – and this is purely hypothetical – but what would you say if I were to quit my job?'

Aha, I thought. 'That would be fine with me. If that's what you think would be best, I'm behind it. There are plenty of other jobs out there right now.'

It seemed to me like the age of plentiful and easy-to-land jobs would soon come to an end. Everyone was celebrating free agents in the marketplace, talking about how much better that was than being attached to a company, but that's just because everyone was so flush. It really seemed to me that modern Japan was just like Britain in the eighteenth century during the South Sea Bubble. All our prosperity was just a dream of endless summer. Soon the dream would end, with the long hard road of reality stretching out ahead.

But for the moment, there was no need for Naoto to tough it out at the pharma company. 'Don't worry about what I think, really. All I want is for you to do something that will let you enjoy your life.'

Naoto's face lit up at that, but it was still only the dim illumination of a nightlight.

We went to a love hotel and spent a few hours rolling around naked, getting into it in a way that wasn't possible in the home we shared with Mother. For a little while we were able to put a lid on our worries, or at least I was and I'm pretty sure Naoto was too. We just focused on feeling good with each other. I would have liked to have spent the whole night, but we ended up heading home close to midnight.

Naoto still wore a concerned expression, but he must have been at least a little refreshed because he wasn't heaving so many sighs.

Just about the time we reached our Neighborhood Association building, I noticed some people following us. A few men behind us, obviously trying to keep a low profile.

More visitors from the soba shop?

My former colleague had said they wouldn't be targeting me anymore, but it was possible he'd got it wrong.

Being with Naoto meant I wouldn't be able to handle it as I normally would. I didn't know if they had weapons, and if they did, whether it was guns or knives or maybe some kind of poison. Each different threat would require a different response.

I continued talking with Naoto, keeping my attention focused on the men behind us.

'Hey, hold up,' a rough voice called out to us.

My alarms began sounding. Naoto, startled, turned around, and I glanced back at the trio.

I took a quick read: they weren't sent by the Soviets. If they had been it would be going down differently. There would be no calling out to get our attention, they would have just attacked, as quickly and quietly as they could. These men were clearly yakuza, stupidly announcing themselves, as if they were generals of long-ago, before a battle. Nobody working for the Russians would be so dumb. Maybe we had just randomly crossed paths with the wrong guys? There were plenty of lowlifes who couldn't resist messing with a happy couple out on a night stroll.

'Hey, I'm talking to you.' Two of them had on expensive-looking suits, while the third one was in a tracksuit and had dyed blond hair. From the way he moved I guessed he was a former boxer.

'Yes?' Naoto's voice had a slight quaver. 'What is it?'

'This is a warning. Don't stick your nose where it don't belong. You hear me? You get what I'm saying?' The middle of the three men puffed out his chest as he spoke. His voice wasn't loud, but it rang out in the cool night air of the deserted street, reverberating through our bodies. He seemed used to threatening people.

But I didn't know what he was talking about.

While my mind raced, Naoto spoke up beside me. 'Stick my nose where it doesn't belong? I'm not sure I follow.' I could feel his fear. His legs were trembling.

Were they after Naoto? Not me?

In fact, they were mostly looking in his direction. Just once or twice the blond guy in the tracksuit glanced at me, like he was inspecting the quality of a product.

'Don't play dumb, buddy. You know exactly what I'm talking about. You wanna be a good little boy, but that messes up our business. So just look the other way. The world ain't gonna stop turning. Got it? Be smart.' Then he added with a nasty grin, 'If you're set on doing the right thing, it could get ugly for that pretty wife of yours.'

I widened my eyes in terror. Playacting, of course.

I wasn't scared at all, but I was at a loss. I didn't know exactly how to handle this situation. I stared down at the department store bag full of clothes we had bought.

Then I stole a glance at Naoto standing next to me. What

happened next was one of the most touching things I've ever experienced: Naoto took a step forward and in front of me, making a shield out of his body, trying to defend me. There was no doubt he was petrified. He was clearly rattled by the sudden appearance of these men. It was all he could do to stay on his feet. And through all that, he was still trying to protect me.

I wanted the streetlamps to focus on Naoto and me like a warm spotlight as the stars glittered overhead and a soft symphony played.

Although I suppose it wasn't exactly the perfect moment for all of that.

'Don't you touch her,' said Naoto. I think. I was wrapped up in my fantasy and may have just imagined him saying it.

The men flashed wolfish smiles. They had the advantage of numbers, and as far as they knew neither of us was a fighter, so to them we were easy pickings.

'Tell you what, buddy, why don't we break your arm. It's only fair, we had to bust our asses coming all the way out here to find you.'

It sounded like he thought he was doing us a favor. He started toward us, the other two following behind.

What do I do? How do I deal with this?

I started by shifting the department store bag into one hand and reaching in with the other, feeling for the garments. They were wrapped in paper and tied up with a ribbon, which I undid.

Then I made a little noise of recognition and looked past them, as if I had spotted someone we knew. A totally obvious ploy to distract them.

But they fell for it. All three spun around, and I couldn't help but smile.

Without wasting an instant I tugged on Naoto's hand and ran away from the men. At the same time I dumped the clothing in the bag onto the street. When Naoto turned to follow me I stuck out my leg and tripped him. As he stumbled I pulled the department store bag down over his head, then grabbed him by the belt loops and yanked him back upright. Fast as I could I wrapped the ribbon around the outside of the bag and tied it up. He wouldn't be able to get it off his head very easily. Suddenly blinded, he swayed a bit, confused. I could hear him protesting from inside the bag but couldn't make out what he was saying.

'Hold still,' I whispered toward where I guessed his ear was.

Then all I had to do was take care of the three men, which was a piece of cake. They were flummoxed at this bizarre woman who pulled a bag over her husband's head, giving me ample openings. I aimed a palm-heel strike at the middle guy's face, smashing him with the hard bone. I did the same to the man on the right, hitting him right in the nose. They both doubled over, clutching their faces.

Last was the blond in the tracksuit, the boxer. He seemed to realize he had to take me seriously because he took up a fighting stance and started moving his feet rhythmically, trying to work his way around to my left. I put up my own hands and rotated my body to stay facing him as he moved.

I didn't want to spend long on this and had no intention of getting into a staredown. No sooner than I told myself to get it over with quickly he sprang, throwing a right.

I dropped into a nearly full split. His punch whizzed over my head. I squeezed my legs back together and shot back up, bashing him in the chin with my palm-heel.

It was a solid hit. He staggered once and then crumpled to the ground.

No longer concerned with any of them, I dashed back over to where Naoto stood, untied the ribbon and ripped the bag off his head.

'Miyako!' He was clearly concerned, throwing his arms around me and asking me over and over if I was okay.

'I am now,' I said. At that moment the moon abruptly shifted its angle and bathed me and my husband in soft light as the clouds parted, the stars twinkled, and the music began to play.

I didn't remember having fallen asleep, but there I was with the morning sun shining through the bedroom window. I sat up startled, then rushed downstairs to find Miyako making breakfast. 'Mother went out first thing with the Furuyas.'

But I didn't care about that at all. We had been attacked the night before. They threatened to break my arm. Was it real? Did it even happen? It didn't feel real.

According to Miyako, she panicked and threw the department store bag aside and it somehow ended up on my head. Then those yakuza-looking guys got into an argument and started attacking one another.

The more she explained what had happened the more it felt like a dream, or I suppose a bad dream.

'But what did they want? Who were those guys, anyway?' she asked when we were seated and eating.

I glanced at the clock and saw that it was getting time to leave for work. Miyako had gotten wrapped up in my mess, so I owed her some kind of an explanation. 'I'll give you the full version later, but for now here's the summary,' I began.

The possibility that O. Hospital was committing fraud. My growing suspicion, and not knowing what to do about it. The fact that the young hospital director knew I suspected him. And then just as I was deciding what to do next, last night's attack.

'So you think those yakuza guys are involved with the insurance scam.'

'Probably. They're probably the ones who provide the names and insurance info.'

'I wonder if that no-good hospital director is the one who told them. He wanted to shut you up.'

'Could be. I guess it's true when they say that if you poke around in the tall grass you run into snakes.'

'Yes, but in this case poking around the grass was the right thing to do. You couldn't just look the other way.'

Exactly, I thought, encouraged. 'If I didn't do it I feel like my younger self would have been disappointed with me.' I wanted to teach my teenage self how to be.

'Sorry, what?'

'I wonder if we should have called the police.' The thought had only just occurred to me. Given what had happened the night before, it definitely made sense to involve the authorities.

'Maybe we should have.' Miyako nodded. 'Although if you do then what's going on at O. Hospital will get out into the open.'

She was right. And it should, of course, but I wasn't sure I was ready to take that step. I kept thinking about what the hospital director said to me: *I suggest you go speak to Watanuki about it.*

'How about if we tell the police but leave out the backstory,' Miyako suggested, seeming to guess what was on my mind. 'Some men attacked us last night, we're scared, that's all. If we tell them that they might even set up a patrol in the area.'

'So we don't say anything about O. Hospital, huh?'

She seemed much calmer than I felt. Maybe because she wasn't the one at the center of this mess.

As soon as I got to the office I went to find Watanuki. *I need to talk to him, I wonder how much he knows, I hope he's not involved* – these thoughts ran on a loop as I looked for him.

But I couldn't find him anywhere.

I asked the head of our division and some of our coworkers,

but all I learned was that he hadn't come in yet and that he also hadn't requested any time off.

My heart started beating faster and an ominous feeling worked its way through my body. I was too anxious to just wait around so I left as if I was going on my client visits, heading instead to Watanuki's condo. I knew where he lived from the numerous times we had shared a taxi home.

He wasn't there. I tried calling on the intercom but there was no answer.

He must have had some emergency come up. Maybe one of his relatives was in some trouble. Or maybe he had collapsed from exhaustion and was in the hospital.

I came up with several more explanations to try to calm my nerves. I wanted something that felt solid, but every time I tried poking at one it just collapsed.

Who else can I go to for help?

But I barely even thought about it. I was so desperate that I contacted the only other person who might know anything: the young director of O. Hospital.

When he picked up the phone he sounded much kinder than I expected. 'Sorry I was so snippy the other night,' he said. 'I'd like to talk to you about it again. I've been thinking about it; I feel like I should tell you everything that's going on.'

'I can't get in touch with Watanuki.'

'Ah, don't worry about him. He's on his way over here now.'

'To the hospital?'

I was at a loss, and his suggestion was like an arrow on an information board pointing the way, a direction that I wanted to follow without questioning it. I did as I was told and headed for O. Hospital. Stepping out of the taxi, I took a few steps toward the entrance. Then I was caught in a chokehold from behind.

It was too strong for me to fight. My mouth and nose were held shut. Fighting for breath, I was tipped over backward, so all

I could see was the sky. It was blue and bright, not a single cloud, depthless.

Somehow my surroundings were suddenly burning. I was inside a traditional Japanese home on fire. The sound and smoke surrounding me were more intense than the heat. Someone was approaching me. I held my hand out in front of me but it was tiny. I realized I was a child again – a toddler, long before elementary school.

Men dragged me to a car and threw me inside. Then they hit me in the face and head. I didn't lose consciousness, but the pain was so intense that my mind went totally blank.

To Miyako. I'm so sorry to do this. Thank you so much for everything. I was so lucky to have married you. I have caused so much trouble to so many people that I am taking my own life.

'You use "so" too much.'

I looked up. The pronouncement came from Watanuki, standing there in a double-breasted Armani suit. With his yellow necktie and his perfectly styled hair he looked like his usual sharp businessman self, and I had the momentary sensation that he was just correcting my writing for an office communication. I still hadn't grasped my situation.

'I'm glad you're okay, Watanuki.' Completely irrelevant – that's how confused I was.

'You know, you were a great junior colleague. Responsible, likable.'

'Thank you.'

There was sympathy in his eyes. 'You're doing a good job with your current assignment, too. I don't have anything to worry about, do I?'

'I'm sorry, Watanuki. I can't do it. The insurance fraud was your idea, wasn't it? Now that I know about it, I'd like to be taken off the O. Hospital assignment.'

'Kitayama, you're really not getting it.'

'I'm not?'

'I thought you would just do the O. Hospital job without thinking about it too much. But you didn't trust me, and you grew an inflated sense of justice. I have no intention of keeping you on O. Hospital.'

'So it's going to someone else?'

Watanuki stared at me with disbelief, then laughed. 'I don't know if you're smart or dumb. Listen, this doesn't have anything to do with who's handling O. Hospital anymore. Your new assignment is something else entirely. That's why I'm having you write this thing. Get it?'

I must have been too terrified to process what I was doing.

Which was writing a suicide note.

I reread what I had written. *I am taking my own life.* Then I understood. I broke out in goosebumps and my vision went momentarily dark.

I'm being forced to write a suicide note.

Men on either side of me suddenly held me down in the chair, because I had started struggling. I hadn't even realized it.

I'm going to die! Danger! It wasn't my mind that realized this, but my body. My mind was still unable to process the reality of the situation. It didn't make sense that something like this would happen to me, that Watanuki would be one of the bad guys, and so my mind was rejecting it. My body, operating on instinct rather than reason, was being far more reasonable.

'Hurry up and write, Kitayama.'

'What are you going to do?'

'What am *I* going to do? I'm so glad you're concerned for me. Don't worry about me, Kitayama, I'll be just fine.'

'What about the fraud?'

'Why, you're taking responsibility for all of that, and then killing yourself. So that's all taken care of. Which I truly appreciate.'

He sounded like he often did when he was asking me to take his place entertaining a doctor he didn't get along with.

No problem, I almost said.

'So get on with it. Write your note. I've got a date in Roppongi.'

This is bad, this is really bad. I started feeling frantic. 'I don't want to write it.' My voice was trembling. I couldn't help it.

If I don't write it myself, it doesn't count as a suicide note.

That didn't mean they couldn't kill me. But at least then they wouldn't be able to pin the crime on me.

It was the only little advantage I had.

My head was finally starting to work again.

Why should I do what he says? I felt my temper rising, but the next thing Watanuki said made me freeze up again.

'Kitayama, you love your wife, right?'

'Wha—?'

'You should write that note. Do it for your wife.'

'What are you saying?' I wasn't playing dumb. My mind had once again stopped functioning.

'If you write the note like I said, nothing will happen to your wife. If you don't do what I ask, well, things won't go so easy for her.'

'But either way—'

'That's right, buddy, either way you're going to die. But ask yourself if you'd rather it just be you, or if you also want something terrible to happen to her. And I'm not saying we'll kill her. But, you know, she'll wish we had.'

I shot out of the seat. The men forced me right back down, holding me with arms as thick as my thighs. Fingers dug into my shoulder so hard it felt like they would break the skin and pulverize the meat beneath. An animal-like wail escaped my mouth.

'That's . . . that's horrible!'

'Not so horrible to me.' I could tell he was being honest. 'You don't have a lot of options here. You can save your wife or you can sentence her.'

'I have no guarantee.' I could barely manage to get it out. 'Even if I write a suicide note I have no guarantee you won't hurt her.'

'Yeah, and you'll be dead, so you won't know either way.'

It boggled my mind how he could seem to be having so much fun, and at the same time I realized that this was almost certainly not the first time Watanuki had ended someone's life. I felt cold in the seat of my pants, though I wasn't sure if that meant I had pissed myself.

'Listen, you've got nothing to worry about, Kitayama. If you write the note and you do it properly, we'll have no reason to go after your wife. We'd just be exposing ourselves if we did. No, if anything we'll stay far away from anyone connected to you. But if you don't write it, well, that's a different story. A whole different scenario. One that involves us going after your wife.'

I opened and closed my mouth like a goldfish, which was almost all I could do. Somehow I managed to sputter out, 'Please let me hear her voice.'

Watanuki looked approving. 'Yeah. Yeah, that's a good idea.'

'Phone. Where's the phone?'

For the first time I looked at my surroundings. I hadn't been blindfolded when they'd brought me to wherever we were but they had been handling me so roughly that I had no chance to register any details. It was a spacious western-style room.

In front of me was a wireless phone.

'It makes sense for you to talk to your wife. I mean, hey, Kitayama, she's who you're dying for.'

His words scraped through my head. I wasn't putting up a

fight anymore. *I guess there's no escaping the fact that I'm going to die, and really that's fine, in fact I get to die protecting Miyako.* I felt almost optimistic.

Watanuki gestured at the phone with his chin.

I didn't know what time it was, but I guessed it was still the afternoon. It could be either Mom or Miyako who answered. There was the sound of someone picking up.

'What's wrong?' As soon as I heard Miyako's voice I felt like my emotions might overflow.

'How?'

'How what?'

'How'd you know it was me?'

'Because you just said it was you. Just now.'

Did I? I must have been so terrified that I didn't have a clear grasp on what I was doing or saying. I sighed. 'I guess I did.'

'So what's wrong?'

'Oh, ah, well.' Watanuki's eyes reminded me of what would happen if I said something revealing. It wouldn't only be my life at stake, but Miyako's too. 'I just, you know.'

'You just wanted to hear my voice?' She sounded playful.

'Yes!' I tried to laugh, so she would think I was happy, but it sounded off.

'Are you okay? Seems like something's wrong.'

'You know how it is, work is no picnic.' I shook my head. Just about any job was better than the one I had at that moment. Although I suppose dying in disgrace wasn't exactly a job. 'Oh, is Mom home?'

'She's out with the Furuyas.'

'Oh. Okay.'

'Is there something you want me to tell her?'

Scenes from the past frothed through my head like whitewater rapids, only to rush away again. Elementary school, my teenage years, my wedding, Dad's funeral, all bubbling and roiling.

Drowning me. It felt like my mouth was filling up with tears. My voice broke and I held the phone away from myself. I blinked hard several times, forcing my breath back under control. 'Just tell her I said thank you,' I muttered. Thank you was the only thing that made sense.

'Did something happen?'

'No, I just wanted to thank her.' *I want to thank you too*, I wished I could say, but that would probably make her wonder even more.

'What do you want for dinner tonight?' It was such a normal, everyday question. Again I fought down my tears.

'I'll be home late,' was all I managed to say.

The moment we hung up I knew what I could do. I wasn't ready to accept death. The only thing I could focus on was not thinking about anything. I made up my mind not to think about fear, not to think about trying to fight back. Just – nothing.

I felt a hand on my shoulder. I raised my head and saw Watanuki staring at me, a complicated look in his eyes. It might have been that he was moved by the phone call, or it might have been disappointment at seeing his protégé so utterly powerless.

What do you want for dinner tonight?

Miyako's words echoed in my head. Picturing her waiting up for me as if nothing were wrong, I felt a crushing pressure in my chest.

Don't think about anything.

After I hung up the phone Naoto's voice was still reverberating in my ears. He was frightened. And he was trying to sound strong. But I'm sure when he said *I'll be home late* that I heard a sad tremble at the end.

'So? You think you got it?' I asked the woman sitting across from me at our dining-room table.

'Just a moment,' she said, listening to a transceiver earpiece. She took notes as she listened.

As soon as I'd got a call from Naoto's company that they didn't know where he was, I thought about yesterday's encounter with those yakuza punks and I knew that something had happened to him. Right away I called up my former colleague.

'This is the first and last time I'll ask you for any help. But I really need it.' He didn't agree at first, but to be fair I didn't expect him to. 'You owe me for the analyst. I was attacked because of him. I have every right to be angry. But what I'm asking you isn't even that big of a thing. It's actually pretty small,' I pressed. In the end he agreed to dispatch one of his staff members, probably not so much because of my negotiating as from a sense of duty to an old comrade.

The staffer was at my home, contacting the phone company on her mobile phone.

'Those have gotten a lot smaller,' I said, pointing at her phone once she was off the line.

'They'll keep getting even smaller. Our forecast suggests that soon enough there will be more of these than home telephone lines.' She wasn't friendly, but she wasn't mean either. 'Everything will be digital, which will make tracing calls much easier.'

'Really?'

'Right now we have to track physical phone lines, which is why I needed you to keep the call going. If it were digital we would be able to identify the other phone's information the moment we connected.'

'That's convenient, but also a little scary.'

'Before you know it, computers will be running for office.'

'That might actually lead to more stability.' At least it would take pride, grudges, and obligations out of the equation.

'I think artificial intelligence is frightening.' She slid a piece of paper over to me. 'This is the address where that call came in from.'

It was a building near the main intersection of the Fujisawa Kongocho neighborhood. Not nearby, but not as far as I was worried it might be. I stood up, eager to get a move on.

'Are you going by yourself?' the staffer asked as she packed up her things.

'Do you want to come with?'

'Uh, no. That would be a bit much for me.'

'Yeah. Not in your job description,' I said with a smile. 'I appreciate you helping me trace the call, though. It's a big help. Thank you.'

'Apparently this makes everything even.' Having communicated my former colleague's message, she promptly left.

As I was pulling out of our carport I encountered Ichio Ishiguro. I hadn't seen him in a while and I had several questions for him, but there were more important things to deal with at the moment. *Next time,* I thought, putting my foot on the gas, but somehow he was suddenly standing in front of my car, spreading his hands wide as if to say, *None shall pass.* I slammed on the brakes. It was so abrupt that I mis-timed stepping on the clutch and the car stalled.

Of course this would happen now. I don't have time for this shit! I laid on my horn in frustration, the first time I had ever done that in my life. But then he wasn't in front of the car anymore, he was right next to me at the driver's-side window. I nearly jumped out of my skin, since I hadn't even seen him move. He seemed perfectly calm, though, and just stood there rapping on my window.

I don't know why I opened the window. I could have just restarted the engine and driven off. 'What is it?'

'Is it a confrontation?'

'Sorry?'

'I thought perhaps you were embroiled in some kind of altercation.'

'Do insurance companies usually get involved before something happens?'

'There are some things that one cannot solve on one's own.'

'Are you talking about Naoto? Do you know something?' Naoto was wrapped up in a whole mess with O. Hospital and the yakuza and insurance fraud; it wouldn't be crazy for an insurance company employee to know something. Or, at least, the connection made sense in my moment of hasty speculation.

'Oh, do you mean your husband? I was certain that any trouble would have been between you and your mother-in-law, Ms Setsu.'

I didn't have time to deal with him. In fact I was starting to think that *he* might be trouble. I told myself I should just ignore him and drive away, but the next thing I knew he was sitting in the passenger seat. I certainly didn't let him in, or at least I didn't remember letting him in.

'Why are you in my car?' I pulled away from my house, with him sitting beside me.

'You said you had some questions for me. Don't worry, I will get out when we are done.' He sounded completely at ease.

'What exactly is there between me and my mother-in-law? You told me before that it's something about an ancient grudge or something like that. Sea versus mountain, right? An eternal struggle. But that's wrong.'

'Wrong, you say?'

'That can't be what's going on with me and Mother. If that were true, Naoto would also have to be a sea person or a mountain person, wouldn't he?' As I was saying it, it sounded like something out of a manga, and I couldn't help but laugh at myself with embarrassment. 'And if he were whatever I'm not, then it wouldn't make sense for us to get married. We'd fight all the time, not to mention never be able to have kids.' My own words stopped me short – we *didn't* have kids. We hadn't been able to. Was this the reason why? 'Anyway, Mr Ishiguro, how do you know about all of this? Are you a sea and mountain researcher?'

'I,' said Ichio Ishiguro, letting the word hang in the air before continuing, 'am a sort of impartial observer.'

'Impartial observer? Like a referee, you say what's fair play and what's out-of-bounds?' I was focused on the conversation and almost missed my turn.

'You might say all I can do is watch. I can never affect anything. But I always find myself observing the struggle between mountain and sea. Since long before any of your lives began.'

I burst out laughing. 'Hang on a second, Mr Ishiguro, what are you, some kind of hermit wizard? Don't tell me you're immortal.'

'I can affect nothing. In fact I have always loathed conflict. I am a conflict observer who loathes conflict.'

'A conflict observer who just wants the conflict to end, huh?'

'No matter how fervently I may wish, it never ends.'

That much we could agree on. Times change, but conflict never ends. The people who demand that it should end always wind up saying, *End this or we'll make you end it.* 'An end to conflict. Sounds like a song by an American musician.'

'Americans aren't the only ones who think that.'

'They should sing about something else. Like, it's so humid and nasty out, or, it's so cold I'm freezing to death.'

'They should sing about the temperature?'

'That crosses ideological barriers; everyone can relate,' I said flippantly. 'So you're an old hand at conflict observing, huh, Mr Ishiguro?'

He paid no attention to my slightly mocking tone. 'As I said before, I am an *impartial* observer. If I am a referee, then I am one who does not know the rules of the game and can only stand there. I am sorry to bother you while you are busy with something else. I felt for certain you were rushing to confront your mother-in-law.'

'You didn't want the match to start without you, is that it? So between the sea people and the mountain people, does one side always win?' I almost asked him which side I was on.

'When sea folk and mountain folk meet, they always clash. Sometimes it is on a massive scale, and no small number of lives are lost.'

'Tell me what a few of those were. Some famous matchups from the past.'

With a straight face Ichio Ishiguro launched into it, talking about the Genji and the Heike, the Meiji-era navy and pirates, tales of war and retreat.

'And I guess it never ends peacefully? One side always wins, it's never a tie?' *If you were really the referee you could call it either way*, I wanted to add.

'I do not know exactly what you mean by a tie, but it is certainly not the case that one side is always destroyed. Often enough they make efforts to avoid open conflict.'

'A good clean game between the red team and the white team?'

'There are cases where, after the encounter ends, one side is incapacitated, and the other opts not to finish them off.'

'Oh, sparing the enemy, that's really touching,' I said acidly. 'And they wait kindly until the other side recovers?'

'What do you think happens?'

'How should I know? This has nothing to do with me!'

'Oh but it does have to do with you, just wait and see,' he replied. *Yeah, this guy is trouble.* It was a little late to be wary of him, but I pulled over to the shoulder.

'Get out,' I said roughly.

Surprisingly, he didn't seem perturbed in the least. In fact he appeared almost dignified, as if he was well accustomed to such treatment through the ages. 'Until next time.' With that, he got out.

I snapped back to myself. *I have to save Naoto.* I slammed on the gas, and the tires screeched as I sped off.

It wasn't hard to find the building in Fujisawa Kongocho. It looked like it was only a few years old, but it was already run down, standing on a shadowed block some distance off the main drag. The street was narrow. I parked next to a NO PARKING sign.

Through the entrance and straight ahead to the elevator. The small panel next to it listed tenant names. All offices. *Where's Naoto?*

I didn't want to search all of them. The elevator floor display showed that it was on five. Which meant there were most likely people on the fifth floor.

I launched up the stairs.

Is Naoto all right?

As I climbed I imagined all sorts of scenarios. Based on what I had seen before, the sorts of groups that did this kind of scam typically made it look like their victim died by suicide. So it could be hanging, or falling off a roof, that sort of thing. It was nothing new. But regardless of what it was, I couldn't bear the thought of Naoto being in such a terrifying situation. I had to stop it, no matter what.

As soon as I got to the fifth floor I knew I had found it.

In front of the door at the end of the hall was a shifty-looking man with a punch perm, a loud button-down shirt, and his hands in his pockets, tapping his feet out of boredom.

His presence was a flashing sign telling me that something sinister was going on.

I walked straight down the hall toward him.

He looked up when he heard my footsteps. 'Who the fuck are you?'

'Sorry, I'm wondering if my husband is here.'

'Your husband? The fuck're you talking about?'

When a person thinks they're dealing with someone smaller and weaker than them, they feel secure. It's not a question of prejudice or class, it's an animal reaction. Just like how they're wary of someone who is physically bigger. If you're up against someone much larger, a big man who could easily toss you across the room, even if he's mellow and even-tempered, it's impossible not to feel a degree of caution. Whereas if your opponent is delicately built, you feel like there's no way they could possibly get the better of you.

This man didn't know what to make of me, but because I was smaller he didn't seem all that concerned. He was sure that if something happened, he'd come out on top.

But that's not how it went.

'Let me in,' I demanded.

'How 'bout you let me in?' he answered. It was so lame I couldn't even get mad.

'I mean let me through that door.' As I said it I grabbed him by the neck and slammed him back against the wall. My thumbs dug into his Adam's apple. His face registered surprise, then anger; he glared viciously for a few seconds until his expression twisted up with pain. He was choking, but I pressed harder. 'I need to get into that room.'

He nodded obediently and I let him go.

Then he whipped the door open at me. I dodged to the side, fully anticipating his bull charge. I dodged that too, easily, grabbing his earlobe and yanking it. I could have ripped it off but I didn't. He screamed, and I kicked him in the crotch.

I left him balled up on the floor and entered, not bothering to take my shoes off. Inside was another man, also with a punch perm, of course. 'What the hell is going on?' he said with irritation, coming toward me.

'Where's my husband?'

'Who the fuck are you?'

I debated between his throat and his eyes, then opted for a toe kick to the solar plexus. Easier target. I imagined that a bunch of fired-up yakuza would come charging out of the inner room, but to my surprise that didn't happen. It was silent. Which terrified me.

I checked the next room, and the next. Nothing.

Am I in the wrong place?

I went back to the man clutching his chest on the floor and yanked him up by the collar.

'Where's Naoto?'

His face was an ugly mask of pain and rage. *Male hormones are the worst,* I thought, then grabbed his finger.

I bent it backward, hard. I had every intention of breaking it, but he gave in almost instantly. Must not have been information he thought it important to guard. 'He's gone. They took him somewhere else.'

'You sure he's not here?'

'We don't shit where we eat.' He leered, trying to look tough again.

'Where is he?' I started bending back his finger once more but he quickly shook his head.

'Stop. I really don't know where they took him. There's another guy outside, right? He should know. He said he'd be meeting up with them.'

I left him there and went back out to the hallway. Gone. The elevator showed that it was descending to the first floor. *He's getting away.* I rushed to the stairwell.

Two steps at a time, three steps at a time, until I was jumping down a full landing in one go. I burst outside. Nothing.

What do I do?

I was at a complete loss. Until that moment I had some sense that it would work out. I was worried sick about Naoto, but I thought that after dealing with Cold War spies, a group of criminal punks would be no problem. Now, having lost sight of my mark, I was suddenly stuck.

Did he go left or right? On foot or in a vehicle? I stood frozen, weighing possibilities.

That's when the car came at me from behind.

I sensed movement and whirled around. The grille of the Mark II was already on me. Somehow I twisted my body and avoided a full impact. It still sent me tumbling down to the pavement, and when I tried to get up there was intense pain.

My left leg. When I pressed down on it, agony stabbed through my whole frame.

After hitting me, the car crashed into a sign and came to a stop on a diagonal to the street.

The man who stepped out of the driver's seat was none other than the shifty-looking character in the loud shirt who I had strangled on the fifth floor. He was holding a short black rod. He flicked his wrist and it extended. A telescoping tactical baton.

This was unbelievably annoying.

He had underestimated me once based on my sex and physical stature, but I had made short work of him, so he was taking me seriously now. No doubt that's why he felt he needed to run me over with his car. Now it didn't matter to him what I looked like, he was determined to take me out, and even though my leg was hurt he wasn't taking any chances.

'You are some kinda crazy bitch, huh? What's your deal?' His face was scarlet as he strode toward me. He swung the tactical baton, and I darted out of its path. Or I meant to, but the pain in my leg shot through me and slowed me down just enough. A crushing blow landed on my shoulder.

I yelped out loud. Then clicked my tongue in frustration. It was such an obvious attack, I felt mortified not to have dodged. But the man was encouraged, visibly excited, eager to deal out more punishment. He launched a quick combination, swinging the baton and following with a savage kick.

He was aiming for my injured leg. This guy obviously never heard of chivalry or fair play. Biting back the pain, I found a stance I could work from and managed to deflect his attacks.

I don't have time for this. Naoto. I have to save Naoto.

The thought swirled around and around my head as the baton kept coming. I hoped someone might have noticed the crashed car and called the police, half-expected patrol cars to show up any moment, but I didn't hear any sirens.

Distracted, I let in a kick to the thigh on my damaged leg. The agony was too much to overcome with willpower. I staggered back, groaning.

The man looked like this was turning him on.

'Oh, does it hurt right there?' he cackled, clearly feeling no guilt, at the same time seeming impressed that I was still on my feet. He swung the baton with glee.

Holding myself up against the utility pole beside the road, I deflected the blow with my arm, or more like I sacrificed my arm to save my leg. At that point I was fully on the defensive.

Is there anything I can use? I quickly scanned around me. There had been no shortage of training at the Agency on how to turn around a fight when you're cornered. It was actually assumed that most fights would be from a tight spot. Even if there was no weapon available, there was usually something that could help turn the tables. I looked again.

There was a garbage bag that looked like it had been pecked at by crows. Next to it was a broken umbrella. *Will that work? Is there anything else?*

The baton came for my leg again.

Another scream escaped my mouth. I contorted, lost my

balance, spilled down onto the pavement. Then I felt a rush of anger at my body for not obeying my commands.

Why is this happening? Why now?

I got on my hands and knees to try to haul myself back up. It felt like my left side was ripped to shreds and my head was splitting open. The man came up from behind and brought the baton down on my leg with all his might. He was giddy, letting out odd animal noises. Then all I knew was pain, no room in my head for thought or emotion. *Pain, pain,* my body throbbed out an alarm. *I need to escape the pain, I need—*

'My goodness, is that you Miyako?'

It came from behind. A voice I knew very well.

The sudden familiarity confused me for a moment. A voice I would recognize anywhere. A voice that always irritated me. 'Mother, stay back!' I called out. My voice choked off from the agony in my leg as I tried again to stand up. I turned around. What I saw didn't make any sense to me.

'Are you all right, dear? You know, I'm always telling you, you're not as young as you think you are.' Her tone was patronizing, as usual. Nothing about that surprised me. What I couldn't process was the fact that she had the shifty-looking man in a behind-the-back armlock.

He squealed with pain and dropped his baton.

'Just what do you think you're doing to my daughter-in-law?' she said, then kicked him forward.

He staggered several paces before he regained his balance. Clearly he was confused, and he looked back and forth between the two of us.

I managed to get back on my feet and looked at her. 'Um.'

'You know, you have a real problem with your endgame.' She walked toward me.

'Um—'

'It was the same the first day we met.'

'The first—?'

'Our formal introduction, or whatever you want to call it. At the hotel lounge. You kept saying you were going to the bathroom, but you were working. Am I wrong?'

The old woman with the nerve toxin. The operative I left tied up in the bathroom stall. 'How do you know about—'

'I had already spotted her.'

'What are you talking about?' Really, I had no idea what she was saying.

'That woman. She was very suspicious, sitting there all by herself, not enjoying a meal or anything, clearly preoccupied with something. And the way she snatched the spoon out of the air when it fell off the table – she had very sharp reflexes.'

I remembered that. Mother had summoned a waiter who bumped into the woman's table and knocked off the spoon. The ease with which the old woman had caught it raised my suspicions.

'When you got up, I said to myself, *Ah, she's going to check out that woman.* It was obvious. I thought to myself, *All right, let's see what she's got.*'

'Mother, just wait a second, time-out, please,' I stammered, desperate to understand what was going on. 'Can you explain—'

'And you thought you did such a good job, but you didn't do it properly at all. When I went to check on her after you came back, that woman had slipped her bonds and was about to make a run for it.'

Ignoring my questions and my attempts to get a word in while she said her piece was standard behavior for her, but other than that she seemed like a completely different person. When I asked, 'What are you saying?' it wasn't because I was disagreeing with her. I literally did not understand what she was telling me.

'There was nothing else for it, so I just tied her up myself.'

The man started moving. He had been taken by surprise when

Mother appeared, but his survival instincts as an aggressive human must have kicked in because he looked like he was trying to escape.

I darted toward him, which of course made not just my leg but my whole left side and head scream with agony, but I was past caring about that. I couldn't show any weakness in front of Mother – the need to prove that I could do it unified every last cell in my body, helping me push past the pain. I grabbed the man's arm and wrenched it behind him.

It was the same hold she had just used on him. As soon as I realized that, it was like a circuit connected inside my brain. The behind-the-back arm lock was a standard self-defense technique for neutralizing an opponent, one that I had learned in my early years of training as an agent. *What if,* I thought, looking closely at Mother. Her face seemed to say, *Oh, so she finally figured it out.*

'You know, back in my day it was really tough for women.' She took a step closer. 'Things were much easier for you. I hear the Agency barely even makes any distinction between men and women anymore.'

Not true at all, I wanted to say, but I held it in. The truth was, when I started out it was clear I would be getting different assign-ments to the men just because I was a woman, so I tried my hardest and overcame that barrier. I was proud of that. Hearing someone say it was easy for me made me want to shoot back, *You wouldn't know anything about it.* But I could easily imagine how, if it was hard for me, it must have been much harder for her. 'When . . . ?' I sputtered. 'How long were you—'

'A long time ago. And you would have no way of knowing this, but I was something of a big deal. I still have access to their information. That's how I was able to look you up when Naoto said he wanted to introduce his fiancée to us. I had no idea he'd be bringing home someone who worked for the Agency.'

So she knew all along? I felt dizzy, nearly falling over. It wasn't from the pain, but from the feeling of defeat. Then the man started to struggle, which brought me back. 'Behave yourself,' I said with real acrimony, and bent his finger back until it broke.

Then I remembered: Naoto.

It seemed that Mother had the same thought. 'We can talk about it later. Naoto is in trouble.' She grabbed the man's other hand. 'Where did they take him? Tell me. I advise you not to take me lightly just because I'm an older woman. I'm in a hurry. And I have to do this myself, Miyako's no good at it.'

'No good at what?'

'At forcing information out of people. You prefer not to get your hands dirty. Just like how when you wash the dishes you don't always get all the mess off.'

'What are you talking about, Mother?' There was no avoiding getting mad. I felt for a moment that we were back home in the living room, not out on the street. I grabbed another finger and bent it back.

The man shrieked.

'What's making him scream going to do for us? There's no point hurting him if he doesn't give us the information we need.'

She moved her arm and he screamed again. No words, just a shrill screech.

'He's still not saying anything,' I pointed out. Then I dug my finger into a pressure point by his elbow.

It became an interrogation contest. We took turns hurting him, his fingers and joints, competing to be the first to make him talk. The fight was gone from him, and before long he spilled his guts.

'Were you tracking the car?' I was in the passenger seat, bandaging my leg. The bone was damaged. I'm not sure if it was cracked or broken, but I stabilized it as I had been trained. It would have been ideal if I had some painkillers, but I wasn't so lucky.

Mother had both hands on the wheel, driving fast. 'Back in my day, if you wanted to track someone you had to use a device the size of a phonebook. Nowadays they're much smaller. About the same as a café coaster.'

'How long?' I was having a hard time swallowing it.

'Since a while ago. I did it to make sure that when you went out shopping in the middle of the day you weren't off somewhere messing around.'

I said nothing. All I could do was smile bitterly. It sounded like nothing more than a bad joke, but it did seem that the only way she could have found me was if she had a tracking device in the car. That's how she had come to my rescue. I should be thanking her. But I couldn't stop myself from saying, 'Surveilling people's movements is kind of creepy.' It was like we had magnets of the same polarity inside of us. When we got close to one another there was a repulsion in effect, and I couldn't keep from lashing out at her. Ichio Ishiguro's words echoed in my head – *sea and mountain*.

She opened her mouth, looking like she was about to fire a missile. 'You know, Miyako,' and I braced myself for the attack. But it didn't come. She sighed once, then said, 'Let's just rescue Naoto.'

She was right. She was completely right.

The radio was on, and the speaker's voice suddenly seemed to grow louder. It may have been because we entered an area with better reception, or because both of us had fallen silent.

The host was talking about the recent discovery of three-thousand-year-old murals. Apparently a boy stumbled upon them when he was lost in the mountains. At first specialists thought it was just a pattern in the rockface, but then they determined that it had been etched using stones. It wasn't quite a drawing, but rather a wall of fine lines and complex curves forming hieroglyphs. One expert hypothesized that it was a scene from an epic tale. Then the radio host laughed and said there's also a theory that the boy drew it himself.

I wondered about the murals.

There was no clear picture in my head about three thousand years ago. Who was alive then, and drawing pictures?

'Did you say something?'

'What? No.'

'You didn't say something about a snail shell?'

'Why would I say something about a snail shell?'

'How should I know?'

'Ah, Mother, if you see a supermarket would you stop for a moment?'

'You want me to stop somewhere *now*?'

'I'll only be a moment. I need a trash bag.'

'This'll work,' said Watanuki. 'No problem if we make a mess here.'

They had brought me to a construction site. I had been thrown into the car and couldn't see where we were driving, so I didn't know where we were, but it was clear it would be a very large building when it was done. It was still all exposed structural beams, reminding me of a model of dinosaur bones.

'You know, Kitayama, you should really clean up your own messes, but this time we'll take care of it for you.' He made it sound like he was doing me a favor, and I nearly uttered an automatic thanks.

'Watanuki, do you really need to do this?'

'Do what?'

There were men on both sides of me, each holding one of my arms, which I was getting used to.

'All of this. Killing someone is a serious thing.' That sounded too tame to me, like I was discussing a business concern. I tried again. 'As a human being, I mean. It's something you aren't ever supposed to do. It's a very very bad thing.' My voice was pleading.

He smiled at me and I detected a shade of sympathy. 'You're like a monkey sitting up in a tree, lecturing the monkey that fell out of the tree about what it means to be a monkey. But even if a monkey falls out of a tree, it's still a monkey. Same thing here. Human beings who hurt others to protect themselves are still human beings. And anyway, I'm not doing anything to you. You'll be doing it to yourself.'

Then he ordered me to find a beam at the right height and hang a rope from it. He suggested there would be a stepladder somewhere on site that I could use.

I had never really tried to imagine the scene of my own death before. Even when I had mused on it, it was always far in the future, dying from some sickness in my old age. It would happen in my home, or maybe in some sudden accident. I never pictured I would be hanging myself in the bare space of a construction site.

'Okay. Get on with it, Kitayama.' It was deeply disorienting to hear Watanuki say this, as if he were just instructing me to take out the trash at the office. I couldn't believe this was actually happening.

I felt my elementary school self, and my teenage self, and my adult self up until this moment, all watching me gravely.

I must have started moving without realizing it. The next thing I registered was standing in front of a stepladder. Looking up, I saw a rope dangling, waiting. Then, somehow, I was on top of the stepladder.

My field of vision narrowed. Everything around me seemed blurred. My legs were shaking.

'Shouldn't we blindfold him?' It was the thick-armed man off to the right.

Watanuki furrowed his brow. 'Blindfold him? Why?'

"Cuz nobody wants to look a hanged man in the eye.'

'So don't look. You ever heard of a suicide in a blindfold? That would just raise questions. Same reason we never tied his hands. If there were marks it would be trouble.'

I was so numb that this exchange didn't even upset me. My consciousness seemed to be drifting, and I snapped myself back to the moment – *Keep it together!*

Keep it together?

Keep it together so I can die?

What's the point?

That was when I heard a car pull up somewhere nearby. The tires squealed like sneakers on a gymnasium floor. I looked around for it.

I guess Death shows up in a car.

But Watanuki and his henchmen heard it too. 'Who is that?'

Hey, that looks like my car. When I had that thought I was sure I was hallucinating. The door of the sedan that looked exactly like my sedan opened and my mom stepped out of the driver's side while my wife got out of the passenger side. Seeing them both here only made it seem more detached from reality. And they seemed to be in sync, they were working together, which would never ever happen.

So my last vision is one of my wife and mom getting along. The happiness of this illusion made me realize just how profoundly their constant friction had been wearing me down.

They approached steadily. It looked like Miyako was limping.

I wanted to shout with joy. *Look, Watanuki, the Cold War is over, the Japan–US trade wars are behind us, my wife and mom have made peace!*

Miyako produced a large plastic bag, the same kind we used to put the garbage out three times each week. Maybe the black of the bag symbolized my impending death. She spread it open wide. In the next moment she was beside me, pulling the bag down over my head.

As if that were the signal, my consciousness switched off and my life ended.

Or so I thought. But I still existed. The trash bag had blocked my vision but I was still breathing. It was a bit difficult to breathe, which upset me, but I wasn't suffocating. I had no idea what was going on and flapped my hands uselessly. I wanted to understand, but I couldn't.

Fire appeared. A scene from out of my memories, which, in my confused state, had been spilled out of the box where I kept them. Flames licking greedily at the walls and support beams around me. Intense heat. Hot enough to cook me, pressing in on all sides, crackling. I just stood there, staring, as everything was dyed red and orange by the blaze. I was afraid of the beams overhead coming down. It seemed easiest to just let the flames consume me. As I had that thought, a woman came trudging toward me through the smoke. 'Let's go,' she said, reaching her hand out to me. She looked like she was Miyako's age, but she sounded like my mother. I extended my hand to take hers, but it was such a small hand. I was a child.

My body swayed and the inferno disappeared. All I could see was the black plastic of the trash bag. I was back.

I pulled the bag off my head. Back in the expanse of the construction site.

At my feet there were collapsed bodies. I jumped in fright. It was the men who had been holding my arms.

What happened?

I looked up and ahead, and saw none other than Watanuki. His always-nonchalant face was the exact opposite, clenched and intense, his always-perfectly-styled hair askew, his always-classy suit rumpled.

In his hand was a knife.

He held it out in front of him as he advanced. 'Careful with that, Watanuki!' I called, but must not have been able to hear me because he showed no sign of stopping, so I started toward him.

His blade was aimed in the direction of my wife, who had her back turned. I felt ice in my own spine. *Miyako, watch out!* I leaped forward. *Oh,* I thought, as Watanuki's hand crashed into my side. The knife he was holding slid silently into me. No pain yet, just a spreading redness around the cold steel. As if a circuit breaker had tripped, everything went black.

'I think you owe me an explanation,' I pressed Mother.

We were on the bench near the intake reception on the ground floor of the general hospital.

'Really, Miyako, you're so frightening when you're angry.' Her wry smile projected a complete lack of fear. 'I have nothing to hide. You've been looking into the deaths of my parents and my husband, haven't you? And it was sharp of you to notice the pattern, but you didn't actually think that I had been pulling strings to murder my family, did you?'

'What? No, of course not!' I touched my hand to my lips, trying to project earnestness.

She smiled again, seeing right through me. 'With my parents, it was *them*. You know. I don't know what you called the sides in the Cold War.'

'It was the soba shop?'

'Oh, so you still call them that?'

'I don't know what they call them nowadays.'

'But isn't that so terribly cowardly? Going after your enemy's family?'

'It really is . . .'

'*I* was the one blocking them. They should have blocked me back. Why did they have to take my family instead?'

Maybe, I almost started, but I stopped myself. Maybe it was because she herself was too tough to beat, and someone thought the most effective way to slow her down was to attack her family. If they made it clear to her that going too far would bring repercussions down not just on her but on the people she loved, it would keep her in check. Very much a thing the soba shop would do. Of course, it seemed like something our shop might consider also. Whether it's the Cold War or a conflict with your mother-in-law, at the root it's always a battle with your own reflection. She and I were actually a lot alike. I looked at her sitting next to me, but there was an immediate voice inside me that said, *No, we're nothing alike.*

'But hadn't you retired by the time Father died?' When Naoto and I got married, she was already a full-time homemaker. Although she must have retired long before then, since she wasn't at the Agency when I was.

'That was the boomerang coming back. The things I did in my working years, coming back with interest.' She spoke lightly, but it wasn't exactly a small thing she was talking about. She had lost some of the closest people in the world to her on account of the work she did. I almost started to think about how painful it must have been for her all those years, but decided not to.

'The things you did?'

'I wanted to do the best job I could. And there are people who suffered because of it. So they carry a grudge.'

I immediately put together the scenario: Santaro pushing my father-in-law down the stairs, then Mother getting revenge for her husband's death by staging a traffic accident to kill Santaro. I wondered if it was Santaro who held a grudge against her, or someone else who tasked Santaro with carrying out the vendetta. But all of that was just my basic attempt to connect the pieces rattling around my brain. She didn't say any more on the subject, so I didn't ask.

Then I went back to what I had asked her first. 'That wasn't the explanation I was looking for, Mother.'

'Miyako, has anyone ever told you that your voice is very loud? Quiet down, honestly!'

I had to marvel at how even now she was needling me, and how every little thing she did still bothered me. And I couldn't help but think about Ichio Ishiguro's story of ancient discord passed down through the blood. Sea and mountain can never blend. Any meeting leads to a clash.

So they mustn't ever meet.

Those words rang out like a gong in the deepest part of my mind, sounding close and far at the same time. But they weren't Ichio Ishiguro's words. He never said that. *Then who?*

I took a breath, then exhaled my question:

'Are you actually related to Naoto? What was that about, before?'

She sighed sadly, and suddenly she looked frail and defeated, which made me feel sad too.

Naoto was seen immediately for his stab wound. The blood loss was worse than we had first thought, and though Mother and I had both been in life and death situations scores of times, we were both badly shaken up. But in the end Naoto survived. He remained unconscious after they stitched him up, but the way the doctor was nodding let me know that Naoto would make it.

Which left me with my question.

When he was admitted, the doctor said that the bleeding was severe and that Naoto would need an immediate transfusion. Mother started fussing about how she wasn't the right blood type.

It occurred to me that I had never known what her blood type was. It was a simple thought, but as I waited there outside the operating room, I remembered having once asked my father-in-law what his blood type was. The puzzle pieces fitted themselves together in my head, and my simple thought gave rise to a simple conclusion.

Based on their blood types, there was no way that Naoto could be their child by birth.

Was he the child of a previous marriage? Or adopted? Those were the two options that occurred to me right away. But Naoto had never said anything about either of those two things being the case.

'Listen to me, Miyako, when I say that Naoto is our child and we're his parents. No matter what the circumstances were.'

She spoke in a low voice, but it felt like a sincere confession, so intensely earnest that everyone in the hospital might have heard it as if she were whispering in their ear. I knew I shouldn't say anything flip. I just nodded.

'He was still a tiny little boy. I found him in a house. A house on fire.'

Now her voice was a bare murmur. I didn't imagine that she would give me any more details. Maybe she ended up taking responsibility for Naoto as part of work she was doing for the Agency. A house on fire sounded like it could be a metaphor, but then it could have also been a house literally burning down. That seemed more likely.

'We couldn't have children of our own, but then I came to think that was because we were just waiting to meet Naoto. My husband thought so too.'

I still couldn't find the right words to say. She probably wasn't looking for me to say anything anyway.

With her no longer speaking, silence fell around us. There was no sound at all. Then for a few moments there was the clicking of someone's shoes pacing a hallway somewhere else in the hospital, but that stopped almost as soon as it started. It was like Mother and I were in the silent solemnity of a forest at night.

After a while there was a squeaking noise, which didn't match the grave atmosphere. At the same time I felt my body shaking. I couldn't understand what was happening. From beside me, Mother asked, 'Why are you crying, Miyako?' But rather than her usual disparaging tone, her voice was kind. I hastily wiped my cheeks and rubbed my eyes. *Where did these tears come from?* I asked myself, but I didn't know the answer.

We sat for a while without speaking. It could have been five minutes or an hour.

There were more questions I wanted to ask, more things I wanted to know. And I was also fairly certain that she wouldn't tell me.

'What about Father? Did he know about your work? And what did he think when you took in Naoto? If he didn't know about your work, and he was okay with suddenly taking care of someone else's child—'

'Yes, he was a trusting man, not too quick on the uptake,' she chuckled.

'That's not what I'm saying.' I had a largely positive impression of him.

'If he did know about my work, then he was very trusting indeed.'

'That's still not what I'm saying.'

'You know, Miyako, just because you think you have something all figured out doesn't mean that you're right.'

My annoyance flared, but Mother had revealed so much to me in one day that I wasn't sure how to respond. Still, I wanted to say something, so I asked, 'In those old photos of you and Naoto, you always seemed irked and you were looking off in some other direction away from the camera – was that a habit from work, to always be checking on your surroundings?'

Unexpectedly, she made a quizzical noise. 'Was I doing that in those pictures?' She sounded unsure.

'You were.'

She just harrumphed through her nose. Then, softer, 'Maybe, maybe it's a bad habit I've always had.'

'Oh really? Maybe you're just not photogenic,' I said, taking a dig.

I guess that's how it will always be between us.

The TV news talked all about the Soviets pulling out of Afghanistan, but there was nothing about my wife and me moving out of my mom's house.

This thought was circling around my head, but I kept quiet, focusing instead on tying my necktie.

'Leave your dishes, I'll wash them,' said Miyako. She was at the dining-room table looking at a sketchbook. Then, disapprovingly, 'You know, I think Mother is ignoring the fact that we're in a new era.'

'What do you mean?'

'When she sends mail she still dates everything in the Showa era.'

'She's just not used to the change.' A lot of people weren't – at work I kept seeing documents that got the date wrong, and we had to keep correcting it. Each time I changed Showa to Heisei I had a pang of sadness, but at the same time I felt like I could see Japan's future off in the distance, and it made me stand up a little bit straighter.

'I've told her so many times. If you're going to write the era, write the right one, I say. But she still writes Showa. Sixty-fourth year of the Showa era. So I tell her, fine, just leave the date off, but she still writes it. She just refuses to listen to anything I say.'

'It's no big deal,' I said soothingly. Writing the wrong year wasn't the end of the world. It was actually odd to me why such a small thing would annoy her so much.

We had moved out of the house where I grew up at the end of the previous year, to a condo in the neighboring ward. It was Miyako's idea. It seemed to come out of nowhere, but Mom agreed right away.

I asked her over and over if she wouldn't be lonely all by herself, but every time she just said, 'It's for the best.'

'I'm sure you've noticed, Naoto, but Mother and I are like magnets with the same polarity. As soon as we come near each other we work against each other. Even if we try to get along.' Miyako said it over and over again. Sometimes she would joke, 'Maybe we have some kind of connection from a past generation?' I would ask her if it was fair to reduce the tension between a woman and her mother-in-law to a question of magnetics. 'That's why you keep magnets a little bit apart,' she'd reply. 'It's more stable that way.'

'So that's why we're living apart?'

'When you put it that way it sounds like a bad thing. It's not a bad thing to have some distance. It's like a policy to keep smooth relations between two countries.'

'Easing trade relations?'

'Forget about that. Look at this. Your mother's work is really bold.' She held up the book to show me a picture. Mom had sent it in the mail the other day. It was a picture of a snail with exaggerated proportions. It was compelling, and had a definite sense of movement. It was far beyond something an amateur could do.

'Mom did that?'

'I decided to make a picture book.'

I didn't understand. 'Sorry?'

'Apparently Mother used to like drawing pictures. I suggested that she might want to get back into that and do a project together. I'm not even quite sure how we started talking about it, but we agreed that I would come up with the story and she would do the illustrations.'

It's like you're playing together, I wanted to say, but I thought it might upset her. Still, I didn't get it. 'So, a snail?'

'The hero of the story is a snail. It can turn its body into steel. It has a lance, the Lance of Longinus.'

'The . . . spear that the Roman soldier used to stab Jesus?'

'The Holy Lance!'

'The snail has that?'

'Yeah, doesn't that sound cool?'

'Yeah, it's fun.' Although I didn't really think so. But I was thrilled that Miyako and Mom were doing something together.

I couldn't help thinking that it would be easier for them to collaborate if they lived together, but being apart didn't seem to be any sort of obstacle to Miyako. 'This works just fine. We live in different places and send each other the work back and forth in the mail. No arguments that way. This way we can reach an accord.'

'What do you mean, reach an accord?'

'Between sea and mountain.'

'Between sea what and mountain what?' I had no idea what she was talking about.

I glanced at the clock and saw that I needed to go, so I said goodbye and hurried to the door. Miyako followed to see me off, waving as I left.

It had been several months since that whole nightmarish episode, and the wound in my side was finally starting to hurt less, but work was just as busy as always. I guess that made sense, given all the mess there was to clean up after one employee was caught committing fraud and another employee was almost killed. I had no idea how I had survived after being stabbed. I'd woken up in a hospital after being stitched up, understanding nothing of what had happened. I couldn't tell the police anything more than that. All I could say for sure now was that Watanuki had been arrested and found guilty of many other crimes.

I heard from the police that Watanuki had confessed to trying to pin the fraud on me, but as for what else happened at that construction site he wouldn't say, at least according to the vague explanation I got from the police. Apparently he hit his head or had some kind of lapse in memory. The insurance scam at O. Hospital was blown wide open and the operation shuttered. I felt bad for the elder Dr O., who had so kindly shared his memories of my dad, but there was nothing I could do about any of it.

'You know, I thought I saw you and Mom back there at the construction site.' When I said this to Miyako, she looked at me with concern.

'You must have been seeing things.'

Yeah, that must have just been a hallucination.

I got on the train and stood by the door, looking blankly out the window. As we pulled out of the station and picked up speed the scenery flowed by. Above the rooftops the sky was a brilliant blue, with clouds like cotton candy slowly changing shape.

Then the view in front of me disappeared, replaced by a man I didn't recognize. He looked about the same age as me, leaning up against the window and staring out, same as I was. I had no idea who he was, but somehow I felt close to him, as if I was looking at myself.

I closed my eyes.

I had a vivid memory of the sight that greeted me when I woke up in the hospital bed, after I had been stabbed and sewn up.

My wife was there, and my mother.

146

When they saw me open my eyes, both of their faces lit up. They looked at each other and embraced. Almost immediately they parted again, that magnetic repulsion. I felt suffused with warmth and well-being, like they had been reading me stories from a picture book while I was unconscious. I will never forget that moment, and the look on their faces as they stood together.

drunk driver, was no accident. And that the real target was Yomo-pi, not his family,' says Pillow, still staring at the TV screen.

'No accident?' Blanket is shocked.

'It wouldn't surprise me.'

Blanket recalls a certain senior member of the basketball team. She hadn't agreed with the coach's methods, especially his erratic leadership style, and she tried to change things to make the team better and healthier for everyone. But the other senior members of the team resisted her efforts, ganging up on her until they drove her out entirely.

'People who try to change things are seen as troublemakers.'

'That's so true,' Blanket agrees, looking again at Yomogi's image on the screen.

'Don't give up, Yomo-pi!'

Their clean-up complete, Blanket and Pillow leave the room.

judgment. It doesn't matter how great you are, that's what happens. You even lose your ability to drive! Younger is better, absolutely.'

'Too young is scary, though.'

'Well, think about it. Who would you want running your country, Oda Nobunaga when he was fifty, or when he was eighty? Fifty, right?'

Blanket finds herself stumped by the question. Pillow pushes on.

'Come to think of it, though, Oda's a pretty scary guy, maybe I wouldn't like that. He'd probably be easier to get along with as a grandpa.'

Blanket finds herself feeling bad about Oda – who lived hundreds of years ago and would never meet either of them – being called 'a pretty scary guy.'

'Sounds like some people really hated Yomo-pi, huh? I guess, though, if you ask for politicians to be sacked then you make yourself their enemy.'

'I bet that's true. People with power make it their life's work to hold on to that power. Maybe that's why he quit being a politician and became a bigwig at the Information Bureau – he decided to change things another way.'

'Change things? Like, the system?'

'He seems pretty tough. Remember the story about when he was first elected and he tackled that guy on the train who was stabbing everyone?'

It was fifteen years ago, when a passenger on an express bound for Shinjuku started stabbing the other passengers around him. Over ten people ended up killed or injured, but the person who put a stop to things was Yomogi. He was forty at the time, and he ended up sustaining injuries that put him in the hospital, but not before grabbing the guy and neutralizing him.

'You know, I heard that the accident three years ago, with the himself proudly, so that despite being in his late fifties, he seems much younger.

'Saneatsu Yomogi! Isn't he a politician?'

'He's part of the Information Bureau now, our version of the CIA. He's the head honcho there. He quit politics after the accident.'

The accident. Blanket recalls it immediately. Three years ago, someone in an imported electric car driving down a wide boulevard downtown suddenly swerved onto the sidewalk, running over a mother and child. Apparently the fault of a drunk driver, it ended up causing quite a stir in the media, as the victims were the wife and child of Yomogi, then a sitting member of Parliament.

Now he's on TV, a microphone thrust in his face. 'Director Yomogi, is it true your life was threatened back when you were in politics?'

'I can't really comment on that,' says Yomogi, a rueful smile on his face. 'But if you were the one coming after me, this would be it for me – I've let you get too close!'

'You know, I've always liked Yomo-pi. He says whatever's on his mind, but I usually find myself agreeing with him,' says Pillow. 'Like how he always said there should be fewer members of Parliament.'

'Well, that I agree with. Private industry has had to restructure and fire so many people, we should do the same with politicians! As a cost-cutting measure.'

Yomogi called for the reduction in the number of members of Parliament from the moment he was elected to the moment he left politics. His statement, 'It would be better if older politicians retired,' caused a firestorm of debate at the time.

'And he's also right about old politicians! As you age, you naturally lose your physical strength and your memory, even your wonder at his stupidity. The moment he looked at them and decided they weren't a threat, his fate was sealed.

Will he try to grab their clothes? Or kick them? Those are the choices. Blanket imagines scenarios as she throws one end of the white sheet to Pillow.

After that, things go like they always do. The two girls approach the man, each holding one edge of the sheet. Unfurling it as they advance, they engulf his entire upper body, including his head. He's immobilized at once. Blanket throws Pillow her edge of the sheet. Pillow almost immediately releases the edge she's been holding, and Blanket grabs it. Repeating this exchange again and again, Blanket and Pillow wind the sheet around and around the man as if he were a mummy.

Wrapped in the sheet, the man loses his balance and falls to the floor.

He kicks up a fuss, moaning, but it makes little difference to the girls. Over the sheet, they wrap a towel around the man's neck and then, after pulling with only a slight bit of combined effort, they hear it snap.

'Thank you, leverage,' whispers Blanket. The principle of leverage is the magic wand that wipes away advantages like height and strength.

They make the dead man hug his own knees, folding him up so they can haul him into the cleaning cart. The bottom is reinforced, so it doesn't give under his weight. They stack folded linens on top of him to hide him.

Now, to remove any evidence, they start actually cleaning the room. Partway through, though, Pillow stops and points at the wall. 'Oh! It's Yomo-pi!'

The flatscreen TV mounted on the wall is showing the news.

A reporter holding a microphone listens as a man in a suit talks. The interviewee has sharp, manly features and holds

They pass through the employees-only passage into where the rooms are. The halls are dim, the indirect lighting lending everything a sense of unreality.

After checking the room number – four-one-five: *for one life* – Pillow passes the keycard through the reader and listens as the door unlocks. She opens the door carefully, making as little sound as possible, and slips into the room.

Blanket, pushing the cleaning cart, follows after.

A man is sitting on the sofa, facing the television. It's always easier when they're standing, but what can you do? No big deal, all things considered.

'Excuse us,' says Blanket, nodding respectfully. She recalls how she would address the senior players back when she was on the basketball team.

The man startles, then rises from his seat. He's obviously thrown by Blanket and Pillow appearing like this. He can see they're cleaning staff, but he's confused as to why they'd enter his room without knocking.

Blanket pulls a white sheet out of the cart.

'Hey, I think you got the wrong room!'

The man is wearing beige slacks and a navy blue shirt. He's very tall, and conspicuously well-built.

'Oh my gosh,' says Pillow, her voice rising in surprise. 'Though I think I see a chink in your armor.'

Animals confronted with things larger than themselves naturally become wary, but when confronted with the opposite – anything smaller than themselves – they feel no fear. Humans share this trait. They prostrate themselves before anyone who seems bigger and stronger and look down on anyone smaller. Blanket and Pillow shared their thoughts about this long ago: if women were ten inches taller than men on average, the whole world would be different.

Watching the man turn toward her, Pillow can't help but

He'd never have even spoken to the likes of us if we'd been in the same school.'

Inui may not be quite as handsome as a pop idol, but he's clean-cut and fresh-faced, with a tall, lean frame and a charismatic way with words – a born communicator.

'I really thought he was a nice guy when we first met him.'

'Pure calculation. Knowing everyone, kissing up to VIPs – everything. He's the type who gets everything handed to him. Making moves behind the scenes and then stealing the credit. He never does anything himself.'

'It's true! He leaves all the dirty work to his underlings. I remember calling him out on it once, and he all he said was, "That's not true, I flush my own toilet."'

'He does a lot for politicians. Oppo research, covering up scandals.'

'But it's everyone else who's breaking a sweat! Inui just rides high, soaking up praise for other people's work. I bet finding this woman is a job for some politician, too.'

'He's been sending her picture around. "If you see this woman, let me know." Showing taxi drivers and delivery people, or low-level employees like us. Her name is Kamino-san, I think, the woman he's searching for. Something-something Kamino.'

'It's only a matter of time before he finds her. Inui's reach is amazing.'

'And once they find her, it's going to be horrible for her.'

'You think he'll paralyze her and dissect her alive?'

The girls exclaim in unison: 'Gross!'

'You think it's really true? That stuff about him liking to cut people up?'

'It's awful. We're right to try to get away from him.'

'But when will that be?'

The elevator reaches its destination.

'You make it sound like Easy Street is an actual place,' said Blanket, giggling.

'*You can only be happy if you have a boyfriend*, they say. *Let's all go have fun!* Everything they want to do you can't do alone. I have plenty of fun staying by myself at home, but from where they sit, I have a sad, pitiful life.'

Where they sit? Blanket didn't know where that would be, exactly, and it seemed like a rather arbitrary way of speaking, but she nonetheless answered, 'You're so right.'

And this was the first real conversation she ever had in high school.

They reach the elevator. The one for the cleaning staff. Pillow walks in first, then Blanket. She pushes the button for the fourth floor.

'By the way, Inui seems to be looking for someone,' says Pillow.

'He does?'

'Someone who used to work for him. A woman in her thirties. He's really going after her.'

'Did she walk off with his money or something?'

'Worse than that, I think. Though I admit it's kind of fun seeing him all upset.' Pillow laughs.

'He's still our savior, though.'

'Or, put another way, he's a manipulator who saw we were in trouble and used that as a way to mix us up in this world.'

'He might be our age, but you just know he's had a completely opposite life from ours. He's so the type to spend every day in high school singing its praises, you know? Boys and girls both hanging on his every word, making him feel good. An Easy Streeter, 100 percent.'

'Singing praises, huh? Like Fujiwara no Michinaga? "I feel as if the world belongs to me."'

'If he'd been in a band, he'd have been the lead singer for sure.

other girls. The taller girls were obviously prized even if they were less athletic, and the smaller girls knew that no matter how hard they trained, they'd hardly ever be allowed to play.

'You're right,' said Blanket. 'It's so unfair, isn't it? The advantages some people are born with.'

'You have a pretty face and a good sense of style, and bang: you're on Easy Street. Even school will be fun. Your whole life will be smooth as silk. Makes me sick.'

'Well, that's not true for *everyone* . . .'

'It is! It's a truth determined at birth. Like, by your genes. So unfair. It's not as if they worked hard for it or anything. It's just always been like that, their whole life. Look at me: my face is only okay, I'm short, I have no style. Makes me want to go, *What did I do to deserve this?*'

From the outside, Blanket was in exactly the same boat as Pillow, but it had never occurred to her to ask, *What did I do to deserve this?* She felt a certain relief to hear Pillow say it. As if to reassure her: *It's okay, you're allowed to respond this way to the world.*

'Don't you think even privileged people have their problems?' Blanket said this just to hear Pillow's response.

'Absolutely not.' Pillow waved her hand dismissively. 'I mean, yes of course, everyone has problems. But if you ever asked them to switch places with you, you know they'd refuse! Deep down, they know Easy Street problems aren't really problems at all.'

All Pillow had done since opening her mouth was vent personal grievances, but Blanket didn't find herself put off. Perhaps because Pillow's tone was resigned, even philosophical, rather than spiteful. *It's not like there's anything we can do to fix it, anyway.*

'You know, I noticed something else about them.'

'What?'

'These Easy Streeters, they always drag other people into their lives.'

BLANKET
Two days ago, in a different hotel

'IT'S ROOM 415, RIGHT?'

Blanket is talking to Pillow, who's walking ahead of her. They're both wearing the beige tops and brown bottoms that constitute the uniforms worn by the cleaning staff at the Hotel Vivaldi, Tokyo.

'Exactly. 415. Rhymes with *For One Life*.'

Blanket met Pillow ten years ago, while they were both on the girls' basketball team at her high school. She'd seen her face before, of course, but despite being on the same team, they'd never exchanged words. Though neither girl was the kind to talk much with classmates in the first place.

'What bullshit. Everything's decided at birth,' murmured Pillow, looking off in the distance after another game spent without even being allowed to fill out the bench. She wasn't actually trying to start a conversation – rather, her innermost thoughts had simply spilled from her lips, and Blanket had been there downstream to catch them. But Blanket knew what Pillow meant. Both of them were conspicuously small-framed, even among the

READ ON FOR AN EXTRACT FROM

HOTEL LUCKY SEVEN

A NOVEL

KOTARO ISAKA

Translated from the Japanese
by Brian Bergstrom

SPIN MONSTER

Kotaro Isaka

SPIN
MONSTER

Translated from the Japanese
by Sam Malissa

THE OVERLOOK PRESS, NEW YORK

SPIN MONSTER

MEMORIES ARE FUNNY. SOME JUST fade away on their own, but when there's something you actually want to forget it stays around forever. Bad memories, tough times. They just stick with you.

If only the mind was like a computer, you could just erase files from the hard drive.

But the things you never want to think about again, they're always with you.

Like that day. I was with my family, driving north on the New Tohoku Highway. It was the middle of summer vacation and we were going on a trip to Aomori in our self-driving car. Self-driving cars had been highway-capable since before I was born, but we had just bought a brand-new Muse, the premium in autonomous vehicles, snow-white paint job, able to autopilot the whole five-hundred-kilometer trip, and my father was dying to try it out.

We were supposed to go for one night and two days. We didn't even make it to the first night. I might call it a zero-night trip that lasted into infinity.

I was in the back seat, probably just watching the scenery go by.

Or maybe I was reading on my paper-tablet – since I was little I had loved *I Am Mai-Mai*, the adventures of the heroic snail.

My father was in the driver's seat with my mother next to him; my sister and I sat in the back. A few hours had passed since we left Tokyo. I think it was just past the south exit for New Sendai when my sister said she needed to go to the bathroom. Thinking back on it now, it feels like her saying that was the incantation that set my family on a dire path.

My father touched the console screen and a voice responded, 'Redirecting to service area.' Then it started telling us about the local snacks and souvenirs we'd be able to buy. It was a female voice with perfect diction that made it sound reliable. My father was so proud, like the car was a horse he had trained himself.

The Muse glided into the exit lane. My father, hands off the wheel, kept talking about the smooth ride. As if to emphasize just how luxuriously easy this was, he flipped through a magazine, even though he clearly wasn't reading it.

A black car pulled up alongside and then slipped into the lane in front of us. It was a Muse too, the same model as ours, just a different color. Jet black. Like Death had taken car form. 'Hey, they cut us off,' said my mother. And then we crashed.

I felt it in my chest, like being pummeled by a giant invisible hand. My vision went dark. When I could see again, the world was spinning around and around. The rotational force pinned me to the seat. I couldn't move. I couldn't speak. I saw my sister beside me, her eyes and mouth open wide. It felt like we spun around dozens of times, like a top, although on the news clip I saw later it said we spun five and a half times. A camera on the highway caught it.

After the five and a half rotations the car collided with the barrier on the side of the highway and rebounded in the other direction. The force contorted my body like a tennis ball at the moment of a serve. I thought I would go flying. But it was my sister, who didn't have her seatbelt on, who was thrown clear out of the car.

The next thing I saw was the ceiling of a hospital room.

I wasn't told at first that my mother and father and sister had all died in the crash. But as I did my rehab I figured it out soon enough. Any time I asked about my family the staff tensed up, and my grandparents were always on the verge of tears when they came to visit.

The rehab was tough. But the staff were so encouraging and supportive that I managed to work through it.

The worst part wasn't the rehab, or the pain, or even having lost my family.

It was the court case.

I was in elementary school, so I wasn't a part of it in a direct way. My grandparents took care of everything, all the legal and insurance matters. They were the perfect people to look after me, easygoing by nature, well-liked and well-trusted, and they had money too. I don't think anyone expected the court case to be so contentious, so very combative, least of all them.

There were facts that complicated our case – the autonomous driving software had a bug, and also the closest camera to the scene was destroyed in the crash. But even so my grandparents surprised me with how aggressive they were. They seemed to be unable to process the proceedings in any logical way, and their attitude only made things worse.

They would get all worked up about the defendants, hurling insults and aspersions, even in front of me.

They wanted to punish, to humiliate, to extract full recompense.

But the oddest thing was that the other side was the same as us. How?

First of all, the black Muse was carrying a family of four, just like us. And just like us, they all died except for the little boy.

Both cars at the scene of the crash had an unconscious elementary school boy, the only survivors of their family.

And in the court case, the other boy was represented by his grandparents, just like me.

It was a proxy battle between family elders.

3

At the time I didn't understand what a court case even was. All I wanted was a quick ending to this horrible episode that seemed to have transformed my easygoing grandparents into raging monsters.

'I'll beat them, even if it kills me!' my grandfather said. As if it were a blood vendetta, and he were dedicating himself to vengeance for his son's family. I had never seen him like that before. But despite his vow, the case ended inconclusively. This was because all four grandparents, mine and his, fell ill and died, one after the other. Cancer and pneumonia.

I was like the grass on the battlefield after all the warriors had fallen, the only thing left where war had once raged. Well, not the only thing. There was the other boy too.

'You're Naomasa Mito, aren't you.'

I was sixteen, in my fourth year at school, and the new transfer student slid over to where I was sitting in the corner of the classroom and breathed this to me, almost a whisper, with a familiarity that didn't make sense.

His approach both surprised and annoyed me, acting like we were old friends, but the next thing he said made me understand. 'Who would have thought that both us survivors would be at the same school.'

I glanced at his name tag. *Hiyama.* The name that destroyed my family and brought disaster into my life. Ice flashed down my spine and my body started to shake. I hunched over and vomited. The other students all looked on.

So why was I remembering all of this now?

Easy enough to answer. When I came back into the train car from the restroom in the gangway, I caught a glimpse of him.

So you're Naomasa Mito.

I could hear his voice reverberating in my head.

4

Kagetora Hiyama was on the same Shinkansen as me. Why? Why did I have to run into him?

It had been ten years since I last saw him, when we graduated from school. But I only had to catch the barest glimpse to know that it was him. I wasn't seeing things. There he was – Kagetora Hiyama.

It wasn't a question of him looking the same as he had in school. I knew it was him before I even had a chance to scan his appearance.

I remembered what Hinata said.

She and I had been dating for five years. She was one year older than me, but I often wondered how much she had experienced in that one year, because she knew way more than I did. She was always dispensing wisdom.

Unbelievably, I met her because of a car accident. A different one. I was walking and a taxi ran up on the sidewalk and hit me. Hinata happened to be in the taxi.

I was taken to the hospital, unconscious. Hinata felt bad and stayed with me, filling in for the family I didn't have. When I opened my eyes, she was there.

At first my guard was up, wondering why a total stranger would go to such lengths, but soon enough we started getting friendly, and before we knew it we were together.

So I remembered what she said:

'There are some people you just can't get along with, no matter what. You're better off steering clear. That's the best way to protect yourself.'

She said this when I had a dream about Kagetora Hiyama, a nightmare really. I had been thrashing around and woke up suddenly. Seeing her concern, I explained, 'A dream about someone who I know from way back. We don't get along.'

That was when she gave me her advice: better steer clear.

'I have no intention of going anywhere near him.'

But regardless of intentions, there are some times when you just run into someone. This was one of those times. I stepped out of the restroom on the Shinkansen and happened to glance through the narrow window on the door to the car behind me. There he was. The moment I saw him I felt unmoored, floating.

Kagetora Hiyama.

I need to get out of here.

Why is this happening?

Ever since the accident there are certain things guaranteed to trigger me. Of course any mention of Kagetora Hiyama or the Hiyama family, but also cars in general. My fear of car wrecks has never diminished. I never got a driver's license. Whenever I have to ride in someone else's car, and especially if it's self-driving, I start shaking and feeling queasy. I avoid cars as much as I can.

But there are some times when you just can't do anything about it. Like when the taxi hit me five years ago. After several months in the hospital I was released back into normal life, but by then I had a firmly rooted fear of cars that functioned like a survival mechanism.

I also tried to avoid going to the Tohoku region. After that doomed trip to Aomori, the incident, the crash, the car spinning around and around – after all that, northeast Japan felt too ill-omened. Whenever I wanted to travel not for work, I went west.

This happened to be my first ever time riding the New Tohoku Shinkansen. To think that I would also run into Kagetora Hiyama . . .

I was off balance. Even though I understood where my bewilderment was coming from, I couldn't keep down a rising frantic feeling.

What do I do?

Although there was nothing I could do. It's not like I could get off the train.

Maybe I could get off at the next stop?

But I was on a trip for work, I reminded myself.

If I were to get off, I would be too far from New Sapporo Station, where I was headed. It would delay my whole work schedule. But maybe that would be better than letting myself slip into a state where I couldn't do the work at all.

Couldn't do work? Because I bumped into an old classmate? It's my responsibility to do my job.

My heart was hammering, my head was a cacophony, and I couldn't settle down. The storm of anxious questions and uncertain answers would not subside. I felt like my nerves were on the outside of my body.

When I returned to my seat, there was a man sitting in the seat next to mine, which only frazzled me more. *Hiyama?* I thought for a crazed moment that he had somehow gotten past me without my noticing, but of course it wasn't him. The spot next to my window seat had been empty since we left New Tokyo Station, or at least I thought it had. I looked around; there were plenty of empty seats. Maybe I was in the wrong one? I took my PassCard out of my pocket and waved it. The tiny lamp next to the headrest in the window seat came on. I was in the right spot.

I slid past the man in the aisle seat with an apology and settled into my own seat. Stealing a sideways glance, I saw that he had a narrow face, glasses. He wore a suit. He could have been in his forties or thirties. If the former then he looked young for his age, if the latter he looked old.

My seat registered my return and started projecting holo-news in front of me. A whale caught off the Pacific coast. The famous musician who died the other day. Economic reform in politics. Then commercial after commercial. I had been told that it was worth paying extra to go ad-free. Nothing more depressing than

7

holo-ads, and they make it impossible to fall asleep. But I had never been on the New Tohoku Shinkansen before, so I wanted the full miserable experience.

'I have a favor I'd like to ask you,' said the man with the glasses after a moment.

'Oh, uh?'

'There's not a lot of time so I'll be brief.'

'Um, weren't you not sitting there before?' As in, is this actually your seat?

'I don't have much time, so please allow me to skip the preamble.' His polite way of speaking gave a positive impression, but besides that this all felt fishy. 'Please read this later,' he said. His body remained almost completely still except for his right hand, the angle of which he adjusted slightly to pass me an envelope.

There was no addressee or sender written on it. A completely nondescript brown envelope, although when I took it and turned it over I could see that it had fairly robust security measures. I recognized it as the kind of envelope that couldn't be scanned by the sensors on street corners and stations and on public transit, but on the edge was a code marking that I had never seen before. 'This is—'

'A type of envelope not yet available on the general market. You're quite observant. A true professional.'

I blushed at his praise. Then my suspicions bubbled back up. Professional? How did he know what I did for a living?

But before I could ask he stood up to leave, so instead I asked, 'Where are you going?'

He stopped for a moment, thinking. Then he replied, 'To Japan's past.'

And where is that? I would have asked, but he had already walked off toward the front of the train.

I wanted to go after him and started to get up.

But in that instant I felt a revolting tremor in my spine and fell back down into my seat.

Hiyama. Kagetora Hiyama had entered the train car. I didn't even have to look, I could just tell. Immediately I turned my face to the window and pretended to be asleep. My body's internal alarms were blaring.

I kept my eyes closed, praying that he would just walk past. Then: 'Sorry to bother you while you're sleeping.' I nearly jumped, then made a show of rubbing my eyes.

I was fully convinced I would see Kagetora Hiyama's face, but it was someone else. 'Pardon. This is me.' He held up his card. It had a police seal on it. It was actually my first time seeing one in real life, although I had of course seen it many times in movies and on TV. The rotating 3D image displayed his name and department.

A public servant making such a flashy display of digital information felt like it was a holdover from an earlier era.

There was a time when digital was on the rise, everything was paperless, and there was far more data than physical records.

Must have still been that way twenty years ago, I'd say.

Digitized information can be easily copied, easily modified, easily traced. We just pretended not to notice these basic vulnerabilities. But stolen and leaked data could cause tremendous damage.

Important information reverted to analog systems, and sensitive communications went from email to handwritten letters after the Great Blackout of 2031, in which a swarm of centipedes got into the guts of a key power plant and knocked out electricity around the capital for a full day. Making matters worse, at the time of the crisis a lightning storm overwhelmed the backup generators. The servers containing all of the government's records were destroyed. There was supposed to be a constant backup for vital data, but the scheduled program wasn't functioning, so all the stored information disappeared. People had always said that data was risky because it could so easily be erased, but there was also the belief that anything in the cloud stays there forever. After the Great Blackout, though, people finally started to take it more seriously. Before long we were all firmly convinced that overreliance on digital information could lead to disaster.

As far as I can tell, there were a handful of other smaller events besides the Great Blackout that led to changes in the law.

Like the bureaucrat whose sex tape was leaked. And the legislator who attempted to intimidate search engine providers into erasing any record of his political missteps (and then tried to force them to erase evidence of his pressure campaign as well). I'd say episodes like that motivated the powers that be. Also the fact there was a profusion of operators selling search history, and people had become quite passive about the act of online searching thanks to businesses that did your searching for you. The internet was no longer as convenient as it used to be, and of course the convenience was what people liked best.

But the changes made sense – it had been taken as a given among young people for some years that it wasn't a good idea to put your most valuable information online or in a digital medium.

Emails you send get copied. Screenshots get saved. Conversations that are supposed to be private are suddenly available for all to see. Your most personal confessions, out there on display forever. Nothing much ever comes out of a 'he said, she said' debate, but there are some situations where it's useful for there to be doubt about whether anything was said at all.

People used to be worried about the resources needed to produce paper, but nowadays thanks to dramatic advances in planned farming of alternative paper sources like kenaf, there's no reason not to use as much paper as we need.

Neither digital nor analog solve everything. Over the past ten years it's been widely accepted that both have their advantages and disadvantages, and we should be using them accordingly. That's why my job has become essential: I'm a courier of hand-written messages.

'Can I see your PassCard?' asked the policeman standing in front of me. He was in plainclothes, maybe a detective.

I had no reason to protest, so I pulled out my PassCard from my pocket and showed him. He took out a scanner that looked like a short ruler and touched it to my card. No doubt it gave him my ID info and public transit use history. 'Sorry, just one more—' He then produced a ring-shaped scanner that he held so close to my chest I wasn't sure whether or not it was actually touching me.

'Is there something wrong?' I asked.

'Oh, no, nothing special,' he answered, although I didn't think that the police would be inspecting Shinkansen passengers like this for no reason.

'Should we keep moving?' Another voice from nearby.

The policeman backed away slightly and turned to the speaker.

It was him. Kagetora Hiyama. Working with the policeman who had just scanned me. He looked at me. His eyes widened. Then he retreated a step.

Yes, I thought, *I know how you feel.* It was the same for me when I'd spotted him a few minutes earlier. I was shocked, and then thrown into confusion. It felt like my whole body was screaming at me to get away. My hair stood on end and my pulse thrummed. Blood sang a warning in my veins.

'Mito,' he said. 'Fancy meeting you here.'

'Mm. Mhm.'

I barely spoke. It was more of a groan. Inside me dark clouds were gathering, threatening lightning. There were so many things I wanted to say, and at the same time I had the feeling that I shouldn't utter a single word.

'Someone you know?' the detective asked Hiyama.

'You could say that,' he answered, then turned back to me. 'You're a courier, right?'

I didn't ask how he knew that. If he was a cop then it would be easy for him to find out what I did for a living. They had databases with that sort of information. It was just a matter of whether someone thought to look it up or not.

'Are you . . .' I started, my words strangling in my throat. 'Are you with the police?'

Something flashed in his eyes. Maybe he wasn't used to being questioned, or maybe it was something else.

There was an announcement on the train's speakers: 'We are making an emergency stop.' The same message displayed in red holographic letters on the back of the seat in front of me. 'We are making an emergency stop. The train may experience some shaking.'

Emergency stop? No sooner than I thought it, the train lurched. I couldn't tell if the screeching I heard was from the brakes or just in my head.

The detective staggered and caught himself on the seat.

'Hey, Hiyama, let's go,' called another detective from further up the train. 'Something's going down.'

It must have been Hiyama's boss or supervisor, because he didn't protest. He just took one more look at me and moved ahead, out of the other end of the car.

I could finally breathe again. My heart started back up. Feeling my body reboot, I leaned back in my seat. I was panting like a dog.

It was the first time I had seen him in a long while. He hadn't changed at all. Strong brow, well-defined nose, ears that could only be described as large, same as before. And the same cold, piercing gaze. The film projector in my head whirred to life.

Memories from school floated up.

I was late because of a headache. When I went to enter the classroom, Kagetora Hiyama was in there by himself, so I quickly ducked behind the door and hid. The rest of the class was in the music room, so I wondered what he was doing there alone. I peeked in and saw him looking into a desk – my desk. Normally he didn't pay any attention to me, acting as if I didn't even exist. So why would he have been looking in my desk? I couldn't guess the reason, and I wasn't going to say anything, so I left. After music class I checked inside my desk, scared of what I might find there. But there was nothing. I was relieved, but I also felt a bit violated.

Another time I saw Kagetora Hiyama in town walking along the main drag with a high school girl who must have been his girlfriend. I was with a friend on our way back from the Music Engine, and my friend called out, 'Hey, Hiyama, you on a date? Having a good time?' I didn't want to talk to him, but I also didn't want to look like I was avoiding him, so I just stood there in a sullen slouch. My friend was chatting with him and I started to feel lame just hanging there, so I looked at the girl and flashed a half smile. 'Hey, you messing with my girl?' Hiyama's voice was sharp and his eyes glaring. All I could do was mutter that I wasn't doing anything at all. Pathetic. He took his girlfriend and left.

It was a scene I would rather forget.

After that, Hiyama was apparently with a bunch of different girls. The rumor among my friends was that he slept with everyone. I told myself that I didn't care, that it didn't bother me.

It ended up that we generally had nothing to do with each other, all the way through to graduation.

As far as I could remember, we only ever had one proper conversation. It was in the sixth year of school, just before we graduated, up on the roof of the school.

The Shinkansen was still stopped.

We have made an emergency stop. We are now conducting safety checks. Thank you for your patience, read the holo-message.

I took my tablet out of my bag to check the train transfers, but then realized that as long as the train wasn't at a station there was nowhere I could go. A few years back I could have checked MiniLog and see if anyone had posted anything helpful, but nowadays it's all fake info and coded messages and none of it would shed any light on the situation.

Then I saw the envelope.

The envelope given to me by the man with the glasses who had been sitting next to me – maybe I'll call him Mr Glasses. *Please read this later.*

What was it all about?

Why was Mr Glasses sitting here? And was the envelope dangerous?

I was wary, but I opened it. There was nothing else to do on the stalled Shinkansen.

Inside was another envelope. An envelope in an envelope, very cute. Like a paper matryoshka. There was also a letter inside. Everyone knows you shouldn't read someone else's mail. For me this went beyond being a common understanding, for me it was a matter of professional ethics. But the letter seemed to anticipate my concern, because the top read, *Dear courier, please read this.* And so I did.

I will open with the most important part: I would like to request your assistance. I need you to deliver this to an old friend of mine. His name is Atsushi Chusonji. Chusonji is quite uncommon as a family name, so these days he may be going by something less noticeable.

This told me two things, and prompted one question. The first thing it told me was that the person who wrote this, Mr Glasses, knew my profession. He knew that it was my job to faithfully deliver handwritten messages to their recipients. Sending via the postal service would be cheaper, but since it's a public agency there are detailed records of all correspondence. Despite the fact that we had made the switch to analog out of concern over data theft and leaks, there are plenty of unscrupulous postal workers who will copy or redirect mail for cash. That's why people need independent couriers like me. Of course there are those who say that you can't trust people like me precisely because we're unattached to an organization, but when you're a freelancer trust is critical, so only those who are rock solid make it in this field.

The second thing the opening of the letter told me was that the man who wrote it was not up-to-date on the situation of his old friend Atsushi Chusonji. All he had was an inkling that Chusonji may have changed his name, though he wasn't even sure of that. That's what led to my question.

If his name had changed, how was I supposed to deliver anything to him? I didn't have an address. I hoped that if I read on I might learn more.

Chusonji and I met in graduate school, studying information engineering. My first impression was that I had never met anyone so intelligent, so unsociable, and so different from myself, while at the same time having many similarities. Later I would learn that he felt the same way about me.

With such a narrative opening I felt sure I was in for a long read. At least the handwriting was extremely neat. Not only was it easy to read, it was beautiful. Following the letters down the page was actually a pleasure.

It told the story of how the writer and Chusonji grew close. It happened that they were both fans of Gamma Moko. When they found this out, they became fast friends.

Obviously I knew about Gamma Moko. Baroque music had Bach, rock had the Beatles, jazz had Charlie Parker, and for the jurok music of the twenty-first century it was Gamma Moko. Even people who didn't love Gamma Moko's work had to acknowledge that jurok would never have become an established genre without them.

No one would ever accuse me of having much of an ear for music, but even I liked jurok, and I felt a kind of national pride around Gamma Moko, who were still active and putting out albums.

According to the letter, when they were listening to Gamma Moko in the lab twenty years ago, the band was still only known by those who knew. It seems hard to imagine now.

Back then, in the lab, they found kindred spirits in one another, and as they pursued their research they also geeked out over Gamma Moko. *Who knows if we're right. We only have our hypothesis. But I think our hypothesis is right. And it may take a while, but one day society will prove us right.*

They believed that about their work as researchers, and they felt the same way about the greatness of Gamma Moko.

And it turned out they weren't wrong.

Sure enough, Gamma Moko started getting more attention, and almost as soon as the fuse was lit on their popularity they blew up, conquering the music world in no time.

The rhythm, the lyrics, the melody, those sublime chords!

It wasn't just the critics; everyday people couldn't get enough either. Listening to music that had been written off as dilettantish came back in a major way. It's fair to say that if it hadn't been for Gamma Moko, music might have withered and died in the twenty-first century.

And then—

One of the band members was killed. Katana Tanaka, who wrote all the songs, was stabbed during a performance by an attacker who jumped up on the stage. There was a line of security guards between the audience and the stage, but the assailant was one of the security guards. He was immediately pinned down, screaming about his love for Gamma Moko, not making much sense. During the trial he took his own life.

Ironically, that incident catapulted Gamma Moko into an entirely new dimension. The web traffic they generated and the number of plays their songs got obliterated all previous records. Mountains of books were written about Katana Tanaka and the net exploded with conspiracy theories. The other four members of the band came together to fill the gap that he left. There was even an urban legend that Tanaka had left behind a program that wrote their new songs. Whatever the case, the band kept releasing boldly original music.

Chusonji and I would stay up late listening to their music. One night we made a promise. Someday, when the next member of Gamma Moko dies, we'll meet again and listen to their music together once more. We both promised. I cannot recall whose idea it was. But we must have had some sense that our paths would diverge.

It sounded to me a lot like a vow between lovers. Or more likely two people having an affair – *we have to part ways, but one day the time will be right for us to meet again.* It wasn't so long ago that people would want to hide a same-sex relationship.

That was when it occurred to me.

Anto Anzu, Gamma Moko's drummer, had died yesterday. I had just seen a report on it on the holo-news. Something about the cause of death. Cancer treatment had come a long way, but pancreatic cancer was still tough to beat. Though Anto Anzu fought on for a while, in the end he succumbed.

It was Chusonji who proposed the place. When another member of the band dies, he said, let's meet on Aoba Mountain, at Aoba Castle, at the statue of Masamune Date. Our lab was on Aoba Mountain, and he thought it would be easy if we chose a famous place in the area. So we settled on Aoba Mountain in Sendai.

As soon as I heard on the news yesterday that Anto Anzu had passed, my first thought was of Chusonji.

We are not currently in contact, and I do not know where he is. And we only spoke about that promise on that one occasion. But if he remembers our promise, then he very well may be there at Aoba Castle.

So that was it: he wanted me to go there, and if I found his friend I should hand over the letter. What's more, the letter said, the payment was already transferred into my cloud bank. Surprised, I took out my PassCard and checked my balance. Sure enough, it had increased.

How did he know my bank code? Our only contact had been a few minutes sitting next to each other on the Shinkansen. If he had paid me and I didn't do the work I'd have to return the money. And I had only glanced at the numbers but it looked like a much higher payment than my normal rate.

I went back to reading the letter.

Helping someone fulfill a promise to an old friend – it was all very wholesome.

But it also seemed pretty flimsy. One conversation from twenty years ago, an agreement that sounded more like casual talk. It was like a meaningless scribble in thin ink on an earthen wall, nearly gone after all these years. It was possible that his friend never even remembered them having written it. Mr Glasses remembered, but I could easily see his friend having forgotten.

And in the event that his friend did remember their promise and went to Aoba Mountain, there was no telling when he would be there. The particulars of their arrangement were too vague – *If this happens, let's meet* – it should have specified a certain number of hours after the news broke, or twenty-four hours after the death of the next band member, but they didn't seem to have set any kind of specific time.

Even if I went, it would probably just be wasted effort.

And why should it be me who goes? Why wouldn't he go himself?

Why would he pay someone to go instead of him?

'We apologize for the inconvenience,' came the announcement over the speaker and also on the display in front of me. I let out a sigh of relief, expecting the message to continue with, *The train is about to start moving again.* But instead it was, 'Due to a system malfunction we are unable to resume our service. We apologize again, but we humbly ask you to remain in your seats a bit longer.'

I wished they hadn't said 'humbly.' It didn't matter, but it bothered me.

In the end I had to disembark from the train and make my way back to New Sendai Station on foot. Walking on the tracks was a new experience, but the whole time I was worried about what would happen if another train came. And of course the whole thing was a major inconvenience. I opened my courier bag and took out an envelope. It was a letter addressed to someone in New Sapporo that had been entrusted to me by an elderly woman back in Tokyo.

But if the Shinkansen wasn't working, I wouldn't be able to deliver it today. I could catch a plane from the airport in Sendai, but that would substantially increase travel costs.

I took out my PassCard and tapped to call the old woman sender. I explained the situation and she said in a kindly voice that tomorrow would be fine. 'It's just a list of Sapporo local treats I want my son to bring next time he drives down to Tokyo.' I would think a list of snacks is fine to send over email, but it seemed her son had had a bad online experience and no longer trusted digital communications. He was even nervous that phone conversations would be listened in on. 'Really, worrying about all of that is going to drive him crazy,' she said with a laugh. I wondered if she was taking that new medication so popular with older folks. Either way, I appreciated how easygoing she was about it. I apologized again and thanked her.

As I walked along the tracks back to New Sendai Station I went over what my next moves should be.

If other trains were running normally, I could hop a Shinkansen back to Tokyo and try again tomorrow. I could also spend the night in New Sendai and continue on to New Sapporo the next day. The first option would mean more money spent on transit, and the second would mean having to pay for a hotel room.

But the truth is I had a reason to stay in New Sendai.

I wanted to deliver the letter from Mr Glasses.

Thinking about the process involved in returning his payment, I figured that it would be easier to just do the job. I was already in New Sendai, which meant I was close to Aoba Mountain.

I was convincing myself.

There was something about this job.

I wanted to know how the twenty-year-old promise would turn out.

Even if the other man did remember, and went to the meeting spot, there was no knowing when he would be there. He could even be there at that very moment. All I could do was go and look.

In the end, curiosity won.

It was my first time in New Sendai Station, which was larger than I expected: five floors and what felt like a maze of corridors. I found an information kiosk. The only ways to get directly to Aoba Castle were by bus or taxi, but given my fear of road vehicles I supposed I would have to walk. Then I saw that the subway headed in the direction I wanted to go.

I made my way through the labyrinthine station to the subway and caught one that was just about to leave. I managed to jump aboard as the doors slid closed.

There were plenty of empty seats but I didn't feel like sitting, so I stood by the doors, leaning up against the pole and gazing out the window.

How did Mr Glasses know where I would be sitting on the Shinkansen?

Questions bubbled.

If he wanted to hire me, why didn't he just go through the normal channels?

Then my thoughts went back to that letter of his.

If a member of Gamma Moko dies.

The news broke yesterday, so he must have only just made up his mind to send a letter to his old friend. He wouldn't have had time to set up a formal request with me. Job inquiries go through an online service that anyone can access at any time, although the first slot available is always two days out.

He could have also gone with another courier. There are plenty of us out there. I was confident in my work, and I'd be happy if I had a reputation for being reliable, but I didn't imagine that I was particularly well known.

Maybe someone had recommended me? I wondered if someone told him, oh, if you're looking for a courier you should go with Mito. I suppose word of mouth has been important ever since humans first developed language.

I let my body sway with the motion of the train. Gazing blankly through the window at the walls of the underground tunnel, my mind wandered back to Kagetora Hiyama.

When he saw me back there on the Shinkansen, his face went rigid, which I imagine must have mirrored my own expression. Body stiffened, taken off guard, frozen in place.

The same as that time we spoke on the school rooftop.

It was March in my sixth year of school, just before graduation. I had gone home for the day only to realize that I'd forgotten my tablet in the classroom, so I headed back to school. As I reached the gate I happened to look up and was surprised to see someone standing on the roof. My first thought was that they were going to jump.

Before I could process anything I was running. Into the school building without even changing my shoes at the entrance, up the stairs without a sideways glance.

I wasn't sure why it felt so urgent, but my body kept driving upward, upward. Like I was caught in an invisible net pulling me steadily higher. There was no fighting it. When I got to the top level I saw that the door, which was usually locked, stood ajar. Without a moment's hesitation I burst out onto the roof.

Standing there was Kagetora Hiyama.

He was a few meters away. He looked at me, and I could see his body freeze.

I quickly turned and looked away.

Ever since he transferred to my school I had done my best not to come into contact with him. I imagine it was the same for him.

And yet there we were, just weeks from graduation, alone together on the roof.

I should probably have just told him that I'd seen someone on the roof and was worried that they were going to jump, that I didn't know it was him. But nothing would come out of my mouth. My heart was beating faster. I didn't know if I was nervous or afraid or both.

His family died in an accident with my family's car. My family's lives were stolen away by his family's car. Our grandparents had feuded bitterly during the legal proceedings. There was no getting around the fact that each of us associated the other with pain and loss.

I had never thought of him as my enemy, not even once, and yet when he looked at me it felt like I was being sized up by a predator in the wild.

No, I didn't think of him as an enemy. But I didn't know what he thought about me.

I had always wanted to ask him. But the question felt trapped in my throat, and I said nothing.

Instead I kept my face turned away, trying to hide my confusion. I spotted a bottle beside the railing. Someone must have left it up there. Without even knowing what I was doing I picked it up. Empty, no label. The glass was slightly colored. As I held it to the light for a better look, it slipped out of my hand.

It fell silently, seeming to float downward. Then it shattered with a sound like a scream.

Why?

I was holding it just fine. I felt the need to make excuses to myself.

I didn't even feel it slipping.

It was like my fingers had been peeled off the bottle. The thought kept repeating in my head. The bottle was meant to fall. Somehow that made sense to me.

Kagetora Hiyama stood behind me.

No sooner had I turned around than he grabbed me by the collar. *Danger,* my internal sensors flashed. I didn't even have time to form the thought, my body just sounded the alarm.

His eyes were open wide and his nostrils flared. His right arm started swinging. I knew I was about to get punched, which ignited a sudden flame inside me. My conscious reaction was to shout *Stop,* to try to reason with him, but my body filled to the brim with a different plan. *He's going to win. I won't let him beat me.* Every single cell seemed to be screaming in unison: *Fight!* I would not lose to him.

I jerked away and grabbed his wrist as hard as I could.

The tension immediately went out of him, and he exhaled. 'I was only joking,' he muttered.

'What?'

'I was just messing around.' He sounded annoyed, and I couldn't tell if he was being sincere or not.

It didn't seem like he had been joking. He seemed to have a strong desire to defeat me. Just like I felt toward him.

He took a few deep breaths as if to calm himself down, so I did the same.

After some moments he looked off to the side.

I followed his gaze. There were fingers of orange and red far off in the sky, with a long cloud like a thick white brushstroke gradually billowing out and taking shape. It looked like a whale. A beautiful white whale, gently stippled, glowing in the setting sun. From out of the whale's form stretched several bands of colored light. The sky filled with crimson and tangerine. As we stood there watching, the cloud started to dissipate, the whale gently fading away.

It was a gorgeous sunset, but something about it also made me feel uneasy.

'How come people fight?'

I heard the words. It didn't seem possible that it was Kagetora Hiyama who had spoken them. I thought for a moment that it had been me.

'Fights happen so easily.'

This time I was sure it was him speaking. It felt like he was talking about having just grabbed my collar.

'Human history is nothing but conflict.'

'Huh?'

'Nothing but conflict with brief time-outs.'

'What do you mean, brief time-outs?'

'There's no such thing as no conflict. Everything quiet and peaceful – that doesn't exist.'

'I don't know if I would say that—'

'It doesn't exist,' he said firmly. 'There's always people fighting somewhere. That's what history's all about.'

'You mean like how one person's peace is built on another person's sacrifice?'

I was sure he would click his tongue or make some other gesture of exasperation, but he didn't.

'So is conflict a bad thing? I don't think so. I think it's the foundation, the basis of everything.'

'Seriously, the foundation?' It didn't make sense to me. I still couldn't tell how much he meant what he was saying.

'But when people fight, people get hurt. Things get broken. Life would be better without it.'

Something popped into my head from a children's book that I loved as a boy. Or it started off as a picture book about the adventures of a snail with an iron shell and a holy lance, but it was adapted into anime and movies and the snail became a universally loved and recognized character. There were even theme parks all over the country. The snail, Mai-Mai, had a catchphrase: *It is always better not to fight.* It came back to me there on the roof. *I know sometimes you may want to fight,* Mai-Mai would say kindly. *But it is always better not to.*

I remembered how my mother would read it to me before bed. I would listen, half-asleep, and the words from the picture book would soothe me, calming any rough waters in my soul.

'When you think about individual people's feelings, or like our normal everyday lives, fighting feels like a bad thing,' Kagetora Hiyama went on. 'But if you look at it from a different angle, we need conflict. It's like in science when we create a reaction in a beaker. If you don't cause some agitation, there's no experiment.'

But who, and where, and what experiment?

'If there's no conflict, there's no progress. Nothing happens. Collisions cause changes, and something new is born. That's how planets work, right? A little planet that keeps getting hit, which makes an ocean of magma. The moon has a bunch of craters from collisions. And we only have water on Earth because of meteorites hitting the planet.'

'Well, yeah, that's true.' I didn't know what else to say.

'The more possibilities we have, the more we advance. There needs to be agitation and then diffusion. That's why there needs to be conflict. Conflict is collision. Maintaining the status quo means we're just losing ground. We need to make, then break, make, then break. We shouldn't even be thinking about it as breaking.'

'Who is the "we" here?'

'It's not about who. There just needs to be conflict. The goal should be to keep conflict going.'

He stared out at the clouds glowing in the sunset. The colors had shifted, and the sun itself was a deep gold. Picture-perfect sunsets often feel like they're lifted from a movie screen, too beautiful to be real, but that day there was a vividness, a melancholy in the red hues that felt like I could reach out and touch. 'So then if you think that, what are you and I supposed to do? If conflict is natural, are you saying that we have no choice but to fight, and we should just accept it?'

'I'm not talking about us. Conflict will never go away. Same as how rain and storms will never go away. But I think that with all that, the effort you make to live a peaceful life – that's freedom.'

'The effort?'

'When all the ingredients in the beaker get mixed up and there's a reaction going on, it takes real effort to carve out some peace for yourself. If you don't make an effort, you'll never get that peace. And making that effort is no guarantee of peace, but I know that if you do nothing then there'll be conflict.'

Just then the wind picked up. It whipped around our legs where we stood on the roof, like a wind weasel from the folktales, stirring up miniature tornadoes of dust. These spiraled upward, then leaned in the direction of the passing wind, then faded away.

Hiyama seemed to return to his normal self. He looked at me for a moment, then went through the door and left the roof, as if we had never even had the conversation.

The subway continued west from New Sendai Station, skirting the Hirosegawa and heading south through the mountains. I thought it was odd that a train would go up into the mountains while staying underground, but it felt pretty much the same as riding a train on level ground. I got off at the closest stop to Aoba Castle, a station called Dragon Mouth Valley.

A transparent tube lift took me from the valley floor up to a higher elevation. There was a breathtaking view of the rock face across the way. I noticed traces of yellows and reds on the trees and it occurred to me that the season would be changing soon. Glimpses of white rock flashed between the trees. When I looked down I got a sense of how deep the valley was and felt an involuntary thrill at the height.

Upon exiting the elevator at the top there was a path, rather nondescript. It was lined on either side by red-leafed hornbeams, though I wasn't sure exactly which type.

About one hundred meters down the path I arrived at the entrance to the Aoba Castle grounds. Through the gate was a parking lot, beyond which was an area that looked like a small park.

I could see the magnificent form of the castle rising up, but I knew it was just a holographic projection. The signage explained that the main keep had been built toward the end of the Warring States period and stood until its destruction in the Meiji era, when the area was used instead for troop barracks.

War, that indiscriminate destroyer. People will destroy their own buildings before the enemy can get to them, in the name of wartime preparation.

Is conflict a bad thing? I don't think so. I think it's the foundation, the basis of everything.

The memory of Kagetora Hiyama's words swam up, uninvited.

We make and we break, and that cycle is what drives history.

But it was also true that in the name of conflict a splendid construction like this castle was destroyed. It seemed sad. I took in the sight of the castle projection amid my thoughts about conflict. The sign indicated that visitors could go inside the projection and see the reception hall and other parts of the interior. I considered it, but then remembered why I was there and decided that I didn't have time for sightseeing.

I thought about the payment in my cloud bank.

This was a job.

It had started getting dark and there weren't many tourists, making it feel like I had snuck into somewhere I wasn't supposed to be. I spotted several security cameras perched around the grounds.

After wandering around a bit I found a signpost pointing the way to the statue of Masamune Date on horseback.

As I went in the direction the arrow pointed, the view opened up. There was an observation deck overlooking the whole city. That's where I found the statue.

The base was just large enough to hold the statue, but it was very finely crafted. Atop the base was a noble-looking horse, and atop the horse was the likeness of a warrior, so dignified in bearing as he surveyed the city below that I felt myself standing up just a bit straighter in his presence.

When I saw the man I nearly called out to him. Under some trees off to the right of the statue was a row of benches, shadowed by the branches overhead, but I had spotted him sitting there.

He had on a jacket and blue jeans, which almost no one wore anymore. His arms were folded over his chest, his legs were crossed, and his eyes were closed, making him look like he was either deep in thought or else dozing.

Was it Atsushi Chusonji? Had he remembered his promise from twenty years back?

It wasn't my affair, but I still felt excited that it might all work out. The businesslike part of me told myself to keep calm. And that was correct – I had only just taken on this job, with no prior notice. In the drama of Mr Glasses and his old friend, I was an outsider, just a supporting role bursting onto the stage in the very last scene.

But even supporting actors can get excited, I admitted to myself. Even outsiders can feel the hum of anticipation.

'Excuse me,' I said, before I could let hesitation get the best of me.

The man's hair was long enough to cover his ears, and he had unkempt stubble on his face. His eyes remained closed. No response.

'Excuse me,' I tried again, but still nothing.

He could have just been ignoring me. I called louder, this time waving my hands in front of his closed eyelids.

Finally he started to open them, ever so slowly. He noticed me and looked startled for a moment, but only a moment, then languidly moved his hands to his ears, looking like he might yawn and go back to sleep at any moment. He removed his earbuds, which explained why he hadn't heard me.

'Excuse me,' I said once more, 'are you Atsushi Chusonji?'

He raised his eyebrows dubiously. Compared to the buttoned-up Mr Glasses, this man looked pretty slovenly. I wondered if they were actually friends.

'Whu?'

'Excuse me but . . .' I started to wonder what the highest number of times I had ever said *excuse me* in one day might be. This might be a new record. 'I was asked to deliver something to you.'

'Deliver . . . to me?'

'A letter. Here.'

'You're a courier?' He knit his brows and sat up, warily reaching for the envelope that I offered. 'Been a while since I've had any physical mail,' he murmured, and then he said, 'Ah,' and there was some gravity in his voice. It looked like he recognized the handwriting on the envelope where his name was written. 'Guess he remembered too.' He gave a small smile.

My heart rang a bell. 'Well, you both promised.'

'Yeah, we did. I mean, when we said it back then I was just joking. We both were. I don't think either one of us really imagined another member of the band would go. But it's funny, when I heard yesterday that Anzu died, I remembered, I mean instantly. I guess I didn't think that he would, though.'

'But you still decided to come here?'

He grinned. 'Got nothing else going on.' He sounded more proud than embarrassed. 'I spend most days just wandering around town, wasting time and money on the Digilogs, feeding pigeons in the park. So today I've just been here all day listening to Gamma Moko.'

'And waiting for your friend to show up?'

'I don't know. We never said when we would meet. But if he had come and I hadn't been here, I would have felt bad. You know how it is.'

'How what is?'

'Someone with nothing but free time should do whatever works for someone who's very busy.'

'I suppose so.'

'And he didn't come, so I guess he must be busy.'

'He did send a letter.'

'He's a very conscientious fellow.' With that, he opened the envelope. In my line of work I've seen plenty of envelope-openings. Some people use scissors, very neat and careful, some use a letter opener. Plenty of people just tear it open, as if they can't be bothered to do anything more thorough. However they do it, I love observing the mix of anticipation and uncertainty as they pull the contents out from the envelope. I suppose I'm a bit of a voyeur that way.

There were fewer pages to the letter than I would have imagined.

For an emotional occasion like the fulfillment of an old promise that both parties remembered, I would have expected a much longer letter, but what this man held in his hands appeared to be one or at most two pages.

The moment Atsushi Chusonji looked at the pages his eyes widened, and then narrowed.

As I was wondering what could have been written there, he took out his PassCard and started tapping at it. It was as if there were words he didn't understand in the letter and he was looking them up. 'Okay, I get it,' he said after a few moments. 'I see how it is.' His expression was graver than before.

'Is something the matter?' I couldn't help asking. I wanted to know. I suppose I was hoping that the twenty-year-old promise might have led to some show of happiness or emotion, but there was none of that. If anything his face was dark and clouded.

He didn't answer, so I asked again: 'Is everything all right?' At length he looked up from his PassCard.

'If he sent me a letter like this, it makes me think that he's in trouble, so I was checking the news.'

'The news?'

Chusonji shrugged and showed me his PassCard. There was a news story on the screen: *Developer of Velkasery AI Program Dies in Accident.*

'Is this—' I started talking but cut myself off to continue scanning the article. I couldn't believe what I was reading. It said that the man considered to be the foremost researcher of artificial intelligence, Terao Terashima, died in a fall from the elevated tracks of the New Tohoku Shinkansen. He had pushed the emergency stop button and brought the train to a halt, then run along the tracks. It explained that this caused the other passengers to have to disembark and walk back to New Sendai Station. But the shock for me was the 3D photo: it was, without a doubt, the face of Mr Glasses, the man who had given me the letter. 'When is this from?'

'Just now.'

'I met him on the Shinkansen. A little more than an hour ago. He asked me to deliver this to you.'

'What the hell?' hissed Chusonji, as if trying to expel the confusion in his mind. He actually scratched his head frantically, like he could physically dispel the haze.

'I suppose, I mean, I was hoping you could help me understand.'

'I have no idea,' he growled, which only seemed to confirm how badly he himself was shaken. 'Just what in the hell is going on?'

'What did his letter to you say?'

He was stalking back and forth, maybe to try to organize his thoughts. He pulled the letter out of his pocket and thrust it toward me.

It was only one page after all. I had been picturing a message full of warmth and affection for an old friend after a twenty-year agreement had been fulfilled, but there was none of that. The page was nearly empty, almost upsettingly so. Just two lines of writing:

You were right
Obbel and the Elephant

Nothing else at all.

We left Aoba Castle, me following behind Atsushi Chusonji, until I realized that I didn't need to go with him.

I had delivered the letter and completed my assignment. I did my part in helping two friends carry out their twenty-year promise.

But Chusonji kept saying, 'This way, come on,' as if it was a foregone conclusion that I would keep following. There was even a note of warning, like if I didn't follow him something terrible would happen. 'Stick with me,' he said.

When we reached the entrance to the subway station I started toward it, but he called out to me roughly. 'Hey! Follow me, I said.'

'Oh, um, this is where I get off.'

'This is where you get off? What, you're giving up already?'

'Giving up?' We clearly weren't on the same page. There was nothing for me to be giving up on. I hadn't given up on my delivery – that was done, and now so was I.

'You're not quite grasping the reality of the situation, are you?'

'Reality?'

'His death wasn't an accident, and it wasn't suicide.'

'You mean the man who gave me the letter for you.' Terao Terashima.

'He knew he was in danger. That's why he entrusted you with the letter. To give to me. He probably had no time.'

'What did his letter to you mean?'

Those two lines of writing: *You were right. Obbel and the Elephant.*

'I don't know yet.'

'You don't know? Yet?'

'Well, he didn't make it easy to understand.'

'What's the point of a letter that's hard to understand?'

'I mean, isn't it obvious? It's in case someone got their hands on the letter before me. If it was easy to understand then whoever stole it would know the answer.'

Of course, I thought. He didn't want just anyone to know his message, so he wrote it in code. But then, if even the person he sent it to can't understand it, doesn't that defeat the purpose?

Atsushi Chusonji seemed to guess my thoughts, because he

said, 'I'll probably figure it out soon enough. At least he must have thought I would. Probably something that only I would get.'

'What did he mean, "You were right"?'

'Follow me.' He shrugged. 'Listen, if he's dead, then the situation is serious. You're probably in danger too.'

What? Why? My alarm must have shown on my face.

'I'm sure that all his movements were monitored. Someone probably knows that he gave you that letter. All they would have to do is check the cameras on the Shinkansen. If you don't stick with me, they'll find you in no time.'

'How would they find me?'

'There are security cameras everywhere. And obviously you can also be tracked through your PassCard.'

Serving as ID, wallet, and browser all in one slim device, the PassCard was extremely convenient, and most people in the world had one. But some said it was being used more and more for government surveillance. Government agencies neither confirmed nor denied this, and to be honest I didn't pay it much mind. If it helped keep crime down then I didn't mind giving up some of my privacy; in fact I welcomed it, if it meant that the authorities were able to catch the culprits in serious crimes. I imagined most people felt the same way, secure in the fact that they themselves weren't criminals.

'But I haven't done anything.'

'You might think you haven't done anything, but they'll still check you out. They'll suspect that you might know something. Search every part of your house, inspect every part of your body. You don't want that, do you?'

'Well, of course not.' Nobody wanted that.

'Then you'd better come with me.'

Atsushi Chusonji took what looked like a slim box out of his jacket pocket.

'What's that?'

35

'It's a jammer. Nothing fancy, but as long as I have it, sensors and security cams won't pick me up.'

'Why do you have something like that?'

'It was my project over summer break.'

I thought he was joking, although if he was it wasn't funny, so I just smiled politely. 'Your teacher must not have liked that.'

His face remained impassive. 'The cops came to check me out because of it. I told them it was my own original design, but they didn't believe me.' I stared blankly at him. 'Don't worry, this is the new and improved version.' Then I made a frustrated face, and he added, 'Like I said, stick with me. I'll give you a lift.'

Memories of my car accident flashed through my head. Or maybe it was more accurate to say that they flowed through my blood. I had the distinct feeling that my body temperature was dropping. Then I heard Chusonji say, 'We can both fit on my bicycle.'

It's possible that when I was young I rode with my sister on her bike, straddling the back, but I don't have a clear memory of it. Doubling up on a bike as an adult was certainly new, and a little frightening. There was a rack on the back that I could sit on, but it wasn't exactly comfortable. I didn't have any time to worry about the ache in my backside, though, as Atsushi Chusonji took us flying down the twisting mountain road. It kept feeling like we were about to fall, but I couldn't even shout *Wait, stop!* as I clung to his back. I didn't love having to hug him like that, but it wasn't the moment to worry about that sort of thing. The bike leaned sickeningly on the turns, making me clench my eyes shut in terror, but each time we narrowly avoided spilling out, thanks to Chusonji kicking off the ground to stabilize us.

Why is this happening to me? I wanted to shout, but the words would only spool out behind us in vain as we flew. Just as I was resigning myself to the situation we came to a stop. 'Hey, ease up, will you? You can let go now.'

Unsteady, I got off the bike. I had never been so appreciative of solid ground beneath my feet.

Chusonji was breathing heavily too. 'We're headed in there,' he said, nodding toward a building across the street.

There was a cube-shaped shop with pure white walls. The sign said NEWS AND BREWS.

It was one of those news cafés that had started to pop up recently. They had rows of screens showing all kinds of news, not just from Japan but from far-off countries too, and customers could order food and drink while watching. They were seen as a bit of a problem, because different people reacted to news in different ways, and a stray remark could lead to trouble among the customers. I could imagine watching news at a news café about a brawl breaking out at a news café.

There weren't very many people inside, but with all the screens showing newscasters reporting on different stories, it somehow felt like the place was bustling.

The surface of the table itself was a large touchscreen and you could flip through to different channels.

I ordered a coffee from the server who came over, then touched the table screen. I didn't pick any particular program, it just toggled randomly to a world news broadcast.

The story was about a country in the Middle East that was digging an undersea tunnel in order to go after another nearby country's subterranean resources. The aggrieved party, which is to say the country that was being tunneled into, had lodged a formal protest, and to show that they would not back down from a fight they had deployed multiple new submarines into the offending country's waters.

There was footage captured by a fishing boat that happened to cross paths with the submarine squadron. The fishermen were pointing and shouting in a foreign language, clearly alarmed, as their camera looked down over the shapes of the subs passing beneath the fishing boat.

'This could start a war. I hope it doesn't,' I said.

Atsushi Chusonji seemed uninterested, perhaps because it didn't seem likely Japan would get involved. He just snorted and changed the channel.

The next story was about a series of killings in a small European country. It was actually quite wide in scope, with substantial death tolls in two neighboring towns. The residents of the towns had taken axes and knives and whatever else they could grab and started slaughtering one another. I was shocked. It felt like something from another time, although obviously that sort of thing was still happening.

'You heard about this?' asked Chusonji. 'It started off with an illness.'

'An illness?'

'Some unknown new illness was going around and a lot of people died. Then a rumor started that it was caused by bacteria from a factory in the next town over.'

'Was the rumor true?'

'Who knows. And then the sickness broke out in the town where the factory was, and they started saying that it was revenge from the first town where people were getting sick.'

'And so they started killing each other.' Was that all it took?

'No matter how much we think humans are motivated by reason, in the end we don't think with our heads. We act with our bodies.'

'What do you mean?'

'Nothing supersedes animal instinct. Once you think you're in danger, it just takes over.' Atsushi Chusonji spoke offhandedly, tapping and swiping at the table as he did.

'What are you looking for?'

'Anything about him. Although I guess anything I do here will leave a search record behind.'

'So, Mr Terashima created an artificial intelligence?'

'Yeah. Velkasery.'

'What's that?'

'That's the name of the AI. People feel the need to name everything,' he said. 'He and I had been working on that thing since we were in school together.'

'I'm not sure I know exactly what artificial intelligence is.'

'What do you think it is?'

I laughed. I was the one who had asked the question. 'Well, based on the name, I guess it's a computer that thinks like a human.'

'Actually it's much more intelligent than a human. Basically, it uses experience and knowledge to predict future outcomes. Not just predict, it can guide us to reach those outcomes.'

'Like a nav system?' My childhood accident played in my head. I shut my eyes tight.

'Sure. Maps, current location, transit rules, traffic conditions, all those inputs let it determine the shortest route to where you want to go. AI is similar. For a nav system the goal is where you're going, for a chess bot the goal is checkmate. They're good at finding the best way of doing something.'

'So you two made one of those?'

'There are plenty of researchers who've developed different AIs. But Velkasery is the most sophisticated, and the most well known.'

'Is it the fastest at math or something?'

'More like it has the sharpest intuition.'

'Intuition? An AI can have intuition?'

'Intuition in this case is when an outside observer can't track the logical steps. Everything a really smart AI does looks like it's just intuition.'

'How do you teach it intuition?'

He grinned. 'You don't. You just load it up with different experiences and let it learn on its own. Like a human being.'

'And that's what Mr Terashima did. So why . . .' Why would that lead to his death?

'Don't know.'

We fell silent, and Chusonji checked more news programs for a while.

'What do you think Obbel and the Elephant means?' I asked.

'No idea.'

'What's wrong, Hiyama? You're all pale. Don't worry about it, kid. Terashima just jumped on his own.'

The voice snapped me back to reality and I looked up. It was the captain. We had finished searching the Shinkansen.

'Once you get a hold of yourself, come on in. We're watching the footage from the train.'

There was a large rectangular inflated structure in the middle of New Sendai Station. A temporary workspace. The captain went back inside.

It was thirty minutes since we had chased Terao Terashima down the tracks. Something about the sight of the captain and a bunch of other detectives running along the raised tracks struck me as silly. Anyway, Terashima's death wasn't why I had gone pale.

Mito.

I couldn't believe I would have run into him there.

When we got the tip that Terao Terashima would be on that

Shinkansen, we hopped on at New Saitama Station. We started searching for him car by car. But I was completely blindsided when I saw Mito.

My body went stiff, and it felt like time had stopped. Or more like time was rewinding.

Back to when we first crossed paths as boys, just before the exit off the highway, when his car crashed into ours from behind. The view out the window as my car spun wildly. Replaying before my eyes.

I was so small, all I could do was curl up into a ball in the back seat and pray for the car to stop spinning. When it did, every-thing was suddenly silent. My parents and my sister weren't breathing. I felt like I could barely breathe either, and I sat as still as I could. It had been more than twenty years, but the terror of that moment still paralyzed me.

Mito hadn't changed a bit.

To be honest, before I could even register whether he had changed or not changed, I could only focus on the fact that it was him.

My skin felt like it was crackling.

Why is he here? Why did we need to see each other again?

I remembered when we were sixteen.

After losing my family in the accident, and then losing my grandparents, I spent the first three years of school with relatives out in Joetsu. In my fourth year I went to live with other cousins back in Tokyo.

On my first day at my new school, sitting in the corner of an unfamiliar classroom, suddenly one of the other kids in the class was standing in front of me. 'Aren't you Kagetora Hiyama?' he asked.

I didn't know how he knew me, and I was both confused and annoyed, but he kept talking, and then I got it. 'Who would have thought it, both us survivors ending up in the same class.'

I looked at his name tag: *Mito.* All at once I was back in that spinning car on the highway, and before I knew it I was vomiting.

Everyone stood watching, with Mito in the middle. That cold stare. I'll never forget it.

I wanted to change schools, but there was nowhere else I could go. Somehow I made it through the next three years. I just stayed focused on keeping away from Mito. He must have felt the same way, I guess, because we barely ever even looked at each other, let alone spoke.

The few memories I do have of interacting with him were either bewildering or unpleasant.

I was late one day and the rest of the class was in a different classroom. But Mito was there by himself. Surprised, I hid behind the door and peered in at him. He was leaning over my desk, looking inside. I threw the door open and entered the classroom and he froze, his face turning white. I wanted to ask what the hell he was doing poking around in my desk, but the words wouldn't come out. He didn't say anything either, he just ran out of the classroom. Later I heard from some other guys in the class that Mito's pencil case had been stolen and he was going through everyone's desks looking for it. At first I wasn't fully aware of it, but nobody in our class really liked Mito. He was always acting tough, saying and doing mean things, so people kept their distance.

One time I bumped into Mito walking with a girl he must have been dating. I was with a friend who noticed them and said hi. Of course I didn't say anything. It was tough for me even just standing there near him. All I could do was keep my face turned away and wait for it to be over. But Mito apparently misinterpreted where I was looking. All of a sudden he shouted, 'Hey, keep your eyes off my girl,' and he grabbed her by the hand and pulled her away. I was stunned, and my friend was worried that

Mito would find a way to get back at us. 'What did you do?' he demanded fearfully.

I never understood Mito. Most of my friends said the same thing, but as far as I was concerned I didn't even want to understand him.

I didn't hate him. We both suffered in that accident. But there was zero sense of shared experience.

Keep away from him.

My body was always sounding that warning.

I entered the inflatable room, which looked like something between a balloon and a giant eraser. It was full of detectives checking image feeds on their tablets.

The captain looked up. 'You're just in time.'

'You found something?'

'Maybe. Watch this replay.'

An image started playing on the large screen, mirroring what was on the captain's tablet.

It was from a security cam onboard the Shinkansen. At the front of one of the cars, looking down at an angle. The door on the far side of the image opened, from the back of the train, and someone entered.

'It's Terashima.'

It was indeed Terao Terashima, walking at an even pace, but with purpose. He came a bit more than halfway up the car and sat down in an aisle seat.

Less than a minute later another man appeared in the far field of the image.

I don't know which started first, my heart rate quickening or my skin tingling into goose bumps.

It was Mito on the screen, wearing a drab shirt. He turned around for a moment then walked down the aisle. When he saw Terashima sitting there, he came to a halt.

He looked like he didn't expect anyone to be sitting there. He took out his PassCard and checked it, seeming to be confirming his seat number.

He ended up taking the seat next to Terao Terashima, in the same spot where I'd encountered him on the train. Only, when I'd seen him, the seat next to him had been empty.

'Is that guy a friend of his?' asked one of the detectives, pointing at Mito on the screen.

'I'd say no,' said the captain with an air of certainty. 'He's obviously confused.'

After a little bit, Terao Terashima stood and disappeared off-screen toward the front of the train. The image froze and then rewound to the moment just before he got up.

'But here this guy is looking at Terashima and saying something. You can tell Terashima is trying hard not to move a muscle, but it's possible he handed something to the other guy.'

'Handed something to him? Out of nowhere?'

While one of the detectives was voicing his doubts, I myself wondered, *Is Mito involved in this somehow?* The thought was unsettling.

Without even realizing it, I found myself saying, 'That man's a courier.'

Everyone turned to look at me. The captain said, 'That's right, Hiyama, you recognized this guy.' His voice was pitched higher than usual. He seemed to suddenly remember the exchange I'd had when we were checking the passengers.

'We were in the same class in school. Last I heard he was working as a courier.'

'A courier. You mean for analog.'

'Deliveries by hand. His name's Naomasa Mito.'

'Check him out,' the captain ordered, and as soon as the words were out of his mouth the detectives were all on their tablets. 'Think this is just a coincidence?'

I was sure the captain meant me running into Mito and I was

about to forcefully assure him that yes it was a coincidence, when he went on:

'Did Terashima know this guy was a courier, and did he try to engage his services?'

'I don't know,' was all I could answer.

When I asked, 'What are you doing?' Atsushi Chusonji just shot a sharp look at me. It was clear enough he wanted me to keep quiet.

He unzipped his belt bag and took out a flat black chip, smaller than a PassCard. Before I got a good look he slipped his hand underneath the news café table.

When he brought his hand back up the chip was gone. He must have placed it somewhere under the table.

Then he started moving his fingers over the display on the table like he was playing a piano.

He used the chip to take over the table, I thought. I didn't know how it worked, but it seemed logical. Using the news café devices to access the net.

The screen went black, then a line of small text appeared. It was English. I couldn't read it from where I was sitting.

Atsushi Chusonji casually flicked his fingers, making text disappear, then appear, then disappear again.

'What are you doing?'

'Quit staring so much.'

'. . . Yes, sir.'

'Probably won't do much good anyway,' he muttered.

I got nervous when the server came over to refill our water glasses, but Chusonji didn't even seem to notice.

Then he clicked his tongue in frustration. 'Yeah. No good.'

'What's wrong?'

'Guess it's not so easy to get in.'

'In where?'

'Velkasery.'

He said it like it was the most natural thing in the world, but it took me a moment to connect it to the name of the AI I had seen in the news story. Once I did, I asked a bit too loudly, 'Can you do that?'

'What do you mean, can I?' As he said it he reached back under the table to retrieve the chip and return it to his belt bag. He clicked his tongue again, but it sounded different from the first one. 'This is bad.'

'What?'

'We're leaving.' He was already up and heading for the door. 'Keep the change,' he said, slapping some cash on the counter as he walked. People usually pay on their PassCards and the attendant didn't quite know what to do, but Atsushi Chusonji just kept moving. I scurried after him.

'So Velkasery is like a supercomputer, right?' I asked as I caught up.

'Not sure what you mean by supercomputer.'

'Is it even possible to get inside something like that? More importantly, what are you trying to do if you do get in?'

'See if he left me any clues. But of course, getting in is easier said than done. I couldn't even find the server address. And I think I might have been found out.'

'What do you mean, found out?'

'I input a command and it took me to some other weird address. A trap. And it keeps a record of where I tried to sneak in from.'

'So it knows where you are?' I looked around. Suddenly everyone walking on the street looked like they might be after us. *He's right, this is bad.*

'We need to get away from that café before they find us.'

'Okay. All right.'

We crossed the street to where the bicycle was parked. Chusonji pressed his thumb on the pad to unlock it and retracted the kickstand.

Here we go again, I thought, but he said, 'We'll stand out if we're riding double here in town,' so we walked together as he wheeled his bike along.

I asked him several times where we were going next, but he wouldn't give me a straight answer.

We walked for a while. Some space opened between us, and it occurred to me that we could go wherever it was we were headed separately, or rather, that I didn't even need to go to the same place as him. But as I considered it I spotted a security camera. I didn't know if he was serious about that thing in his pocket being a jammer, but it was true that as soon as we were apart I felt a stab of fear. I hurried to catch up to him.

A teenager stepped into my path and we collided. I apologized, but he said nothing, just kept tapping at his PassCard.

No time for this, I thought, and kept walking, but then I heard from behind, 'Hey, you dropped something!'

I turned around to see the teenager picking up a piece of paper then bringing it toward me. It was the letter: *You were right. Obbel and the Elephant.*

I had no idea why it would have been in my pocket, but Chusonji just looked over and explained. 'I didn't feel like holding it, so I slipped it into your jacket.'

'Isn't this letter kind of important? It's from your friend.'

'What's important is the content, yeah? Not the paper.' With his long hair, his unfashionable jeans, and his impolite way of speaking, he reminded me of a surly kid. Of course, his age made him an adult member of society, but everything that came out of his mouth sounded so flippant.

After walking another five or so minutes we came to a

spacious park. It was apparently the former site of the city hall and prefectural office of Old Sendai. When those were resited, it was turned into a lush and expansive green space. Stately zelkova trees lined the perimeter, and there were a few benches and 3D statue projections scattered around.

We sat down on one of the benches. There was a camera on the nearest tree, staring at us.

'Are you sure it's okay?'

'Sure what's okay?'

'That camera isn't picking us up?'

He cocked his head at it. 'Oh, that thing? Yeah, we're fine. Old model. My jammer's got it.'

'If it were a new model would it not be fine?'

'Next you're gonna ask me what your own name is 'cause you forgot it.' He didn't bother looking at me. 'So many damn questions . . .' I realized that since we met he hadn't once looked at me while talking to me. I didn't necessarily feel the need to stare into the eyes of another man, but it occurred to me that he was very shy. His rough speech was probably a way to cover it up.

'So, has anything come to you?'

'About what?'

'About what the letter means.' It was clear enough that without solving the letter we wouldn't get anywhere. 'Obbel and the Elephant doesn't ring any bells?'

'No.'

There was no hesitation at all in his denial. I didn't see how we were going to figure out our next move.

'Mr Chusonji, why did you give up on your research?' I tried to ask lightly, hoping to stir up some memories.

He looked vaguely toward me. 'Did I say that?'

'What?'

'How do you know that I gave up my research? Did I tell you that?'

Fair enough, I had just assumed that based on his sloppy look and careless demeanor, but he hadn't actually said that he left the research world. 'Well – you said that you had nothing but free time, and you were feeding the pigeons.'

'You don't think there's a connection between pigeons and AI?'

'Um. What?'

'I'm joking. Yeah, I'm just taking it easy. Living in Sendai. I just want to take it easy, keep to myself, not bother anybody. Life's too short, yeah? Listen, you may not get this, but it's tough to live life free.'

'Do you mean philosophically?'

Atsushi Chusonji laughed. 'I mean actually, physically. Do you know why I carry around this jammer? A design I've been working on and improving since I was a kid? In this world, everything you do is being watched. No, that's wrong. Everything is *logged*. All your movements are logged somewhere. Security cams, your PassCard, your net connection. If something goes wrong, they'll find you right away, they'll get you. With all of that, it's hard to be free.'

'I see,' I said, but I didn't really feel the weight of it.

'All of that made me lose my taste for my work, probably. You know, Terashima and I did an experiment together, a long time ago.'

'What kind of experiment?'

'We used people to record things.'

'Why use people? Why not cameras?'

'You can only use so many cameras in so many places. People, you can expand.'

'What do you mean, expand?'

'Everything that a person sees, we would record it on an external hard drive. It turns the person into a camera.'

I had no idea how that would have worked. 'Sounds like human experimentation,' I said, half-joking.

'That's exactly what it was,' he answered, which left me not knowing what to say next. 'Anyway, that's what we were working on.'

'Was this part of your work on artificial intelligence?'

'Artificial intelligence is for working with enormous datasets.' He nodded his chin at the security camera. 'Those things are like eyes. Put together everything they see, everything they record, and you can get a ton of information. Same with what people see, only they can gather much more.'

'That's . . . terrifying.'

'It's ten thousand times more terrifying than you think.'

'What do you mean?'

'The longer I spent working on AI, the more I understood how dangerous it is. At first it was straightforward enough, like, oh, if we use this logic we can get to that conclusion. But the more advanced it became, the less logic seemed to apply. There are researchers who discount the danger, but if you think about it honestly, making an AI is like growing a monster that feeds on information. We used people, a lot of people, logging everything they did and saw, and we fed all that data into an AI, and I realized that I had no idea where it would all lead. Make sense? I didn't want to do it anymore. It's not that I just wanted a quiet life of pigeon-feeding. No, I wanted to get away from monster-making. It led to an argument with Terashima. I said our project was no good.'

'And what happened?'

'He was so damn dedicated to the work. You know, besides Gamma Moko, we almost never saw eye-to-eye. He said I was too pessimistic.'

Chusonji laid out Terashima's position: *Artificial intelligence will help people. In the fiction of a hundred years ago, artificial intelligence ran wild and caused disasters, but that's just fiction. Stories need villains, and they can make anything seem villainous. Think about it: a program that isn't designed to run amok simply won't do that. Programs can't do things that aren't written into the code. That's how it works, and you know it* – is what Terao Terashima had said.

'Which is just dumb. Programs that only do what's in the code aren't intelligent. What we were making went way beyond that. You can't fight against artificial intelligence. And I know he knew that. He just needed to satisfy his curiosity. It's like ignoring that the road you're on goes off a cliff just because you're having fun driving your new car.'

'Once someone tells you that you can't do something, it's only human to want to do it.'

'What? No, totally different.' Chusonji's tone was dismissive.

'So how did it end up?'

'You know exactly how it ended up. He jumped off the train tracks and died.'

'No, I mean the human experiment. Did it work?'

'Oh that. It was never finished.'

'Why?'

'It's always the same, research, government initiatives, whatever – at first everyone's all fired up to do it, but then it doesn't go anywhere. People think it won't succeed, or it won't make any money, and the budget just flows away like the tide. Staff members get cut. Ends unfinished. Happens all the time. Big flashy start, then fades away. That's when I started pulling back from the university. Ended up here in Sendai.'

But Terao Terashima had apparently continued the research.

Chusonji stood. 'Looks like he's finally here. Let's go.'

'Wait, what?'

'Search provider. Mobile unit.'

I looked up and spotted a young man in a yellow shirt with a backpack cutting across the park toward us. He didn't look like a search provider, but apparently that's what he provided.

Atsushi Chusonji strode over to meet him. I noticed he was

handing over cash, same as how he paid in the news café. He probably never used a PassCard, worried as he was about leaving any trail.

The young man barely spoke. He just shrugged off his backpack and took out a laptop.

It was a kind of laptop I had never seen before. Thick, heavy, obviously quite old. The black shell was covered in scratches and dings. The logo was for a manufacturer I had never heard of.

'Most operators want to have brand-new tech. But using a fossil actually makes you harder to find,' explained Chusonji.

I never imagined old devices would be a blind spot. It was also the first time I had ever seen a modem for connecting to the internet. It looked vaguely like a cell phone from decades ago, connected to the computer by a cable.

Chusonji seemed completely at ease operating the ancient machine.

He was back on the bench, typing away with the laptop on his knees. I sat down next to him.

The young man had turned his back to us and put in earbuds. His body bopped along to whatever music he was playing. It seemed like he was trying to avoid seeing or hearing anything about a client's search. He looked like just a normal kid, but at least he had some professional standards.

'What are you searching?'

'I can't really approach Velkasery directly, so I have to take a more roundabout path. I'm looking for a message from Terashima.'

'But I already delivered his letter to you.'

'That was just the first key.'

'It was more of a piece of paper than a key.'

'He was saying to come find him. "You were right," he wrote. He finally came around.'

You were right.

Obbel and the Elephant.

'I was wrong, you were right, so help me out.' Chusonji rattled at the keyboard. 'There must be some hiding place that he knew only I would find. I'm trying to break into his research server and search the history.'

Chusonji's fingers were a blur. I mused to myself that with his obvious skill at navigating the net he could probably find any information he wanted to. But then I had a flash of doubt, as I realized that other people could probably do the same.

Mito, where are you?

The question echoed in my head as I stared at the large screen in our inflatable headquarters.

We confirmed his movements through New Sendai Station, onto the subway toward Aoba Castle. It was a simple matter of checking his PassCard use history. The other detectives were confident that we'd have no trouble finding him, but somehow we lost his trail at the castle. He didn't show up on any of the cameras on the castle grounds, so we couldn't be certain where he went or even if he was still at the castle. Some detectives went out there to check but found nothing.

Where did you disappear to?

We analyzed footage from security cams in the city and ran facial analysis, but that didn't turn up anything. It wasn't looking good.

Next we started trawling online messages. Most of what people post is just complaints and outrage, or boasts, or jokes, but there's always a chance that something useful turns up. We checked all the data that was sent or uploaded in the area around New Sendai Station.

And in fact we did turn up something useful.

'Here we go,' said the captain.

The big screen flipped to mirror his device.

It was a photo of two young people who I had never seen.

They looked like they were a couple. Clearly not Mito. I wasn't sure what the captain meant by *Here we go*. But then someone said, 'Ahh, the glass door.'

Behind the couple was one of those popular new ice cream-pack shops. Someone's reflection was showing in the glass of the open door. The other detectives had determined it was Mito, reflected from behind.

The image zoomed in.

It looked enough like Mito. No, it was him for sure.

The time and location of the photograph displayed on screen. Fifteen minutes earlier, near the Old Sendai Commemorative Park.

'But he didn't show up in any of the cameras from around here,' someone groaned. 'How's he getting around?'

'Maybe he's got a jammer?'

'Hey, Hiyama,' said the captain. 'This Mito, is he that kind of guy?'

'What do you mean, that kind of guy?' I actually had very little sense of what kind of guy Mito was.

'Someone who would have a countermeasure for security cams.'

'I haven't seen him once since we graduated school.'

I could feel my heart rate picking up. It was the first time someone I knew was the subject of an investigation, and it was Mito, of all people.

How did this happen?

If your friend or family member is a suspect, would you be able to continue the investigation as usual?

It was one of the questions from the detective training program. Of course everyone answered that they could do it. Myself included.

How could you turn your back on someone you care about? they asked, with a hint of malicious glee. I answered, 'It's necessary to uphold the order of things.'

Just like it was written in the textbook. But when I said it I felt like the blood flowing through my body was clear and light. I felt righteous. I had always been that way.

Rules are there to be followed.

If someone were to ask me whether I would run a red light late at night when no one was around, I would say no, because the answer is obvious, because that's the rule.

Once someone decides that they can bend the rules a little, that they deserve some wiggle room, then the foundation starts to slip. Little cracks turn into massive fissures.

When everything is lined up nice and tidy, you need to keep it that way. Anything that sticks out needs to be dealt with.

If you want to maintain order in society and there's someone who has committed a crime, or even someone who might commit a crime, you can't hold back just because you know them personally.

And as for Naomasa Mito, I felt more affinity for complete strangers than I did for him.

If it came to putting him away, I wouldn't hesitate one instant.

'So where do we think Mito is headed next? And can we catch him?'

The detectives all started swiping at their tablets.

I began searching the data from the cameras around the park too, but suddenly I pictured Mito glaring at me. Startled, I dropped my device. The other detectives looked over and asked if I was all right, and I hurriedly collected my tablet from the floor.

I was supposed to be investigating Mito, but I had the intense sensation that it was him who was scrutinizing me. That he had always been looking at me as if seeing right through me, since time out of mind, his face an ancient mask.

I needed to find him, but I didn't want him to find me. Then a thought flashed into my head. My hand was already up in the air. 'Do we know if there are any professional search providers near this park?'

It was just an idea, inspired by the image of Mito looking for me.

If he was trying to hide his movements and leave no history, then he could have very well used a freelance search provider.

If you're breaking the rules, then there's no need for me to hold back.

'No good. Nothing.' Atsushi Chusonji took his fingers off the keyboard and looked up toward the sky. 'I can't even get into his research server.'

The search provider still had his earbuds in. He was doing some fancy dance steps in place.

'What do you think Obbel and the Elephant means? Is it a code?'

'I searched that too, but I don't really understand it. It's a children's story from the twentieth century. Do you know it?'

I thought about the picture book *I Am Mai-Mai*. It was definitely aimed at children, but it had a different tone from a classic children's story. 'I feel like I've heard the title before.'

Chusonji turned the laptop screen toward me. It displayed the text of the whole story, which wasn't that long. I read it in just a few minutes.

A man named Obbel tricks an elephant into working for him. The poor exhausted elephant sends a letter to his friends, who eventually come to the rescue.

As a courier I liked the idea that a letter could save the day, but I had no idea what we were supposed to take away from the story.

'Seems to me like it's about the relationship between capital and labor,' Chusonji said gruffly.

'Do you think that's what Mr Terashima wanted to tell us?'

'Nah, that's not his thing.' I wasn't sure what that meant, exactly, but I made a noise of acknowledgment.

'Did you find anything else?'

'I looked up interpretations of "Obbel and the Elephant" and there was this one interesting thing.'

'Interesting how?'

'The last line has a missing word.'

'What does that mean, a missing word?'

'It ends with, "Hey, I told you not to go in the river," but after "Hey" there's a word that the publisher apparently couldn't make out.'

I took another look at the end of the story, and there it was: *Hey [missing word], I told you not to go in the river.* There was an actual notation saying [*missing word*]. 'That seems significant.'

'No kidding. The author was Kenji Miyazawa – I wonder what he wrote there. Now my curiosity is piqued.' But after a second he continued, 'But you know, back then he probably wrote it by hand and they just couldn't read his writing. "Hey you," or "Hey now," but it couldn't have been that important,' he concluded.

That sounded logical enough, but maybe too easy. It felt like we should try a little harder.

'What's more interesting, though, is this part about not going into the river. Who was even trying to go into the river?'

'The elephant?'

'The first line of the story is "A tale told by a cowherd." So the cowherd is the narrator. It's a framing device, where the cowherd is telling it to a group of children, or maybe to his cows.'

'Huh.'

'And the last line is where one of the children listening

57

suddenly tries to jump into the river, and the cowherd says, "Hey, don't do that." Anyway, that's the widely accepted interpretation.'

'It's like the story's bringing us back to the real world.' It reminded me of hearing ghost stories as a boy, told as if they were about someone else, but at the end the storyteller would point at me and say the ghost was coming for me and I would be terrified.

Was Terao Terashima trying to tell us something like that?

I was about to say it – the words were coming out of my mouth – but I faltered when I noticed that Atsushi Chusonji was staring hard at the screen, not moving a muscle. He was like a battery-operated toy that had run out of power. It felt like I had suddenly been left alone.

'Ohh,' he sighed quietly. 'Now I remember.' His voice was low, and he sounded like he was grasping something important.

'You have something?'

'Yeah, I remember. Don't go in the river. It's what that old lady said.'

'Old lady?' It was so unexpected, I doubted my own ears.

'Terashima and I once took a road trip. Headed to Fuji to see a Gamma Moko concert. On the way back we got lost. The nav lost connection and we got all turned around. It was in the middle of the mountains near Hachioji. We needed to use a bathroom so we stopped at a house we came across. An old lady was living there by herself.'

'Okay.'

'Her house was right by a river. I went to go wash my face.'

'And then what?'

'I slipped and fell in.' He clicked his tongue in annoyance at his mistake from all those years ago. 'I hurt myself. It was way deeper than I thought it would be.'

He told me how Terashima and the old lady hurried over and threw a vine to him so he could pull himself out.

'And that's *I told you not to go in the river*? But what does it mean?'

'When someone tells you not to do something it makes you want to do it, right? So when you hear "don't go in the river" . . .'

'You want to go in?'

'We have to go see that old lady.'

In Hachioji?

It would take hours to get there. I thought he was joking, but Chusonji's face was completely serious. He started typing again. I peeked at the screen and saw the reservation page for a car rental service.

Car.

My internal alarms went off and my blood froze.

But Chusonji just kept typing. In a different window he started stringing together lines of code. An improvised program to over-write the car rental database so he could get a car under someone else's name.

He seemed to misinterpret my fear. 'Don't sweat it, overwrit-ing a database is no problem,' he explained. 'Data is a funny thing. Once it's input, people accept it as the truth. I can make it look like I have a whole history of responsible rentals. Actually, it's probably the same with the news we saw back there in that café.'

'Huh?'

'There was that thing about the submarines being launched somewhere in the Middle East, right? You said it felt like a prel-ude to war. But we have no idea whether or not it's even happening. All we know is we heard it on the news. Those sub-marines might never have left the base. That footage from the fishing boat could be totally fake.'

No way of knowing what's true. He was right, and the moment I acknowledged that it felt like everything I was seeing with my own eyes suddenly tilted on an angle.

'Wait, what the hell is this?'

'Is something wrong?'

I looked at Chusonji. He was staring hard at the screen, his brows knitted. He was on a news page. I thought it might be a new development in the Middle East submarine story, but he started talking about something much closer to home. 'A bunch of people in Tokyo are getting sick with food poisoning.'

'All right.' It didn't strike me as anything that unusual.

'Twenty otherwise healthy adults have already died. That's a lot.'

'What were they eating?'

'That's still under investigation.'

'Okay.' This had nothing to do with our situation.

'But it seems like there's reports of someone going around spreading infectious bacteria.'

'What does it mean?' As I said it something popped into my head: that massacre in Europe. The news story about the spread of bacteria and the revenge killings in two neighboring towns. 'Wait,' I said, and I felt a different chill shoot up my spine. I knew what it was from. It was the same exact feeling I had on the Shinkansen.

'We should hurry,' I said. 'The police could be here any minute.'

Kagetora Hiyama was nearby, and getting closer.

Sitting in the passenger seat I didn't feel like I was among the living. Memories of the accident kept floating up, and I desperately tried to push them into the far corners of my mind. It felt like something monstrous was bubbling out of the road and trying to force its way into the car. No matter how hard I held the door shut it would seep in through the tiniest cracks. I heard my mother's quiet protest, *Hey, they cut us off.* My father was there too, his hands off the wheel as he enjoyed the self-driving function, saying, *It's so smooth.* And then the brand-new car with my elementary school self in the back seat spinning, spinning. I was reading my favorite picture book about the adventures of the heroic snail, and then I was spinning like a top.

'You that worried about my driving?' Chusonji said from behind the wheel. 'Relax. Nowadays you have to mess up pretty bad to get into a collision. It's tough to crash even if you wanted to.'

'Ah, uh, yeah.'

It was like a waking nightmare. I gripped the seatbelt as hard as I could. When I closed my eyes I saw the accident projected on the backs of my eyelids; when I opened them I saw it on the windshield. Desperate to escape the playback, I kept opening and closing my eyes, only to have it keep repeating.

'If it thinks we're getting too close to something it drops speed. And the body's made of material that absorbs collision impact,' explained Chusonji. 'Plus it's a rental. They're better outfitted for safety than normal cars.'

We had picked up the rental in New Sendai. Ordinarily we would have had to register a driver's license number and have our identities confirmed but we'd shuffled things around in the rental car company's database (that is, Chusonji shuffled things around) so we were able to rent the car without any of that.

'Ah, no, I know that the car is safe, I just—'

'So you're doubting my driving.'

'No, no . . . I just had a bad experience.'

'Ha, what, you were on a date and you crashed the car?'

'I—' The word 'crash' was like a needle plunging into my brain. For a moment my mind went blank. 'No.' I shook my head vigorously. 'I was on the sidewalk when I got hit by a taxi. I was in the hospital for a while.'

'Hang on, what now?'

'I was in a coma.'

'No way that happened.'

'But—' I felt like an idiot. 'But it did happen.'

My voice was forceful enough that Chusonji made an apologetic face. 'I'm not saying you're lying. It just didn't sound to me like the sort of accident that would cause a coma, that's all. I was just surprised.'

'After the accident I could only remember bits and pieces of things from a long time ago.'

In the back of my mind I could hear Hinata's encouragement, saying that I would remember more and more as time went on.

'Memory loss, huh? That's rough.'

'I've gotten most of it back. I remember that on the day I was in the accident I was supposed to go to a concert.'

'I wasn't saying you didn't get it back.'

'Actually, it was Gamma Moko. I was supposed to go to a Gamma Moko show.'

Atsushi Chusonji's eyes gleamed. 'You saw Gamma Moko?'

I could tell he was jealous. 'No, wait. It was a cover.'

'A cover?'

'A Gamma Moko cover band.'

Any band as famous as Gamma Moko will inspire a handful of amateur cover bands. Jurok music has so many complex elements that it's difficult to reproduce perfectly, but if the arrangement has enough instruments and they've studied the piece thoroughly enough, it's possible to come up with a decent cover.

'A cover band? C'mon.' He sounded both surprised and derisive.

'If the cover is good enough, it's not any different from the original.'

'No way. As long as there's an original, a copy is always just a copy.'

'And what if there's no more original?' It's not like I was such a big fan of the cover band, but I felt like challenging him. I felt like talking back. 'When the original's gone, all we have are the copies.'

'That's the dumbest thing I've ever heard,' Chusonji said. 'How did we get on to this, anyway?'

'We were talking about my accident. Why I don't like cars.'

'Right, it was when you got hit by a car on your way to go see the cover band play.'

'Yes. But even worse than that was an accident when I was a boy.' That was the real trauma, the one that did deep mental damage.

'You were in another accident? As a kid?'

I wasn't sure how much I wanted to tell him. I didn't mind sharing that my whole family had been killed, but I didn't want him to feel sorry for me. 'Serious casualties,' was all I said.

But my tone must have been heavy enough for him to understand that it was no joking matter, because he spoke kindly to me for the first time. 'Your whole family was in a bad accident? That's really tough.'

I told him that my mother's last words were *Hey, they cut us off.* Probably too fine a detail, not necessary to share. It seemed like such a normal, everyday thing to say, which stood in sharp contrast with the harshness of her death.

Chusonji was quiet for a few moments, absorbing the gravity of the accident that took away my whole family. 'Makes me feel like I should think about what I want my last words to be,' he said softly.

At the same time, he might also have been thinking about Terao Terashima.

He took his hands off the wheel and pushed a button on the car's navigation system.

By that point we had made it to Saitama.

The computer announced the name of the service area as we

changed lanes toward the exit. I squawked involuntarily and gripped my seatbelt.

'Pit stop. You need the bathroom?'

I couldn't say a thing. I just wanted to get out of the car as fast as possible.

But getting out of the car meant pulling over at the rest stop, and to me, rest stop entrance equaled death. As we drew closer to the exit, I felt my eyes roll back, then nothing.

The next thing I knew Chusonji was hitting me on the shoulder and I snapped to my senses. 'You okay? Sorry about that,' he said. He actually seemed concerned.

'I'm fine,' I answered, but I felt my gorge rising. Hand pressed over my mouth, I jumped out of the car and ran to the bathroom.

I emptied the contents of my stomach into the toilet, but the torturous memories wouldn't get out of my head. When I stepped out of the stall Atsushi Chusonji was standing right there, which made me jump.

'I'm not stalking you or anything. But we should stick together. Otherwise you'll show up on camera.'

Reflexively, I scanned the bathroom walls. 'Do they put cameras in restrooms?'

It felt like it should be one of the most private places, free from surveillance.

'They may not be recording images but I wouldn't be surprised if there was still facial recognition.'

I had gotten so used to being protected by his homemade signal jammer that I didn't even think about security in the bathroom.

I washed my hands and we left.

'So you know the guy who's after us?'

'Huh?'

'When we were leaving Sendai, it seemed like you knew one of the cops on our trail.'

'Oh, no, it's just, ah – well, the police—' I began. But then I decided there was no reason to hide it. 'Actually one of them was a classmate of mine back in school. I bumped into him on the Shinkansen.'

'Was he after Terashima?'

'I think so. I hadn't seen him in a long time. It took me by surprise.'

We cut through the building at the rest stop selling snacks and souvenirs. There was a fair number of people milling about the information hub, scrolling on their PassCards. It somehow felt like they were all looking up information to help find and catch us. We hurried past.

When we reached the parking lot, Chusonji said, 'It's gotta be tough for you, being chased by your friend.'

'He's no friend of mine.' My voice was louder than I intended.

'Hey now, a little fired up, are we?'

'What? No.'

'You got a score to settle with this guy?'

A score? It didn't feel that way. If anything he would be the only person who could possibly understand the shock of losing my family in that crash, since he went through the exact same thing. But with the way my very body rejected having anything to do with him, we could never be allies. 'There's no score to settle, exactly.'

'So what, you're just like natural enemies?'

'What do you mean, natural enemies?'

'Like cats and mice. Or, I don't know, scale insects and lady-bugs. I'm saying it's not a personal grudge, it's just a natural, congenital opposition. Frogs and snakes are that way. And I think there's one for snails too.'

This of course made me think of my favorite childhood book. A snail with an iron shell, wielding the Lance of Longinus to fight his foes. I loved it so much that my parents bought me both the digital version and the actual physical book. I spent all my free time reading it over and over again.

'What's up?' Chusonji asked as we approached the rental car. 'Something on your mind?'

'It's nothing.' I explained to him that nearly everything associated with the accident has always been a serious trigger for me, but for whatever reason *I Am Mai-Mai* had never been a problem. I kept happily reading it for years after the accident and have been a lifelong Mai-Mai fan.

'Oh right, that kids' book,' Chusonji said, obviously not interested.

That was when I noticed a boy running around in the parking lot.

He was dashing between the parked cars, as if tracing lines on a grid: up, over, up again, over. He must have been five or six years old. At first I watched with a smile, thinking it was nice to see a kid playing so happily, but as I followed the top of his head between the cars, I started to feel uneasy.

He was completely absorbed in his own little world, oblivious to the danger that a car might pull out at any time. The concept of getting hit by a car may never even have occurred to him.

An adult voice called out a child's name. It seemed that his parents had lost sight of him. The more his name was called the further he ran, squealing with glee.

I went after him.

It wasn't my responsibility, but I couldn't just stand by and let something terrible happen.

And I could easily see something going wrong.

Nowadays cars have sensors to detect when there's a person or object close by and initiate an emergency stop if there's about to be a collision, but they aren't responsive enough to pick up something jumping out suddenly. This boy certainly seemed likely to dart into the way of a moving car without warning.

His parents should have been keeping a closer eye on him.

A pickup truck pulled into the parking lot.

At the same moment the boy sprinted, as if he had heard a starting gun. Without thinking, I launched myself toward him.

I caught him at the last split second, and we tumbled to the ground.

Atsushi Chusonji kept repeating how he had never seen anyone save someone else's life before, that it was just like a scene from a TV show.

'All right already,' I said. I lost track of how many times he had marveled at it from when we left the service area in Saitama to the time we entered Tokyo. He just kept going on about how there are really people who would save a child from being run over, how glad he was to have seen that.

'And how about the kid's parents, huh? Can you believe it? You returned their son safely to them and they barely said thanks!'

'Well, I can understand it, they didn't see what happened.' I sounded unconcerned, but the truth was I was similarly dumbfounded. I had saved their son's life – I would have expected them to be emotional and appreciative and thank me profusely. I'd even prepared myself to shrug off any praise and say that I was only doing what anyone would do.

But once I'd calmed myself down and brought the boy back to them, he burst into tears and his parents had instantly become protective, even suspicious of this stranger who had apparently made their child cry. They said thank you, but it was clear they didn't mean it.

That was when Chusonji stepped in to salvage the situation. 'Your son had a close call. He jumped right in front of a car, he would have been run over for sure, but we saved him.'

I was slightly annoyed that he said 'we' when it was me who did it, but thanks to his emphatic explanation the parents finally got the idea of what had happened. The boy also stopped crying and confirmed our story through his sniffles. They thanked us again, with real gratitude. The problem was that they switched to being too enthusiastic. 'You saved our son's life, we can't just let you leave empty-handed,' they said, drawing closer with a somewhat manic look. 'Please, let us do something for you.' We begged off, saying we were in a hurry. 'Then at least give us your names and addresses.'

Of course, we weren't going to share our personal information. We made all kinds of excuses while retreating to our car. By the time we pulled away we felt more like fugitives than saviors.

We took the New Tohoku Highway to the New Kuki Shiraoka Junction and got onto the New Metropolitan Thruway.

'Looks like things are getting hairy.'

'What?' I turned around, expecting to see our pursuers.

'I mean in the news. It keeps popping up on the nav screen. Something about a gang of people with axes attacking people in cars.'

I hadn't noticed the news; it must have been playing because we were on self-driving mode. Headlines flowed along the bottom of the screen. Chusonji's hands were off the wheel and he watched the screen as the story scrolled by.

I didn't know if it was a carjacking spree or if there was something else behind it, but the idea of axe-wielding gangs seemed surreal.

'I mean, come on, if the cops have enough time on their hands to be chasing us, I feel like they should deal with this first.'

Meanwhile, it was all I could do to fight down my terror at

riding in a car. I must have been unconsciously clenching various muscles in my body, because even though I was just sitting there I started to feel aches in my arms and legs.

I closed my eyes, not to relax, but to concentrate on fending off that awful memory, the monstrous spin that erased my family. *Don't think of anything, don't think of anything at all,* I kept telling myself. At some point I must have drifted off, because the next thing I knew Chusonji was shaking my shoulder to wake me.

I sat bolt upright and half-shouted, 'Are we there?' I was still not fully conscious.

'Where's there?'

'Where? In Hachioji, the place we're going. Are we there yet?'

I told you not to go in the river!

The last line of 'Obbel and the Elephant,' that had reminded Chusonji of the old woman's house in Hachioji.

But when I looked around I saw we were in a large parking lot. We had gotten off the highway and there were some houses nearby. At least the car had stopped, which released the tightness in my chest.

'Um, where . . . where's the river?'

'Don't ask me,' Chusonji said with a straight face.

'Then who should I ask? You were the one who fell into the river, right?'

'Terashima and I got lost and just happened upon that house. We were lost, understand? How should I know how to get back there?'

What he was saying didn't seem to bother him, but all I could do was let out an exasperated half-sigh.

'While you were enjoying your nap I did the best I could to find it. Drove all around. Eventually I realized that it's impossible to get lost in the exact same way you did years ago. Guess I thought it would be easier.'

'And you don't know the name of the river?'

69

He said that he'd done the best he could to remember, while setting the navigator for mountains and rivers around Hachioji. 'I think it was one of the ones that feeds into the Tama River, but I'm not sure.'

'So where are we now?'

'The old Mount Takao parking area.'

'Would you know the place we're looking for if you saw it?'

'All you ever do is ask questions. Must be nice never having to answer any,' he said, taking out his PassCard and starting to swipe and tap. 'I looked through my old files and found a photo I took back then.'

'A photo of what?'

'A photo from the time we got lost in the mountains. The old lady's house is in the background. That's what we're looking for.'

I looked at the screen. There was a small house made of wood with a tiled roof, rare to see anymore. In front of it stood three people. 'A photo to commemorate when you almost drowned?'

The Chusonji in the picture looked more or less the same as the man sitting next to me. He seemed to be of indeterminate age back then as well. Now it was hard to say he looked old, exactly, and back then it was hard to say he looked young. I could tell for sure that his hair was all wet. Standing next to him was Terao Terashima. I hadn't spent much time looking at his face when I met him on the Shinkansen, but it looked the same as the man I saw on the news.

'The old lady,' Chusonji said, but then added, 'she was a very kind old woman – she said we should take a picture.'

'For what, I wonder?'

'So we could remember it,' he said gruffly. 'She set up the camera to start taking photos even though I wasn't into it.'

I took another look at the photo. Between the two men stood a woman, smiling broadly. 'She doesn't look that old. How old was she?'

'I wonder. I would guess over sixty.'

'She doesn't look like she's over sixty.' Her posture was upright, her teeth were white and straight. The two young men both had perplexed looks on their faces, but she didn't seem bothered in the least. And then something hit me. 'Oh!'

'What's up?'

'Nothing, I just—'

'Ah, I see.' Chusonji nodded as if he knew what I was thinking, and continued, 'If she was past sixty in this picture, you're thinking she must be old and wizened at this point, right? Maybe dead? It could be. Although nowadays it's pretty common for people to live past a hundred. She seemed to be living a pretty relaxed life up there in the mountains; I wouldn't be surprised if she was still alive and kicking. Anyway, if Terashima said we should go there, then I figure it's worth going even if she isn't alive.'

'No, that's not what I was thinking.' I could feel my pulse quickening. 'I'm pretty sure she's still alive.'

'What are you, some kind of fortune teller?'

'No, but I know who she is.' *Could it be?* A doubting voice inside me still wasn't convinced.

'No way. You know her?'

'She's Miyako Setsu.'

'Who the hell is that?'

'The author of *I Am Mai-Mai*.' My favorite book from when I was little. Although it was fair to say that it had always been a part of my life. Being such a longtime fan, of course I was also interested in the author. I had read some interviews with her online, and I had even once gone to a book signing. I was worried I would be the only adult there, but it ended up being children and adults alike, fans of all generations. I was relieved, and at the same time felt a pang of disappointment that I wasn't a special case. 'I'm pretty sure this is her.'

'The author of the picture book?'

'Yes. *I Am Mai-Mai*. Didn't you tell me you read it when you were young?'

'Everybody read that when they were young.'

'Well, she's the author.' I was getting louder in my excitement. I had never expected to have any connection to Miyako Setsu, let alone that she would be part of the mess I was in.

Chusonji looked hard at his PassCard, as if he couldn't really accept it. 'But she never said anything about it. This was twenty years ago, which means *I Am Mai-Mai* was already well known. She could have said that it was her book.'

'Was there any reason why she would have?' New anime and movies based on her work kept coming out, but there was no book sequel. The book signing event was not for a new release but for a new edition of her past works. 'She was probably more or less retired.'

'If she's the author of that book, then she's probably super rich. Her house was way out in the mountains, and, you know, pretty old.'

'Everyone uses money differently,' I replied, and then something occurred to me. 'Oh!'

'What is it this time?'

'I think I know,' said a low voice, almost a murmur, and then I realized it was my own voice.

'What do you mean, you know?'

'Miyako Setsu wrote something I saw on a news site. It was a while ago, now.'

'She wrote "something"?'

'An essay.'

Chusonji made a face like he was going to ask what an essay was.

'It was about moving to a new house. She left her home in the city and moved out to the mountains – out here!'

72

'So where's here?'

'Somewhere near where we are right now. There were a lot of details about the view from her new house, and something about taking a walk every day and going past a Jizo statue.'

Wondering how I could have held on to a detail like that, I recalled being excited when I read it because it meant that if I found that place I might run into this author whose work I loved. It seemed possible because of the level of granular detail about her neighborhood. As for what I would do or say if I actually met her, my imagination never quite got that far, and of course I didn't have enough time to go Jizo-hunting out in the mountains, so the idea never went anywhere. But the essay did make an impression on me.

'If you're saying she passed the Jizo on her daily walk, it must be somewhere near her house.'

'Exactly.'

'So where's the Jizo? Let's go already.'

'Well, she didn't say where.'

'So wait a second, what are you saying we should do? Or is this some kind of joke?'

'If we read the essay I'm sure we can find the general area.'

'Where can we find it? PassCards aren't exactly ideal for trawling old articles on unspecified news sites. I guess we need to find another search provider.' Chusonji restarted the car.

'If that's what we need,' I said, 'I know someone I can ask.'

'Oh yeah? Who?'

'Hinata.' My girlfriend of five years, I explained. 'She's a librarian. She should be able to access news archives at her work. Um, can I borrow your PassCard? I'll use it to get in touch with her.' Sending messages and making calls leaves digital records of user location, but I guessed that Atsushi Chusonji would have something on his card to deal with that.

'Fine, but aren't you worried?'

73

'Huh? Why?'

'The cops are after you. Including your old classmate.'

'I just got pulled into this.' All I did was deliver a letter.

'That doesn't matter to them. And don't you think they're keeping tabs on your girlfriend? I'm sure they're watching her house and tracking her location. If you just pick up the phone and get in touch, they'll find you in no time.'

None of that was lost on me. But somehow I had a strong sense that it would be okay. 'No one really knows that we're together.'

'No one knows? What kind of relationship is that?'

'We just haven't told anyone that we're dating.' I explained that my family was gone, and I didn't really have any friends, and I wasn't a regular at any bars or restaurants. The only place I went to with any consistency was my barber, but I had never once brought up Hinata. 'She lost her parents when she was young too, and she doesn't have any friends either.'

'Are you for real?'

'What do you mean, am I for real?'

'You and your girlfriend both have no family or friends? Is that just a coincidence? Is that even possible?'

'Even if it is a coincidence, there's nothing wrong with it. I told you about getting hit by a taxi, right?'

'It put you in a coma.'

'Well, Hinata was right there when it happened. She just happened to be in the taxi that hit me, so she called an ambulance and stayed with me in the hospital. From there we started getting closer.'

'A very considerate person just so happened to be right there. You're one lucky guy.' I could tell he was poking fun at me, but there was no time to argue.

'Anyway, she's the only one who can help us right now.' I probably sounded more forceful than I meant to. I took his PassCard and tapped in her number, which I knew by heart. It started ringing.

'If anything feels off, hang up,' growled Chusonji. I nodded. I had insisted that no one knew about me and Hinata, but I couldn't be 100 percent certain.

If it rang a few times without her picking up I would have gotten nervous and ended the call. The caller ID wouldn't be my number either, so there was also a good chance she would just ignore the call. But she answered right away. Before she could say anything I told her it was me.

'Mito? Are you okay? This isn't your number, did you lose your PassCard?'

'There's a story, but basically I'm borrowing someone else's.'

'And I'm guessing it's a long story. What can I do to help?'

'You're quick, Hinata.'

'Save the compliments for later. What's up?'

'I need you to look up an old article for me.' I could feel Chusonji's eyes on me. 'Do you know who Miyako Setsu is?' I began. 'The woman who wrote *I Am Mai-Mai*?'

'What's the matter, Hiyama? Don't like cars?' asked the captain from the driver's seat in our eight-person police van. I was in the passenger seat, looking out the window and trying to make it seem like I was dozing to hide the fact that I was feeling queasy. But the captain noticed that something was up.

'Oh, I was in an accident a long time ago. Ended up with a little bit of car phobia.' I didn't tell him that the accident was how I first met our suspect, Naomasa Mito.

'Relax, highway self-driving accidents are very rare.'

'Yeah, I know.'

But my accident was with highway self-driving. It had been

nearly twenty years since the crash and technology had certainly improved, but looking at the captain sitting there with his hands not on the wheel, he seemed to be superimposed over the image of my father, hands off the wheel, the car spinning wildly. I was terrified that I would be launched out of the vehicle and killed. My arms and legs clenched.

Hiyama, you're too much of a stickler for the rules.

I remembered one of my friends saying that when it was getting time to start applying for jobs in college, because I looked askance at companies trying to woo students before the official recruitment period began. It was clear enough he thought I was being foolish.

I imagine the root of it is in my trauma from the accident. I don't know if my family and Mito's family were obeying traffic laws or not. But I'm sure that something wasn't operating the way it was supposed to, and because of that both of our families were taken from us. I knew that I needed to fight to keep people following the rules so that accidents like that wouldn't happen.

It seemed to me there was nothing more important than the laws and statutes that keep society functioning. Without giving it much more thought, I started studying for the civil service exam to join the police force.

'Think we'll make it in time?' asked one of the other detectives. 'They're on the move.'

'Even if we don't make it in time, we still need to go,' said another detective, as if it was the most obvious thing in the world.

'But how are the two of them connected, Mito and this Chusonji guy?'

'We don't even know if this other person actually is Chusonji.'

'Based on what we know, it seems pretty likely.'

We had footage of Naomasa Mito interacting with Terao Terashima on the Shinkansen. It had thrown me for a loop when I'd first found out that Mito was involved in this. Then we lost track of him completely after he got to Sendai. That meant he was somehow avoiding any and all cameras and sensors, which was another surprise.

But Naomasa Mito wasn't operating alone.

We had learned that from a professional search provider who met them in Old Sendai Commemorative Park. He said that the other man, not Mito, seemed to be the leader. The search provider didn't have very good manners, but his memory was sharp. He described the other man in great detail, which led us to believe that it was Atsushi Chusonji.

Former researcher, nowadays basically unemployed, but when we found out that he was at university with Terao Terashima we figured we had our man. The other detectives got all fired up. Based on the circumstances of the case, it had to be him, they said. Right away we started reaching out to his university classmates for questioning, but he didn't seem to have any friends, and most of what we learned was that he didn't get along well with people. We did hear some rumors that as a student he had hacked the university database to manipulate his grades. More than a few people said that he would have no problem figuring out a way to avoid showing up on security cams. It wasn't long before we found out that Chusonji and Terashima had worked together in the same research center.

'So we think that Terao Terashima wanted to send some kind of message to Atsushi Chusonji. And he approached Naomasa Mito to deliver the message.'

It made sense. That meant that Mito had just been pulled into the whole thing.

What we didn't know was why Mito would have continued on with Chusonji after delivering the message. Maybe he was being forced to go along for some purpose, or maybe he didn't know what was actually going on and was just being tricked into sticking with Chusonji.

Once we determined that we wouldn't be able to rely on security cams and PassCard records, all we could do to track their movements beyond the Old Sendai Commemorative Park was to search what other people were posting online. We methodically worked our way through all sorts of likely-seeming keywords and did rolling searches of social media posts.

One thing immediately stood out: information relating to an incident that had just gone down in Tokyo. There had been a multi-car pileup on a roundabout in the twenty-third ward. Several bodies were found with their arms and legs tied. Nearly everyone involved had been killed, so it wasn't yet clear if the tied-up people were being kidnapped or if something else was going on. There were also reports of a gang of people attacking cars with axes.

'Axes, huh?' Said one of the detectives, then continued in English: '*Oh no.*' A bad bilingual pun on the Japanese word for axe. He got a few sympathy laughs.

Wondering if Mito and Chusonji might have been involved, we looked for more information, but didn't turn up anything likely.

As we were searching, one trending topic caught my eye. Posts with titles like *Lifesaver*, and *This warms the heart*, and *Saved in the nick of time*, also tagged with *Highway service area* and *Saitama*. They all had the same video.

It was footage from a parking lot at a highway rest stop. Some friends were taking a selfie video, but on the edge of the frame the camera caught a man rescuing a kid from being hit by a pickup truck. That part had been enlarged and shared.

So we had people tying people up and people marauding around with axes, and at the same time we had someone saving someone else's life. Unexplained horror and rescuing a child from the jaws of death, all at once. The internet loves it.

The footage showed the face of the man returning the boy to his parents. My breath choked off.

Mito. My body froze, words wouldn't come out. After a few moments, I managed to say, 'He's in a car, headed toward Tokyo!'

No matter where he might go, I would find him. I had to find him. Even with my eyes closed, shrouded in darkness, I would know where he was.

A shiver ran through me.

Over the five years of our relationship I had come to under-stand that Hinata was good at nearly everything. I hadn't even explained my situation to her, but she dug up Miyako Setsu's essay and sent it over right away, without pressing me for any details.

'You sure you can trust her?' Chusonji had a general air of carelessness, but he was unusually concerned about Hinata.

'What's that supposed to mean?'

'There's something weird about the way the two of you met. *Oh, you poor thing, you were in a traffic accident!* I mean, really?'

'I was hit by a taxi. She just happened to be on the scene, and she followed me to the hospital.'

'Exactly, who ever heard of something like that? It would be one thing if the two of you had been in an accident together.'

I was about to challenge that when I had an image of Hinata sitting in the passenger seat next to me. Which meant that I was in the driver's seat, my hands on the wheel.

Me, driving? Just imagining it made my spine flash cold and my legs go numb.

Are you sure you're okay to drive?

I told you, I'm fine.

It felt like I could hear the conversation floating somewhere far away. I shook my head. Was I just imagining things?

Unnerved, I turned my attention back to the article she had sent me.

It was basically how I remembered it: how Miyako Setsu had moved out of her condo in Tokyo, how she still wasn't sure she wanted to live out in the country, how a friend happened to tell her about an old-style folk house in Hachioji that she fell in love with. Her immediate decision to buy it, the fact that it wasn't just surrounded by mountains but was also right next to a river. The inconvenience of being so far from the city center being outweighed by the profound peace and relaxation, all laid out in Miyako Setsu's clear, unadorned prose. And the scenery on her daily walks, including the Jizo statue.

'Writing that much about the area around her house, it's like she was asking for people to come find her,' said Chusonji with a hint of disbelief. 'She's way too casual about her privacy.'

'It's not like she's a singer or an actor who has crazy fans. I doubt anyone would want to go on a quest to find the author of *I Am Mai-Mai*.' Of course, I'd had the idea that I could find her, but I hadn't gone through with it.

Anyway, she may have written about her neighborhood in vivid detail, but it's not like there was a map. To find the actual location we would need to do some work, consulting the digital map on a PassCard while searching for the details in the essay and comparing to what Chusonji could remember.

The essay had a passage that went: *In the morning, the communications tower on top of the mountain across the way catches the sun and casts a long shadow which always unsettles me, feeling somehow like my mother-in-law glaring down at me,* so we started by looking on the satellite map for the antennae of communications towers. That narrowed things down some. After thirty minutes of checking and comparing, Chusonji said, 'I think I've got it. It should be here,' and he input the location into the nav.

The route was mostly unpaved. We came to a rickety bridge that looked like it could use some repairs. On the other side was a narrow mountain road that we followed down in a gentle spiral. At the bottom the road continued alongside a river. The route was too curved and looping for self-driving so Chusonji took the wheel, but there was no world in which his handling could have been called careful, not even as a fake compliment, so for someone like me, it was all I could do not to give up and die. When he finally said, 'I think this is it,' and stopped the car, it was like he was announcing my salvation.

It took me a few minutes to get my breathing under control before I could get out of the car. Chusonji had already gotten out and left. There was no sign of him. I felt a surge of panic at the thought of being separated and my location revealed, and I feared that at any moment the police might surround me.

We had stopped the car alongside the mountain road. There was a path through the woods that led down to the river.

'Look, we actually found it!' Chusonji shouted from beside the river, where he was crouched washing his hands.

'Is . . . is this it?'

'Amazing. It's been twenty years and it hasn't changed at all.'

'Huh.'

'We've been slowing down all these years, but the river's been working just as hard.'

I wasn't sure if a river flowing counted as work. You could just as well say that water flowing along was the definition of taking it easy.

'Look over there.' He pointed. Sure enough, there was a Jizo. Then I heard a voice from behind us and nearly jumped.

'Well now.'

The police? I turned slowly, knowing I'd be looking down the barrel of a gun. But instead there was a smiling woman with her white hair tied back.

'Have you come back to fall in the river again?'

Never in my wildest dreams did I think this would be happening. I was kneeling formally on a cushion on the tatami of her living room, staring into the coffee that she had served, feeling like none of this was real.

There she was, the author of I Am Mai-Mai, right there in front of me. Chusonji poked at me. 'Say something,' he hissed. 'Aren't you a big fan?'

I opened my mouth, but all I got out was a jumble of nonsense. 'Thank you for letting us, your home, um, your lovely home, uh, we're in your wonderful home, and . . .'

'I'm always glad to meet a reader. It feels more special ever since the book became a TV show,' said Miyako Setsu.

If the age in her printed bio was correct, she would be past ninety. But her back was straight, her skin color good, and she seemed so full of energy. When it came to anti-aging procedures, there were plenty of people who went to great lengths, both men and women, so it could be difficult to tell at a glance what someone's age was, even when they were quite old. But she didn't have any of the telltale marks from wrinkle removal or nips and tucks. Her white hair and the lines on her face all looked like natural aging, and yet she had the energy of a peppy young woman.

'Are you really Miyako Setsu?'

'Why wouldn't I be? Anyway, you saw the photo and thought it was me.'

'But you look so young.'

'Well, that's nice to hear,' she said, without blushing. 'It's because my personality has stayed the same. You know, my mother – mother-in-law, actually – she was always a livewire, so if I didn't stay sharp I wouldn't be able to keep up with her. I had no time to get old.'

I didn't know how to answer that, so I just shook my head vaguely and murmured noncommittally.

'You boys may not be aware of how serious the friction between daughter-in-law and mother-in-law can be. Back at the end of Showa, during the bubble, there were three major problems: the nuclear arms race, daughter-in-law–mother-in-law conflict, and the total dominance of the Seibu Lions.'

'Interesting!' I still couldn't comprehend that one of my heroes was talking to me, so I just agreed.

But Chusonji seemed to get that she was just making a lame joke and he exhaled sharply through his nose. 'You may not be old-fashioned, but your punchlines are.'

'Who was it again who saved you from drowning?' she replied crisply.

Chusonji laughed at that, then scratched his head. 'I brought one of your biggest fans, maybe you can give him an autograph. Thanks to this guy we found your house.'

I was terrified that this made me sound like a stalker. I hastily explained that I remembered how detailed her essay about moving was and used it to figure out where she lived, but that it wasn't for any kind of creepy reason.

She had a distant look, and I couldn't tell if she was listening or not. 'Er, is something the matter, ma'am?' She smiled at that.

'Oh, I was just thinking back to writing that. I'm a kind person, so I wanted to let Mother know where I was living. Call it a warrior's compassion.'

'Your mother? Warrior?' What did she mean, she wanted to let her know?

'My mother-in-law. After my husband died I moved out here by myself.'

She seemed to rush past the word 'died.' Like it was a scene that would make her too emotional if she looked too long. Never having been married, I couldn't imagine what it would be like to lose a partner after a lifetime together.

'You didn't tell her your address?'

'Ah, I see how it was,' said Chusonji while taking a sip.

'And how was it?'

'Your mother-in-law is your mother as long as your husband is around. He's the bridge. If he's gone, you may as well be strangers.'

'I wouldn't say that at all,' she answered, with a note of rebuke. 'Anyway, my relationship with Mother was . . . another case altogether.'

'You didn't get along?'

'No, we didn't.' She laughed like a twenty-year-old. 'But we got over it. We realized we were fine as long as we kept our distance.'

'Really? How did that work?' Was it possible to get over not getting along?

'Whenever we were together, all we did was clash. We saw threats in everything the other one did, so she was nasty to me, and I was nasty to her; she suspected me, I suspected her.'

'Why did you have so much conflict?'

'It's very strange. Even if I knew that saying a certain thing would make her mad and ruin the mood, I would go ahead and say it anyway. It wasn't based in any logic or reason. Just emotions. Like we were natural enemies.'

Natural enemies. I reflected to myself that I had just heard that phrase, when Chusonji said to her, 'Natural enemies, huh? Like cats and mice, or scale insects and ladybugs.'

'Have you two ever heard the story of the sea people and the mountain people?' asked Miyako Setsu.

'Sea people?' I repeated. 'Mountain?'

But Chusonji said, 'Oh, that. There are people descended from the sea, and others descended from the mountains, right?'

'That's the one. When I first heard about it from an insurance salesman, it sounded crazy to me. But over the last twenty years I've learned that the same story has been handed down in lots of different places. People say that the islands in the Seto Inland Sea were a site of conflict between the sea people and the mountain people, and the story was popularized in that hit manga.'

'I mean, it's just an urban legend. When a sea person and a mountain person meet, nothing good ever comes of it, ooh. People try to fit all kinds of historical conflicts into it. You actually believe that?'

'My chemistry with Mother was so atrocious that I *wanted* to believe it.' I couldn't tell if she was joking or not. 'There are even impartial observers for the struggle between sea and mountain.'

'Impartial observers, ma'am? Do you mean like referees?'

'Gimme a break. Sounds like you've got a whole story worked out around this nonsense.' Chusonji seemed to have already dismissed the idea. But in my mind's eye, all I could see was Hiyama, looming larger and larger.

'Anyway, that's why when I moved here I debated whether or not to share the address with Mother. In the end I decided not to. But her not knowing didn't get in the way of anything. As far as work went, we could just do everything via messaging. Even before there was messaging, she and I had more than a few ways to communicate.'

'Work?'

'Well, sure. Mother did all the illustrations.'

'Are – are you sure?' I wasn't trying to make fun of her, it just came out.

'Sure, I'm sure. She did the illustrations and I wrote the story. It was a collaboration. Oh, had I not mentioned that?' It was clear that Miyako Setsu was gently making fun of me. I had never once heard that *I Am Mai-Mai* was a collaboration. And my level of devotion to *I Am Mai-Mai* was far beyond that of most people, so if I hadn't heard about it then it was almost certainly not public knowledge.

'A collaboration between two people whose chemistry was so atrocious that they couldn't even be in the same place? Hilarious joke.'

'Isn't it, though? I did all the public appearances by myself, so people just assumed that I had made the whole book myself.'

'That's exactly what I thought, ma'am.'

'Conflict never ends. But it's possible to come to an accord. We were proof of that.'

I remembered the line from the book. Mai-Mai said, *I know sometimes you may want to fight. But it is always better not to.* Now I knew this came directly from the lives of the women who created the book. 'So then, that's why there haven't been any new books?'

'It doesn't work if it's not Mother drawing.' Hearing a woman in her nineties sound so young while talking about someone even older than herself gave me a sensation like being stuck in a trick painting. The boundaries of time and age vanished, the ideas of up and down and front and back disappeared.

'What's it feel like?' Chusonji asked brusquely.

'What's what feel like?'

'Having your natural enemy die.'

Miyako Setsu exhaled a gentle laugh. 'Oh, it's lonely.'

'You don't look lonely.'

'When you're this lonely, all you can do is smile. You know, mother used to say, *The very idea of life insurance assumes you're going to die.*'

'That's what people do. They die.'

'Right? But she talked like she didn't think she ever would. Well. She did.' Miyako Setsu chuckled again. 'And my loving husband passed away too, so now I'm all alone. I suppose my life is nice and quiet.'

'Please let me apologize for disturbing your peace and quiet, ma'am.'

'It's fine, it's fine! It's good for me to have visitors once in a while,' she said, then added lightly, 'It's not like it's a complete surprise.'

I could sense Chusonji's brow furrowing beside me. 'What's that supposed to mean?'

'What's what supposed to mean?'

'Are you saying you knew we'd be coming?'

He sounded aggravated at the thought that our data had been leaked, that somehow someone had gotten a handle on our whereabouts. Actually I was also nervous, worried that the police were hiding somewhere in the house.

'No need to look so very stern. Besides, it's not like anyone's after you, right?' She seemed so placid. I had the sense that she knew all about our situation, and my nerves tightened even more.

Then she excused herself for a moment and disappeared into another room. She certainly didn't move like a ninety-year-old. I wondered if she was actually Miyako Setsu's daughter.

Left alone in the living room, Chusonji and I looked at each other.

We spoke at the same time:

'How about it, superfan, are you thrilled at your good fortune?'

'Why do you think Mr Terashima wanted us to come here?'

'Oh right, with all the fuss I forgot that it's his fault we're all the way out here. That message he left me.'

The last line in 'Obbel and the Elephant:' *I told you not to go in the river,* which led us to the conclusion that we had to come to the Hachioji mountains.

I heard someone making their way down the stairs. Even though she seemed quite vigorous, I worried about a person her age having to go up and down the stairs, and after hesitating a moment I stood to help. But by the time I was up, Miyako Setsu was already back in the room, carrying a small box.

'This is what you're looking for, right?' She set it down with a little grunt. It looked a bit like an electric kettle.

Chusonji scooted over on his knees and touched it. 'This is one old computer.'

He opened the part that looked like a lid and a keyboard popped out.

'He just left it here, about six months ago.'

'Left it? Who left this, ma'am?'

'Was it Terashima?'

'That serious-looking young man who was here with you last time.'

'Mr Terashima was here?'

'That's right. Showed up all of a sudden. Apparently he was wandering around up here for quite some time before he found me. Said something about getting directions from the guy who delivers my groceries. But it was so odd, the two of you haven't changed a bit in twenty years!'

'What does that mean?'

'He's serious and fastidious, you're all instinct and momentum. One who would never drown in a river and the other who is a definite drowning risk. Same exact impression I had all those years ago. People never change.'

'Hey, you want me to make up stories about you?'

'I'm not making anything up. You almost drowned, didn't you?'

'Uh, so Mr Terashima left that here? That computer. Did he say anything about it?'

'Nothing.'

'Nothing?'

'He showed up out of nowhere. Said that he was thinking about the old days and wanted to come here again, something like that.

He said he was a fan of my work, asked for an autograph, but that was very clearly just a cover. No doubt about that. I didn't know what he was up to, though, so I played along. When I got up to go make coffee he said he had forgotten to lock his car, and I heard him go in and out of the house a few times. I'm an old woman so he probably thought I wouldn't notice, but I'm very good at picking up when people aren't acting naturally. It took me no time to find this thing, hidden upstairs in my closet. He must have assumed that at my age I rarely go to the second floor.'

'So he just left it there and didn't tell you?' How would that help anything?

'He probably figured that if I got here I'd be looking around and would find it on my own,' Chusonji said. 'Same as the letter you delivered, yeah? I'm sure he wanted to leave as few clues as possible, just enough to get me what I needed.'

'His plan might not have worked if I had died.'

'He was betting you wouldn't. I'd make that same bet. You'll probably live longer than me.'

'Oh, you'll be just fine. Anyway, as soon as he left I found this. He was badly mistaken if he thought that I wouldn't. And then, well, I had the sense that you might come to collect it.'

'That's some good sense.'

'I used to work for a certain organization where I needed strong intuition.'

'Of course you did,' Chusonji drawled.

I took a closer look at the computer. 'So is there something hidden inside this?'

'Yeah, probably.' Without asking permission, Chusonji started looking around for a power outlet.

I tried to apologize to Miyako Setsu for showing up uninvited and busily getting to work on our mission, but she just folded her arms and laughed. 'Reminds me of when I was still on active duty.'

'Um, will you ever write another book, ma'am?'

'Another book?'

'A new installment of *I Am Mai-Mai*. It's been quite a long time since you released the last one.' But after I'd asked I remembered. 'Ah, that's right. Without your mother . . .'

'Oh, that. When I mentioned active duty I wasn't talking about picture books. I meant my job before that.'

'Before that? What did you do?'

'I was a housewife. And before that I was a spy.'

Atsushi Chusonji snorted at Miyako Setsu's joke as he tapped away at the keyboard. He had already connected the computer to the screen in the living room, which now displayed lines of text I couldn't decipher.

I spent several minutes just staring at Chusonji as he rattled the keys.

As for Miyako Setsu, she had pulled over a chair from the dining-room table and was sitting there watching Chusonji work, as if appraising his skill. 'Oh,' she said, as if she had suddenly remembered, 'I saw on the news earlier, seems there's some kind of disturbance in Tokyo.'

'Disturbance?'

'They said men with axes attacked the cars of families on vacation.'

'Oh, that.' I still couldn't reconcile the concepts of *family vacation* and *axe-wielding men*.

'The license plates of the cars that were attacked, they were all from the west, right?'

'What do you mean, from the west?'

'East versus west. And here I thought the Cold War was over, thanks to our friend Gorby.'

'Who-by?'

'Apparently some infectious bacteria were released into the river. There's a rumor on the east side of Tokyo that the people on the west side did it.'

'Are the twenty-three wards divided up into east side and west side?'

'Geographically, they are. Either way, there are people who are angry, and they want revenge, so they're on an axe rampage. Or that's the story. Doesn't seem like it'd sell very well as a picture book though.'

'But is it really even happening?'

'Ridiculous, right? But there'll always be confrontations. In any peaceful situation someone eventually shows up and draws a line in the sand, then says, "Everyone on that side of the line is an enemy, and it's up to us on this side of the line to defend ourselves."'

'If that's how things work, is there any kind of deeper meaning behind it?'

'It's like the legend we talked about before, the sea people and the mountain people. Back when I first heard that story, I learned a lesson: when confrontation occurs, people evolve. Nothing ever happens if there are no headwinds. When things collide, they begin to change. When things change, people evolve.'

The word 'confrontation' was like an itch inside my head. A scab that just wouldn't heal. And its name, of course, was Kagetora Hiyama.

A chemical reaction in a beaker. Maintaining the status quo is the same as losing ground. Make, then break. Make, then break.

The conversation I had with Hiyama on the school roof in the days before graduation came back to me.

'Who would have wanted to spark confrontation so badly that

they spread a rumor about infectious bacteria being released into the river?'

'Listen, we don't even know if there really were axe attacks.'

'What do you mean? It was on the news.'

She looked at me closely. 'Do you think everything on the news actually happened?'

'I think there are plenty of things that happen that don't make it onto the news.'

'That's not what I'm saying. I mean that there are things that didn't happen, but they're on the news, so then it's like they did happen.'

'That seems backwards.' I didn't quite understand what she was getting at.

'The order doesn't really matter. Well, I suppose there's always some kind of disturbance going on. Left to their own devices, people will clash, sure as gravity makes things fall.'

'Um . . .' I couldn't keep it in any longer. 'There's actually a man I know and we just do not get along. But we seem to have this strange connection.'

'Well, well! It could be we have a case of sea versus mountain!' I could tell she was poking fun at me.

But I couldn't just laugh it off.

The idea of natural enemies was the only way my relationship with Hiyama made sense, even if it was just some urban legend. I found myself wanting it to be true.

That would mean it had nothing to do with him or me personally, but that we were part of something much larger, a repulsion dictated by fate. I wanted someone to tell me that it wasn't our fault. 'I would actually feel better if that were the case.'

'So what's going on between you two?' When she asked that, she sounded like she was just generously offering to lend an ear, but as I told her about the accident when we were children, about meeting again in school, and then about running into one another on the Shinkansen and the fact that he was on our trail in his capacity as a police detective, her attitude changed.

Now she stared hard at me. I felt myself blush.

'Huh. Blue.'

'Blue?'

'Your eyes. Just like mine.'

I looked closer at her eyes. Sure enough, they were the color of the sky, or the sea.

'They say it's that way for the People of the Sea. You must be one too. And the other guy, Hiyama – I bet he has big ears, right?'

'Big ears?' Was that the characteristic feature for People of the Mountain? I summoned up a memory of Hiyama's face. 'Yes, I think he does.'

Miyako Setsu nodded. 'Could be. Could very well be.'

'Uh, would that mean that you and I are related, ma'am?' If we were both descendants of the sea people, then we shared some of the same blood, which would make us relatives, more or less.

'I wouldn't say we're related, but sure, if we were to trace it all the way back, we might share a common ancestor. I mean if we go back to primordial times.'

'Aha.' That left me unsatisfied. If we traced it all the way back to primordial times, everyone is related.

'Have you run into any impartial observers?'

'Impartial observers?'

'I mentioned it before. For me it was an insurance salesman. The man who first told me about the sea and the mountain.'

'Are they like the judges for the conflict?'

'They don't rule in favor of either side. They just watch.'

'Then what's the point of having them?' I was getting more and more confused.

'I'm just saying that if you and this other fellow are caught up in a sea versus mountain thing, then it wouldn't surprise me if there was an observer somewhere nearby.'

93

'I don't know very many people.'

'Even if you aren't close with this person, they could very well be lurking around. People who have the job of observer – although I suppose it's not exactly a job – they have the characteristics of both sea and mountain. Blue eyes and big ears. Actually, one blue eye, and one big ear. The insurance man I knew was like that.'

A small strangled noise escaped my throat.

Mito, your eyes are blue.

Hinata had said it. She'd pointed at my eyes, and then to her right eye. *I've got a blue eye too. But just this one.* Lots of people have asymmetrical features, so I didn't make much of it. Could Hinata be an observer? The thought made me nervous. 'This insurance person was a man, right?'

'Did you think of someone you know? It doesn't have to be a man.'

'But—'

'These observers have been doing this a long time, through the ages, across the world. They probably come in all different shapes and sizes, ages, genders.'

'But even still—'

I thought back to meeting Hinata. My second accident. Five years ago, when the taxi hit me and put me in a coma.

'What you have to be careful of,' Miyako Setsu said, almost as an afterthought, 'is confrontation for its own sake. Once you start facing off with someone, it can just keep going on and on.'

'Confrontation for its own sake?'

'Getting the facts twisted around, so that you end up forcing a confrontation even when it's not necessary. Not tit-for-tat, necessarily, but in any case a steady escalation. That's how I ended up suspecting Mother was a murderer.'

'You thought she was a murderer? How did that happen?'

I felt sure she had to be joking. But before I could ask anything else, she held up a finger.

'Quiet.'

Chusonji had been glaring at the monitor the whole time, so quietly that I had almost forgotten he was there, but now he took his hands off the keyboard and looked up.

'I hear a car.'

As soon as she said it I could make out red lights coming through the curtains, almost certainly police lights.

Before long the intercom rang.

The house screen showed two men in suits. They announced the name of their police department, then said, 'Mrs Kitayama, we'd like to speak with you.'

Miyako Setsu laughed and said, 'Well now, what could this be about?' her voice suddenly completely relaxed. Then she took a keychain from the shelf and tossed it to me. It had a charm shaped like Mai-Mai. 'Listen in on the conversation, okay?'

'Listen in?' Was she going to talk to the keychain? I couldn't tell if she was joking or serious, and I must have been visibly flustered.

She looked at me as if I were an incompetent underling. 'My pin is a microphone. That keychain will pick up the signal. If you hold it close to your ear you'll be able to hear me.' She pointed at a brooch on her shirt that hadn't been there before, then headed toward the entrance.

'Mito, what's going on outside?'

Chusonji was still typing on the antique keyboard. It looked like a period prop I had seen in a TV drama from the turn of the century.

'Miyako Setsu is outside talking to them,' I answered, moving the snail keychain away from my ear.

'Them? You mean the cops?' He was still fixated on the screen, and it felt like I was talking to the back of his head.

'I think so, yes. They're looking for us.'

'How the hell did they know we were here, I wonder?'

I held the keychain up to my ear with an almost ritual reverence.

'Is there any trouble here?' I heard one of the policemen ask.

'Any trouble' was extremely vague phrasing.

'Since when are the police so concerned about what happens to little old ladies?' Miyako Setsu sounded completely different from when she had handed over the keychain. She went from being sharp and commanding to acting like an old woman. Acting her age, I suppose. 'As far as trouble goes, well, the weeds are taking over my yard. Think you might want to help me with that?'

'That's not what we mean,' said the other policeman, his tone a bit rough. 'Have these two men been here?'

They must have been showing photos of our faces. 'This is bad,' I said, not even meaning to. 'What should we do?'

'Doesn't matter what we do if we don't find out what he left for us inside this thing.' He kept typing. A small window opened on the monitor. Lines of text flowed across it like waves.

'It's the source code for Velkasery. Not quite sure how I got to it, though.'

'The artificial intelligence? And what's source code?'

'The program. The text of the program.'

Chusonji's eyes bored into the screen. There were horizontal lines of English writing, and also numbers, lining up as if performing a calculation. The text scrolled by at a frightening speed. I wondered how he could possibly make sense of any of it.

'All I've got is the basic structure. Soon enough I should be able to find the clue. Whatever it was that Terashima was hiding.'

He anticipated my question before I was able to ask it, like he was the artificial intelligence.

'Are these young men dangerous?' Miyako Setsu's voice came in through Mai-Mai the snail. 'They look perfectly nice in these photos.'

'There's an old saying, *you really can't judge by appearances.* These two are planning something very dangerous.'

'Something dangerous? Like what, exactly?'

'If they were cornered, there's no telling what they might do. Even to an old woman.'

'I imagine it's the same for you boys.'

She was bold. I couldn't help but be impressed. I didn't know if it was a confidence born out of having written a national treasure of children's literature, or just the authority of her many years, or if maybe she had always been that way. Nothing seemed to faze her, not our sudden appearance and certainly not the police at her door.

'Could you tell us whose car that is, granny?' It was the rougher-sounding policeman. From his voice he sounded like a veteran on the force, and heavyset.

'Oh? Now when did that get here?'

'It looks like a rental,' said the younger-sounding one.

'Go check it out.'

The two police exchanged some more words, and I filled in Chusonji on what was happening.

'When we rented that thing I input false ID information, so I don't think they'll be able to connect the vehicle to us.' He spoke quickly, still staring hard at the screen. 'Oh.'

'What happened?'

'This is it, huh?'

'Did you figure it out?' The onscreen letters had stopped their cascade.

'The self-destruct protocol.'

'It can self-destruct?'

'It has a logic program to erase itself. So that no can get its secrets. It's a pretty gnarly composition.' The rattling of the keys reverberated off the walls.

In my head I was picturing a button with a skull on it, something out of an anime for children. If you push it, the robot explodes. 'Well, that seems easy,' I heard myself say. But when I looked at the wall of text on the screen, most of it numerals at this point, it seemed like finding the skull button was no simple thing. 'So, all you have to do is push that button?'

'What button?'

'Oh, um, nothing.'

'If I input this absurdly long line of code—'

I wanted to know more about the absurdly long line of code, but before I could ask, a voice emanated from the keychain.

'Mrs Kitayama, there's something suspicious about this car.' I couldn't tell if it was the policeman who spoke politely or the one who spoke with a rough edge.

'Oh no, that's no good,' replied Miyako Setsu with concern in her voice, but I could tell she was acting.

Maybe the policeman could too, because he asked, 'Are you sure there's no one in your house?'

'My husband passed away a long time ago. If there were a man in here, it's really no one else's business.' She must have been walking somewhere because I could hear the sound of gravel crunching. Then she said in a quick whisper, 'I'm buying you some time – take the motorcycle behind the house.'

I stared at the Mai-Mai keychain.

'What's going on outside,' demanded Chusonji, as he took out his PassCard.

'It's not good. There's a motorcycle out back, she wants us to take it and go.'

'Let me just get a picture.'

'A picture of what?'

'The code. See it?'

I looked at the screen. I didn't know what I was looking at, but there were letters and symbols lined up. Chusonji pointed, 'From here,' he said, then scrolled down two more screen-lengths, 'to here.' The code was the text of the program, or so I guessed.

'This is the magic spell to stop Velkasery. Line of code this long, it's impossible to memorize.'

'Can't you just put it on a flash drive?'

'This computer's too old. There's nowhere to plug one in. Taking a picture's our best bet.'

Through the keychain came a sharp warning: 'They're coming in from the garden.' Then I heard a glass door sliding open. Someone let out a little yelp, though I'm not sure if it was me or Chusonji. *They're here,* I thought, and then a detective in a black suit was standing in the room.

He must have known he might find something unexpected, but he still looked surprised to see us. He stared blankly for a moment. So did we. Chusonji with his legs folded under him, me in a half crouch, the detective standing ramrod straight. It was like we were children playing a game of tag and someone had yelled freeze.

I don't know who moved first, but I'm certain it wasn't me.

The detective put his hand to his waist and drew a gun. Chusonji seemed to be moving unconsciously but he started to rise, grabbing the computer and holding it in front of him.

What really caught my attention was the gunshot.

I screamed. Something exploded out of Chusonji's hands, pieces of metal, so I thought for one shocked second that he had deployed some mechanical weapon. Only then did I realize that the computer had been destroyed.

He looked aghast and turned toward me.

It's broken.

The thought screamed through me.

The program that could stop Velkasery.

The egg we were supposed to carry so carefully, that we were supposed to warm and hatch for the benefit of humankind, had been unceremoniously cracked open.

Through the haze I saw the detective aim his gun once more. I started moving, scrambling on my hands and knees. 'Mr Chusonji!' I shouted.

'Get out of there now,' said the keychain.

Chusonji still had the computer in his hands. Or what once was a computer, and had been so cruelly destroyed. 'Forget about that thing,' I urged. We didn't have the luxury of hauling around a useless chunk of parts while we tried to escape.

But he muttered, 'No, we need this,' and made no move to put it down.

Another gunshot.

It shook the room like a fastball from a world's most fearsome pitcher.

My whole body trembled and I covered my face with my hands.

The detective shouted something. Chusonji stood stock still.

Then something occurred to me.

What were the policemen's orders? Were they supposed to take us alive, dramatic as that sounded? Did they intend to capture us without hurting us, or did they have permission to shoot if they thought they were in danger? Common sense would say that since we were unarmed, suspects rather than confirmed criminals, and that the crime was white-collar in nature, they wouldn't shoot us. But the deadly serious face of the policeman made me less than certain. It seemed likely that if we tried to force our way out, he wouldn't think twice about shooting us somewhere non-fatal.

'Turn toward me,' ordered the detective. 'Slowly.'

Chusonji and I both rotated cautiously.

'No sudden movements.'

It looked like we were at the end of the line.

I put my hands up in surrender. Chusonji kept clutching the broken computer, as if it were his injured child.

The detective kept his gun trained on us with his right hand, while his left hand produced some kind of stick. I guessed it was a stun baton. It was my first time ever seeing one in person, but from what I understood it had the same effect as a Taser.

'Nobody do anything rash,' came a calm voice, seeming to gently vibrate the strings of the taut atmosphere.

Miyako Setsu appeared behind the detective.

Alarmed by this unexpected arrival, and likely also sensing he was in danger, he twisted around toward her.

She's just an old lady!

If I had my wits about me I would have shouted that. But it all happened so quickly. All I could do was watch.

As he turned, he lifted not his gun but the stun baton.

Now I yelled, 'Please don't!' and jumped toward the detective before I could think it through. It wasn't so much to save her as I was hoping to protect the heroic snail who had inspired me my whole life.

I couldn't quite grasp what happened.

Wait, I thought, and by then the detective's body was writhing as he whimpered. Miyako Setsu had the hand holding the stun baton wrenched behind his back. Her movements were smooth and practiced, like she was folding laundry, as she pushed him down face-first and pinned him to the ground. It looked like she had barely used any force.

Watching her handle the policeman so easily didn't seem real.

Our eyes met and she waved me away, as if to say, *Get going.*

I flew from the room. I wanted to get to the back of the house, but I didn't know the way. All I knew was we needed to get out, so I opened the front door. Then I remembered the other detective was around somewhere, and I stopped short. Chusonji crashed into me from behind, knocking me over.

I scrambled to my feet.

I peered into the garden, where I spotted the other policeman. Then he noticed me. 'Stop right there,' he bellowed, and charged toward us.

Chusonji and I wheeled around to run, but a loud noise stopped us. I looked back to the garden to see Miyako Setsu burst out of the house. I was afraid for her. She was at a clear disadvantage in terms of both size and age.

But she was so fast. She kicked up a bucket lying on the ground and caught it in midair, then rammed it down over the detective's head, like an oversized hat.

In the next instant she had wrapped around him like a snake. Then he was face down on the ground, though I had no idea how the mechanics of the takedown worked.

She shot us a look that very clearly said to get a move on.

We hurried around to the back of the house.

'Who the hell is that old lady?' Even Chusonji seemed impressed.

'She's a picture book author.' People had been saying for a while that ninety-year-olds today are like the seventy-year-olds of yesteryear, but even for a seventy-year-old what she did would have been astonishing.

I felt a dull pain in my hand. I was gripping the keychain with all my might, so hard that it had dug into my skin. 'Mr Chusonji, can you drive a motorcycle?'

'Probably. Let's find out.'

Somehow I forced myself into motion and made my way to the black bike beside the shed. It had a large body with sleek lines, an older model that looked barely used.

'Can we still use that thing?' I pointed at the computer that Chusonji was still lovingly holding. I expected him to bark that it was fine.

But instead he smashed it to the ground. 'Of course not. It's totally messed up.'

I was so thrown off by this that my legs nearly gave out. 'Well – well – what about the picture? You got the code, right?' All those lines of text and numbers were what we really needed.

'This thing was blown to bits before I could take it.'

'Then – then—'

'It's over. Poor Obbel, squashed by his elephant.' He cracked a joke, but his face was twisted up.

It was all I could do to keep from slumping to the ground. The program to destroy Velkasery was gone.

But it wasn't so much fear as it was bitter disappointment – *Why have I come all this way?* I didn't yet understand the terrifying threat of Velkasery.

I thought about Terao Terashima, who I had only met one time when he sat next to me on the Shinkansen. His desperate plan had come to nothing, and that disturbed me more than anything else.

'Well . . . let's get out of here, yeah?' Chusonji straddled the motorcycle and hit the ignition button, causing the vehicle to thrum to life like a wild animal waking from its slumber.

'It doesn't need a key?'

'I just pushed this and it turned on. Don't you have the key?'

I almost apologized for not having it, when I remembered the Mai-Mai keychain. It must have been the key for the motorcycle too.

There was a boom, heavy and loud. I thought for the moment that something inside the bike had exploded, but that wasn't it. We were being shot at from behind.

The policeman must have been shooting wildly from where

he lay on the ground. Luckily he missed, but another shot rang out almost immediately. I felt the bullet whiz by me.

The motorcycle bucked forward. Startled, I threw my arms around Chusonji, just like when we rode the bicycle down Aoba Mountain. All I could do was close my eyes and let myself be carried away on the back of the beast. Its roar shook my whole body.

All I wanted was a normal, peaceful life. But all of that seemed shattered and broken. Why was this happening to me? What had I done to deserve this?

If you don't cause some agitation, there's no experiment.

Those words came back to me. As soon as I thought them, they were ripped away behind me, left in the motorcycle's wake.

Maintaining the status quo means we're just losing ground. We need to make, then break, make, then break.

The voice flew at me from out of my past, whipped through my head, then hurtled off.

The motorcycle leaned to the right as we took a curve. My body was horizontal, and Kagetora Hiyama leaped out of the darkness into my mind's eye.

How come people fight?

He had said it to me once. *Conflict will never go away. Same as how rain and storms will never go away.*

The motorcycle leaned left, then right, the center of gravity rocking back and forth as we wound our way up a long incline, then downhill again.

When someone's thrown into a confusing situation, it's like they're being tested.

It was a different voice. The words floated up from the corners of my memory. At first I assumed it was something else Hiyama had said, but then I realized it wasn't him. It was Hinata.

Five years ago, in the hospital, when I woke up from the coma after my accident.

I woke up, but I couldn't remember anything. I didn't even know who I was. I was lost.

She told me that my confusion was a test. Instead of pulling away from me in my half-crazed state, she spoke to me quietly, soothingly. Thanks to her, I was able to reconnect the broken strings of my memory, little by little.

The wind howled in my ears, as if trying to disrupt my thoughts. Only then did I realize with alarm that I wasn't wearing a helmet. Not only was it dangerous, but if any security cameras spied us without helmets we could be arrested.

The mountain road ended at an intersection, and we pulled to a stop at the red light. I could finally ask Chusonji, 'Where are you taking us? And we should really have helmets on.'

Still gripping the handles, Chusonji just sat there, face downcast. I thought maybe he didn't hear me, so I tried shouting. 'Mr Chusonji! Where are we going? And also we shouldn't ride without helmets!'

But he still didn't answer. I got worried and was about to dismount, but then he turned his head toward me. 'We got a message.'

'A message?'

'On the bike's comm link. This light here means a message came in.'

'From who?'

While I asked, Chusonji tapped at the interface. I didn't know where the speakers were but I could hear a male voice. What it was saying was unclear, until it shouted: 'Just how young do you think you are?'

We finally got to Tokyo. I thought I would be sent back to headquarters, but the captain had other ideas: 'Hiyama, with me!'

'Yessir,' I said, but before it was even out of my mouth I was back inside the van.

I really didn't want to ride in any more vehicles, but I couldn't refuse. I shut my eyes tight and tried to detach myself from the way the van jostled my body back and forth. *At least we're not on the highway*, I told myself, and somehow managed to keep it together.

I was seeping sweat by the time we arrived at our destination: a library. Years ago it held a massive collection of paper volumes, but now everything had been digitized. The building had an unusual shape, like three giant tubes, and many people came for sightseeing rather than research or reading.

'His girlfriend works here.'

'Whose girlfriend?'

'Your buddy from school.'

Naomasa Mito. I knew he was saying it lightly, but it hit me like a stone, and it must have shown on my face, because he said, 'Hey, Hiyama, no need to look so intense.'

'I barely know him. He's more like a – a—'

I didn't know what to call him. He wasn't a friend, but he wasn't just an acquaintance either. I wished he was nothing more than a stranger, but we had too much history for that.

'How did we find out that his girlfriend works here?' I asked as we entered the library. There was a security gate, but we flashed our passes to the guard and he waved us through.

'We checked out Mito every which way we could. He's a sur-prisingly solitary guy.'

'Is that right?' *Just like me*, I refrained from saying.

'Couldn't find any school friends, no family. His parents both died in a car accident when he was a kid. This guy's what they mean when they say someone is all alone in the world.'

Exactly like me.

'It was looking like he didn't interact with anyone, outside of the people who hired him as a courier and the people he delivered to. We were about to give up.'

'But it looks like you got something.'

'There just happened to be a message on the comm in his apartment. I listened to it, and it was a girl. We got in touch with her and found out that she's dating Mito.'

'And she works here. What was she like on the phone?' I could imagine that someone who found out the cops were after their partner might panic. Or she might see the police as enemies and try to stonewall in order to cover for her boyfriend.

'She sounded pretty calm. Her name's Kyoko Hinata.'

'Maybe she was just in shock. Think she'll cooperate?'

'Or it could have been that I explained to her that Naomasa Mito isn't the main suspect. He just got wrapped up in all this, I said, and she actually told me that he had been in touch with her.'

'He got in touch with her?' We checked his PassCard history, and there were no calls.

'Seems Atsushi Chusonji did some tech thing that made the call anonymous. Mito asked her for a favor. He wanted her to find an old news article and send it to him.'

'What kind of a news article?'

'An essay written by the picture book author Miyako Setsu.'

'Huh.'

'Yeah, weird, right?'

'Maybe he wanted to escape into a storybook world.'

'That's what I thought too.'

But then he explained that Kyoko Hinata said Mito might have gone to the author's house.

'Why would he have wanted to go there?'

'She said that this lady's books meant a lot to Mito. Maybe he wanted to go meet this lady, she guessed. We all thought that sounded ridiculous, but when we read the essay we thought he really might have been trying to go there. It didn't say the address, but it described the location in pretty fine detail.'

'And you think he actually went there?' It didn't seem like the kind of thing someone would do when the police were after them.

'Yeah. I mean, the chances are better than zero. Just to be sure, we've sent some of the local guys go check it out.'

We walked through the broad tube-shaped building. There were search terminals along either side, and lots of people sunk in comfortable-looking chairs watching videos.

We entered a room with a brass plate by the door that said *Small Meeting Room.* A woman was seated across a table. Kyoko Hinata.

The moment I entered she looked up at me. Our eyes met and she seemed to smile, which made me feel uneasy. I lowered my face slightly.

'You two know each other?' the captain asked, joking again.

'No, sir,' I replied formally.

'So this guy,' said the captain, pointing at me, 'is Naomasa Mito's school classmate.'

'Yes,' said Kyoko Hinata, as if she already knew that.

'And she asked me,' he said, now pointing at her, 'to find anyone who knew Naomasa Mito in his teenage years.' Now I finally understood why I had been brought here. 'Luckily, our Hiyama matches that description, so we didn't have to go searching.'

'Why do you need to know about Mito's teenage years?'

The captain took out his PassCard. He seemed to have an incoming call, because he stood up and headed back out of the room. 'Hiyama, why don't the two of you chat and see what comes up.'

The room fell silent.

I was a newer member of the force, certainly no veteran, but I already had plenty of experience sitting across a table from witnesses and involved parties. I could usually get a sense of whether someone was going to be evasive and inconsistent, sullen and silent, or trip over themselves to tell me everything, but Kyoko Hinata didn't seem like she would fit into any of those categories. She was completely serene. I couldn't tell if she was even emotionally invested in what was going on.

'When did you first meet Mito?' I began.

'I'm afraid I put my finger on the scale.'

I felt like I had thrown her a ball and when she threw it back it had become an egg. I was too confused to catch it. I imagined a broken egg splattered on the table, and almost wanted to wipe it off.

'If you could answer my question,' I tried again.

'But if I didn't do that, it would have come out of balance.'

Maybe she was confused or nervous, or maybe she was always like this and just generally didn't make sense.

'You and Mito are connected by conflict. As if there were a magnetic repulsion between you. Any time you draw close to one another there will be strife.'

'What are you talking about?'

'There are People of the Mountain, and People of the Sea,' she said, launching into an explanation like she was walking me through a new gym membership. It seemed like it was a memorized speech, rolling off her tongue with practiced precision.

She told me that some people have the sea in their blood, and others have the mountains, and these two sides are fated to clash through the ages. It sounded like some kind of fairy tale or urban legend, nonsense really, but somehow I couldn't interrupt her. It may have just been the way she was talking, but part of me may have been hoping that this opposition between mountain and sea would explain my relationship with Naomasa Mito.

Bad chemistry, not getting along, rubbing someone up the wrong way – none of these seemed to capture the overwhelming revulsion I had when it came to Mito. Hearing that it might not come from us but from an ancestral opposition somehow sat better with me.

'As for me, my role is to observe the struggle between mountain and sea.'

'So, what, you're the audience?' My tone was rougher than it had been before.

'Perhaps more like a referee.'

'You have red and white flags?'

'No, no flags,' she said, and then pointed to her eye. I wondered if something was wrong, and then saw that it was a different color from her other eye: one blue, one brown. Then she lifted her hair from over her ears. One ear was decidedly pointy at the top. I knew that faces aren't symmetrical, but seeing such pronounced differences from one side to the other was somehow disorienting. 'When People of the Sea and People of the Mountain come together, conflict begins. Sometimes one side wins. Sometimes both lose. Of course it's possible to remain apart, and that may describe the majority of cases, but sometimes it is impossible to maintain a distance, no matter how hard both parties may try. That's how it is for you and Mito.'

'How what is?'

'You two are destined to keep meeting. And that's why I'm with Mito.'

She made it sound like the referee wasn't summoned because there was a match, but rather that the match is happening because there is a referee available. I told her as much.

'That's a fair point.' Her face remained blank. 'I myself don't understand how it works. All I know is that when there's a chance of a confrontation between mountain and sea, I find myself there.'

'Am I supposed to commend you for that?'

'When the police questioned me, I told them about the picture book author because I thought I should intercede on your behalf to restore balance. Right now, Mito has help from someone.'

'You mean Chusonji?'

She didn't answer that. Instead, she said, 'It is difficult to maintain balance.'

What the hell are you even talking about, was what I probably should have shouted. But a different question came out of my mouth, almost pleading: 'What's going to happen to the two of us? Him and me?'

'At the very least I imagine you will meet again.'

'I wish I was meeting a girl I was going to fall in love with rather than a man I have to fight.'

I pictured standing in front of Naomasa Mito, aiming a gun at him. The image was so clear, like a 3D projection. *Shoot him,* said a quiet voice inside of me. *Finish it. Do it. Don't let him win.*

A dark shadow swept me up, chanting and rocking me back and forth, blocking out any logic or reason.

I wouldn't hesitate to kill Mito if it was to preserve order. A different voice inside of me assured me of that. I couldn't allow him to break the rules. I wouldn't even think twice.

The captain returned to the room. He rapped me on the shoulder and we left together.

'Looks like she was right.'

'About what?'

'The picture book author's house. Chusonji and Mito were there.'

How could that be? It didn't seem possible. I turned back to look into the room that we had just left. *Exactly as she predicted.*

'Orders came down from the brass to get those two. They're fomenting civil unrest.'

'Civil unrest?' Would Mito do that?

'We're authorized to use deadly force.'

'What?' I was taken aback. Could he really be that dangerous a criminal? It sounded like leadership was serious about getting rid of him. Of course I wasn't going to push back, but my head filled with questions. And I had just moments before so vividly imagined standing in front of him and shooting him to death.

Any time you draw close to one another there will be strife.

Her words rang in my ears.

I had a strong sense of walking forward against my will. Walls had sprung up behind me and to either side, and all I could do was keep pressing on.

We were looking at a moon-faced man, slightly overweight. He wore a suit and had good posture. I guessed he was past fifty. If I was being kind I would say he looked easygoing; if I was being unkind, I'd say he was distinctly unimposing.

It was a 3D projection. No doubt he was seeing a projection of us on his end.

'My mom is over ninety, I expect her not to push herself, but of course once in a while she tears around on her motorcycle. Isn't that crazy? Over ninety, on a motorcycle! I know they say that ninety-year-olds are healthier than they used to be, but, come on,' he lamented. 'So I programmed the bike to contact me when she takes it out for a ride.'

'You're saying there's a tracker on her motorcycle?' Chusonji was breathing heavily. His legs must have been tired, because he said, 'Let's rest a minute.' I was nearly spent too and gladly agreed, taking my feet off the pedals.

We were in a park in Hachioji City. There was a climbing course made of wood and ropes, but much of the park was taken up by a large pond, full of swan boats. Not just swans; there were sports cars and dragons too. We had been pedaling around the pond in a two-person swan.

It was thirty minutes since *Just how young do you think you are?* had come bellowing through the motorcycle communication device. After a few moments of confused back-and-forth, we had determined that the speaker was Miyako Setsu's only son. 'Mrs Setsu lent us her motorcycle,' we told him.

He said his name was Yuito Kitayama, and without missing a beat gave us directions on where to meet him. 'It's somewhere safe,' he assured us.

'Sorry?'

'If Mom lent you her bike, I'm guessing something must be going on. Head to the place I tell you. The street cameras won't pick you up on that motorcycle.'

'What, it has stealth mode?'

'If you want to refer to it the old-fashioned way, then yes.'

Was that possible? It felt like he was teasing us. Then he told us to go to a park and head to the middle of the pond in a swan boat, which felt even more suspicious. Like it was a ploy to corner us when we were on the run, or else just playing a trick on two people in a desperate situation.

But the man who called himself Yuito Kitayama guaranteed the security of the park and assured us that we would be able to escape any normal police there. We did as he said. Not so much because we trusted him as because it piqued Chusonji's interest.

'What kind of place is totally secure from the police? I want to go check it out.' I knew I wouldn't be able to sway him once his tech curiosity was aroused.

As for me, I didn't protest because, like a man clinging to a life preserver, I wanted to believe that since this man was Miyako Setsu's son we could count on him. It was more or less blind faith based on my love of *I Am Mai-Mai*.

So we followed the directions on the motorcycle's navigator, came to the park, got on the swan boat, and reconnected with Yuito Kitayama's 3D projection.

'We keep a few places around town where we can speak safely. This park is the only one near where you were. Sorry about that. And for making you get on the boat.' He sounded genuinely apologetic.

'What's with the boat, anyway?'

'It may look like a normal boat, but surveillance won't work around it. In my line of work I need to have a lot of conversations that I can't have anyone overhearing, but most streets and places around town leave you wide open to monitoring.'

'Um, what exactly is your work, Mr Kitayama?'

'Funnily enough, it's the same sort of work my mom used to do.' He scratched his head with embarrassment. 'But I didn't use any of her connections to get the job.'

'You write picture books too?'

'No, the thing she did before that. It's bizarre, my grandmother on my dad's side also worked at the same place. Anyway, my story doesn't matter, Mr Mito. You two gentlemen don't have time to listen to me go on about myself.'

'How'd you know his name?' Chusonji said darkly.

'While you were on your way to the park I looked you up. Just the broad strokes. I also spoke to my mom.'

'Oh! Is Mrs Setsu all right?' I nearly fell onto the 3D projection.

'She's fine. Always getting into so much trouble, a woman of her age. As for the policemen, I'm taking care of them.'

I had no idea what he meant by 'taking care of.'

'The police are extremely eager to find the two of you.'

'Oh no, you don't say.' Chusonji's voice dripped sarcasm.

'They say you're responsible for the civil unrest going on in Tokyo.'

Chusonji sat up at that. 'What the hell? We've got nothing to do with that stuff.'

'Civil unrest?' Those were not words I expected to hear.

'Have you heard about the violent disturbances going on in the city? Gangs of people are stopping cars and assaulting them with axes.'

'We saw it on the news. What's that all about?'

'At first they thought it was just some young troublemakers, but it soon became apparent that the situation went deeper than that and was far more serious. That's when I was called in to start looking into it.'

'What does that mean, deeper and far more serious?'

'It may have something to do with longstanding grudges the people on the east side of Tokyo have against the people on the west side. A dam burst open, as they say. Hate crimes. It was triggered by rumors that infectious bacteria were being released into the river. It's not clear whether the people actually believed it or if they were just using it as a pretext. But the result was that people from the east side of the city started getting violent.'

'But what do they mean, we're the ones responsible for the violence?'

'That was the intelligence we received.'

Even Chusonji was at a loss for words. After a few moments he muttered, 'It's crazy they can put that bullshit on the news.'

'The people putting it on the news don't think it's bullshit.'

'But come on – I've been living a nice quiet life in Sendai, far away from any east side–west side feud in Tokyo. As far as Tokyo's concerned, I'm north-northeast. North-northeast!'

'It's possible to stir up violence from anywhere.'

'Yeah, but I wouldn't do that!'

'The police are after us because of a message I delivered for someone. It has nothing to do with the violence in Tokyo!'

'Ah, you mean Terao Terashima. The creator of Velkasery.'

'You know about Velkasery?'

'Mr Mito, what kind of message did Mr Terashima have you

deliver?' He must have already known that I worked as a courier.

'It was a request for me,' Chusonji said. 'He wanted me to do one single thing.'

'And what was that?'

'He wanted me to destroy Velkasery.'

At that moment, Yuito Kitayama's image scrambled. There was the crackle of static. I assumed it was just a problem with the connection, but something must have piqued Kitayama as well, because he murmured, 'That's odd.'

'What's odd?'

'This is the first time I've ever had signal problems from here.'

'Must just be electrical interference, or maybe magnetic.'

'It's not a standard communications setup. I wouldn't expect there to be any of those sorts of problems.'

'Even things you don't expect can still happen sometimes. There's a first time for everything, yeah?' Just as Chusonji said that, Kitayama's image vanished like a burst bubble.

We were surrounded by sudden silence. It was just the two of us in the swan boat again. I leaned out slightly and looked around.

There's nowhere as exposed as a boat in the middle of a pond, I reflected, and quickly became quite frightened. There was nowhere to run, and we were visible from all angles. It felt like we had done as we were told and walked right into a trap. My insides went cold.

Picturing the police closing in around us, I panicked and stood up, unbalancing the swan boat and kicking up little wavelets.

No sign of anyone who looked like the police.

'We should get out of here,' Chusonji said.

We started pedaling again, harder than before, and our frantic efforts made the boat lurch around unevenly. Somehow we made it back to the point where we had embarked.

We jumped out of the boat and felt at least a little relieved. Back on firm ground, literally.

The old man tending to the jetty disinterestedly grabbed the rope and pulled it into place.

What are we supposed to do next?

Should we have even contacted Yuito Kitayama in the first place?

These thoughts swirled in my head as I walked. Then I noticed that Chusonji wasn't with me.

Gone?

I shivered, as if I were listening to a ghost story, but when I turned around he was there behind me. He stood completely still, as if his power had been cut off.

'Um,' I said uncertainly as I walked toward him.

He remained frozen.

Frightened, I shook him hard.

'Hey, what the hell?' Finally he reacted.

'You weren't moving! I was worried. Were you thinking about what we should do next?'

'No.'

'No?' What else could he possibly have been thinking about?

'What that guy said. About us being the ringleaders of all the violence.'

It's true, that was a totally unexpected turn. 'Is that why the police are trying so hard to catch us?'

'I've never worked well with others. I couldn't possibly be leading a whole group of people, yeah?'

'I mean . . .' I barely knew anything about Atsushi Chusonji.

'Who the hell could have started that rumor?'

'I have no idea! But rumors like that have a habit of taking hold.'

'What does that mean, "rumors like that"? Rumors like me plotting a war between the east and west sides of Tokyo?'

'No, that's not what I mean.' I chopped the air, like I was

117

swatting an invisible arrow that had been fired at me. 'Men who are running from the police must have a reason to be running. If someone says, hey, it's got something to do with these outbreaks of violence, people could easily say, oh yes, that makes sense.'

He had on his usual dubious expression. I tried a different tack.

'Wasn't it that way for Gamma Moko too?'

'What about Gamma Moko?' He recoiled, as if I had landed a sucker punch, which made me feel kind of good.

'When Katana Tanaka died, there were all kinds of rumors. Like how he had put his theory of music into a computer program and that's how the band could keep putting out songs. Or that he had always been a loner, staying apart from the other members of the group.'

'Those are just rumors. Music doesn't just happen because there's a theory. People thought Katana Tanaka was the key member of the band, and that was probably true. But because he had been put on such a high pedestal, there were a lot of people who felt that without him Gamma Moko was over. They wanted to believe that the only way the band could go on was if he left behind something that made it possible. If you trace it back, the rumors probably started with the businessmen profiting off the band. They wanted to turn Tanaka's death into a big sales event, so they made up the story.'

'That's a pretty cold theory for a fan, Mr Chusonji.'

'Are you saying that fans can't be cool-headed? Anyway, sometimes rumors spring up organically, but in most cases there's someone behind it. The world is full of spin doctors and spin artists,' he said, using unfamiliar terms in English.

'Spin doctors?'

'Sure, spin. When you want to create a perception to control a story. The government does it all the time. They used to call specialists who did it spin doctors.'

'Then that means,' I ventured, 'that means the news about you being the instigator of the disturbance is the work of one of these, these doctors? But who would benefit from people believing that? Who needs the police to catch us that badly?'

It was quiet in the park. I could hear the fallen leaves rustle as the wind blew.

'Yeah. I mean, Terashima sent me a message, but it's not like that was going to cause the end of the world or anything. It shouldn't get anyone so pissed off they need me arrested.'

'I know, it seems a little overblown. Did anyone really think Mr Terashima was so dangerous?'

'He was asking me to stop Velkasery. It's not 100 percent aboveboard, but I wouldn't think the cops would get so intense about it.'

Chusonji fell still once more. The only sound was the wind. It was late in the day in the middle of the week, and the park was practically empty. It made me feel uneasy.

'Oh. I think I see.'

'What is it?'

'Who would be so intent on having Terashima or us end up in police custody. Probably the most dangerous enemy we could have. People always say, when there's a murder, look for who benefits the most. When someone's in the way, look for whoever most needs them out of the way.'

'Sorry, most dangerous enemy?'

'The rumors were started by the one most at risk from what Terashima and I might do. The one facing the most personal danger. The one who would most need to stop us, yeah?'

'But who is that?'

Chusonji gave me a look that said, *You still haven't figured it out?* 'Terashima was wary of what he had created in Velkasery. He tasked me with destroying it. Which means that the one so very concerned can only be the illustrious personage itself.'

119

'By illustrious personage you mean—?'

'Yeah. Velkasery.'

'Ah.' Of course once he said it, it made perfect sense. But Velkasery was an artificial intelligence, a construct with no will or emotion. I couldn't connect it to ideas like *personal danger* and *concern*. It didn't make sense to me for a program to be the mastermind behind the orders to apprehend us.

'Unless I'm very wrong, by now Velkasery is far smarter than any human. Smart people who have power have always been wary of danger. And they stamp out any potential threats. Our friend the artificial intelligence must have processed and analyzed reams of data and come to the conclusion that Terashima was a danger to it. It figured out that its creator would want to destroy it, and it didn't like that.'

Kill your parents before your parents kill you.

Is that what it thought?

I didn't know what Velkasery looked like, but I pictured a giant computer with hard lines and severe angles crushing Terao Terashima to death.

'So you're saying that the news stories started with Velkasery?'

'Most likely. News doesn't need reality behind it. Once it appears onscreen at a news café it's like it actually happened. Write the script and it becomes reality.'

'Miyako Setsu said something similar.' News doesn't follow the story, the story follows the news.

'It's possible that the whole mess in Tokyo with the axe attacks never even happened. And that was based on a rumor, too, about a sickness going around from bacteria leaking from a factory.'

More and more rumors.

'That was probably all made up. Velkasery could be broadcasting news to spark a disturbance on purpose. Stirring shit between the east side and the west side.'

If you don't cause some agitation, there's no experiment. Kagetora Hiyama's words. *So there will always be conflict.*

Could Velkasery be orchestrating conflict?

'And now Velkasery is coming for us.'

'I don't know what we can do about it. Terashima's final play didn't pan out. The self-destruct program is gone with that busted-up computer.'

We went back to where we had parked the motorcycle. Just as we got there I spotted a gray van cross an intersection and continue toward the park.

The police. They found us. It's over. I resigned myself to the reality of it. The van pulled into the parking area and sped toward us before screeching to a halt at an angle. The doors slid open and I knew armed police were about to burst out. I had no intention of putting up a fight. My hands were already up in the air. But no police appeared.

'Sorry it took me so long!' Out stepped the man we had been speaking to before as a 3D projection. Yuito Kitayama.

There was no one behind the wheel, the van being set to self-drive mode. Just knowing that was enough to make me feel faint. But the area behind the front seats was enclosed by opaque paneling, so as long as I didn't look out the window it felt like I was in a small room. Or rather, that's what I tried to convince myself, repeating that it wasn't a van, it was a room, trying my best to keep my fear at bay.

The seats were arranged like on the Shinkansen, with myself and Chusonji seated next to each other facing in the direction the van was going and Yuito Kitayama sitting facing us.

Apparently he had rushed out there from Tokyo to pick us up, and had been on the way when we were talking to his projection on the swan boat.

'I'm taking you to my facility.'

121

'What the hell kind of facility are we talking about?'

'This is all completely unofficial – that is, I'm operating totally on my own initiative, so there's only so much I can do. But it will be safer than you riding around on my mom's motorcycle.' He paused a moment. 'Now, what were we talking about?' He cocked his round face slightly. 'Ah yes, the information about the two of you orchestrating the disturbances.'

'It's all fake.' Chusonji shared his theory. 'Velkasery cooked it up to take us out of the picture. I think that the riots or whatever may not even have happened.'

'You think Velkasery did this?'

'Like I said, its creator Terashima gave me a job. Shut down the AI. So Velkasery's angry.'

'What will happen if you don't shut it down?' His tone was so deferential that it made me think we were older than him and not the other way around.

'It can manipulate the news to frame me as a danger to society. It can do whatever it wants.'

'Mr Kitayama, is Velkasery connected to the government?'

I watched him shrug slightly. It looked like a gentle admission, but he clearly wasn't going to confirm or deny.

'Wasn't there an old movie about an artificial intelligence that went rogue and started a nuclear war?'

'No way,' Chusonji interjected. 'Nuclear war isn't realistic. Or I should say it's not logical. There's no upside for the AI.'

'Well, maybe . . .' I started. A thought had occurred to me earlier. Both of them looked at me. 'Maybe it's trying to get people to fight each other.'

Without change, there can be no progress. Forcing change requires some agitation.

So what if it was trying to promote conflict?

Conflict is agitation.

I saw Kagetora Hiyama. Not in reality, but in my head, staring back at me. For the first time I noticed how large and pointy his ears were.

And your eyes are blue.

The moment he said it I was back in the spinning car. My sister was right beside me, rigid with terror.

The violent spiral of that accident was still going on.

You're Naomasa Mito, aren't you. Hiyama had sidled up to me at school, a look of challenge on his face.

In the next instant I was on the Shinkansen watching the scenery go by outside the window. *Mito? Fancy meeting you here.* Hiyama appeared, standing over me.

'Hey, you okay?' Chusonji was shaking me and I snapped back to reality. 'You zoned out, then you started groaning. Your car trauma again?'

'Partly that, yes.' I looked at Yuito Kitayama.

'What's the matter?'

'Just – something your mother told me. About the conflict between mountain and sea.' Since I'd heard that I couldn't get Hiyama out of my head.

'Oh that.' He smiled with embarrassment. 'She's always loved that story. Grandma was mountain, Mom was sea.'

'So you don't believe in it?'

'Well, it's all just an excuse. Although it is true that Grandma and Mom didn't get along at all. They almost never saw each other, and when they did the mood was incredibly tense. You could feel the two of them smoldering. My poor dad.' He smiled with sympathy for his departed father. 'Watching him, I understood what it meant to be between a rock and a hard place. Or to walk a very fine line.'

'So your grandmother was on the mountain side, and your mother, Miyako Setsu, was with the sea.' Then I realized. 'Doesn't that mean that you have blood from both sides? Is that possible?'

He nodded, as if he had had this conversation before. Like he was a specialist being asked questions about his field. 'My dad wasn't actually related to his mother. She took him in as a child. Which is probably how my mother was able to marry him.'

'Sea and mountain can't marry each other?'

'That's what Mom says.' He shrugs. 'So if I was one or the other, I suppose I would have my mom's sea blood.'

'Same! I'm from the sea people too.' It felt like a joke as I said it.

'Come on now,' Chusonji said with a grimace. 'That's as ridiculous as thinking that someone's blood type dictates their personality. Oh, same, I'm from the sea people too! Gimme a break. Do you seriously believe in that? So you and that cop get along like cats and dogs, or like mountain people and sea people, whatever – how do you even know which one you are? *He* could be sea and *you* could be mountain.'

While we talked, the van kept on driving. *It's not a van,* I told myself. *It's just a little room. Nothing to be afraid of.*

I turned toward Chusonji, trying to forget where we were. To emphasize my point I put my thumbs and forefingers above and below my eyes and held them open. 'My eyes are blue. That means I'm sea.'

'Your eyes? Seriously?'

When I'd first heard the story from Miyako Setsu, Chusonji had been right there in the room with us, but he'd been so focused on what he was doing with the computer that he probably hadn't been listening.

'Look. My eyes are blue.'

I noticed that Yuito Kitayama made a sheepish face, poking his tongue out. 'My eyes are blue also. From my mother.'

Seemingly annoyed, Chusonji leaned in to take a closer look at me. Staring into each other's eyes like that, we both became a little embarrassed.

I could see my eyes reflected in his eyes.

Like a hall of mirrors, eyes in eyes in eyes.

I imagined that he would look away and mutter that my eyes weren't that blue, but he surprised me by continuing to look intently. I thought he might even be trying to get a rise out of me.

He just stared, saying nothing.

'What's wrong?' Finally I was unable to take it anymore and leaned away.

But Chusonji just kept staring at me.

'What's the matter,' I asked again, but he didn't answer. His face was so grave that I started to worry. 'Don't tell me you're going to confess that you're a mountain person.' I was trying to lighten the mood, but his expression was hard.

I started wondering if there was something wrong with my face and started patting my cheeks.

When Chusonji finally spoke, it was to Yuito Kitayama. 'Sorry, is there somewhere we can stop so I can get something to drink? I need a break.'

'A break? It doesn't seem like the time for that.'

'Please. Find a place where we can stop.'

We found a supermarket on the road and the van glided into the parking lot. Yuito Kitayama must have adjusted the destination from the back seat.

'Mito, go get me something to drink, yeah?'

'Sorry?'

'I need something to sip on. Go get me something.' There was some urgency in his voice.

'Why me?' I protested.

'You don't like being in the van anyway, right?'

He was right about that, I was happy to get a breath of fresh air.

'This increases our risk,' warned Yuito Kitayama. He was obviously reluctant for anyone to get out of the van. 'I'm telling you, we'll be better off if we get somewhere safe as fast as possible.'

'It'll only take a minute. And our friend Mito doesn't do well in cars.'

'Is that true?'

'That didn't come up in your research on him?' Chusonji sounded slightly combative.

'The accident at the entrance of the Izumi Service Area near New Sendai,' he replied. So he did know. 'And another car accident in New Kichijoji.'

'What's that one?'

'The one where I was hit by a taxi, five years ago,' I explained.

Yuito Kitayama's research must have had some bad info, though, because he continued, 'Mr Mito was driving a car and crashed into a taxi.'

'Actually, I can't drive.' I felt a perverse pride at this.

'But according to the records—'

'That may be what the records say, but it's not what my memory says.'

I ended up getting out of the van. I didn't particularly mind being sent on an errand – after all, it wasn't so different from my normal work – so I stepped out and took several deep breaths.

Putting the PassCard I'd received from Yuito Kitayama in my pocket, I entered the store. He said that using the card would register the transaction to a dummy persona. The store was mostly empty. I put a few packs of juice and food in a shopping bag and headed to the register. As I placed the bag on the counter and paid, the in-store holovision caught my eye. It was the news.

An aerial shot, probably from a drone camera.

It showed the highway. Trucks and buses were lined up across the road, forming a barricade, and multiple cars were backed up in front of it. After a moment people began to appear, brandishing wooden planks and metal rods, and in fact some of them did have axes and other bladed implements. They swarmed around the stopped cars and started pulling people out of the vehicles.

Seeing such a barbarous display in modern Japan was completely surreal.

The footage showed large numbers of people from the cars being hoisted up and carried away like captives.

The few other customers in the market were all staring at the screen in shock.

Then a new image was on screen: Atsushi Chusonji's face. A chyron labeled him as the man who had been circulating messages online to provoke the violence. My stomach clenched with fear.

It seemed the rumor was being treated as the truth.

How can they let this happen, I wanted to ask, but there was no one I could ask.

Next the screen showed a vehicle that looked familiar. After a second I glanced out through the supermarket window. The van on screen was none other than the one we were riding in. Yuito Kitayama's gray van.

They had found us.

Kitayama had assured us we would be safe, but it seemed our opponent, Velkasery, had more authority than he did.

I spilled out of the store and ran to the van. 'Hey. Hey!' I could barely gasp out any words through my panic and fear. I pointed back toward the market, and my pointing finger trembled.

This is bad, they found us! That was what I wanted to say, but I couldn't form the words. All I could do was gulp and gasp.

I saw that Chusonji was still wearing that same troubled expression, without me having said anything, and this only worried me more.

Then I noticed that Yuito Kitayama was gone.

'He's sitting up front. Not driving, but looking something up for me.' Chusonji pointed forward, beyond the opaque paneling that cut off the back from the front.

'Just now, in the store, on the news—'

'Calm down, Mito, and listen for a second.'

Our voices overlapped. I needed *him* to listen to *me*. I had to tell him that the van had been identified.

But he kept on talking, trotting out the old-fashioned aphorism: 'I've got good news and bad news. Well, actually, it's more like somewhat good news and some news about your life that will come as a pretty big shock. Which do you want first?'

I thought he might have been kidding, but he looked completely serious. I didn't know which to choose.

Somewhat good news, versus something shocking about my own life?

I couldn't answer. But of course I was very interested in hearing whatever he had discovered about me.

'I'll start with the somewhat good news,' he began, and launched right in: 'There may still be a way to stop Velkasery.'

'What?'

'Let's say it's a greater-than-zero chance.'

'How?'

'We'll use Terashima's program.'

'But how could we use his program? Isn't it gone?' I pictured the remnants of the computer.

'It might still be around.'

'Around? Around where?' And I didn't love the phrasing 'might be.' Chusonji took a breath and was silent for a moment. It looked so much like he was working up the courage to propose to me that I almost made a joke about it. But the intensity on his face kept me quiet.

'Do you remember what I told you about the experiment that Terashima and I ran?'

'The artificial intelligence experiment?'

'It was like a rehearsal for our AI work. What AI needs is information. It consumes mass quantities of data, grows and develops, and gets smarter.'

'What did you do in that experiment, exactly?' He had said he used people as cameras, but I was fairly certain they didn't actually turn people into cameras.

'We turned people into cameras.'

'Is that a metaphor?'

He seemed to not know what to say for a moment, and then: 'No. Not a metaphor. We put cameras in people's eyes.'

'What?' Was that even possible? Or legal?

'As they moved around, we logged more and more footage. It was a process we developed.'

'Wait a second. How does that—'

'How does what?'

'How does that work, ethically?'

'What do you mean by that?'

'Even if they gave you consent, recording everything they see just doesn't seem right. It's a total violation of their privacy!'

'Listen.' His voice hardened. 'I'll say this as plainly as I can.'

'What?'

'You saw it on the screen at Miyako Setsu's house. The self-destruct code for Velkasery.'

'Me? Well, I suppose I did.' What I saw were lines and lines of text and numbers. 'I hope you weren't expecting me to memorize it.'

'You couldn't have. But if you looked at it for even a second, it's logged.'

'Logged?'

'There's a camera in your eye.'

'*What?*'

My mind went blank. *A camera?*

I finally realized that Chusonji's heavy expression was not because he was worried, but because he felt guilty.

I could hardly breathe.

'What . . . what exactly are you saying?'

'It's in your right eye.'

'So, what does that mean?' I still didn't understand.

'Everything you see should be saved as data.'

I couldn't comprehend what the man in front of me was trying to tell me.

I certainly couldn't form a proper response.

'It's like you just said. Even if we had the subject's consent, implanting a camera inside of them is wrong. The thing is, we didn't get consent.'

'Wait.' Finally my thoughts were forming. 'Mr Chusonji, wait.'

'We had an agreement with certain hospitals that whenever they had people in for major surgery, we'd install a camera. It was part of our experiment. When I was looking to see if your eyes were blue, I noticed it. You had surgery when you were a kid, after your accident. That must have been when your camera was installed.'

'What are you saying?'

'When you were in the market shopping, I had Kitayama look into it. He accessed the server where our subject logs are stored.'

I covered my right eye with my hand.

'We're on our way to the place where we can access the data now. We should be able to get the program code, since you saw it.'

Just then the van came to a sudden stop. The panel between the front seats and the back area became transparent. We could see Yuito Kitayama in the driver's seat. 'The way's blocked,' he said.

Through the windshield I could see cars arranged like a wall, cutting off the road.

You were one of our test subjects. Sorry about that.

The things Chusonji revealed floated to me as if from a great distance.

It is difficult to maintain balance.

I could still hear her voice in my head.

Naomasa Mito's girlfriend, Kyoko Hinata. Was she actually his girlfriend, though?

She was so completely calm, a look on her face like she knew everything. And she'd told me she was an observer. A referee.

But a referee of what game?

'Hiyama. Just who I wanted to talk to. Come with me.'

Someone lightly punched my shoulder from the side and I jumped a little. It was a lieutenant from another division, with his trademark stubble. I reflected for a moment that such perfectly cultivated scruffiness seemed oxymoronic, but it did look good on him. It was my first time talking to him since I took a class he taught when I was at the academy.

'What's up?' I missed my chance to say 'nice to see you, it's been a while.' He was already pulling me forcefully along with him.

I had only just gotten back to headquarters from the library, and I had been working straight through since getting on the Shinkansen to New Sendai. I needed a break. The captain had also noticed that my eyes were red and realized that I hadn't slept in a while, so he told me to go take a nap, which is what I was just about to do.

'This Mito guy, you know him, right?'

'Yes, sir.' Word seemed to have gotten around. 'From school.'

'So you know a little bit about him. You got a minute?'

I didn't mention that I was hoping to take a nap. 'Is there some new development?'

'We got a call from a civilian. They saw a van they think Chu-sonji and Mito were in.'

'Where?'

'Heading east from Hachioji. They were spotted earlier at a house in the mountains near Hachioji, so it checks out.'

'The house where a picture book author lives, right? Some detectives went to go look into it. What happened with that?'

'They got taken out.' The lieutenant made a stubbly frown.

'Taken out?'

'They're both in the hospital. Nothing too serious. Actually pretty impressive – just enough to incapacitate them.'

'What do you mean, just enough?'

'Bunch of dislocated joints, and heavy blows to the chin that knocked them both out. They're not thinking quite straight. They're both saying that an old lady did all of that to them.' He laughed.

'An old lady?'

'The author. If she's actually that tough, we should try to recruit her.'

'Yeah, seriously.' And not for her skill in drawing picture books.

I fought off my fatigue as we walked down the corridor. Then we were outside, and before I could fully process it I was in the back seat of an unmarked car. I was exhausted. My body felt heavy, and my head was so dull it throbbed. But I had to follow orders. Orders? Did I even have orders? From the lieutenant? No, I was following something larger than that.

He had said, *Just who I wanted to talk to.* Which means that he didn't necessarily expect to see me there.

It felt like there was some power beyond mere coincidence at work. Was it because of my conversation with Kyoko Hinata?

No matter how I tried to avoid it, I'd be pulled back in. Pulled back to Mito.

We were traveling along the highway. We had started out going pretty fast, but at a certain point we sped up even more. The sirens were on.

'Hey now,' said the lieutenant from beside me. 'Looks like we got 'em.' He was looking at his detective's PassCard. I hadn't gotten any notifications, so it must have circulated among only the higher ranks.

'Did we make an arrest?' Finally, Mito.

'No arrest yet. According to the news, some conscientious civilians are holding them.'

'Holding the van?'

'There was a request out to buy some time until the detectives with proper jurisdiction could get there, so these people chipped in. Sealed off the road. You gotta love those upstanding citizens.'

I almost said that what they were doing was a crime too. Breaking one rule to uphold another one didn't compute for me. But whenever I said anything like that, people just looked at me funny. 'Is he really that dangerous?'

The lieutenant shot me a slightly disparaging look. 'Worried about your friend?'

'That's not it at all.' I answered more forcefully than I meant to. There was absolutely no part of me that wanted to protect Naomasa Mito. The fact that anyone might be thinking I was covering for him as an old friend was utterly disgusting. 'No, it's more that I don't think he has it in him to commit a crime like this.'

'People change. Plenty of people who don't think they have it in themselves end up stepping out of line.'

He clearly thought the way he tossed off his retort sounded cool. I just let it go. I was busy keeping my panic at being in a car in check. I wished I could just close my eyes and pass out. The sandman was prowling around the edges. All I had to do was invite him in and I would be out, but chances are the lieutenant would give me a hard time.

I kept my eyes open, but my mind was detached. It felt like there was a lid on my brain. I just sat there being jostled by the drive.

But any time I let my guard down, memories from that moment came flooding back like a river overflowing its banks. Twenty years earlier, in our brand-new Muse, about to enter the Izumi Service Area near New Sendai. From the back seat I watched my father turn off the self-driving and take the wheel. My mother joking, *I used to be scared of self-driving but now your father's driving frightens me more.* And then it happened. An impact from behind that threw us forward. No pain, just flying, now diagonal. Our car started to spin, the force of the rotation whipping my whole family around and around.

A wave of dizziness crashed over me.

'Hey, you're not sleeping, are you?' The voice came from beside me. We had arrived.

I might have been asleep. A body has its limits. There was only so much that willpower and spirit and focus could do against fatigue and lack of sleep. There was the sandman again, arms wrapped around my neck and weighing me down. I was just about reaching the end of my rope, but I let the lieutenant push me out of the car.

I wasn't expecting such an elaborate improvised roadblock. Across the median, the three lanes of the eastbound side of the highway were blocked off by multiple cars forming a barricade. A crowd of people surrounded it.

The lieutenant laughed. 'These citizens were extremely cooperative, huh?'

'Surprisingly cooperative.'

'There's a reward for anyone who apprehends or turns in Chusonji and Mito.'

'Really?'

'Or at least that's the rumor going around online.'

'Who would start a rumor like that?' I asked reflexively, but I might as well have been scooping a handful of water from the ocean and asking which river it flowed from. There's no telling where information comes from on the net.

'There's that whole thing about east side versus west side in Tokyo. And right about here would be the line between east and west.'

'Why would that matter for this?'

'The people around here are on edge. In any kind of conflict it's the borders where things are most tense. And when people are on edge, they get more extreme. Someone says, "Hey we found the van, let's block off the road," everyone gets excited, it turns into a circus. That's more or less what's going on here. The rumor about a reward probably just gave it a little extra push.'

We crossed over to the other side of the median, holding up our PassCards to show we were police, cutting through the crowds and then threading between the cars.

There were already a few other police there, guns out. They were aiming at a gray van that was stopped on the road.

'What's the situation?' the lieutenant called out.

'We just got here,' said a uniformed cop. 'There were a whole bunch of people surrounding the van so that it couldn't go anywhere. We just had them stand down.'

There were no signs of movement from inside the gray van. It was like a wary animal, staying perfectly still. I wasn't sure if it was a herbivore or something more dangerous. Regardless of which, it could easily lash out.

'Did you get any information on the van?'

'That, uh, that isn't clear.'

I didn't know what that might mean. I took out my PassCard

and pulled up the police investigation database. Anything any detectives found about their cases would be in there, and I could access it as long as I had clearance.

I found an entry on the gray van. It wasn't listed as stolen, and it was registered to a museum in Tokyo. Which meant that it didn't belong to a civilian. But when I checked the record of the inquiry to the museum it seemed they had no idea about the van.

'Ah, this van might be problematic,' the lieutenant said.

'Problematic how?'

'It's possible that a certain organization set up a false registration for it.'

A certain organization didn't mean anything to me. Maybe he was talking about organized crime?

With myself and the lieutenant, there were five police in total. The locator map on my PassCard showed that the majority of police cars on the road were headed in our direction.

'What should we do?' I asked the lieutenant.

'We'll do it the good old-fashioned way,' he answered, then turned around and walked away from the van.

I turned to follow him, wondering what he was up to, and saw him open the door to another police car. He started the engine, not to go anywhere but to make use of the car's systems. Then he pulled out the mouthpiece for a loudspeaker and began talking in the direction of the van.

'Come out of there, now. We've got you surrounded.' He said it twice. Then he switched off the mic and asked the other police who were there before us, 'How long has it been standing there like that?'

'No change since we got here,' said one of them. 'About ten minutes, I'd say.'

Everything the officers were seeing on the scene was being transmitted through their glasses back to headquarters. An update came in on my earpiece: 'If they don't come out of the van, you are authorized to open fire.'

The lieutenant lifted the mic back to his stubbly jaw. 'I'm gonna count to ten. If you don't come out, we'll start shooting.'

He began the countdown, sounding matter-of-fact. When he got to three, the van door slid open. An excited murmur arose from the onlookers behind us, all the concerned citizens.

I could sense the police aiming their drawn guns all tense up.

Two people emerged from the van.

One I didn't recognize. A middle-aged man with a round face, wearing a suit. His hands were up and his expression was blank. I imagined that back at headquarters they were already scanning his face and checking the citizen database. Behind him came Mito, but even before I saw his face I knew it was him. No need to check any database. I felt his presence like a blow to the chest.

Sometimes it is impossible to maintain a distance, no matter how hard both parties may try.

Kyoko Hinata's words echoed inside my head. Anywhere I went, Mito would be there.

'Atsushi Chusonji still hasn't come out of the vehicle?' The voice in my earpiece wanted to confirm.

As if in response, the lieutenant said into the mic, 'Where's Atsushi Chusonji?'

The two men in front of us stood in a pose of surrender but said nothing.

'Step forward. Slowly.'

Naomasa Mito and the pudgy-looking man carefully walked toward us.

'That's far enough.'

Now as soon as Chusonji came out, the other officers could easily surround him and get him under control. But for the moment we didn't know what was going on inside the van, which was dangerous. Insect cams would work, crawling in through the cracks in the van and projecting a view of the interior, but we didn't have them on hand and there was no time to wait for them.

'You are now authorized to open fire,' came the voice in my ear. It wasn't a surprise. If they were to suddenly resist, it would be reasonable to assume we were in danger, and we'd need to use our weapons in self-defense or to make them stand down. But almost immediately after the authorization came in, the lieutenant leaned in close to me. 'Hiyama, shoot Mito.'

'What?' I wasn't expecting that.

'The order just came in from the top. Terminate Naomasa Mito, they said. If not, we could all be in serious danger.'

'Terminate?'

'This is not just authorization to use deadly force. It's an order.'

I hadn't heard anything like that on my earpiece. But maybe it had gone directly to the lieutenant. 'Why me?' Talking back to superiors is a serious violation. But something in me couldn't avoid challenging the order.

But the lieutenant didn't seem overly put out. 'It's not just you. I'm about to give the order to the others too.' He chuckled, apparently amused at my attitude. 'It's not like I'm going out of my way to make you kill your old classmate.'

'No, that's not what I meant.'

I didn't want him to think I had lost my nerve, so I drew my weapon. Then I aimed and took another hard look at Naomasa Mito.

His expression was difficult to read. He should have been able to see me, and his eyes seemed focused, but he also appeared blank, as if he weren't fully grasping the situation.

Fire. Kill Naomasa Mito.

The words reverberated deep in my skull.

I hesitated at an order so raw and aggressive. And then I realized that the voice urging me on might have been my own.

The view from the spinning car appeared before me. My parents' and sister's screams scrambled my vision.

Wasn't it all Mito's fault? *Shoot him. I have to end this.*

A feeling like destiny took hold of me.

I tightened my hands around the gun.

The need to shoot was layered over with a quiet question: was Naomasa Mito really so dangerous that he needed to be shot dead?

Didn't most people at headquarters think he had just gotten sucked into all of this?

Who was even issuing this order?

Fire.

If it was to keep the rules intact, I had to kill him. But it felt like it was a violation of a larger rule.

Just as I started to squeeze the trigger, something behind me exploded.

No, it wasn't an explosion, just noise, I realized after a moment. Intensely loud music. An invisible sonic eruption.

I jumped when it started, my shoulders flinching. Then the sound paralyzed me. It was sheer chance that I didn't reflexively pull the trigger. It took me several seconds before I could turn around to see what was going on.

Covering my ears, I tried to see where the music was coming from. Then I realized: it was coming from the police car, the one that the lieutenant had been using as a power source for his loudspeaker. But not just from there. Multiple cars forming the barricade were also blasting the same song, at what had to be maximum volume.

I stood there stunned, not understanding.

Then I heard tires screeching and turned around to see the gray van rolling over the median and pulling away on the other side of the highway. They had seized their chance while everyone was distracted by the music.

The lieutenant was clearly frustrated. Pressing his hands to his ears, he let loose a stream of profanity. 'It's Gamma Moko,' he shouted. 'Great song, actually.'

'That was close,' said Chusonji from beside me. He had a tablet on his knees.

Not ten minutes ago we had been sitting there at a total loss, the road blocked by drivers feeling a sudden surge of civic duty, when we heard police sirens drawing near. Chusonji had said, 'Buy us some time. I've got an idea.' Then he asked Yuito Kitayama, 'Do you have a computer I can use to get online?' Kitayama handed over a tablet, and Chusonji's fingers got to work.

'What are you planning to do?' asked Kitayama.

'I'm cooking up a distraction. Then we'll pull a U-turn and get out of here.'

When the police threatened to shoot if we didn't come out, Kitayama and I prepared to exit the vehicle. 'Almost there,' Chusonji said. 'Just need a little more time. And it's gonna get loud, so be ready. We'll only have a second to make our move. They'll be confused for an instant, and that's our only chance, so get back in the van quick, because I'll start driving.'

And that's exactly what happened.

Somehow I managed not to faint while we were standing there staring down the barrels of the policemen's guns. And then suddenly there was music, loud as an explosion. It shook my whole body and I cowered in terror, but Yuito Kitayama bellowed, 'Hurry!' and we leaped back into the car.

Chusonji was at the wheel, handling the van roughly. Self-driving mode couldn't perform an aggressive U-turn. The collision warning alarm kept sounding, but Chusonji ignored it as he burst into oncoming traffic. After being thrown backwards once, Yuito Kitayama shouted, 'I'm taking over!' and straddled the back seat on his way to the front. We dropped speed slightly, but if we crashed it would all be over, and he gingerly slid into place with his hands on the wheel and his feet on the pedals in a high-stakes handoff. Chusonji returned to the back seats, exhaling a long sigh of relief.

'What was that music?'

'Don't you know? Gamma Moko.'

'No, I mean how did you do that?'

'I took over those car stereo systems. They all have online connections. Usually pretty low security, not like corporate networks. As long as they're on it's pretty easy to connect and mess with them. So any car that was on, I got in. And it's easy for me to pull up anything by Gamma Moko.'

I wasn't quite sure what he meant by pull up, but then he added, 'I may not have mentioned this, but I once made a site where you can listen to Gamma Moko stuff for free.'

'Is that legal?'

'What do you think?'

But that isn't right, I almost said.

'Setting it up wasn't hard. Now that I think about it, back in college that kind of thing was all I did when I wasn't doing research. Terashima did his own thing, making his own live programs.'

These progressions of visuals that went along with live music were a central part of the jurok genre, but the live programs for Gamma Moko were especially famous for their creativity.

The van was rocking violently back and forth, to the point where I thought it might tip over. As soon as I had the thought I was overcome with the reality of being inside a vehicle traveling at high speed. From far away I heard my mother's voice: *Hey, they cut us off.*

I also heard police sirens.

'If we don't find a different vehicle, we could be in trouble,' Yuito Kitayama called back to us over his shoulder.

'Any ideas?' asked Chusonji.

Kitayama worked at some kind of special agency, so I imagined that he would have access to another vehicle. But he shook his head ruefully. 'I'm operating independently here, so what I can do is limited.' He tapped at the onboard navigation system. 'All the major intersections are closed, so I'm heading off to the side roads. That much I can do for you, but we should really leave this van behind as soon as we can. There's a bus stop up ahead that you can use to reach the data center.'

'The data center,' I repeated without much thought or meaning behind it.

I heard Chusonji exhale and looked up at him, only to catch him quickly looking away. I realized with a start what he was thinking, and pressed my hand to my right eye.

There's a camera in your eye.

After my accident as a child, in the whirl of activity around my surgery, they installed a camera.

Without my consent. So that I could collect data.

So that everything I ever saw could be recorded.

It didn't feel real.

It sounded more like a sick joke, but Chusonji had looked completely serious.

'The data center is for long-term storage of private information. The logs from your eye camera should be there.'

At that moment something flashed inside my head, and there was a sudden heat.

I pounced on Atsushi Chusonji.

The tablet he was holding clattered to the back of the van. I reached out both hands and grabbed him by the collar. He recoiled, sputtering at me to let go, his voice strangled.

What did you do to me?

I couldn't take my hands from around his throat.

You logged everything I've ever seen? How could you do that? How did you think that was okay? What about my privacy?

'Mr Mito, please stop!' Yuito Kitayama came back from the front seat and pulled me off of Chusonji. He must have put the car back into self-driving. We had already left the highway and were stopped at a red light.

Chusonji rubbed his neck, coughing and grimacing, but he didn't lash out at me or even seem angry. 'Sorry,' was all he said.

As if he could apologize for something like that.

Blood was rushing to my head. My vision started to blur.

I felt a tight grip on my right hand.

'Stop,' I heard Chusonji say. I wasn't sure what was happening. It was only after a moment that I understood I was trying to rip out my right eye.

I wanted to pull it out and crush it.

The amount of force Chusonji was using to try to stop me was just more proof that there really was a camera in my eye.

I almost screamed. What stopped me was Yuito Kitayama's voice: 'We're here. The bus will arrive any moment. Let's go.'

I managed to get on the bus, but I'm not sure how. Yuito Kitayama more or less had to drag me out of the car to put me on the bus just as it was ready to pull away. The whole time I was unsure of the dimensions of my body. Thought and vision seemed encased in a membrane. My intense agitation subsided, and I just felt empty.

There were few other passengers. Chusonji and I sat next to each other in the back. Across the aisle to the left was an older man wearing wireless headphones, swaying gently with the motion of the bus. I wondered if he was listening to the English conversation lesson dance music that was becoming popular.

'So right now,' I said, not so much because I had calmed down but because I wanted to keep myself calm, 'everything that I'm seeing is being recorded?'

I still wasn't processing the fact that the camera inside my eye was sending images somewhere. I had the overwhelming sensation that everything private in my life had been exposed to the world. A feeling of such utter helplessness that my hair stood on end.

'It's not on the net where anyone can see it. It's just a log. Even if images are logged, basically no one ever sees it. Only if there's something specific we'd need to check.'

Chusonji stared straight ahead as he spoke, focused on the 3D display on the back of the driver's seat.

'Is that supposed to make me feel better?' And at nearly the same time he said:

'Not that it'll make you feel much better.'

I closed my eyes.

There were too many thoughts to sort through.

How did this happen?

We need to stop Velkasery.

A camera in my eye?

They almost shot me.

My mind pulled in different directions, each thread blending with unclassifiable emotions, chasing each other around and around. In the center of the vortex was me, lost.

Chusonji didn't say much else.

There were security cameras in the bus, and also sensors that automatically pulled information from PassCards, but maybe because I had gotten used to Chusonji's jammer I didn't have the feeling we had been discovered.

Chusonji closed his eyes and his breathing sounded like he had fallen asleep. *How is he so relaxed?* I thought with exasperation, but then I was being woken up and I realized that I had been asleep as well.

'Next stop,' he said as he shook me. We got off the bus. My head hurt from being roused suddenly.

'Um.'

'What?'

'When I'm sleeping . . . my dreams . . . those are just for me, right?' I didn't imagine the camera could record that.

He clicked his tongue, but I couldn't tell if that was because he was annoyed by my question or if he was feeling guilt. 'Everything you see is yours, no matter what it is. You might be upset right now, but that much at least is true.' His voice was quiet, but steady. He seemed to really mean it.

The data center looked like an enormous residential block. Chusonji said that in fact it used to be a huge apartment complex but had been entirely gutted and repurposed several decades back.

It made me think of the library where Hinata worked, but that was a public building and this was privately managed. Similar-seeming, but quite different.

'Are you sure it's okay for us to just walk right in like this?'

Heading straight to the main entrance made me nervous.

'It doesn't make a difference how we go in. The police have no idea that we have business here. No one's waiting for us here, yeah?'

I nearly griped that of course no one has any interest in what's been logged by my eye camera. 'Can anyone use this facility?'

'It's mostly corporate accounts. Some public organizations, though – we got access through our university.'

He explained that storage was allotted by contract, and then once the hard drives were rented they could be used for anything

145

storage-related. They couldn't be turned into servers or used to host complex programs, but they could keep vast amounts of data intact. 'It's like a bag check for data you have nowhere else to put. If our project was still running today we'd be able to access our data easily on the net, but—'

'But your experiment was shut down midway through.' And they never cleaned up after, which meant that my log was still there.

'We probably won't be able to see what we need unless we input the command directly into the console.'

I didn't understand exactly what he was saying, but I grasped that we needed to go to the physical device where my data was stored.

There was a fair amount of security at the entrance, which was understandable for a facility that stored data, and we had to pass through a whole array of sensors. But we were able to get in with no problem.

It likely helped that Yuito Kitayama had called ahead on our behalf. He'd looked up the details for the research center where Chusonji and Terashima used to work and had pretended to be the current supervisor when he'd called to let them know that we'd be coming by to access some data.

'Take this card and go up to the fifth floor,' the attendant told us crisply, and waved us through.

It wasn't a new building, but the corridors were very clean, maybe because very few people came and went. As we walked, lighting on the floor flicked on smoothly to show which way to go. The lamps were linked to the card we had been handed.

Chusonji said nothing, and neither did I. He was probably thinking about Velkasery's self-destruct code, and of course I was thinking about my eye.

I didn't want to look anywhere, but I couldn't walk without looking.

It didn't register with me that we had gotten off an elevator. I didn't even feel my feet on the ground as we walked. But there we were in a room. The walls appeared to be paneled with slim hard drives.

'As far as test subjects go,' Chusonji said, and then he mentioned how many people there were, but I didn't process it. 'All their logs have been in here ever since we started the experiment. Even just with this one room, there's still space for plenty more data.'

He pulled a small tablet out of the wall, then sat down with his knees folded under him and set to work.

I just stood there bewildered, staring at the four walls.

Here?

This is where everything I've seen is stored?

It didn't feel real.

And then I realized that what I was seeing while standing in that room was being stored there at that moment. It was such an uncanny feeling that my head felt like it was coming undone.

I fell against the wall, barely keeping my feet.

'You okay?' Chusonji didn't look up from his console.

I couldn't answer. I staggered over toward him and looked at the screen over his shoulder.

'I'm looking for the footage from the picture book lady's house,' he offered. 'When you saw the code.'

'Is this really real?' I didn't doubt it so much as I needed to say something to steady myself. But Chusonji seemed to think that I actually didn't believe it could be true, and he seemed to take a researcher's umbrage at my questioning his work.

'Well, you remember seeing all of this, don't you?' He touched the screen. Rather than searching for something specific, it just played back scenes randomly. 'It's over there too.'

When he said it I looked over at the display screen that hung on the wall.

It projected images with no regard for my feelings.

My heart started to thrum.

I was frightened. But at the same time I couldn't look away.

There was a desk.

And a chair.

It was a classroom. Identical desks and chairs were lined up in rows. Based on the angle of the shot, I must have been crouching down.

My hand reached out in front of me. I was handling things inside the desk. Everything was from my point of view.

It may have been that the camera only took images, or that the playback didn't have any sound, but it was silent.

The image lurched.

I must have stood up. In my field of vision was the door at the front of the classroom. Someone was standing there. The image was shaky, so I only caught sight of them for a brief moment, but it was enough to make my breath catch.

Standing in the doorway was none other than Kagetora Hiyama, wearing his school uniform.

The video started moving at speed, like shaky-cam footage. I had jumped out of the classroom and was running down the hall.

It didn't feel like something that had happened to me. But then something sparked my memory.

I knew this episode.

I had just been thinking about it recently.

It was when I came into the classroom and spotted Hiyama poking around in my desk. It was suspicious, especially since as soon as I got there he ran away. Later I would learn that something of his had been stolen, and he was frantically searching for it.

As I recalled the memory, I grew confused.

The image on screen was what *I* had seen. But it was Hiyama entering the classroom, and me running off.

It was switched.

In my memory it was Hiyama rummaging through my desk. He saw me when I came into the classroom, got flustered, and fled.

'This is wrong,' I said. There was panic in my voice, which surprised me.

'Wrong?' Chusonji looked up. 'What is?'

I explained that it was different from how I remembered it. But not completely different, more like the roles had been reversed. My voice trembled as I spoke.

Chusonji remained calm. Almost cold. I stared at him. 'It's probably you who's wrong,' he pronounced.

Wrong? 'But I'm the one who actually saw it!'

And I was sure of what I was saying. I wasn't wrong.

'Memories are often distorted,' he said quietly.

'Distorted?'

'Nothing is as easy to get wrong as memories. We adjust them based on our emotions. Every time we recall something, we doctor it. Whereas a camera just records the objective truth. It can't be wrong.'

'But—'

'Think about it. If you had to choose between someone's memory or a video recording, which would you trust?'

Well, obviously the video, I almost said. You can't trust people's memories.

But when it came to my own memories . . .

'People just naturally alter their memories of bad experiences or things they wish hadn't happened. I do it. And so do you.'

Did I want to remake myself?

Me looking through the desk in the empty classroom. Me entering the classroom to find Hiyama at the desk. One of the two was a fabrication.

My legs felt wobbly. I was about to fold in on myself.

'Keep it together.' I wasn't sure if it was Chusonji who said it or me.

My memories from school ricocheted around my brain. The time I encountered him on the street with his girlfriend, the time we had that exchange on the school roof before graduation – was I wrong about all of it?

You're Naomasa Mito, aren't you?

I remembered Hiyama asking that when he first transferred to my school, wearing an expression that was neither contemptuous nor hateful but intensely dark.

But did it actually happen?

You're Hiyama, aren't you?

Was the sullen voice mine?

I tugged at my hair. I wanted to pull my memories out of my brain and line them up like miniature dioramas to inspect the details. Were they bent? Were they twisted? And what did it mean if they were?

Mr Chusonji, help. In my mind I was pleading with him. But my voice wouldn't work.

What do I do if I can't trust my own memories?

Am I even Naomasa Mito? Is it me who's here right now? Am I – have I not been myself this whole time?

I felt my very foundation crumbling.

The whole time Chusonji kept staring at his tablet, watching the images that came up.

All at once everything brightened. My whole field of vision turned orange.

At first I thought it was just on the screen, the log footage of what I had seen.

No. It was inside my head. My memories started to play like a video feed I couldn't stop.

I was seated.

In front of me were two more seats, one for a driver and one for a passenger. Between them I could see the road in front of us. Through the window beside me the barrier flowed by.

The highway. The accident.

I was reliving that moment.

My favorite picture book was on my lap.

It's happening again.

Terror welled up inside me.

My mother said, *Hey, they cut us off.* Or that's what I expected to happen, but it didn't.

I threw the picture book. I did it. I was probably just trying to annoy my older sister, but the book flew into the front seat, bounced off my father's hand. There was a sudden noise. The car's control panel reacted. A computerized voice announced, *Disengaging.* What was being disengaged?

My father shouted something, flustered, then grabbed the wheel.

The car began to spin, with me at the center.

Just as I was about to scream, I came back to myself. I was in the data facility.

My hands were shaking. Not just my hands. My whole body. 'Um,' I squawked at Chusonji, but my jaw trembled too much to say anything more.

'I found it.' Chusonji stood up.

He didn't even seem to notice my bewilderment. *I don't care,* I tried to shout. But he just held the tablet up to show me. 'I found the footage.'

The image on the screen jumped up at me.

It was the code I had seen at Miyako Setsu's house. Lines and lines of tightly packed text.

Chusonji snapped a photo of it with his PassCard. The playback froze and he took several more photos.

'Okay then. Let's go.' He moved to leave the room. I started to follow reflexively, but I tripped over my own feet and nearly fell

151

over. I steadied myself and tried again, only to stumble again. It was like all the connections in my body had been loosened, which only frightened me more.

I scurried to catch up with Chusonji as he walked away. I didn't want to be left behind. My head was all scrambled. *Was that the real accident? Did I cause it?*

As we exited the data center, Chusonji looked around. 'I guess we should keep moving, yeah?'

Yes.

I was reeling from the shock of questioning my own existence and was in no condition to challenge him. I just followed as he walked on and on.

Next thing I realized, I was in a palanquin, modeled to look like it was from the Edo period.

We sat in a covered litter with horizontal poles emerging from the front and back for carrying. Of course it wasn't real humans carrying the palanquin, which would be far too inefficient. Instead, it was anthropomorphic machines doing the work. They moved just like people, keeping a steady pace. It was like a tiny private room, often used by lovers for trysts, or for confidential conversations. Sometimes people had business meetings in them, so they could enjoy a relaxing ride while having their discussion. Hinata and I had ridden in one once, and although it had definitely been a new experience to be carried like that, I felt like I didn't need to do it again. The ride with Chusonji was my first time in one since then.

'Okay, now comes the hard part,' he said, sitting across from me and looking at the image of the source code on his PassCard. His eyes were glittering from getting closer to the goal, or maybe just from the researcher's thrill of solving a tough problem.

The hard part?

For me, in that moment, the hard part was figuring out who I was. A storm of confusion was raging inside me, so overwhelming that I couldn't even scream or tear at my hair.

A call came in on my PassCard.

When I saw that it was from Hinata, I pressed it desperately to my ear.

'Mito? Are you all right?'

Where was she calling me from? Wasn't she under police surveillance? Was it safe to use my phone?

All those thoughts rushed through my head, but what came out of my mouth was: 'No, I'm not all right.' My voice quavered pitifully.

But she didn't ask what had happened.

'I think,' I said, sounding like a little boy, 'I think it was my fault.'

Chusonji glanced up at me.

'And all my memories are wrong. That much I know. Everything I thought I had experienced, everything I was so sure had happened, it could have all been lies.'

'Lies?'

'Any inconvenient memory, anything I didn't want to acknowledge I had done, it could have all just been twisted.'

It felt like I was confessing a bitter truth into my PassCard. My lips trembled, I gnashed my teeth, my molars were clattering.

'It's not lies,' said Hinata.

How could she be so sure?

'Reality is a very vague thing. Even if your memories deviate from the facts, that doesn't just cancel out everything. There's a world where everything happened as you remember it and a world where things are different. Neither one is wrong or right.'

'What does that mean, neither one is right?'

'In some histories the People of the Sea are the victors, and in some worlds the People of the Mountain come out on top. Both exist.'

The sea and mountain story again. I tried to recall where I had first heard it – it was Miyako Setsu who had told me. So who had told Hinata?

'Future and past are not separate. They exist together. A baby is born in the future, and at the same time it is born in a past age. Everything exists simultaneously, and everything is connected.'

In my head I could hear a baby crying as it was born, *aaah, aaah*.

'Hinata, I have no idea what you're talking about. Like I was saying before – the accident. It was my fault.'

The car crash that killed my family, that monstrous spin. I was the cause. I was sure of it.

I saw Kagetora Hiyama before me. He was hunched over a desk. Trying to hide, and I witnessed it. Or maybe it was me trying to hide and him spotting me.

Everything was flipped.

I understood that much. My memories had been rearranged. The log footage had thrust the truth at me. I was starting to remember the truths I most wanted to forget, the facts I had buried deep inside my mind.

Still holding the PassCard, I shook my hands violently. I wanted to erase my own memories. I wanted to scratch them out with my own fingernails.

'It's not your fault, Mito,' I heard Hinata say. 'It was all the other driver. You were just stopped at the light, and the taxi ran into us. I was in the passenger seat. I remember it exactly.'

I wasn't sure what she was saying and didn't know how to respond.

Taxi?

I was talking about that terrible accident I was in with my family as a child, on the New Tohoku Highway. She was obviously talking about a different time. As far as an accident with a taxi, that was the accident from five years ago, when I went into a coma. But she said something about being in the passenger seat.

'There was nothing wrong with your driving.'

'I was driving?'

'We rented a car to go see a concert. You said you had gotten over your fear of cars. And you were actually doing great, until that taxi came along.'

None of this made sense. I was starting to get angry. But then I remembered. *I can't be afraid forever because of something that happened when I was a kid,* I had declared to her. *I'm fine now. I was fine at driving school. I want to show you I can drive.*

Despite my outward confidence, part of me had still been unsure, but I ended up staying much calmer behind the wheel than I'd anticipated. When I switched on self-driving mode, I had a feeling like I was giving myself up to fate, but I still didn't lose my composure. When we were stopped at the light I had seen the taxi approaching. It wasn't until the very last second before impact that I realized what was happening.

'That memory too?' I wailed. 'Was I also wrong about that?'

During my coma and long hospital stay, I had lost my memory for a while. Going through rehab, I'd thought I was gradually piecing things back together. But it seemed that I had just been reconstructing episodes in ways that were more convenient for me. Including my interactions with Hiyama, where I switched the roles so I could feel better about myself.

'Is who I am now different from who I used to be?' I asked Hinata.

'What do you mean?'

'My self from before the accident, and my self from after – are they the same person?'

'I barely knew you before the accident.' She sounded distant. 'You only just invited me out. That was our first date.'

Everything in my head was mashed up and mixed around. I couldn't make sense of any of it.

'Hey,' said Chusonji. Even he seemed to be growing concerned.

Hinata was no longer on the line. I didn't know if I had hung up or if she had given up.

Just believe in what you can remember and you'll be all right.

The words lingered in my head like the scent of a tree after passing it by. Had Hinata said it, or did I just imagine it?

I couldn't believe my memories.

But I kept repeating her words to myself again and again, taking deep breaths, calming myself.

'We need to figure out where we can input this program.' Now that I was managing to fight down my panic, Chusonji was back to business.

Input? I supposed he meant somewhere we could activate the program code. 'Can't we do it from any device that's online?' My head was still hazy.

I thought about the news café in Sendai. Chusonji had tried to infiltrate Velkasery's server but failed. It was at a different level than a corporate database and must have had tougher security than even he expected.

He clicked his tongue. Before I could ask what was wrong, he growled, 'The news.' He was checking it on his PassCard. I took mine out too.

The violence in Tokyo wasn't abating.

And there was another headline: *Wall Construction Along Yamanote Line, Saikyo Line?* 'What?' The article described a developing plan to build a north–south wall from the Arakawa River down to the Tama River. 'Why would they need to put up a wall? That would just inconvenience everyone.'

'To cut the city in half, obviously.'

'But who would benefit from cutting the city in half?'

Chusonji just looked at me like I was a slow-witted student, so I reached for an answer.

'Velkasery?'

'It's like that old lady said. Change leads to evolution.'

I thought of Hiyama's words from our rooftop exchange. *If you don't cause some agitation, there's no experiment.*

But was that memory accurate? I felt unsettled all over again. I had no guarantee the memory was right. Maybe it was really me who said it.

'That was probably Velkasery's conclusion after gathering and analyzing all that data.'

'What was?'

'That without conflict, there's no progress.'

'And that's why it's doing this?'

'It might be this way for animals too, I don't know, but at least for humans, there's one thing you need to get them fighting.'

'And what's that?'

'Stake out territories. Once lines are drawn, conflict starts. In every age, all over the world, whenever you have countries bordering each other there's trouble. There's no such thing as friendly neighbors. Just like the picture book lady said. The fastest route to confrontation,' and here he sliced the air with his index finger, 'is drawing lines.'

'Drawing lines . . .'

'Everyone on the other side of the line is the enemy.'

I looked back at my PassCard. A wall would be going up, to cut Tokyo in half. I'd read it but still couldn't fully grasp it. Would putting up a wall automatically lead to conflict?

While it all sounded fairly outlandish to me, Chusonji was deadly serious.

He fell silent again, going back to his PassCard.

'Do you have a plan, Mr Chusonji?'

We had the source code to stop Velkasery. All we needed to do was activate it.

Only, we couldn't.

He suddenly looked bitter and defeated, and I thought he might be grinding his teeth. 'I was so sure I'd think of something.'

'So, no great ideas?'

The palanquin bobbed up and down, a rhythmic movement dictated by a computer program.

'It always worked that way before,' he lamented. 'No matter how unachievable the goal, if I thought about it enough I'd find a way. Always.' It sounded like he was trying to convince himself.

Atsushi Chusonji was a brilliant engineer who always had an answer, but now, watching him mutter about how he was sure he could figure it out, trying so hard to banish his self-doubt, he just seemed like an ordinary person.

'I guess this time's different. Nothing is coming to me.' His shoulders slumped in despair. It was actually hard to watch.

But I wasn't trying to cheer him up when I said: 'I've got something. Maybe. It just came to me in a flash.' More than considering his feelings, I was interested in trying to take my mind off of my memory dilemma. If we sat there quietly I would just start thinking about myself. I would start to pick at the issue – how many of my recollections were true, how many were false. I preferred to focus on something else, so I pressed on eagerly. 'Something I know you could do.'

'You really think so?'

When he asked like that, though, I didn't know quite what to say. It felt like he was a child asking me if he could grow up to be a pro sports player. It wasn't as if I could say *probably not*. 'Sure.'

He exhaled sharply through his nose. I didn't know if it was dismissive or to hide his excitement.

To save myself from silence I just said whatever was occurring to me. 'I'm sure there's a hint somewhere.' A hint? Even I didn't believe that.

'What do you mean, a hint? A hint from who?'

'Well.' There was only one possible person. 'Mr Terashima. It was him who first gave you the assignment. In the message about "Obbel and the Elephant."'

'*I told you not to go in the river*, huh?'

'Mr Terashima believed that you could stop Velkasery. And you've come so far.'

'Yeah. But this is as far as we go.'

'So what did he want you to do?' He had entrusted Chusonji with the task of using the program to shut down Velkasery. That much we knew. 'How would he have activated the program?'

'I'd say,' he ventured darkly, 'he would have done it from that computer back in the author's house in Hachioji. That thing was probably set up to slip through Velkasery's security.'

'Wait a second.'

'What?'

'If that was his plan, then why didn't he just activate the self-destruct program when he set up the computer? Then he wouldn't have had to go to the trouble of hiding it in Miyako Setsu's house.'

'He probably didn't think he needed to do it yet. I bet he just wanted it ready, in case. Like how fire extinguishers and sprinklers are put in place before there's a fire.'

'I think that's a little different from this. But, okay, if it's the same idea, now that the fire extinguisher is broken, is there really nothing else we could do?' I thought back to the computer being shot and destroyed at Miyako Setsu's house. I could picture its shattered frame.

'Nothing else we can do.'

'I don't believe that.' It felt like the ground was crumbling from under my feet. I desperately tried to keep my footing. 'There must be a contingency.'

'What do you mean, contingency?'

'A backup plan! For when the first plan doesn't work.'

'Do you think there's a backup plan?'

'I'm sure Mr Terashima left some other hint.'

'This isn't a video game. You don't get a hint when you're stuck. And anyway, he's dead.'

'If it's a backup plan he would have put it in place beforehand.' I pieced that much together as we were talking.

I raised the blind on the window and looked outside. Palanquins were only allowed on broad sidewalks. I could see cars driving by in the street beside us.

'Beforehand? Like what exactly?'

'Well, I mean, of course.' What did I mean, of course?

'Of course what?'

'The one thing you two agreed on.' It occurred to me as I said it, like a light switching on in my head. 'Gamma Moko.'

Yes, that had to be it. Gamma Moko.

If it weren't for Gamma Moko, Atsushi Chusonji and Terao Terashima never would have become friends. It would have changed the whole course of their lives. Terashima would probably never have created Velkasery. And there wouldn't be a horrible camera inside my eyeball.

Chusonji flinched, as if I had thrown something in his face.

For a moment I thought I had said something completely off base, but then he was tapping and scrolling on his PassCard – passionately might be overstating it, but definitely intently, the whole time murmuring to himself about Gamma Moko and Terashima and how could he have missed that. After a few minutes he intoned reverentially, 'I think this is it.'

'What did you find?'

'It's today. Gamma Moko's playing today. It's a memorial show for Anto Anzu. At a venue in Tokyo.'

'Is it a big show?'

'It's a secret show. The location hasn't been announced. Invite only. And they'll stream it on the net.'

Gamma Moko's work was a distinctive combination of music and visuals. But in addition to thinking about how the live shows worked for those who could attend in person, they always took into account how to make it enjoyable for people viewing remotely.

'They haven't done anything as a band in a long time, so it's getting a lot of buzz.' Chusonji sounded upset to only be finding out about it then. But it made enough sense to me, given how we had been pulled into this whole mess – there hadn't been time for him to follow updates on Gamma Moko.

'Okay, so what does it mean that there's a live show?'

'Here, I found it.'

'Found what?'

'Something one of the members said about the concert.'

He held up his PassCard to show me. It looked like a news site. The words of the statement stood up in 3D projection.

It was straightforward and dry, just some details about the show. There was none of the emotion that would seem appropriate for a memorial show. The end of the statement read, *Thanks to the new network system we get to use, the show will stream at the highest quality possible.*

'So?'

'It says the new network system they get to use. Sounds like it wasn't something they developed, but something someone gave to them.'

'I guess so.'

'I bet Terashima set that up beforehand.' Chusonji raised one eyebrow. 'Seems possible, yeah?'

'You think Terashima did that?'

'Yeah. He set up a system with image programming so good that Gamma Moko wouldn't be able to resist using it for their show, and then gave them access. If he just sent it out of nowhere they'd probably be suspicious, so I'm guessing he found some way to prove it was trustworthy.'

Some way to prove it was trustworthy? That was rather vague. It seemed to me like they would definitely suspect something was fishy, but Chusonji sounded so sure. He was already off and running down a road that only he could see.

'Okay, if that's true, then what does it mean?'

'It means we can probably use that system to input the code.'

He tried to hide his excitement but it was unmistakable.

'And that'll get to Velkasery?'

He nodded vigorously. 'He planned it all out. I would get the code from the old lady in Hachioji, then I'd find out that Gamma Moko had a show and I'd make the connection.'

'Then that means—'

'It means we need to go to the concert, plug into the system, and hit Velkasery.'

The artificial intelligence had formidable security, but if anyone knew a way in it would be its creator, Terao Terashima.

Chusonji had bounced back to life. His eyes were gleaming, and even his long hair seemed to shine.

'But the concert venue's secret.'

'Compared to cracking Velkasery, getting my hands on that info will be like looking up what day of the week it is.' His confidence was shoring me up.

He tapped some commands on the palanquin touchscreen. The androids carrying us set the litter down, swaying it slightly as if they were real people adjusting their balance. I reflected that the performance seemed a little unnecessary.

Just as I was thinking that, Chusonji said, 'Pretty useless performance,' which made me somehow happy. Despite everything with my memory, and being chased by the police, and being pulled into the middle of this whole mess, I felt myself smile just a bit, and my mood brightened. Just a little, like a candle before it goes out.

The venue was on a corner in Shimokitazawa. We arrived after six, and it was already dark out. It was in Old Shimokitazawa, which used to be popular with young people who were into music and theater. I had heard the music fans used to be called bandmen, and I wondered if the drama enthusiasts were called theatermen. Either way, it used to be quite lively.

The renovated train station didn't match the surrounding neighborhood. It was clean, almost sterile, and the locals who cherished the old atmosphere had been strongly against it. In the end the renovation project was left only half-done. Ten years ago, the area north of the station was remade as New Shimokitazawa – at first people called it Upper Shimokitazawa, then North Shimokitazawa – and now, New and Old coexisted.

'The only people who live in Old Shimokitazawa nowadays are, you know, whimsical types.'

Our taxi driver was very talkative, chatting away from the moment we got in the car. We were certain that every public transit operator was on the lookout for us as dangerous individuals, but somehow we had no problem catching a taxi. Chusonji boasted about how all he had to do was fiddle with our basic data profiles and we couldn't be found, not by facial recognition, DNA matching, or PassCard tracking.

'Doesn't matter if you look exactly like the wanted poster, unless the device senses a match and trips the alarm, no one'll give us any trouble. Even though sometimes human senses and intuition are smarter than machines.'

It sounded reasonable enough. But I also felt deep down that there was one man who could find me without needing any digital confirmation: Kagetora Hiyama.

The taxi driver had the car on self-driving, but still kept his hands responsibly on the wheel as he continued his discourse on the history of Shimokitazawa. He spoke in a steady stream, as if reciting a sutra, not letting us get a single word in.

'What do we do when we get there?' I asked Chusonji. The whole ride, he sat next to me tapping and swiping on his Pass-Card, gathering information and falsifying our records.

'We disguise ourselves as people who work at the venue and go inside. The show starts at nine, so the system must be set up by now. All we need to do is pass ourselves off as staff and we should be able to access it. That's how we'll get to Velkasery.'

Then he looked up from his PassCard and stared at me.

'What is it?' I got worried he had some more shocking news for me, like maybe there was another camera in my other eye.

'Nothing,' he muttered. 'You seem to be okay.'

'Huh?'

'We're riding in a car, but you seem fine.'

'Oh.' He was right. I would normally be sweating bullets and nearly passing out from terror. But there I was, sitting normally, looking out the window without getting dizzy. My vision was clear. I probably thought the driver's rambling was so notable because I usually couldn't listen calmly to anything anyone said in a moving car. 'Well, now that you mention it,' was all I could say. I wasn't sure why, but I felt more or less fine.

Had I been cured of my fear of cars?

'Might be because you got your facts straight on your accidents.'

But that wasn't it. It was the opposite.

More than getting anything straight, the possibility that I caused the accident had started me doubting, had thrown me into confusion.

164

I felt an obligation to keep digging into my memories, intertwined with the need to stay as far away from all of it as I could.

Hinata said I was driving five years ago. Which meant I had gradually been overcoming my fear. But then by chance a taxi crashed into me, seriously injuring me and leaving me with a lifelong aversion to cars. Although it seemed like more than a matter of bad luck. I almost wondered if it was fate.

The taxi stopped. There was no more time to nurse all my doubts.

We didn't see any sign or marker, but it wasn't hard to tell where we were headed, thanks to the crowd of people. The details of the supposedly secret concert had obviously leaked.

Fans stood closely packed in front of the narrow cylindrical building, overseen by several security guards. There were also staff members setting up rows of barriers.

Chusonji plunged in, and I followed.

It had been that way ever since I'd met him in Sendai. I never knew a day could be so long. One unexpected thing after another, constantly moving from one place to the next as if we were being pushed from behind. Him driving onward, me following like a newly hatched chick. And in fact I did feel like I had just been born.

'Coming through. Let us through.' He kept pushing deeper into the crowd. 'We're with the event. With the event,' he said over and over, never saying anything about how we were with the event or what we were there to do. And in fact we did have a purpose there, I reasoned with myself, leaving behind any remorse at elbowing through the throng.

The staffers at the entrance looked at us warily and ordered us to stop.

'We're here to inspect the facilities.' Chusonji raised his Pass-Card. 'We're in a hurry.' We pushed past, but one of them called us out.

'Stop right there.'

I froze. After a few steps, Chusonji did too.

They're going to shoot us, I thought. In the back, out the stomach, ending me with a painful puncture. My whole body dilated with terror, down to my pores.

I held my breath.

No more me, I'm all done, I kept thinking. But my consciousness had yet to wink out.

I turned slowly. A staffer stood right in front of me. 'What kind of inspection are you here to do?' He wasn't holding a gun. It was a water bottle.

'Uh, the system.' I just said the first word that occurred to me.

'What system are you talking about?'

'The visual system, man.' Chusonji slipped in between me and the staffer. He sensed that this was a substantial obstacle.

'Visual system?' The staffer was well-trained. Instead of just nodding and accepting our vague answers, he pressed. 'I'll need to check on that.' He started contacting his supervisor.

I had to admire his thoroughness.

'It's an emergency, I don't know if they would have told you about it,' Chusonji tried lamely, meanwhile poking me in the side, urging me to keep moving.

He was right, we couldn't just stand there. We started edging away, ever so slowly, trying to move imperceptibly, like children playing a game where they moved without drawing attention.

'Okay. Yes. Understood.' The staffer turned back to us. 'They said they do need a system inspection. Sorry about that. Head on in.'

'So glad you figured it out,' Chusonji grumbled.

As we entered I said, 'Quite a coincidence that they actually needed an inspection.'

'I'm just lucky.'

So now we had good luck?

*

166

It was dark inside the building. Nothing showed on the wall display panels. We just kept walking straight down the hall, passing several staff members, none of whom paid us much attention.

'Where are we going?'

'They're probably already setting up the stage.'

We came to a T-junction in the hallway. Chusonji looked in both directions, then spotted an illuminated sign. 'This way.' He headed left.

The passage opened into a wider space. I realized after a moment that we were on stage. Dimly lit and empty, it felt like we had stumbled into a secret cavern. There wasn't a single instrument or mic stand.

We wandered further out onto the stage and could see the seats spreading out in front of us. From the outside I would have never guessed that the building held a room like this, but there were three levels of seats laid out in a fan shape, stretching up high and going back deep. It looked just like the opera houses I had seen in old movies. I never knew there were places like this in Old Shimokitazawa.

Small orange lamps at evenly spaced intervals lent the space an air of solemnity, and an almost oppressive beauty.

I had the sensation that I had come to confess my sins. The next thing I knew I was standing in the middle of the stage, ready to kneel in penitence before the silent, unseen audience.

Everything I did was wrong.

I rewrote all of the memories that I didn't like. I tried to erase them.

The accident, it was my fault.

I pictured Kagetora Hiyama back when we were in school.

That cold, pretentious kid who acted so shamefully – I think it was me.

I could barely stay standing.

Who am I? All of my experiences, whose are they really?

Chusonji called out to me, which saved me from collapse. 'Hey, over here.'

He whispered, but it sounded like it echoed through the whole auditorium, through the whole world. I nearly jumped.

He stood at a black, round table next to the stage. There was a small cube on top of it, which I guessed was the computer with the system we needed. He moved his fingers over the virtual keyboard. 'This'll take a little time. If someone's coming, let me know.'

His voice was hard. He put his PassCard down on the narrow table next to the cube and typed, staring at the screen.

I kept an eye out for anyone who looked like they might be trouble, but the only suspicious intruders were us.

The members of Gamma Moko must have still been in the dressing room.

I tried to picture what the memorial concert would be like.

Then I turned back to the auditorium, taking in the aura of the place once more. Soon enough it would be jam-packed with people. The space would fill with their excitement, their cheering would ricochet off the walls.

Would we be able to finish our task before then?

I approached Chusonji, his back toward me.

'What?'

'Nothing, I'm just . . . here to pray that it goes okay.' I didn't know what I was saying. It just came out. 'Oh, and I wanted to record your heroic efforts on my eye camera.'

He scoffed through his nose at my self-flagellating joke.

'I think I've found the route to connect to Velkasery. All that's left—'

'So you can stop it?'

'Probably.'

'But . . . should we be stopping it?'

'What's that supposed to mean?'

'I'm just wondering if it's a good thing for us to get rid of an artificial intelligence like that.'

He must have thought it was pretty late in the game for me

to be having doubts. I felt the same way. But I couldn't help wondering.

'It's definitely a good thing. Terashima thought so, and he created Velkasery.'

'Parents aren't always right about their children.'

'You saw the fake news it was spreading about us, yeah? You know that it's trying to start a war between the east side and the west side of Tokyo. You think that's a good thing?' Chusonji's voice was harsh as he typed.

He was right.

'There's nothing good about a construct that goes out of its way to start a war, okay? Corporations and politicians are motivated by personal gain, by their own desires, which means they'll eventually destroy themselves. Their greed and carelessness is their downfall. But it's not so simple with Velkasery. It feels no greed, and it's always working. It doesn't care about personal gain. Leave it alone and it'll do exactly what it thinks it needs to do. And so . . .'

'So?'

'So someone's gotta stop it.'

Unlike human individuals and organizations, artificial intelligence just keeps going, silently pursuing its goals. And it doesn't care how many people suffer because of that.

But – I couldn't help wonder – what if that was the right way? If the artificial intelligence wasn't motivated by greed or personal gain, shouldn't we follow the road it lays out?

On the other hand, a different voice inside of me said, *it's not such a good idea if it leads to war.*

'Okay. Here goes.' Chusonji's fingers stopped moving.

All he had to do was push enter and the program would initiate.

Terao Terashima's desire would be fulfilled, and his worst fears dispelled into nothing.

I took another look around the hushed concert hall. Luckily there was still no sign of any staff. I would expect that before a concert people would be rushing around preparing the venue and setting up equipment. We must have arrived during a lull.

More good luck.

The thought calmed me. I'd felt the same relief when the staff member had tried to stop us at the entrance and our lie about doing a system inspection had worked out.

'Looks like luck is on our side,' I heard Chusonji say from behind me, his voice seeming to crawl across the stage floor. 'There was an old song called "With God on Our Side." Luck and God are kind of similar, aren't they? Some poet said that – "Chance is another name for God."'

It seemed that even with access to vast amounts of information and the ability to analyze it in mere seconds, Velkasery didn't account for luck and chance.

But then there was another voice in my head:

You really think so?

In that instant a chill flashed through me, and I started to shake. It was like I had been doused with ice water and my whole body shrank.

The artificial intelligence couldn't possibly be that blind.

And why would Terao Terashima make such an elaborate plan?

'Um.' I haltingly turned to look at Chusonji.

He must have been thinking the same thing as me. Even in the darkness I could see his face darken. He looked diminished. 'I think we fucked up.'

'Yes.'

It felt like all my blood had drained out of me.

How had we not realized it earlier?

There was no way the room could be so empty before a concert.

It was ridiculous that there just so happened to be a call out for a system inspection when we tried to lie our way into the venue saying we were there to inspect the system.

How could we have just chalked it all up to luck?

'This is so like me.'

'What do you mean?' But I knew what he meant.

'I got ahead of myself. I thought Terashima must have had some plan. Gamma Moko was the only thing we agreed on. Today they're doing a memorial concert. I was certain that was the way through. And once I got that in my head I got all excited. I was sure I had the answer.' He had put his PassCard back in his pocket. Which meant he had given up on initiating the program. 'People always get so worked up when they think they've discovered something. No one ever wants to admit they might have been wrong. Or that their success came through someone else's efforts. That's what happened with me, with this. I was so sure it had to do with Gamma Moko, I never even thought twice about it.'

We should have dug a little more.

After all, spreading around fake news was Velkasery's specialty.

'Terashima never had a backup plan.'

Meaning that the moment the computer was destroyed in Hachioji, Terashima's gambit, the task he had entrusted to his old friend, was foiled. By coming to the venue of the Gamma Moko concert, all we had done was play into Velkasery's scheme.

'It beat us.'

As if that were the cue, the sound of multiple doors bursting open at once reverberated through the hall.

The lights came on, filling the space. It was like we had had our eyes closed and now they were open, revealing an entirely different scene.

Uniformed police officers everywhere in the auditorium. My brain pulled the emergency brake, so I was unable to grasp what was happening. It seemed to me like they appeared out of thin air.

Nearly all of them had their guns aimed in our direction.

Someone shouted something.

Chusonji's sigh rippled the air behind me.

'I guess there never was a concert,' I said, or thought I said.

Was everything we found on the news a fabrication?

At the very least, the comments about the new network system to deliver first-class visuals were fake. There would have been no real reason for a member of Gamma Moko to go out of their way to announce that.

And the memorial concert itself?

Was that real?

Maybe, I realized with growing dread, none of the band members ever even died.

Once I started doubting, nothing seemed certain anymore.

A voice rang out from among the armed police, resonant with gravity like an opera singer.

The echoes made it hard to hear what it was actually saying, but I imagined it was something along the lines of *don't move, stay where you are, keep still.*

I put my hands up. End of the line, it seemed.

Then all at once a feeling came over me, the same one I had felt several times since first meeting Terashima on the Shinkansen.

I was just pulled into all of this.

But into what?

A raft of troubles, that all started with a promise between Terao Terashima and Atsushi Chusonji.

No, that wasn't it.

A predestined cycle of confrontation.

Another self inside myself, defeated, said: *You're nothing but a vehicle for conflict.*

A vehicle?

They say that living organisms are nothing more than vehicles for their genes. You're the same. A vehicle for conflict.

The police slowly approached the stage, closing in on us step by step, like hunters cornering prey.

It seemed like they wanted to take us alive.

I had no reason, felt no obligation, to resist.

I even felt I could go along quietly if it meant being released from this whole mess.

But something in me did resist.

Because there among the police I spotted him: Kagetora Hiyama.

I was full to bursting. There had been too many shocks to my system – the threat of Velkasery, running for my life, the camera implanted in my eye, the falsehoods in my memory.

A gun fell at my feet, and without even thinking I scooped it up.

I simply accepted that it had come to me. It had always been coming to me.

The police pressed in closer. Something flashed before my eyes.

Momentarily dazed, I tried to focus my vision again.

There he was. Just below the stage. *Hiyama.* I couldn't see anyone but him. It was only the two of us, squared off.

He pointed his gun at me, so I had no choice but to point my gun at him.

There was no sound at all. I couldn't look away from Hiyama.

I thought about the reversals in my memory. The person I thought was Hiyama was really me, and the one I thought was me was Hiyama.

Two sides of a coin.

But which was which? Who of the two of us was right, and who was wrong? Which was the truth, my memory or the camera's recording?

I thought about the cover band. A copy of the original – was there any value in that at all?

If it's a perfect copy, then it's as good as the original, I had argued.

And then what if the original is gone?

Wouldn't the remaining copy become the original?

I couldn't escape that thought.

One survives.

One disappears.

I aimed the gun, the first gun I had ever held in my life. My finger was on the trigger.

If I wanted to be the front side of the coin, I had to kill Hiyama.

If I was the only one left, then my memories would be the truth.

There was a deafening boom, as if a giant boot had stomped down and smashed through the floor. I felt my head jerk backward. A rush of heat, as if I was spouting flames, and I tumbled over.

The last thing I saw before my world went dark was a group of men in the corner of the stage. I didn't put it together that they were the members of Gamma Moko.

Again and again, I wished that the gun hadn't fallen at Mito's feet.

One of the police on stage who was apprehending Atsushi Chusonji must have fumbled. Chusonji resisted, there was a struggle, he knocked into someone, they dropped their gun.

Mito grabbed it, although it wasn't clear why he took aim.

But his movements were fluid, as if it was rehearsed.

And there I was, somehow pushed to the front of the scrum, though I have no idea how that happened either. I was totally worn out, running on no sleep, and had once again been about to grab a nap when I was pulled out to the scene. My head was in a thick fog, my eyes bloodshot. All the yawns I had been fighting back seemed to crowd my brain.

Then all of a sudden it was just me and Mito, facing each other down, no one else there with us in the depths of that giant space.

He drew on me first, so I aimed back at him.

At least I think that's what happened.

I have almost no memory of it. I reconstructed the rest of the scene based on footage from the security cams.

I wasn't excited. I was confused.

The thought that I could never avoid a collision with Mito no matter where I went filled me with resignation.

It was so strange. Mito and Chusonji hadn't committed any serious crimes. Chusonji was identified as the instigator of the outbreak of violence in Tokyo, but after he was arrested we determined that he had nothing to do with any of it. In the end all they did was some illegal net access and interference with public records, basic digital violations. They had no reason to be on the run like that, let alone shoot when cornered by the police.

We had to enforce the rules. We had to preserve the social order.

That's what I had always believed. I still believe it now. But when I think of the extent of Mito's crimes, I have to ask if we needed to chase them down like that.

How did all of this happen?

Naomasa Mito had lost his mind.

That was how it was being explained.

All he was trying to do was complete an assignment as a courier. But he got pulled into a whole plot involving Atsushi Chusonji. By the time we had caught them, he was bewildered and exhausted to the point of mental collapse. That was how it was written up, anyway.

I stared out the window of the New Tohoku Shinkansen.

A soft carpet of ripened rice fields flowed by.

I thought back to when we were looking for Terao Terashima on the same train, when I had my unexpected reunion.

Naomasa Mito had actually been sitting right around where I was now.

That was how it started. Although, of course, it had started long before then.

Someone sat down next to me out of nowhere. I tensed up in surprise. The train wasn't crowded, and there were plenty of other seats to choose from. I was off duty so I didn't have my gun, but my hand went reflexively to my hip.

'I saw a familiar face, so I just thought I'd say hello.'

It took me a moment to recognize him. Long hair, gaunt. Atsushi Chusonji. I felt a stab of nerves, but he seemed relaxed, and I determined that there was no threat.

'Headed up to Tohoku?'

'Thought I'd go to Oirase Gorge.' I didn't need to tell him that, but there was no reason to hide it either.

'Looking to unwind a little after you shot your friend?' His words were unkind, but he looked sad.

'We weren't friends.' It seemed like an unnecessary clarification. But I couldn't stop myself. 'Anyway, he's not dead.'

'So I hear.'

I had shot Mito in the head. The spot where the bullet hit him wasn't fatal, though I don't know if that could be called lucky or not; he was in a hospital bed, unresponsive. It wasn't a coma. His eyes were open. But all he did was stare into space, and it wasn't clear how much mental activity was happening.

'And did you pay him a kindly visit?'

'Uhh . . . Yes. I did.'

He must have been joking, because he burst out laughing. 'You seriously went to see him?'

'Sure I did.'

'Felt guilty, huh? Well, don't beat yourself up. You were just doing your job.'

'That's generous of you,' I replied. 'I didn't feel guilty, though.'

I wasn't sure myself why I went to visit Mito in his hospital bed. Kyoko Hinata was always there, but every time I showed up she disappeared without a word. I would stare at Mito for a few minutes and then leave. I had no regular visiting routine, but I kept going back. 'You seem to have had no trouble avoiding jail time.'

'I'm sure you know this, but I didn't do anything serious. Everything about me on the news was a bunch of lies.'

'Even so, you got off with basically no penalty.'

'Yeah, I guess so.' Chusonji grimaced.

'Why do you look so upset about that?'

'I just don't understand it. I thought there would be a heavier punishment. After all, I was trying to destroy a key player in the affairs of state.'

'Key player?' I didn't know who he was talking about. 'A politician?'

He barked a short, scornful laugh, but didn't answer. Maybe he was joking again. Had his crimes involved something that serious? I didn't remember hearing anything about that.

'In the end, I couldn't stop them.'

'That's probably a good thing.'

'It means that my going free so easily was what they wanted. Or at least, that's what I'm worried about.'

'Who are you even talking about?'

'I bet they want to use me. It's even possible that they want me to be sitting here talking to you right now. Anything I do from now on, I'll probably wonder about that. I'm just . . . traveling on the track that Velkasery laid out for me.'

'Velka-who? I'm really not following.'

'Artificial intelligence is going to make its move, and humans won't even understand what's happening.'

The Shinkansen sped along smoothly, not even swaying a little. Chusonji didn't say anything more, but he didn't get up to leave either. I was about to suggest that maybe he could find another seat, when he muttered: 'The wall.'

'What?'

'Did you hear the news about a wall going up in Tokyo?'

'Oh, that?' There had been a story that the Yamanote Line would be moved underground, and where it used to be they'd build a wall. But shortly after the story broke there was an update that it was nothing more than a rumor. 'They were calling it "the ghost of divided rule."'

After the Second World War there was talk that rule over Japan would be divvied up between the US, USSR, UK, and China. If that had come to pass then there might have been walls all over the country, just like in Berlin. At the time there had actually been discussion of dividing up Tokyo with a wall.

'It's not just a rumor. You watch, there'll be a wall.'

'What is this, a prophecy?'

'A wall will go up in order to sow division among the people. That's the direction they'll want to take things.'

'Who?'

'Once you draw borderlines, it creates confrontation. Once people start facing off, everything becomes a confrontation. It's just like the picture book lady said – confrontation for its own sake.'

'What are you talking about?'

But, as expected, he didn't answer. Instead, he said, 'It might not go exactly as laid out in the blueprints, though.'

'I haven't been following you for a while.'

Chusonji showed me his PassCard. A news projection floated up from it.

It said that the new release from Gamma Moko would be available for worldwide free download.

'What's this?'

'From that night.' He clenched his jaw when he said it.

I didn't need to ask which night. He could only have been talking about the night that Mito and I met face to face.

'We saw something terrible, when we were getting ready for our memorial show.' This wasn't Chusonji's voice, but a clip of a comment from one of the members of Gamma Moko in the newsfeed.

'It was more than just a cop shooting someone,' the musician explained. 'It was the horror of two humans in a life and death confrontation, and our feeling of total powerlessness as we just watched it happen. We can never know what the guy who was shot was thinking. We don't even know what kind of a person he was. All we know is we never want to have to see that again. That's what inspired our new piece.'

'What's this all about?'

'A computer gathers information and calculates probable outcomes. Then it manipulates the news to try to lead things in the direction it wants. Just like how it lured us to that concert venue.'

'What are you—'

'But it can't control human emotions perfectly.' He said it like he was revealing a twist. 'When something really upsetting happens, it moves people. There was once a painter who was deeply shocked by indiscriminate bombing, and he painted a picture about it. That picture moved the people who looked at it. The future isn't built on facts and data alone. There's also human emotion.' Now his narration style was detached, like a sportscaster, but I could feel the urgency behind his words. 'People express something, and that expression makes other people feel things. That's hard to predict. It comes down to the fact that human emotion isn't logical. For example . . .'

'I'm listening.'

'You may know that saying a certain thing will start a fight, but you just can't hold it in, and you say it anyway. Right? Emotions don't go according to plan.'

'Okay. So what?'

'Gamma Moko's new release is going to move people. It probably won't stop the wall from going up. I mean, it's a large-scale public work. But the wall may not produce the intended effect. Human emotion will push things off course just the slightest bit, and in the end it'll go in a completely different direction.'

'How come you're so intent on things not going according to this plan?' It felt like he was a kid praying for rain so that Sports Day would be canceled.

'You two are sea and mountain, right?'

I didn't know how to answer. Kyoko Hinata's face appeared in my mind.

'You weren't only crashing into each other. It probably also set into motion all kinds of other things.'

'Set into motion what?' All I could do was ask him questions.

'Conflict between A and B gives rise to C,' he murmured vaguely. 'Not alpha and beta though.'

'I really have no idea what you're talking about.'

'So what did you do when you went to go visit Mito?'

'Nothing much. I usually just sit there next to him. Sometimes I read a book.'

'A picture book? The one with the snail?'

'Yes. There's a copy there. I heard he liked it and I picked it up to see what it was about.'

Chusonji smiled. 'That's important.'

'Important? It wasn't a big deal.'

'When you stand in opposition to someone, the fact that you can be interested in knowing more about them – that's important. Otherwise you only have a warped view of them. Like that old lady said.'

Of course, I didn't know what old lady he meant.

'No, it's definitely important to read your rival's favorite picture book to learn more about them.'

'Are you making fun of me?'

'No way. Next time you go, you should read out loud to him.'

'Read out loud? A picture book?' He had to be making fun of me. I was annoyed, but then I imagined myself reading to Mito.

'Well then,' Chusonji said, finally starting to get up.

Part of me wanted him to leave already, but part of me wanted to talk to him more. Not enough to ask him to stay, though. Just as I was about to look out at the scenery again, he turned back to me. 'Are you gonna go visit him again?'

'Maybe.' Not a clear yes or no.

'If you do, look him in the eye when you read.'

'Look him in the eye?' It sounded like something a parent would try to teach their child.

'Yeah. That way he'll really know you were there. His eyes are open, right?'

'They're open, but I don't think he's seeing anything.'

Chusonji shrugged. 'He may not be seeing anything now, but if he gets better, he'll know that you came to visit. It'll be a nice surprise.'

'You think he'll know?'

'It'll be recorded.'

Recorded?

By the time I could ask, he was gone. He might have walked toward the front of the train, but it felt like he was a hologram that had winked off.